MEDICAL
Pulse-racing passion

The Vet's Caribbean Fling
Ann McIntosh

Her Forbidden Firefighter
Traci Douglass

MILLS & BOON

THE VET'S CARIBBEAN FLING
© 2024 by Ann McIntosh
Philippine Copyright 2024
Australian Copyright 2024
New Zealand Copyright 2024

First Published 2024
First Australian Paperback Edition 2024
ISBN 978 1 038 91065 3

HER FORBIDDEN FIREFIGHTER
© 2024 by Traci Douglass
Philippine Copyright 2024
Australian Copyright 2024
New Zealand Copyright 2024

First Published 2024
First Australian Paperback Edition 2024
ISBN 978 1 038 91065 3

MIX
Paper | Supporting
responsible forestry
FSC® C001695

Published by
Harlequin Mills & Boon
An imprint of Harlequin Enterprises (Australia) Pty Limited
(ABN 47 001 180 918), a subsidiary of HarperCollins
Publishers Australia Pty Limited
(ABN 36 009 913 517)
Level 19, 201 Elizabeth Street
SYDNEY NSW 2000 AUSTRALIA

Cover art used by arrangement with Harlequin Books S.A.. All rights reserved.

Printed and bound in Australia by McPherson's Printing Group

The Vet's Caribbean Fling

Ann McIntosh

MILLS & BOON

Ann McIntosh was born in the tropics, lived in the frozen north for a number of years and now resides in sunny central Florida with her husband. She's a proud mama to three grown children, loves tea, crafting, animals (except reptiles!), bacon and the ocean. She believes in the power of romance to heal, inspire and provide hope in our complex world.

Visit the Author Profile page
at millsandboon.com.au.

Dear Reader,

Anyone involved with animal rescue is a hero to me. But if a rescuer happens to read this book, they'll probably laugh themselves silly at the idea of an island vet who somehow also has time to run a shelter. Believe me, having seen both veterinarians and rescue workers in the trenches, I was fully aware making my heroine, Mellie, juggle both occupations *and* find time to fall in love was stretching it!

Yet I wanted to highlight the world of animal rescue. It's not all cute kittens and puppies. It's hard, heartbreaking work that most of us wouldn't have the stomach for. The woman I've dedicated this book to had a dream of rescuing animals in Jamaica and, against all odds, made it a reality. Montego Bay Animal Haven is dear to my heart, and their Hiking with the Hooligans program is a must if you're visiting the island!

Rescuers suffer along with the animals, and mourn the ones they can't help or don't get to in time. In *The Vet's Caribbean Fling*, Delano and Mellie find love and healing in each other, and that's my wish for all the animals and their rescuers.

That love prevails, and heals us all.

Ann McIntosh

DEDICATION

To Tammy Browne Ogden, one of the kindest, strongest, most amazing and beautiful women I know. You make the world a better place just by your existence (and I know a plethora of animals that would wholeheartedly agree!).

CHAPTER ONE

THE CALL CAME at nine in the evening and, although not unexpected, it made Dr. Mellie Roscoe sigh.

"Snugums is nesting," Karyn Williams said, the fear in her voice obvious. "I think you should come."

Mellie bit back both another sigh and a sharp reply. Although she was fed right up with Karyn and her drama, the probability that her Yorkie, Snugums, might have problems delivering her pups was high.

Fighting annoyance, and keeping her voice as calm and level as possible, she said, "What's Snugums doing?"

"She's off her food—hasn't eaten today at all—and she's pawing around in the nursery, pulling all the towels and blankets together. I read that's a sure sign that she's about to give birth."

"Those are some of the indicators," Mellie agreed. "Is her belly really hard?"

"I'm not going to touch her to find out," Karyn all but wailed. "She growled at me earlier."

There was no way to stop herself from rolling her eyes, and Mellie was glad she wasn't face-to-face with the client.

"Well, you're going to have to be brave because

I want you to put her in the car and meet me at the clinic."

"Why can't you come here?" Panic laced the other woman's tone.

"Because if Snugums or the puppies are in distress, I want to be able to operate immediately. You're twenty minutes away from the clinic, and those minutes could make all the difference."

"If Snugums bites me when I try to get her in the car, I'm holding you responsible," was the unreasonable reply, followed by the unmistakable click of the phone being hung up.

It was only then that Mellie allowed herself to growl, and mutter a couple of curses. As she trailed into the kitchen to make herself a quick cup of coffee before going to meet Karyn, pairs of interested eyes followed her every move.

"Sorry, guys," she said to the three dogs, opening the back door so they could go out and do their business. "I'm heading right back out again to meet up with a princess and her Karyn, so make it snappy."

Under normal circumstances she'd be more sympathetic toward the other woman. After all, it was Snugums's first litter, but it was also an ill-advised one.

When Karyn had first approached Mellie about breeding the tiny bitch, Mellie had been blunt with her opinion.

"I wouldn't advise it, since any of the available males on St. Eustace will be related to her, and that is a risk in itself. Also, Snugums is rather small, and I can't think of a male smaller than she is, which is advisable when breeding a bitch of this size."

"I've never heard anything like that before," Karyn had scoffed, despite Mellie being the vet and Karyn a first-time pure-bred dog owner. Mellie was sure all Karyn was interested in was the idea of the money she could make from the puppies, which longtime breeders would say was a lot less than people thought. "Why would she need to be mated with a male smaller than she is?"

"Because if she mates with a male larger than she is, there's the risk that she can't deliver the puppies naturally. Then we'd have to do a Cesarian section."

Despite huffily saying she understood the difficulties, the next thing Mellie heard was that Snugums was in the family way.

It still rankled that Karyn would have ignored her advice. Having grown up with a hypercritical mother, it had taken a lot of hard work on Mellie's part to learn to speak up firmly. Once she'd mastered the art, it was a source of annoyance when people dismissed what she said.

"Don't worry about Karyn," Dr. Milo said, when Mellie brought it up with him. "I told her the same thing, so it wasn't just you she didn't listen to."

Worse, once it was confirmed Snugums was expecting, Karyn immediately went from cocky potential dog breeder to manic grandmother-to-be on steroids. Every few days, she'd brought Snugums to the clinic, quite sure that her "baby" was on death's door.

Even the ever-patient Dr. Milo, who Karyn insisted take care of Snugums, had begun to get testy about the whole situation. When the older vet had what he euphemistically called "a turn"—in reality a myocardial infarction—just a few days ago, Mellie had found herself in the unenviable position of taking over the Yorkie's care.

As if she didn't have enough on her plate, worrying about her mentor and friend's prospects of recovery, along with taking care of all the veterinary patients.

In fact, she'd just walked in the door after going across the island to drench a herd of cattle, which she'd only managed to get to after the clinic closed. Thankfully, being summer, she'd had enough light to get most of the herd done, and the farmer had brought out a standing light so she could do the last few.

Exhaustion dragged at her, but there was no way she would abandon a patient.

Thank goodness for her right-hand man, Johnny Luck, who'd fed all the animals after Mellie had called to let him know she'd be home late. Without the elderly man keeping an eye on things here at the shelter, she didn't know what she'd do.

After letting the dogs back in, Mellie poured the coffee into a travel mug. Sheba trotted over to come to stand beside her, big brown eyes looking up at her as if to ask, *You're going out again?*

Reaching down, Mellie scratched the little mongrel dog between her ears. "Sorry, girl. Mama's got another doggy to take care of."

Then, suppressing a yawn, she grabbed her tote and coffee, and went back out into the warmth and darkness of the Caribbean night to her car.

At that time of the evening it was only a ten-minute drive to the clinic, which was on a low hill on the road to downtown Port Michael, and Mellie spent the time mentally prepping for the upcoming delivery.

Since Dr. Milo's medical emergency, Mellie had been fretting about her ability to keep the Prospect Vet Clinic running by herself. Over the five years since she started working there, she and Dr. Milo had worked out a system that ran like clockwork.

They each had their own patients, but were always on hand to help each other out when needed. They'd shared the ubiquitous dogs and cats, but Dr. Milo did a lot of the large animal work, while he preferred to leave what he called the "exotic" animals to Mellie.

On St. Eustace, "exotic" was anything other than dogs, cats or farm animals, and consisted of rabbits, guinea pigs, birds and the occasional hamster—all well within Mellie's sphere of competence. So far no one had brought in a pet iguana, for which she was secretly grateful. She hadn't had any practice on a reptile since leaving vet school.

And even if before this last illness Dr. Milo had been showing definite signs of slowing down, but while Mellie had been handling more of the patients, he'd still been there to call on.

Now, as she drove through the night toward who knew what drama, Mellie couldn't help a shiver of apprehension. She'd be alone to deliver the pups—Karyn would be no help—and if she needed to do the C-section, it would be so much better to have someone there with her. The chances of finding a vet assistant willing and able to come back in to help were meager, at best. What if she lost the puppies? Or, worse, Snugums?

Then, on an inhale, she thrust her fear aside and tightened her grip on the steering wheel.

For the last couple of years, she'd been working and planning toward buying the seventy-year-old Dr. Milo out when he was ready to retire. Yes, it seemed as though that time might be coming sooner than she expected and, sure, she was finding the sudden plunge into being the only vet at the clinic harrowing. But in the final analysis, she was definitely ready if that was the way things panned out. The last four days had been chaotic, as she tried to fulfill all the obligations they'd committed to, but going forward things would smooth out.

She was sure of it.

Turning into the clinic parking lot, she drove around to the back and parked in her usual spot. The building exterior was lit by a number of lights, and the resident dogs in the kennels attached to the rear of the building let out a volley of welcoming barks as Mellie got out of the car.

Taking out her keys, she let herself into the kitchen/mudroom, and paused after pulling the door closed behind her.

"Who left on the light in the office?" she muttered, gazing at the triangle of light visible from the hallway, just as a shadow split it for a second, causing her heart to jump.

Frozen in place, her breath sawing in and out of her suddenly laboring lungs, she strained to hear anything from the office, anything at all, over the lingering barks and the rush of her own fear.

The dogs outside settled down somewhat, and in the sudden pocket of silence Mellie heard something like a bottle fall to the floor and a male voice grumble, as though in response.

And suddenly, ferociously, she wasn't afraid anymore.

She was livid.

How dare someone break into the clinic to rob it?

Without another thought, Mellie moved on near-silent, sneakered feet toward the corridor leading to the office, pausing only to pick up the machete used to trim the bushes around the building. Then she walked along to the door, and stepped into the office she and Dr. Milo shared.

"Who are you?" she barked. "And what do you think you're doing?"

The man, who was leaning into the medicine closet, jolted upright and spun around, whacking the side of his head on the open cupboard door so hard that even Mellie winced. But it didn't make her drop her aggressive stance—machete held up and out, as though prepared to do battle.

"What the hell?" The man stood glaring at her, rubbing his cheek. "You scared the daylights out of me."

"I'll do a lot more than that," Mellie retorted, lifting the machete a little higher and giving it a threatening swish. "How did you get in here, and what do you think you're doing?"

But a couple of thoughts hit her just then, shaking her assurance.

Firstly, the burglar was very large. At least four inches taller than her own five-foot-eight-inch height, very broad in the shoulders and overall muscular.

Taking him on in a fight wouldn't be easy.

Secondly, there was something vaguely familiar about him, although she knew, for a fact, she'd never seen him before. He was also—well—rather *dapper* for a burglar.

"Tall, dark and handsome" was such a cliché, but absolutely suited him.

With his neatly barbered hair, unwrinkled and expensive-looking polo shirt, "sleek and sophisticated" did too.

Sweat trickled down her back beneath her scrub top, as the man silently stared at her, his gaze shifting between her face and the machete. Instead of feeling scared or intimidated, Mellie was shocked by a rush of attraction, bordering on lust.

It took every ounce of determination she had

not to devour his delicious body with her eyes, and to remind herself he was some kind of criminal. By the time he finally spoke, Mellie was about to scream with the tension that had built up inside her.

"My name is Delano, and I'm Dr. Logan's son," he said calmly, his dark gaze flicking one more time to the machete before fixing on hers. "And, Dr. Roscoe, I'd suggest you put down that machete before you hurt yourself."

Over years of working with large animals—especially horses because of their almost psychic ability to read emotion and mood—Delano had learned to project nothing but tranquility.

Even when, like now, his instincts were screaming at him that this was a monumental moment, although he wasn't sure of what kind.

The woman standing in the doorway looked downright Amazonian—all bristled up and ready to defend herself and the clinic, no matter the cost.

And even from across the room, the keen edge on the blade in her hand was obvious.

He recognized her, of course, from the pictures his aunt and father had sent over the last few years. Dr. Mellie Roscoe, his father's junior associate and obvious favorite vet, present company not excepted. While they hadn't met before, Delano could only hope that someone had alerted her to his existence, and it wouldn't come as a shock.

Surely his father hadn't completely excised him from all conversation? Although there was always that possibility. For too many years to contemplate, since Delano was twelve and his mother had died, there had been a huge chasm between him and his father that felt too wide to cross.

Pushing that depressing thought away, and hoping his words would defuse the situation, he kept looking at her face and therefore saw exactly when his statement sank in.

Her eyes widened, and her mouth fell open slightly as her gaze scoured his face. Most importantly, the machete was lowered, so it hung by her side. But she didn't put it down.

Then, instead of apologizing, or offering any kind of friendly overture, her eyes narrowed and her top lip curled.

"Dr. Delano Logan..." She drew his name out, making the hair on the back of his neck rise at her laconic and somehow insulting tone. "Well, that's a bit of a surprise. What are you doing here?"

Taken aback all over again, Delano rubbed his still stinging cheek, wondering how to answer her rather rude question.

It shouldn't be a surprise to her that Delano had traveled to St. Eustace from Trinidad to be by his father's side after the elder Dr. Logan had a heart attack. Yet, she'd worked with his father for five years, and no doubt also knew Delano hadn't been back to his homeland for a very long time.

Not when Dr. Milo got an award from the chamber of commerce for his contributions to island life, nor when the Caribbean Veterinary Council honored him for his years of service. Delano had even missed his father's sixty-fifth birthday bash, although from the pictures it seemed almost the entire population of St. Eustace had been there.

He'd never even come back for any of the biennial dog shows his father organized in memory of Delano's mother, Iris, who'd had a passionate love of all canines.

She probably was also well aware of the problems within the Racing Commission back in Trinidad. Their press releases had been carefully uncommunicative, simply saying there had been some irregularities they needed to investigate, and that they were canceling race meets until further notice. While Delano knew the full story, he'd been asked not to speak about it, and hadn't; however, the rumors and gossip had flown and stung them all, even the innocent.

Just thinking about all those issues had guilt and shame crawling up in a heated wave from his chest into his throat, but he kept his face expressionless. There was another way to interpret her question regarding what he was doing there, and Delano quickly chose it.

"I'm looking for the broad-spectrum dewormers." Her eyebrows rose, and her head tilted to one side, as though his reply came as the surprise he'd hoped for. "For my dog, Baldur. I forgot to bring any for him, and he's due a dose now. I didn't want to wait until I got back to T & T, so Dad suggested I come down and get some from here. I walked down rather than bother driving such a short way."

She didn't respond immediately. Instead, she looked over her shoulder, and Delano saw a shaft of light that he thought was from an approaching vehicle travel across the wall outside the office.

"That'll be my patient coming in." Mellie glanced back at him, but there was no mistaking her dismissive tone. "Dewormer's on the right-hand side of the other cupboard."

Then, before he could say another word, she exited, thankfully taking the machete with her, and Delano took the first deep breath he'd been able to since he'd turned and seen her in the doorway.

His aunt had described Mellie Roscoe as a warm, fun, lighthearted person, who worked and played equally hard and got along well with everyone. Her pictures had shown a good-looking, smiling woman, almost invariably with her arm slung around some else's shoulders.

Somehow, now, he couldn't decide whether his aunt had misrepresented the vet's personality, or if it were he who brought out the worst in her. What he did have to acknowledge, though, was that she was far more beautiful in person than in those photos. Rich, brown skin stretched smooth and silky over an oval face. Full lips made him think of kissing even when she was frowning, and flashing light brown eyes seemed made for drowning in. In all honesty, their encounter had impacted him in ways he hadn't expected at all.

Even as she threatened him with a machete, he'd felt a definite thrill of attraction. One that was both unwanted and highly inadvisable. There was no room in his life for any kind of entanglement, especially not here in St. Eustace.

With a rueful headshake, Delano turned to the cupboard Mellie had indicated to hunt for the medication, all to a backdrop of muted conversation from one of the examination rooms. Thank goodness he only planned to be on the island for a couple of weeks, so he wouldn't be too tempted to try and figure Mellie Roscoe out.

"Hey."

He hadn't heard her come back to the door, and only narrowly missed whacking his head again when he spun around to face her.

"What?"

"Make yourself useful, and help me do an ultrasound on a dog? She may need a Cesarean section and I need someone to keep her calm while I take a look at the puppies' placement and size."

She still didn't look friendly. In fact, she looked as though asking him was the last thing she wanted to do, which made Delano feel even more annoyed. Let her handle her business on her own, then.

"Sure," he heard himself say, contrary to his thought. He even threw in one of his best, most charming smiles for good measure. "I can do that."

From her little snort—which sounded suspiciously like disgust—you'd think he'd refused instead. And Delano found himself smiling as he followed her out of the office and into the examination room.

This just might be fun, after all.

CHAPTER TWO

Delano Logan.

Here in Port Michael, at the Prospect Clinic, acting as though he somehow belonged.

No. As though he *owned* the place.

He even had the nerve to be cheerfully accommodating when she asked for his help, and charming enough to turn Karyn Williams's head. There'd been no mistaking the double take and kittenish behavior the other woman had immediately exhibited on being introduced to the handsome vet. And even though neither Mellie nor Delano was really paying her any attention, Karyn was droning on behind them, clearly trying to attract his attention.

Worst of all, while he was leaning over the examination table, whispering sweet nothings to an adoring Snugums and Mellie shaved the Yorkie's belly, he smelled like a dream...

A very naughty dream, in fact.

The last time she'd been attracted to a man of this type, in this way, the result had been embarrassment, heartbreak, financial devastation and a protracted lawsuit aimed at getting restitution.

There was no way her heart should be thumping with awareness, or that her focus wanted to stray away from her patient to the man beside her.

The unwanted physical reaction to him was just one more reason to be angry with him; not that she needed additional stimulus. While her emotions about his sudden advent into her life were confused, none of them were positive.

As she got the ultrasound machine set up, she tried to get her feelings under control but kept cycling back to the crux of the matter, which didn't help in her effort to calm down.

Dr. Milo meant the world to her. He'd given her a spot in his clinic when she'd desperately needed a job, on just her father's assurance that she knew what she was doing. His illness had affected her profoundly—the same way, she suspected, as it would have had it been her own father. She knew Milo must be over the moon to have his son come home to be with him at a time like this, and under normal circumstances she would be too.

But who could trust Delano and his motives when he'd ignored his father for years?

When he'd turned up only after his job as a race-course veterinarian seemed in jeopardy?

Coincidence? Happenstance?

Mellie didn't think so, and it made her blood icy to think of him causing his father additional hurt, should it come out that he was simply here with an eye to the main chance.

But she also had to admit she felt hurt by the fact Dr. Milo hadn't even let her know his son was back on the island. She thought they were closer than that.

Hard not to feel rejected, like the other brother in the story of the Prodigal Son. The one who'd kept on the straight and narrow—was dependable—and couldn't understand what the fuss was about when the wastrel son came home.

There was, she thought, a lesson in there somewhere, but she was too busy just now to figure it out.

As she pressed the transducer into Snugums's distended belly, her gaze on the monitor, she was desperately trying to ignore the warm, spicy scent emanating off Delano's skin. Then, as she shifted the transducer, her heart did a little dip toward her stomach, and Delano let out a soft grunt.

"What? What is it?"

Apparently Karyn had been paying some attention to what they were doing, and had picked up on their reactions. Mellie took a deep breath, knowing if she exhibited any of the anxiety shivering along her spine, Karyn would probably lose it.

"In my opinion, the puppies' heads are too big to pass through the birth canal." There was no way to soft-soap it. "If we let Snugums try to deliver them vaginally, we'd be risking both her life and the lives of the pups. I'm suggesting I perform an emergency C-section, rather than take the risk."

Karyn immediately turned and asked Delano, "What do you think I should do?"

Mellie raised her eyebrows, but stayed silent. It would be instructive to see how Delano responded.

"I think," he said slowly, "you should listen to your vet."

"No." Karyn swept her carefully straightened hair back over her shoulder and gave her head a toss. "You're a vet too. I want to hear your opinion, before I make a decision."

Remember you're a professional.

Mellie's jaw clicked with the pressure she put it under, and she turned her back on the other woman, firmly keeping the words fighting to come out behind her teeth.

It wasn't the first time someone had tried to do an end run around her, usually appealing to Dr. Milo rather than listening to what Mellie said. But no matter how often it happened, it never failed to rile her up. After all, casual misogyny wasn't confined to men. Some of the worst she'd experienced had been at the hands of women.

"I don't have an opinion," Delano said, his voice quiet and deep. "I'm not your dog's primary veterinarian. Dr. Roscoe is, and she's given her diagnosis."

Karyn seemed set to continue arguing, but just then Snugums whimpered.

"Oh, all right, do the C-section, but I'm holding you responsible—"

"Yes. Yes. I know." Fed up, Mellie couldn't stop herself from interrupting the familiar refrain. "If you'll wait in the reception area, I'll get the paperwork together for you to sign."

Thankfully, Karyn stomped off, and Mellie let

out a long exhale. The part of her that appreciated Delano supporting her, rather than taking the chance to undermine her, insisted that she thank him, but she knew it would sound grudging, so she didn't.

"Can you stay with Snugums for a little longer?" she asked instead. "I need to see if I can locate one of the vet techs, and print out the waiver for Karyn to sign."

"Will any of your techs be available on a Friday night, at almost ten o'clock?" he asked in response. "I can assist, if you need me to. I'll just need to call the house and let them know what's happening."

His mentioning Dr. Milo squelched any softer feelings Mellie might have started to develop toward him, and she frowned. But as she was about to refuse his offer, Delano continued.

"And before you ask, I do small animal work in Trinidad too, not just work with horses."

"I actually wasn't going to ask that," she huffed, picking up Snugums and placing her back in her carrier, where she'd be safe for the moment. Turning to face Delano, she crossed her arms. "However, I was going to suggest that your father is probably looking forward to you coming back to the house to spend time with him."

The expression that crossed his face was fleeting, and she wasn't sure exactly what the emotion was—only saw the way the corners of his mouth turned down slightly. Then he smiled and shrugged.

"He was already getting ready for bed when I

left. Aunt Eddie will still be up, though. She's a night owl."

Somehow, although she still wanted to refuse his offer of help, now she felt as though she couldn't, and those conflicting impulses made her huff out an annoyed breath.

"All right," she said, aware she was more miffed with herself than him, but knowing it probably didn't sound that way. "Let's get this done."

It had been a while since Delano had performed a C-section on such a small animal, but he remembered the routine well. You had to move quickly, not just for the health of the dam but also so the anesthetic didn't get to the puppies, or at least their exposure was minimized.

Because of his lack of familiarity with the operating theater, which hadn't been set up this way when he left, he felt a bit useless when it came time to prepare. However, Mellie proved patient and organized, directing him to where he could find all they needed in her brisk, if cool, way.

"Do you feel comfortable intubating?" she asked. They'd already inserted the IV and done a preliminary scrub of the site. It had also been decided that she'd perform the surgery, of course, while he took care of the pups once they'd been removed from the uterus.

"Yes."

Mellie took one last look at everything laid out,

as though going through a mental checklist, and then gave a decisive nod.

"Okay, let's go."

She administered the anesthetic, then they secured Snugums to the table. Once Delano had intubated the dam, he had a few moments to watch as Mellie began the operation. Her movements were deft, displaying both confidence and competence, which weren't always mutually inclusive. The technique she used was different from the one he generally favored, but wasn't unfamiliar to him, and soon she had exteriorized the first uterine horn and the uterine body. After packing the abdominal cavity with moistened laparotomy pads, she incised into the uterine body and used scissors to extend the cut.

Then the first puppy was extracted and handed to him, and he was too busy to look over Mellie's shoulder. He had to work quickly to free each pup from the amniotic sack, clamp their umbilicus, clean them up, suction their noses and mouths, and assess their conditions. Thankfully, each of the first three began breathing on their own and went into the incubator. The fourth, however, needed a dose of doxapram, but quickly thereafter started breathing without Delano having to do chest compressions or mouth-to-mouth resuscitation.

"Four healthy puppies," Delano commented, ligating the last pup's umbilicus and disinfecting the stump.

"No thanks to the owner," Mellie muttered. "I warned Karyn about mating Snugums, but…"

Her voice tapered off, ending on an exhale. She was closing the skin in a subcuticular pattern with dissolvable microfilament, so there would be no need to have the stitches removed later. It also stopped the puppies sucking on external sutures and aggravating the wound site.

"All's well that ends well," he said absently, which earned him a snort from Mellie.

"Don't jinx us now," she replied, with the first hint of humor he'd heard from her. "Let's get Snugums up and taking care of her pups before we pat ourselves on the back."

"Are you going to send Snugums home, or keep her under observation here until she comes out from under the anesthetic?"

Mellie sent him a sideways, one-eyebrow-up glance.

"Do you honestly think Karyn will be a suitable supervisor?" She gave another snort, and a brisk headshake. "I'll take them home with me and keep them until morning."

Was that weariness in her voice? Dad had made a point of saying that Mellie had somehow been able to take care of everything at the clinic since his heart attack, despite it usually being two of them working. If Mellie took the Yorkie and her pups home, she'd have to stay up a minimum of two hours more, to make sure the anesthetic had worn off completely and Snugums didn't inadvertently hurt her puppies.

Mellie gave Snugums the reversal shot, and then

removed the endotracheal tube. Delano helped her remove the restraints, and then asked, "Where do you want her?"

"Over in the recovery cage," she replied, gesturing to one of the top two built-in kennels against the wall.

It didn't take more than a moment to do as directed, but when he asked about reuniting the puppies with their mother, Mellie said to leave them in the incubator for a while longer.

"I want to keep an eye on all of them before I put them in with her." She paused beside the incubator and looked at the pups, a little smile tipping her lips. "They're so tiny, even Snugums could do them an injury if she were to step on them."

"Like tiny little sausages," Delano agreed, drawing an abbreviated chuckle from her.

After stripping off her gloves and washing her hands, she rubbed at the back of her neck as she turned to him, and he was sure the bags under her honey-colored eyes were from exhaustion.

"Why don't you let me take them back to Dad's?" He wasn't sure where the idea came from, but it seemed a good one. "I slept on the flight coming over, so I'm not tired at all."

"No." Her tone was abrupt, snappish, and her lips tightened for an instant before she continued, "I can manage."

Obviously she didn't want his help, but something prodded Delano to persist.

"Really, it's no problem."

She turned from where she was standing by the sink, and glared at him.

"I said I don't need your help taking care of Snugums and her puppies. Now, excuse me while I go and inform Karyn of what's happened. You can go home now."

Stung, and feeling as though she'd dismissed him like a pesky gnat, Delano couldn't resist taunting her in return.

"What? No, *Thank you for your help and kind offer, Delano*? Just, *Be gone, foul fiend*?"

Whatever response he was expecting, it wasn't for her to not even miss a beat on her way to the door, and he was beginning to wonder if she'd even reply when she opened the door and paused for an instant.

Without even looking his way, she simply said, "Exactly. By the way, that's not even a real quote from Shakespeare."

And having had the last word, she continued on her way, leaving him shaking his head in her wake.

CHAPTER THREE

DESPITE NOT GETTING to bed until after one, Mellie was up and checking on Snugums and her puppies by six the following morning. The Yorkie dam had taken longer than expected to shake off the effects of the anesthesia the night before and, once she had, at first showed little interest in her pups. Eventually Snugums started sniffing and licking the puppies, and didn't object when Mellie got them suckling in a nice little row.

"Don't get used to the organization," she muttered to Snugums. "It won't be long before they're all over the place, driving you nuts."

The little dog just looked up at her, before putting her head down, as though exhausted. Thankfully, that had signaled Mellie's chance to go shower and then go to bed.

Heavy-eyed and yawning, she was happy to see everything was fine—none of the pups bleeding from their tied-off umbilical cords, no sign of infection in the mother. Snugums couldn't be coaxed to leave the pups to go outside, and Mellie didn't try to force her. In fact, it was a bit of a relief. With all the other animals around, it was better and more sanitary the Yorkie stay sequestered in the powder room until Karyn came to pick her up.

After letting Sheba, Smudge and Ursa out, Mellie shuffled into the kitchen to make herself a much-needed cup of coffee. Outside she could hear Johnny Luck whistling as he released the other dogs from their kennels and started his day too. Between the two of them, they'd feed and water all the animals, clean the kennels, stable and fowl coop, and administer any medication necessary.

Thank goodness she didn't need to tackle the pigsty today.

As used to it all as she was, Mellie couldn't help contemplating the day ahead with dread brought on by exhaustion. She'd also been too tired the night before to stew on the latest drama unfolding in her life, but now that she was awake it all flooded back.

Delano Logan was charming, handsome and smooth, and Mellie didn't trust him farther than she could throw him. Although strong and fit, she didn't think she could even pick him up, so while the thought of tossing him like a caber was a pleasant one, it was firmly in the realm of imagination.

Mellie considered herself something of an expert on untrustworthy males. How could she not be, after her experience with Kyle? She'd learned the hard way that charm and winning smiles often went along with selfishness and questionable, or lacking, morals.

No one could have told her anything bad about Kyle back when they were together and make her believe it. He'd been sweet, winning and loving. He hadn't showered her with gifts, but had done little things to make her feel treasured. She'd been charmed enough to buy into a fantasy of happy-ever-after, which included her moving to Miami with him and providing the downpayment on a fixer-upper house. She hadn't been able to go on the title, because she didn't qualify for a mortgage, but Kyle had assured her that once they were married, it would all be legally taken care of.

Kyle had also convinced her to hold off finding a steady job. She'd had some experience working in her stepfather's construction firm, so she'd spent most of her time doing repairs to the house, getting it close to completion.

Then it had all fallen apart.

He'd gone behind her back and sold the house.

At Christmas, no less.

And that's when she'd found out it had all been one big scam.

Homeless and broke, she'd learned the hard way never to put her future into anyone else's hands. And the way things were shaping up with Dr. Milo and Delano, she couldn't help thinking she was heading right back into a similar situation.

That Delano was a threat to everything she'd worked for.

Last night her first thoughts had been for Dr. Milo, who might be hurt by his son no matter what Delano ended up doing. Now, however, Mellie had to admit to herself that her true feelings weren't entirely selfless. She was also worried on her own behalf.

Almost three years ago, Dr. Milo had spoken to her about the fate of his practice when he retired.

"Once, I'd hoped Delano would come home and take it over," he'd said, trying to sound matter-of-fact, but just sounding stilted and a little sad. "But now I realize I have to accept that he's settled in Trinidad and has no plans to ever live here again."

"So what's plan B?" she'd asked, holding her breath, hope swirling in her chest like dog hair in the groomer's drying room.

"Well," he'd replied, dragging the word out. "Hopefully I'll find someone willing to buy me out, and I can retire with a little nest egg."

She'd let out a long, silent exhale, before saying, "If that's the case, Doc, I'd like right of first refusal."

Dr. Milo had smiled then, his eyes starting to twinkle, and he'd replied, "Okay."

With that one word of agreement, Mellie had seen her future clearer than she'd ever been able to before.

She'd always hoped to have her own clinic one day, but just then—here on the island she'd come to call home—she could actually envision it.

But suddenly, now, when his job seemed to be hanging in the balance and his father might just be about to retire, here comes Delano sniffing around.

And threatening to make all of Mellie's hard work be for nothing.

Truthfully, she felt horrible even thinking that way. After all, it was a good thing that Delano was here to be with his father during the older man's illness. But no matter how she looked at it, Mellie could see no upside for herself.

If Delano decided to stay, she had no doubt Dr. Milo would hand the clinic over to him without hesitation, ignoring all that Mellie had put into it. Keeping her to an associate position, rather than an owner.

If Dr. Milo recovered enough to come back to work, and Delano went back to Trinidad, the visit might give Dr. Milo hope that his son could be convinced to eventually take over.

The final analysis, she decided, was she couldn't trust Delano to do right by his father or, if his decision affected her, do right by her either.

With that depressing and rage-inducing thought in mind, she took a sip of her coffee before going to change the cat litter and fill the feeding bowls.

Once that was done, she took the rest of her now lukewarm drink out into the yard so as to get to work.

By seven thirty she'd just finished feeding the pigs, Jane and Bingley, and was standing by their pen when Dr. Milo called. After a deep breath, she answered.

"Dr. Milo. How're you feeling today?"

"Good-good, Mellie." She could hear the joy and good humor in his voice. "I'm ready to go dancing, but Eddie won't let me."

Mellie snorted with laughter. "Glad to hear that

your sister is keeping you under control. You can't be trusted to stay quiet, the way the doctors want."

"Cho, them doctors just beating up their gums." He chuckled, then continued, "I hear you met Delano last night."

The change of subject caught her off guard, and Mellie had to take a steadying breath before she replied, "Yes. We surprised each other at the clinic."

"If I'd known he was coming, or that you'd be at work at that hour of the night, I'd have called to let you know, but he just turned up around dinnertime. Gave me a bit of a shock, can I tell you?"

Ridiculous to surprise a man who'd had a heart attack like that. Another indication in her books that Delano might just be a narcissist. Or a sociopath.

Keeping her dislike out of her voice took some effort, but she thought she did credibly well when she replied, "You must have been happy to see him."

"I was. And I'm sure you were happy for the help with the C-section on Snugums Williams."

"I was glad for the extra hands," she admitted grudgingly. "At least two of those puppies' heads were bigger than Snugums's pelvic canal. She'd have never been able to deliver them naturally."

"Delano said he offered to bring them all here and keep an eye on them for you, but you refused." Was that a hint of a reprimand in the older doctor's voice? It seemed as though it was, as he said, "You should have taken him up on the offer. I wouldn't have minded at all."

"It was no problem," she lied, keeping her voice light. "I put them in the powder room, away from all the other animals, and as soon as I get off the phone with you, I'm calling Karyn to come get them and take them home."

"Well, with everything you've been having to do since I've been ill, I'd have preferred you taking the opportunity to get some rest, but you know your own mind. What do you have going on today? I know there's no spay and neuter clinic this week, but are you giving a talk anywhere?"

Since starting her small animal shelter, Mellie had networked like crazy, getting sponsorships so she could offer low-cost and, in some cases, free spay and neuter days. They, along with educational outreach programs, would hopefully go a long way to curb the incidents of unwanted puppies and kittens as well as stray dogs and cats roaming the streets.

"No. I don't have anything planned today." Never had she been more relieved to have something of a free day, once all the animals were taken care of. But she didn't say so, knowing Dr. Milo was already stressing over the amount she was working.

"When is the next spay and neuter clinic?"

Wondering why he was asking, she replied, "In two weeks, in Grand Harbor."

"Well, I've asked Delano to help out while he's here—at the clinic and anything else I can't manage—so put him down for a shift. He can run the obedience classes too."

Biting back the sharp retort that rose to her lips, Mellie took a moment to get herself under control.

"Thanks, but you know I have things well in hand, right? Why don't you take the opportunity to spend time with your son, instead of farming him out like a workhorse?"

"Yes," was the decisive answer. "I know I can depend on you, but I don't want Delano sitting around all day, doing nothing. And if he doesn't take over the obedience classes, the dogs will forget all they've learned."

It sounded like Dr. Milo was clutching at straws, and although Mellie wanted to argue, she also didn't want to upset the older man.

So, suppressing a sigh, she said, "If he's serious about it, tell him to come into the clinic on Monday. I'm sure we can find something for him to do."

And there was no mistaking the satisfaction in Dr. Milo's voice as he finished the conversation and hung up.

As she punched the telephone screen to disconnect the call, Mellie muttered a string of curses.

The entire situation was going from bad to worse.

Delano retreated into the house without his father knowing he had even been there, and wandered toward the kitchen with Baldur, his Doberman pinscher, shadowing his steps. Hearing his father say he didn't want Delano sitting around the house doing nothing all day should be infuriating but, in reality, it just confirmed what Delano already suspected.

His father didn't want to spend more time with him than he had to.

Who could blame him? Having to see the person responsible for your beloved wife's death day in and day out must be excruciating. Which is why Delano had stayed away so long.

The guilt and sorrow that always flooded him whenever he'd thought about returning to St. Eustace filled him again now. In the past he'd used it as an excuse not to come home, but when he'd heard about his father's heart attack, he knew he had put off returning for too long.

Delano loved his dad, irrespective of how his father felt about him, and there was no way he'd shirk his responsibility of love just to avoid his own pain.

If all his father wanted was someone to take over his myriad occupations, and that would help keep him calm and well, then that was what Delano would do.

Although, he couldn't help wondering how the icy Mellie Roscoe was going to take having to interact with him all the time.

She'd made it absolutely clear that, like his father, she didn't want him around. But while his father's attitude made him sad, the thought of tweaking Mellie's tail was somehow highly amusing. Softening her up, charming her in whatever way he could, would give him a sorely needed distraction.

He was so lost in thought he almost ran into Aunt Eddie as she came out of the kitchen.

"Where you going?" she asked, putting her arms akimbo. "You just finished breakfast. Don't be going into my kitchen to mooch."

Delano couldn't help laughing and teasing his father's sister. "Cho-man, Aunt Eddie. But I hungry."

Her face softened into a fond smile. "You know how long I've been waiting to hear you say those words to me again? Come. Let me see what's in the fridge."

Slinging his arm around her shoulders, Delano confessed, "I'm not really hungry, Auntie. I just said so to annoy you. I could use another cup of coffee, though, but I can get that myself."

"Let me spoil you a little, at least today," she said, tiptoeing to kiss his cheek. "Tomorrow you can start looking after yourself."

Sitting at the kitchen table, Delano watched his aunt smoothly moving around the room, his heart swelling with love for the woman who'd moved in and helped raise him since he was a teen.

"So, you had a baptism by fire, eh? Delivering puppies on your first day back home."

"It was a surprise," he replied. "But not as much of one as being accosted by a machete-wielding woman out of the blue."

Aunt Eddie chuckled, shaking her head as she got the coffee maker going. "That Mellie is something else, isn't she? A real firecracker. Hard worker too.

You know she has an animal shelter at her home, don't you?"

"I don't think you mentioned that to me." Even if his aunt had, it wouldn't have meant too much to him. Everything about his homeland—with the exception of his father and aunt—had felt way too distant to be of much interest.

"When she came here, her father, Charlie—you remember Charlie Roscoe? He's a friend of your father—he gave her the old farm cottage he'd inherited from his uncle to live in. It sits on two acres, and once Mellie started taking in strays, everyone was bringing all kinds of beasts. Everything from cats and dogs to pigs and a turkey. She had to figure out a way to keep it going, so she turned it into a nonprofit, and gets donations to help run the place."

"Ahh…"

"She was saying it's getting crowded now, and she's contemplating buying a piece of land she's seen for sale, a bit farther up Long Hill, but I think she's waiting to see how things pan out first."

Aware that his aunt was looking at him out of the corner of her eye, Delano raised his eyebrows, and asked, "Things? What things you mean, Aunt Eddie?"

"Well, like whether you plan to stay here and take over your father's place at the clinic, or not."

The shock of her words left him speechless for a long moment. Is that what everyone was thinking, that because of the trouble back in Trinidad, he was looking to come back to St. Eustace and take over the clinic? His physical reaction to the thought made him have to swallow as a sickly sensation tickled the back of his throat.

Then he got himself under control and, well aware of his aunt's eagle eyes on him, he forced a smile and shook his head.

"If that's the case, then you should let her know I don't plan to do any such thing."

And, although he really wanted to walk away, he stayed where he was, pretending not to notice the frown his aunt sent him from across the room.

CHAPTER FOUR

MELLIE CAME UP with a plan of action to deal with Delano Logan at work.

Cool, calm and distant were the bywords, but there was no way to know beforehand just how difficult he would make it to stick to her guns.

The damned man was a force of nature: full of smiles, jokes and the kind of casual charm that no one seemed immune to.

Except Mellie, who was determined not to succumb.

He came strolling in on Monday morning, his red and rust Doberman, Baldur, heeling by his side despite being off leash.

"Good morning."

Just the cheerfulness of his voice made the hair stand up on the back of her neck, and Mellie suppressed a shiver. Looking up from the paperwork she was doing before her first patient, she nodded.

"Morning." In contrast, she made her voice sound brisk and impersonal. "Will you be bringing your dog with you to work every day? Is he sociable?"

Delano looked down and scratched the Dobe on the top of its head.

"Baldur? He's very chill. Not nosy or aggressive,

and since I take him for long runs each morning, he'll be happy to spend most of the day lazing about in here." With a hand signal, he released Baldur from his heel, and the Dobe gave a vigorous shake and started investigating the room. "He doesn't mind strangers, but usually chooses not to engage with people."

"Really?" Mellie retorted, trying not to laugh, since Baldur had stopped beside her and plopped his head into her lap, his ears lying back almost flat and his golden eyes beseeching pets. There was no way to ignore such a winning appeal, and Mellie happily gave in. "Yes, I can see how aloof he is."

Delano snorted. "Traitor, making me look like a liar right out the gate."

There were several thoughts that popped in her head, but Mellie kept them to herself. No need to start the day off on a sour note.

Instead, she asked, "Why did you decide to crop his ears? He's not a show dog, is he?" She didn't try to hide her disapproval, but Delano didn't seem to mind.

"No." Delano dropped into the other office chair and spun it to face her. "His conformation isn't right. He's too long for his height, and his ears sit too low, but he's actually a rescue, of a kind. His original owner thought he'd make some money off him if he won dog shows, and once he realized that wasn't going to happen, he wanted to put him down. I took him, instead."

Horrified, Mellie bent to hug Baldur. "I'm glad.

He's lovely, no matter what anyone else—or the conformation standard—says."

"I agree," Delano said, easily. "If I'd had him from a pup, I wouldn't have cropped his ears, and he'd have a tail too, if I'd had any say in the matter. Thankfully, it seems more people are turning away from those types of cosmetic changes."

Giving the Dobe another squeeze, Mellie replied, "It's illegal in some countries, but getting animal-based laws passed is an uphill battle in so many others."

Perhaps the embrace was too much for Baldur, because, after giving Mellie a lick, he eased out of her arms and lay down under her desk, taking up all the space where her feet should go.

Feeling as though her interaction with the dog had already undermined her determination to keep Delano at arm's length, Mellie made her tone cool again as she said, "We should discuss what you're interested and willing to do while you're here."

"Oh, I'll do anything," he replied, twisting his chair back and forth as though unable to keep still. "Just tell me what you need."

That felt like a completely loaded suggestion, and Mellie had to force herself not to let her mind wander down a dangerous and delicious path. Clearing her throat, she leaned back in her own chair and narrowed her eyes at him.

"Usually, your dad takes the larger animals and I do a lot of the small animal work, but I don't think we have anything with cattle or horses on the schedule just now. So why don't you see patients, while I check up on the animals we're monitoring here? Later, we can alternate with the patients. If you're comfortable with that, I'll tell Jackie, the receptionist, that she can book additional appointments. We'd cut back this week because of your dad being ill."

"Sounds good," he said in that easy way, as he put one ankle up onto the opposite knee, apparently about to settle in for a chat. "Aunt Eddie tells me you have an animal shelter? How many animals do you have?"

"A lot," she replied, knowing she was being abrupt and borderline rude. Getting up, she shuffled the papers into a neat pile, and said, "I'm heading down to the kennels, and you should probably take some time to figure out where everything is. The vet techs will help you."

Then, trying to ignore the way her skin felt tight and hot, and the tantalizing scent of his cologne lingering in her nostrils, she walked out as quickly as she could without seeming as though she was running away.

Although, since she'd effectively taken herself off to another part of the clinic, it did kind of feel like she was fleeing Delano's company.

There was something about his dark, twinkling eyes and the hint of a dimple in his cheek when he smiled that made her heart beat faster and threw her into a state of confusion.

And her determination to ignore Delano's presence as much as possible turned out to be almost impossible.

The first three days they had such an influx of clients—both old and new—that they were kept jumping. Even Mellie's best friend, Amity, was amongst the crowd.

"You'd believe every puss, dog and hamster suddenly needed to be examined," Mellie said to Amity on the phone after the second day. "I think we've had every female animal owner we've ever seen, and some new ones too, coming in once word got out that Delano was working at the clinic. Including you."

Amity just giggled. "Kitty-Puss needed her medication. Did you want her to run out?"

"Usually you call and ask me to bring it home for you, but this time you just had to come and pick it up yourself, eh?"

"Of course." Amity was still snickering. "After the way you'd been going on about him being here, I had to judge him for myself. I couldn't trust you to be impartial."

"For goodness' sake. You're as annoying as he is."

"Are you sure he's annoying you?" Amity asked, and Mellie knew if she could see her friend, there'd be a devilish sparkle in her eyes. Amity was such a brat. "Or is he turning you on? He's hot like fire!"

Mellie wished she could disagree, but her friend was right and they both knew it. And Mellie found herself more and more fascinated by Delano as the days passed. Although they mostly worked separately, in between patients their paths crossed continuously.

Then, at lunchtime on Wednesday, they had an existing canine patient, Rufus, come in having been hit by a car. Unfortunately Cecil, the surgical tech, was out of the clinic. When Mellie called and found out he was actually on the other side of Port Michael, she realized they couldn't wait for him to come back.

"Call the patients that have appointments right after lunch," she told Jackie, the receptionist. "Tell them we have an emergency and might be running late. They can come in and wait or reschedule."

Then she and Delano rushed the large mongrel down to surgery.

After they'd sedated Rufus and started hydrating him with Lactated Ringer's, they were able to examine him thoroughly and staunch the bleeding. X-rays showed the extent of the damage to his right hind leg, and Delano whistled.

"Yeah," Mellie said, pointing to the image. "With this amount of damage to the tibia and fibula, and the break in the femur…"

She trailed off, contemplating what to tell the dog's owner. They certainly could repair the damage but, as bad as it was, it would be an expensive operation. The procedure would involve painstakingly rebuilding the bones, pinning the repairs in place, and affixing the pins to external plates. She wasn't sure the elderly Mr. Brixton would be able to afford the surgery, or provide the dog with the appropriate aftercare. Yet, she also knew how attached the gentleman was to Rufus.

"What are you thinking?" Delano asked, as Mellie stripped off her gloves and tossed them into the garbage. He was lightly stroking Rufus's head, and Mellie found her gaze following the slow, tender movement of his fingers for a moment.

Then she sighed, and looked him in the eyes.

"I'll get Jackie to calculate the cost of surgery, but I think both poor Rufus and Mr. Brixton would be better off if we amputate the leg. The aftercare will be less extensive and the bill would be far less."

"Agreed," he replied. Then he turned toward the autoclave, as though ready to set out the necessary surgical instruments. "Just let me know what he decides, and let's get this fellow sorted out as quickly as possible. I'll keep an eye on him and watch for signs of internal bleeding while you deal with the owner."

She shouldn't feel relieved just because Delano agreed with her diagnosis, but the truth was that she had a real soft spot for Rufus, and it hurt to see him in pain and suffering. Hearing Delano say she was giving Mr. Brixton the best possible options somehow eased the stress she was under.

"Thanks," she said, completely forgetting her determination to keep her distance and touching his arm as she passed. A shock of warm electricity rushed into her hand, and she couldn't help noticing the firm muscles that bunched beneath his flesh. "I'll be back as soon as possible."

And she found herself absently rubbing her thumb and fingers together as she went back toward reception, trying to stop them tingling in reaction to the sensation of his skin beneath hers.

Delano released a rushed breath as the door closed behind Mellie, and looked down at the spot where she'd touched him. There was no mistaking the heat lingering on his arm, and the goose bumps that her light caress had caused to flare out across his back. But he pushed the sensation aside to consider another facet of Mellie's personality he thought he'd just figured out.

One of the things that had been emphasized by a professor at veterinary college was the fact that loving animals and wanting to help them all wasn't a secure enough basis to be a vet.

There's nothing wrong with having empathy for both animals and owners, she'd said. *But equally important for your own sanity is the understanding that you will not be able to cure or save every patient. Getting emotionally involved with all the animals you treat will eventually cause burnout.*

She'd gone on to explain that the suicide rate among animal welfare workers was one of the highest—on par with police officers and firefighters.

Watching Mellie examine Rufus, knowing she was both familiar with the animal and passionate about animal rescue, he'd found himself hyperfocused on her demeanor, trying to get a read on her emotional state. What he'd seen was a veterinarian who knew her job, was compassionate toward the patient and thoughtfully considerate to the owner's financial situation. Somehow she seemed to have found a balance between sentiment and the realities of her profession.

It made him feel much better about his decision not to ever come back to live on St. Eustace.

Just having to interact with the clients today had been emotionally exhausting. Many of them had known him when he was younger, and he swore a bunch only came into the clinic to be nosy. He'd examined animals that exhibited not one sign of disease, nor did they need any kind of preventative care. However, if the owners wanted to waste time and money just to get a look at Dr. Milo's errant son, who was he to complain?

The fuss would die down soon enough, when Delano left again.

In the meantime, he was beginning to think it would be politic to let Mellie know his plans didn't include taking over from his father. It seemed terribly unfair to him that she, who had put so much time and effort into the clinic, might be worrying about her future there.

He wasn't sure how to bring it up, though, without putting her back up.

Ten minutes later, the door swung open, revealing a sober Mellie.

"Mr. Brixton agreed that amputation is the best

option," Mellie said. "Although he's terribly upset at the idea."

"Rufus looks to be in good overall condition. I'm sure he'll do fine as a tripod, once he gets used to it."

Mellie nodded, looking at the chart where Delano had made some notes regarding the dog's condition while she was gone. "That's what I told him, but he's had Rufus since he was a puppy, so he's very attached." She flipped back a few pages of the chart, her eyebrows drawn together in concern. "Normally I'd have blood tests done to make sure he's in the best shape possible to withstand the stress of the operation, but he was in for his annual physical just two weeks ago, and everything was good."

A lucky happenstance, and another indication of the owner's commitment to his pet.

Mellie had pulled back up the X-rays, and was studying them intently.

"With the break where it is, I'll do a proximal femoral amputation," she muttered, talking more to herself than to him. "No need to make it more uncomfortable for him than necessary."

Delano had been thinking the same thing. Rather than take the leg off at the hip—coxofemoral disarticulation—which was necessary if the femur was damaged higher up, she was opting to leave a part of the bone intact. Not only was it a less invasive surgery, but because the thigh muscles would be sewn around the bone, the dog would be able to lie on that side more comfortably than if the entire leg was removed.

"Is Cecil back?" he asked, knowing Mellie usually had the surgical tech assist in delicate operations.

"No. He broke a tooth earlier and went to the dentist. He's still there." The wrinkles between her eyebrows deepened for an instant, and then smoothed out. Her expression, when she turned his way, was determined. "I don't want to wait for him to get back. Let's get started on this. I'll have reception warn clients coming in that there'll be a delay, and when Cecil gets back he can take over."

Glad not to have to face any more scrutiny from nosy patients just yet, Delano hastily agreed.

"While you're talking to Jackie, I'll get Rufus shaved."

And although the smile she sent his way was a little thin, it still gave him a warm sense of satisfaction.

Maybe there was hope for them to develop an easy working relationship, after all.

CHAPTER FIVE

MELLIE CAME BACK so quickly Delano was still using
the shears to clip the hair on Rufus's leg prior to
shaving down to the skin with a disposable razor.
Bustling across the room, she looked over the instrument tray, then went to unlock the cupboard
where the medicines were kept. Selecting the anesthesia, antibiotics and pain medications she'd be
administering to Rufus prior to the start of the amputation, she took them over to the operating table.

There was a kind of controlled efficiency to her
movements that Delano appreciated. She knew
what she was about, and he could almost see the
wheels turning in her head as she went over the operation in her head. And she knew how she liked
everything arranged; Mellie had a system for or-
ganizing all the accoutrements necessary for the
surgery ahead.

Going to the other side of the room, where the
recovery cages were, she turned on the radio. Whoever had used it before had left it on the AM station, and the news blared out.

"...word from the head of the Trinidadian Racing Commission is that the Santa Rosa racetrack
will reopen—"

Mellie hit a button, cutting the announcer off in

midsentence and filling the room with an R & B tune instead.

After turning the volume down to a more reasonable level, she said, "If I hear one more thing about the Racing Commission in Trinidad today, I think I might scream. No doubt you feel the same way."

He looked up at her to see if she was being facetious, but there was nothing but rueful amusement in her expression.

"Why would you say that?" he asked.

Now it was her turn to send him a searching look.

"Because almost every patient owner I've seen today has asked me something about what's happening, as if I have the inside scoop. I'm sure it's been even worse for you."

"Actually, no," he replied, turning back to shaving the last bit of stubble from Rufus's leg. "A couple of people sort of danced around the topic, but no one actually asked outright."

"Huh." The sound was somewhere between amusement and annoyance. "I think that must be some kind of weird instance of good manners overcoming normal nosiness, because I got a comprehensive grilling from everyone. Give them a few days to get used to the idea of you being here, and I'm betting that will change."

Delano couldn't help snorting. "They can hold off forever, if they like." Curiosity got the better of him, and he had to ask, "What did they want to know?"

The Racing Commission had played its cards close to its chest, revealing a minimum of information through the media and naming no names. Speculation had run rampant through Trinidad the day before Delano left for St. Eustace, and he could only figure the same was happening here.

"If it was a doping issue, or a betting scandal. If you were involved, and that's why you're here."

"Outrageous, when they all know Dad's ill." But he couldn't really put much weight behind the words, since there was a certain ugly logic to the speculation. That knowledge made him sigh, and although he tried to suppress the sound, it snuck out.

"Honestly, I had the same thoughts," Mellie admitted without rancor, but Delano was sure there was both an accusation and question behind her words, as though she were feeling him out.

As good a time as any to set her straight.

Focusing his gaze on where he was plying his razor, rather than on Mellie's face, Delano said, "I'm not sure how much information the commission has released, so please don't repeat this." He waited until she agreed before continuing, "They've been investigating a race-fixing ring for over six months, and I was asked to keep my eyes and ears open. I heard about Dad's heart attack, applied for leave and was about to book my ticket when it all came to a head, and they asked me to delay my departure until after I'd given a statement."

"So that's why you didn't make it here until Friday." Her voice was carefully noncommittal.

"Yes." Finally finished with shaving Rufus's leg, he put the razor into the bowl of water next to him, and faced Mellie. "I didn't have anything to do with the problem, other than to have been working at the track at the time it was going on. My job there is secure, and I'll be going back to it when my leave is up. Believe me, I won't be lingering here once I know Dad is on the mend and completely out of danger."

She didn't reply right away, her gaze searching his, as though trying to glean whether he was telling the truth or not. But although the moment should have simply been one that could determine the way they worked together going forward, Delano found himself holding his breath. He didn't understand why it was so important that Mellie believe him, but it was.

Mellie was equally still, her eyes dilated so there was a ring—almost golden—around the dark centers. A shiver worked its way up Delano's back, and had to be ruthlessly suppressed.

When she abruptly turned away, he couldn't be sure whether he was relieved or disappointed, especially when all she said was, "Okay," and indicated she was ready to start the operation.

As they prepared for the amputation, Delano realized he was thinking more about the woman competently readying herself than about the dog on the operating table, and pulled himself out of his ruminations.

There'd be time later to go back over the conversation, and try to figure out exactly what he was feeling, although a part of him whispered that he didn't actually want to know.

While she was concentrating on Rufus's surgery, and keeping an eye on how Delano handled himself during the operation, there was no time to contemplate what he'd said. But it lingered in the back of Mellie's mind nonetheless, awaiting a chance to come forward and be picked over.

About halfway through the surgery Cecil came back and took over from Delano, which Mellie found both a relief and disappointment. He had been a calm, capable presence in the room, handling the instruments and any assistance she needed with no fuss or questions.

It was hard not to appreciate the way he let her get on with her work without offering suggestions or trying to take over. Whatever she asked of him, he did, without any hesitation.

But, Mellie thought to herself after the surgery was over and Rufus was recovering under Cecil's supervision, just because he was a good vet and surgical partner, didn't mean he was trustworthy.

She wanted to believe him, both for Dr. Milo's sake and her own, but had learned a long time ago to be realistic with how she viewed people, and what they were capable of.

Her mother had been the first source of this knowledge.

Even as a child, Mellie had known her mother was difficult—exacting and derisive when her standards weren't met. Muddling through childhood, adolescence and early adulthood, trying to be everything expected of her, even while her self-assurance was being undermined by constant criticism, had been bad enough. Discovering Mom had lied to destroy the relationship between Mellie and her father had created a rift that would never completely heal.

Mellie had been told her father was a bum and deadbeat while, in reality, he'd not only been paying child support, but also sending gifts and letters from St. Eustace to Chicago.

None of which Mellie had received.

Only as an adult had Mellie allowed curiosity about her father to get the better of her, and she'd reached out to him. It had felt like the right time in her life. She'd been about to graduate vet school and, having mostly lived apart from her mother for the last few years, was feeling more confident about her ability to deal with whatever she discovered.

When her father had burst into tears and admitted her mother had told him Mellie never wanted anything to do with him, she'd cried too, but with mingled joy and rage.

When confronted, her mother had had a complete meltdown, calling Mellie ungrateful and a lot of other even more hurtful names, before saying she didn't want to have anything more to do with her.

Over the years, Mellie had tried to keep the lines of communication open, but her mother was always cool, dismissive and on occasion downright mean. When Kyle had conned her, it hadn't even occurred to Mellie to ask her mother for help. Instead, she'd turned to her father, and had never regretted that decision.

It had led her to St. Eustace, and the happiest days of her life. The first place she'd felt completely at home and accepted.

As though knowing she was thinking about him, her phone rang, the distinctive tone telling her it was her father on the other end. Sitting at her desk, figuring no one could begrudge her a few minutes respite after surgery, she answered.

"Hi, Daddy. I was just thinking about you."

"Good thoughts, I hope?"

"Always," she replied, with a chuckle, awash with love for the one person in the world she could say she completely trusted. "Although, when you call me at work, I do worry about what's going on."

His laughter lifted her spirits and she leaned back, rocking the chair slightly.

"You know me too well," Dad said. "Actually, I was wondering if you could come by and take a look at Lawrie? He's favoring his left hind leg, and his fetlock feels hot."

"Oh, do you need me to come now?" Lawrie was

one of her father's polo ponies, and the apple of his eye. "We have a waiting room full of people."

"No. Tomorrow will be fine. We wrapped the leg, and he doesn't seem to be in too much distress."

"I'll come by in the morning, or get Delano to go." It would get the darn man out of the clinic for a while, which suited Mellie just fine. "If that works for you?"

"Sure. You know I'm up from six, so any time after that works." He paused for a moment, then continued, "It would be nice to see Delano again. It's been a very long time."

It was an opening she really wanted to take advantage of. Her curiosity about the relationship between Dr. Milo and his son had grown day by day, and her father was one of Milo's best friends. She didn't doubt he could give her important insight into the situation.

"Dad..." It felt so wrong to ask her father about the Logan family dynamic, but there was something brewing—like a storm on the horizon—and she needed to be equipped to deal with it. "What's the story between Dr. Milo and Delano?"

There was a long pause, as though her father was thinking about not answering, but then he sighed.

"You know how Iris died, right?"

"Yes." Delano's mother had drowned off Ludlow Beach, trying to save a little boy caught in a riptide. At least, that was the story Mellie had heard.

"It tore that family apart." Mellie could hear the

remembered pain in her father's voice. "Milo was devastated, of course, and retreated into himself. And Delano...well, he'd lost both his mother and his best friend."

The sudden pang of sympathy and understanding she felt made her breath catch in her throat. "Janice Gopaul's son was Delano's best friend?"

She knew Janice well, since the older woman was one of the volunteers that helped out with the shelter outreach programs and the spay and neuter clinics. Someone had mentioned the connection between Dr. Milo and Janice to Mellie and, although she'd never discussed it with either of them, the information had stuck in her mind.

It had been such a huge tragedy, even now, more than twenty years later, people still remembered and occasionally spoke about it.

"Everard Gopaul. Yes, he was. Overnight, the relationship between Milo and Delano changed, and I don't think it ever recovered."

"Do you think that would be enough to make Delano not want to stay here, even if he has the chance to take over the clinic? It was a long time ago."

"Mel, he left here after high school, and hardly looked back." As her father was talking, Mellie saw the door to the office start to open, and felt a wash of embarrassment when Delano stepped in. Their eyes met, and he gave her a crooked smile, but she averted her gaze, hoping he wouldn't realize she was talking about him. Thank goodness her father had a relatively soft voice! "I can only think of two times that he's been back here—once for his grandfather's funeral, the other for one of his cousin's weddings. I don't see that antipathy toward the island changing anytime soon."

Although Delano had walked over to the other desk and seemed to be looking for something, Mellie wondered if he'd figured out that he was the topic of discussion. Not waiting to see if her father had anything to add, Mellie quickly said, "Okay, Daddy. Thanks, but I have to go back to work. I'll let you know who's coming tomorrow. Love you."

"Love you too, Mellie-Mel."

As she hung up, Delano turned to face her, and his eyebrows quirked.

"That was your father? How is Mr. Charlie?"

"He's good," she replied, tamping down the flustered sensation making her face feel too warm. "One of his polo ponies needs looking at, though. Do you think you could manage to get up to the farm and examine him tomorrow morning?"

"Sure. He's in the same place, isn't he?"

"Yes. Crispin Farm, in the valley just over the Rio Vida bridge."

"I remember it well. What time is he expecting me?"

"He's up at the barns from six in the morning, so any time after that will work for him," she replied, getting to her feet, and sliding out from around the desk. "I better get back to work. I saw how many patients we still have to see."

"I can manage awhile longer, if you need a break. That was a long operation, and did you even have lunch before we started?"

The expression on his face made another wave of warmth rush through her. It wasn't born from shame, though, but from the sensation that he really cared.

Then she scoffed silently at her gullibility. Hadn't she learned not to be taken in by charm and the illusion of concern?

Yet, she couldn't bring herself to snap at him. Suddenly the man she'd been thinking of as some kind of sneaking charlatan had taken on a more complex and sympathetic aura. So she just shook her head as she reached for the doorknob, and said, "It's all good. Let's get going."

But she could have sworn his gaze was boring into her back as she walked away.

CHAPTER SIX

By the end of the day, Mellie was satisfied with Rufus's progress, although the dog seemed listless and a little down.

"Sorry, fella," she told him, after the clinic had closed and she was doing her last rounds. Rather than taking him out of the cage, she'd sat down on the ground next to it to examine him. Seeing the sadness in his eyes, she stayed a little longer after checking his drain and incision site, just to keep him company. "I know you're not feeling your best, and probably would prefer to be home, but we're taking good care of you."

"He doesn't seem too reassured."

The sound of Delano's voice, low and mellow, startled her, and Mellie's head jerked up as she turned to look at him.

"He's still a bit groggy, and unsure because it's so strange," she mumbled, stroking the dog's head. She still felt weird about what had happened earlier, and it made her revert to her prior stiffness. "I'm sure he'll be okay once he settles in."

Delano moved closer, then sat down next to her so he could also pet the mongrel.

"I always feel bad about leaving the animals overnight in the hospital," he admitted. "Even though I'm pretty sure they'll be okay, there's a part of me that worries anyway."

"I know," she agreed. It was difficult to strike the balance between professionalism and very genuine concern, and sometimes people took her empathy toward the animals as a type of weakness. Yet, she didn't hesitate to confide in Delano. "They can't articulate it the way we can, but I know they fret at being left in a strange place, especially when they're in pain."

"That's true, but he won't be with us for long."

"Hopefully," she replied, determined to break the intimacy of their conversation and move away from his too-close proximity.

What was it about him that drew her in against her will, and rendered her weak in the knees?

No matter what it was, she told herself sternly, she refused to give in to it. And staying here in the quiet of the after-hours clinic, so close that she could feel the warmth from his skin and smell the remnants of his cologne, was a bad idea.

As she rose to her feet, Delano stroked behind Rufus's ear again, and the dog gave him such a sad look he kept doing it.

Looking up at her, he asked, "Are you coming to obedience class tonight?"

She'd been thinking about it, wanting to see Delano take Baldur through his paces. No, actually what she'd fantasized about was seeing Delano in a tracksuit or shorts, running around. The Dobe was beautiful, but to Mellie his owner was even more so.

It would be yummy to see all those muscles in motion. Just the thought sent a trickle of desire along her veins.

For that very reason, she replied, "I don't think so. I need to get home and help Johnny Luck with the animals, and it would be nice to have a quiet evening at home. The last week has been stressful and tiring."

"Understandable," he replied.

He was still sitting on the floor and tilted his head back to look at her. It gave Mellie a new and strangely tantalizing view of his face, and her breath hitched in her chest as her gaze landed and clung to his lips.

Delano had a mouth made for kissing—truly he did. It was full-lipped, but eminently masculine at the same time, with a natural upturn at the corners that took it from attractive into the "sinful" category.

The temptation to bend and put her mouth on his was almost overwhelming, and when the tip of his tongue slipped out to dampen his lower lip, a shudder of desire heated Mellie's skin.

No. No. No.

This wouldn't do at all!

She spun on her heel and, in her haste, wobbled. Delano grabbed her leg, high up on her thigh, apparently trying to stabilize her balance. But what he did, instead, was make her gasp at the strength of his grip and the warmth of his palm evident through her scrubs.

"You okay there?"

His voice sounded even deeper than before, and the tone sent another shiver down her spine. Galvanized into action by the unwanted attraction weakening her knees, Mellie stepped carefully away and swallowed to make sure her voice wouldn't croak.

"Yes." Intent on sounding unmoved, it came out cold, as sharp as ice. "I'm fine."

Hearing the gate to the kennel close, she risked a glance over her shoulder. He'd shot the bolt home and, as she watched, rose to his feet with fluid grace, giving her a fine view of his glutes and thigh muscles at work.

Before he could catch her staring, Mellie looked down at the chart on the table in front of her, although she couldn't for the life of her remember which animal's it was.

"Well, I'm going to head out so I can get ready for class."

He sounded normal again, making Mellie wonder if she'd imagined the change in his tone before.

"Okay," she replied, assiduously avoiding looking his way and keeping her voice level. "See you tomorrow."

"Night."

She stayed where she was, not moving a muscle until she heard him call for Baldur and exit through the rear door of the clinic. In fact, she didn't relax until the sound of his car engine faded into the distance.

Then the air left her lungs with a *whoosh*, and she put her elbows on the table and her head in her hands.

What on earth was she doing? The very last thing she needed or wanted was to be drooling over Delano Logan. Sure, her instinctive distrust for him and his motivations had waned, but if she were smart, she'd hang on to at least some of her suspiciousness.

He claimed to be in the clear with the Racing Commission, and determined to go back to Trinidad as soon as he possibly could, but there was a part of her that still couldn't bring itself to believe him.

Maybe it was because she'd found her place—and her true, authentic self—here on St. Eustace, and found it impossible to fathom why anyone else wouldn't feel the same.

Her life was busy, and fulfilling, but she also had friends and a social life. She worked hard, but there was the opportunity to play just as hard, whenever she wanted. Since arriving here, the stress of trying to be what others expected her to be had finally fallen away, and she could chart her own course.

Or had felt as though she could, until Delano had turned up.

As attracted to him as she was, she couldn't lose sight of the fact he had the power to completely undo almost everything she'd built.

Including, she acknowledged to herself, her hard-won self-esteem. She was honest enough to admit she wanted to sleep with him, but the thought of him turning out to be unworthy of her trust was a barrier she'd find hard to overcome.

The old lesson—that caring for and even loving someone didn't mean they had your best interests at heart, or wouldn't lie for their own gains—was ingrained on her psyche. Carved there by her mother, and reinforced by Kyle. And unless she could trust Delano, and be assured her emotions wouldn't be involved, so when he left she wouldn't be devastated, he was definitely off-limits!

However difficult it might be, she had to revert to her previous manner of treating him: putting aside all sympathy, quashing any overtures of friendship, maintaining her distance.

She could do that, couldn't she?

But there was no great confidence behind her determination, and Mellie knew it.

The obedience class ended at eight that evening, and Delano thankfully waved goodbye to the last participant before heading to the car with Baldur heeling at his side.

The class had been a bit of a shambles. Along with the eight or so people his father had told him to expect, there'd been another five newcomers. Those five, like some of the clients at the clinic, seemed to be there strictly out of curiosity, since the dogs were completely uncontrollable and the handlers had no idea what they were doing.

At least he'd had the satisfaction of getting them started on the road to having well-trained dogs, if the novelty didn't wear off before they got to that point.

Restless, and unwilling to go home right away, Delano decided to pick up some takeout and swing by the clinic to check on Rufus and keep him company for a while. The dog had shown signs of depression—not unusual after surgery and being away from home—and Delano had made a point to visit him as often as possible throughout the day. Just like with humans, an animal's ability to heal, and do so quickly, very often was affected by their mood.

Driving along through the downtown area, he felt a wave of nostalgia at the small food shops and vendors lining the road. The fare on offer in Port Michael reflected the diversity of the St. Eustace population—doubles and stuffed roti jostled for space alongside "pan" chicken, roasted corn and slabs of salted fish. Other vendors offered soups and stews, such as pepper pot, and the children gravitated to the crushed ice covered with syrup, served in little plastic bags, or a variety of sweet baked goods.

No matter what you had a hankering for, you could find it, or something similar, along Garvey Road.

Everard and he used to spend most of the weekends and school holidays riding their bicycles all over Port Michael, and Delano remembered them heading here at the end of the day. By then, having visited the beach or the fishing village at the edge of the city, or whatever other mischief they'd gotten up to, they'd be starving. The vendors knew when they had money they'd spend it all on the street food, but when they were broke Everard, with his careless charm, would often get something for free.

Everard.

As was usually the case when his thoughts turned to his childhood best friend, his first instinct was to push all memories aside. It was what he'd done for over twenty years, since just thinking his name once more brought that agonizing rush of shame, guilt and loss. That had worked in Trinidad, but suddenly felt impossible here.

Around every corner there was something to remind him of Everard.

And Mum.

No.

He wasn't going down that road. Not tonight. Not any other night if he had his way.

Their deaths were far, far in the past, and he refused to allow them to drag him back down into the dark place he'd lived in for years after they'd happened.

Stopping the car next to a chicken stand, he ordered a meal, and determinedly engaged the vendor in chatter while he waited. As he took the foil package from the vendor and thanked him, he saw Baldur's nose go up in the air.

"Oh, no, my friend," Delano told the dog. "You already had your dinner earlier. This is all mine."

Not that Baldur would expect to get any, since Delano didn't allow his animals to eat human food. But the dog was a master of the begging eyes and seemed to always live in hope that his doleful expression would finally bear fruit.

As he drove toward the clinic, Delano mused on his conversations with Mellie earlier in the day, and then again that evening.

He hoped he'd made it plain to her that she had nothing to fear from him, when it came to her place at the clinic. That he had no intention of staying and usurping her position.

It wasn't hard to understand why she worried. Dad had made oblique references to retirement, as though he was sounding Delano out, while Aunt Eddie had been far more direct.

"Your father would be so happy to see his life's work continue on," she'd said. "Especially if you were a part of that."

"The clinic is in good hands with Mellie," he'd retorted. "And Dad hasn't said he's ready to retire just yet."

He'd been hoping she wouldn't pursue the conversation but, of course, Aunt Eddie wouldn't be deterred until she'd had her full say.

"He might not have said it outright, but he is.

And Mellie is completely competent," she agreed readily. "But there's work enough for two."

It made him feel hemmed in and put on the spot. All he wanted was to get back to Port of Spain and away from the barrage of memories.

At least, that's what he had to keep telling himself.

There was something about Mellie that often made him forget that St. Eustace wasn't somewhere he wanted to be.

The thread of attraction he felt toward her, which no matter how hard he tried wouldn't be ignored, overshadowed all else. Even when she was coolly sassing him or giving him the side-eye, he was totally aware of her as a woman…her movements, scent, expressions.

More than once he'd found himself fixated on her lips, the urge to test their softness with his, to taste them, almost overwhelming. Like this evening, when it had felt like an electric current was flowing through the air around them, and it had taken every ounce of willpower he had not to get up and take her into his arms.

Kiss her senseless. Or until he, himself, was senseless, and all his pain, sorrow and guilt fell away.

Yet, he knew himself well. Well enough to admit there was a permanent emotional barrier between him and other people. One he'd carefully built up over the years, and no longer thought could be breached. He'd tried honestly during his marriage to let his wife into his heart, but Stella had known he wasn't all in. She'd said as much, during the trainwreck days as it fell completely apart.

You don't have the capacity to love, Delano. Her words had cut through him, even as he'd had to acknowledge their truth. *You have no heart. You don't care about anyone.*

Realistically, her indictment had made him feel horrible and less than he should be, but he made no effort to change.

Getting too close to others opened yourself up to devastation, and he'd had more than enough of that in his life as it was. Yet, his father's health scare forced him to admit he wasn't fully immune to connections of the heart. It had scared him into realizing how much his father meant to him, even if Milo didn't feel quite the same way.

Turning into the clinic, he was surprised to see lights on in the hospital area, and Mellie's car parked out back. Immediately his heart started pounding in anticipation, and he almost drove back out of the parking lot. Still, although he hesitated for a long moment before turning off the ignition, he knew he would be going inside anyway.

CHAPTER SEVEN

AFTER GETTING HIMSELF and Baldur out of the vehicle, Delano grabbed his dinner and let himself into the clinic via the side door, which led right into the hospital.

Mellie had turned on only one light in the other room, leaving the hospital in low, golden light, and was sitting on the floor beside Rufus's cage, her little mutt, Sheba, lying beside her. Sheba's whip tail beat a tattoo of greeting on the floor, while Mellie gave him a bland stare, without a hint of welcome. The change from earlier, when there'd seemed to be a distinct thawing of her attitude toward him, took him aback and raised his hackles.

"What are you doing here?" she asked, in that cool, distant voice that so irritated him.

He smiled, or tried to, using the baring of his teeth to mask the sudden flood of annoyance.

"The same thing you are, I suspect," he replied, stopping himself from calling Baldur back to his side when the traitorous canine headed straight for Mellie, getting in her face for pets. "We came to keep Rufus company a little."

She glanced at Rufus, who was looking back and forth between them from beneath the edge of the cone he was wearing to stop him licking his wound. Delano looked at the dog too, noticing that his eyes seemed brighter, but his head was low and his tail didn't move.

"He has been a bit down," Mellie conceded. "He misses his owner."

Pulling a stool up to the nearest counter, Delano unwrapped his chicken from its foil envelope, said, "Well, he has as much company as he can get right now. Maybe having Baldur and Sheba here will help too."

The sound she made was no doubt supposed to be some kind of agreement, but to Delano it immediately brought other, more erotic situations to mind.

He cleared his throat, suddenly glad he was on the opposite side of the table, where she wouldn't be able to notice his physical reaction. And how ridiculous that response was, when taken in the context of Mellie reverting to her cool, distancing persona. It was as though the accord they'd achieved earlier had never happened, or had been a figment of his imagination.

"How did obedience class go?"

Delano chuckled around a mouthful of food, then swallowed.

"It was a mess. There were five people there who hadn't a clue. One of the dogs even tangled me in their lead and tripped me. I went down like a felled tree. Never been more embarrassed in my life."

Mellie's gurgle of amusement lightened the atmosphere, and lifted his spirits. In between bites of his dinner, he regaled her with all the mishaps and comedic faux pas of the evening, just happy to hear her laughter ringing through the air.

Finished with his meal, he wadded up the foil and, ignoring Baldur's baleful stare, tossed the refuse into the garbage bin. Then he hesitated for a moment, torn.

Mellie was still sitting in front of the cage, Sheba pressed close to her side, the little mongrel's head on her lap. It would be politic to go back and sit on the stool where he'd been before, but Delano felt drawn to Mellie's side, and gave in to the impulse to get closer to her.

When he stepped over to where she sat, Mellie silently shuffled over to allow him room to sit on her other side. Delano settled onto the concrete, trying to make himself as small as possible so as not to crowd her, but it was impossible for their bodies not to touch in the confined space.

Especially when Baldur came and leaned against Delano, his sturdy weight pressing his master into even closer proximity to Mellie. Now there was no ignoring the warmth emanating from her skin, and the soft, sweet scent filling his nostrils. Mellie shifted, not away, though, but just in place so her arm rubbed against his, leaving behind a trail of fire. Delano's body tightened; a hot shiver started at the base of his spine and ran up to his nape, leaving goose bumps in its wake.

"Baldur, down." His voice was gruff, the sudden rush of desire making him harsher than he meant to be, and he gave the dog a little nudge with his elbow. Then, getting himself back under control, he said to Mellie, "Sorry about that. He weighs a ton."

"No worries," she replied, but she shifted farther over, as though to give him additional room, lessening his discomfort.

They were quiet for a moment and, as he reached out to stroke Rufus, Delano wrestled his desire into submission.

It had been a while since he'd been attracted to a woman as strongly as he was to Mellie, but he knew this was someone he had to tread gently with. Not only was she his father's employer and friend, but he realized he genuinely liked her—cared about her well-being. She was, in effect, the last woman he would want to hurt in any way.

Best and far easier for all involved to keep their relationship friendly, even if he couldn't maintain the type of distance he normally found easy enough to preserve between him and others.

In the dim golden light, Delano gradually relaxed and turned his thoughts to something he'd wondered about for a while, but had never pursued.

"Can I ask you something?"

Mellie shrugged, smiling slightly.

"Sure."

"How come we never knew each other when we were kids? I mean, our fathers are good friends. Even though I know you lived abroad, I would have thought you'd spend some time here. Summers, or Christmas vacation."

Her sudden stillness made him wonder if he'd strayed into an area of her life she'd rather not discuss, and it was on the tip of his tongue to retract the question. But then she drew in a deep breath and released it on a sigh.

"I didn't get to know my dad until I was in my late twenties, so I never had the chance to visit when I was young."

The shock of that made his mouth dry, and although he wondered how that could have been, all he said was, "I'm sorry."

She shook her shoulders, as though sloughing something off. "Don't be. It turned out all right." Sending him a searching glance over her shoulder, she continued, "I'm surprised you didn't know that already." Then she chuckled, and said, "Actually, I'm not. Dr. Milo never gossips about anything."

"He despises gossip," Delano agreed.

"Do you know how many times I've come to tell him something or other, and he's said, 'I already know'? Drives me nuts."

He couldn't help grinning. "You're not the first woman to complain about that. Aunt Eddie does too, and my mother used to, as well. Mum would fuss at him because people told him all kinds of things, but he never passed any of it on. Mum said it was like being married to a priest who couldn't divulge what he'd heard in confession."

Mellie laughed so hard, she snorted, and the vibrations of her amusement transferred through where their legs rested against each other. "That's the perfect description."

While he laughed with her, it took Delano a moment to realize he'd spoken about his mother without feeling anything but love and amusement. Usually he pushed thoughts of her aside to avoid the inevitable sorrow and guilt. But somehow, with Mellie, he could bring out a happy, funny memory, and think of Mum with laughter and fond appreciation for her witty turns of phrase.

Then Mellie's amusement faded and she nibbled on her bottom lip, regarding him through eyes narrowed by a little frown.

"I'm going to say something, and I hope you'll take it in the spirit meant, because I'm not trying to hurt you, or put you on a guilt trip."

Delano stiffened, and the glow of contentment he'd felt just seconds before evaporated.

"Okay," he responded, stretching the word out, wondering where this conversation was going and bracing himself for whatever she came up with.

"Through no fault of his own, Daddy and I were estranged," she started, speaking slowly, as though picking her words with care. "Once we got back in touch and developed a relationship, it was the best thing that ever happened to me. Now my only regret is that we missed all those years of knowing each other."

She was trying to sound factual, but Delano thought he heard an undercurrent of residual pain in her voice. Mellie's gaze was firmly focused on his, and her sincerity was unmistakable when she continued to speak. Yet, his muscles tightened, knowing she was probably about to say something he didn't want to hear.

"Your father is a good man. He's decent and kind and logical. You seem to take after him in that respect, as far as I can see. Whatever happened between you to cause a rift, don't you think it's time to mend it? Even if you're determined to go back to Trinidad, wouldn't it be better to do that with both of you knowing your relationship is solid?"

And the pain her words caused him made him retreat, unwilling to face it or the woman gazing at him with both compassion and determination.

As Mellie spoke, she'd seen Delano's expression change, grow closed and distant, but she knew if she hadn't spoken up, she'd regret it later. Dr. Milo was her mentor and friend, and whether Delano realized it or not, their fractured relationship upset the older man intensely.

Just as the silence between them was becoming uncomfortable, Delano stirred, as though he'd been far away, and the corners of his mouth quirked upward. Not into a smile, exactly, but a facsimile of one—forced and unnatural.

"I'm not sure there's anything I can do about my relationship with Dad, but I'll take what you said under advisement. After all, you know him better at this stage than I do."

It was on the tip of her tongue to ask him whose

fault that was, but although his expression was carefully neutral, Mellie was sure there was veiled pain behind his dark eyes.

She knew better than most people just how heartbreaking estrangement from a parent could be. And while she still had her father to make the situation with her mother a little easier, Delano's mother had been gone for a long time.

No matter how close he might be with his aunt Eddie, there really was no compensating for a mother's love.

Delano looked down to where his hand slowly resumed stroking behind Rufus's ear, and Baldur sidled closer, resting his head on his owner's lap, as though in sympathy.

"I don't know how to make things better with Dad," he said quietly, as though the words were being drawn out of him unconsciously. As if he were talking more to himself than to her. "He won't discuss the past, and I…" For a moment she thought he wouldn't continue, but then he sighed, and said, "And I can't seem to put it all behind me. There were things that happened—that were said…"

His voice faded, leaving Mellie with an insistent sense of empathetic sadness. Without thought, she put an arm around his shoulders and gave him a little squeeze.

"I hear you," she said. "But sometimes even when we can't get at the answers, we really do need to move forward from where we are. Not leave the past behind us, necessarily, but accept we might never know everything we want to, and admit the present and future might just be more important."

He turned his head, so they were face-to-face, and his gaze sought and captured hers.

"Is that what you did—when you came here? After you found your father again?"

He was so close his breath touched her lips, and the intimacy of the moment had warmth blooming in her chest. She wanted—oh-so badly—to kiss him, but the conversation was too serious to abandon.

"It was more than just rediscovering Dad that brought me here. But yes, I definitely had to remind myself I wasn't the sum total of my family's secrets and my own stupid mistakes so as to move forward. And thrive."

His eyebrows rose, but she could no longer see the expression in his eyes, because his lids had fallen to half-mast. Something about the way he looked had her heart racing, and released a plethora of butterflies into her stomach.

"Secrets and mistakes, eh?" He was almost whispering, his voice rumbling and causing an answering echo in her torso. "You tell me yours, and I'll tell you mine…"

"Maybe." She found herself whispering too, and the distance between their mouths was suddenly too far. Or too close. Her addled brain couldn't decide which, stuck on wondering how he would taste, and whether he would be as good a kisser as she thought. "One day. Not tonight."

These moments were too sweet to disrupt with the ugliness of the world outside.

"No," he agreed, his gaze dropping to her lips. "Not tonight."

Was it an invitation? Mellie didn't know, but she was suddenly willing to take a chance and find out. Every inch of her flesh tingled with anticipation, and her heart was set to hammer its way out of her chest.

If she didn't kiss Delano, she thought she might spontaneously combust.

As she began to tilt her head toward his, she hesitated, wondering if she should ask, but it was a moot point since he met her halfway and their lips touched. Softly at first, testing and molding, learning the contours of each other's mouth, breathing each other in with inhalations that grew increasingly rushed.

When the tip of his tongue swept her lower lip, Mellie shuddered, shocked by the intensity of her reaction, which swept out from her belly to heat every inch of her being.

She was insensate to everything but Delano—his scent and warmth, the hardness of his shoulders beneath her arm, the tenderness of his hand cupping her cheek, angling her perfectly for his kiss.

They both jumped, startled, when Sheba let out a sudden volley of barks then took off across the room and out the door toward reception. Baldur, although holding his position beside Delano, added his own deep warning.

Yet, even when someone knocked loudly on the front door, neither Mellie nor Delano moved, their gazes once more meshing, questioning. Was he trying to come to terms with what had just happened, the way she was?

"I should see who that is," she said, shocked by the rawness in her throat, which rendered her voice whiskey-rough.

"Yeah," he agreed, but his hand, which was now on the side of her throat, didn't drop away.

For some reason, that made her huff with a little burst of amusement, and her heart did a strange dip when his lips curled into a smile.

It was Sheba's increasingly frantic barking that had her tearing her gaze away from his and somehow getting to her feet. Her legs felt shaky and, as she followed Sheba into the reception area, she touched the tip of her tongue to her lower lip, searching for one last taste of Delano.

Switching on the light outside the front door of the clinic so she could see who was outside, hyper-aware of Delano coming into the room, she pushed aside the blinds and looked out.

"Who is it?" he asked, standing way too close for comfort.

It made her want to ignore the person outside, and drag Delano back into their office and ravish him.

For the sake of her sanity, she shifted away, putting a modicum of distance between them.

"A taxi driver I know," she replied, turning the

lock. Pulling open the door, she tried to smile at the diminutive gentleman standing on the doorstep and holding a cardboard box. "Hi, Mr. Jolly. What's going on?"

"I was coming down Pepper Hill, Dr. Mellie, and a woman flag me down and ask me if I coming to town and if I can bring you this." From the meows coming from the box, Mellie already had a good idea of the contents even before Mr. Jolly continued, "She say the mama puss disappear yesterday, and she don't see her come back, so she 'fraid the little one's going dead without them mother. If the lights wasn't on here, I'd have take them up to your house."

More kittens, when she'd just found homes for the six she'd bottle-raised over last month! But, of course, there was no way she could or would refuse.

Taking the box from Mr. Jolly, she said, "Okay, but next time you're going back through Pepper Hill, if you see that woman tell her if the mother cat comes back, she should contact me about getting her spayed so she won't have any more kittens."

"I will." The taxi driver smiled, gesturing over his shoulder. "She send you some jelly coconuts too, Dr. Mellie, for your trouble."

"I'll get them," Delano offered, slipping by her to follow Mr. Jolly to the car, leaving a heated spot on her arm where he'd brushed against it.

Mellie told herself to take the kittens back into the hospital yet she didn't move. Instead, she watched Delano walk alongside Mr. Jolly to the trunk of the car. Delano had a confident, sexy stride that commanded her attention.

How much simpler all this would be if she wasn't so intensely attracted to him. And now that she knew he was interested in her too, everything was even more complicated. She was mentally kicking herself for giving in to her desire.

What should she do now? Tell him it was a mistake? Pretend it didn't happen?

As Delano laughed at something Mr. Jolly said, Mellie's heart did a flip and heat flamed up from her belly into her face at the rich, decadent sound.

Maybe he could pretend that kiss was a figment of their imagination, but Mellie knew she wouldn't be able to.

Thankfully, just then Sheba stood up on her hind legs, nose snuffling at the bottom of the box, her tail wagging a mile a minute. It was just the distraction Mellie needed to stop mooning over the most handsome, fascinating and utterly frustrating man she'd ever met.

Slowly making her way to the hospital, Sheba prancing and jigging around her as she went, Mellie was still thinking about their prior conversation and its aftermath.

Delano came back inside and closed the front door, and Mellie heard the click of Baldur's nails on the tile along the corridor as she was opening the box.

"How many kittens?" Delano stood on the other side of the table and leaned to peer into the box.

"Looks like three," she replied, glad he seemed determined not to mention what had happened before, at least for a while. Reaching in, she pulled out the first kitten by its scruff.

"A ginger." Delano touched the tiny body, stroking down its back. "About four weeks old, do you think?"

"Yes, and that's such a relief to me," she said, trying to sound normal, although with the way her heart was pounding, she wasn't sure what that even meant anymore. Replacing the kitten in the box, she took out a fluffy gray one. "I just weaned and rehomed a litter of six and wasn't looking forward to having to bottle-feed another."

Delano nodded, bringing the smallest of the kittens out of the box, a little black ball of fur that gave an almost soundless hiss, which made Delano chuckle.

"Okay, tough guy," he said, juggling the squirming kitten. "I've got you, whether you like it or not."

"Can you confirm it's a guy and not a girl?" she asked. She'd had a look at both the ginger and the gray, and thought they were female, but the gender of kittens of this age was notoriously difficult to determine.

He laughed, whether at her question or the fact that the kitten was trying to run up his shirt, she wasn't sure.

"As confidently as anyone could be at this point," he replied, not putting the kitten back into the box with its siblings, but cradling it between his palms. "What are you going to name them?"

Tearing her gaze away from his hands, she stared blankly down into the box.

"I usually try to do linked names," she replied, her brain refusing to give his question its full attention. It was too busy wondering what it would feel like having those hands on her body. "It makes it easier to keep them all straight. The last ones were *Star Trek TNG* themed—Troi, Wesley, Riker, Worf, Jean-Luc, Beverly. I'm drawing a blank on these."

"How about going really retro?" he asked, actually bringing the kitten up to his face and snuggling it, making Mellie's heart melt. "Ginger, Mary Ann and Gilligan, for this dude?"

"I like that," she said, glad he'd come up with something since her brain was still stuck on their kiss. And the way he was cuddling the little black kitten, which was happily curled up in his hand, wasn't helping.

She wanted to be embraced like that!

Snap out of it, Mellie!

Hadn't she just been thinking how much more complicated life would be if she slept with Delano?

What she needed to do, right now, was make as graceful an exit as she could, and hopefully he'd get the hint and not mention what had happened before.

"I have to get these babies home," she said, making her voice brisk and businesslike. The little black kitten was fast asleep against Delano's chest, and

Mellie almost couldn't stand the cuteness. "I'll see you tomorrow."

"Yes," he replied, in a voice that sounded not one whit upset. He gently lowered the kitten into the box, and closed the flaps, while sending Mellie a little smile. "I'll see you in the morning."

And while she was walking to the car, Mellie was cursing herself for swinging wildly between elation at their sudden intimacy and disappointment at the easy way he'd let her leave.

CHAPTER EIGHT

SEVEN THIRTY THE next morning found Delano crossing the Rio Vida, on his way back from Charlie Roscoe's farm.

The visit had gone better than he'd expected. Mr. Charlie—as Delano had called him since he was a child—was the same forthright man he'd always been, but unlike almost everyone else on the island didn't pry into the younger man's business. He'd been welcoming and chatty, and the only sort of touchy moment was when he'd asked how Delano liked working with Mellie.

Thankfully, Delano was bending over looking at Lawrie's leg when he asked.

"She's a really good vet," he replied, glad that Mr. Charlie couldn't see his face. "Great with patients and their owners too."

And a fantastic kisser!

But Mr. Charlie didn't seem to notice anything strange in what he'd said, and replied, "She is, isn't she? I keep telling her to just concentrate on the veterinarian side of things, and not bother with all this animal rescue business, but she won't listen."

Without thinking, Delano said, "She's passionate about rescuing. It seems to make her happy."

Mr. Charlie sighed. "Oh, I know it, and I wouldn't

do anything to get in her way. I just worry about her emotional health. Rescuers have to have thick skins, and yet the majority—like Mellie—don't."

"She probably has a thicker skin than most," he replied, wondering why he felt as though he had to defend her to her father. "Being a vet isn't for bleeding hearts."

"True." There was a thoughtful tone to Mr. Charlie's voice. "I never really thought about it that way."

They'd left the conversation there, much to Delano's relief.

He'd already spent most of the previous night tossing and turning, thoughts of Mellie making him alternatively confused and aroused. Just the fact that he'd spoken to her about both his parents—especially his mother—without hesitation and without much pain had been surprising enough. But then add that kiss on to it, and he'd been knocked completely for a loop.

The damned woman had well and truly gotten under his skin, and he wasn't sure what to do about it.

He'd done his best to reassure her his plans didn't include staying in St. Eustace. He'd be a fool not to realize his father's heart attack, coupled with Delano's arrival had created an aura of uncertainty regarding the future of the clinic.

And who knew what Dad had said or intimated to Mellie.

Their kiss the night before had been amazing. He'd wanted more and more of her, but, at the same time, it had scared him silly. It had felt so right, so important, he couldn't help wondering if Mellie had felt the same way.

If, in her mind, it had somehow negated what he'd said about leaving.

Not that she struck him as the type of woman to build fantasies out of one kiss.

Maybe, a voice whispered, he was worried not because of what Mellie felt about it but because of how *he* felt.

It wouldn't hurt, though, to make sure they were on the same page—about the clinic, the kiss and the future. And doing it outside of work seemed like the best way.

All in all, it was far too easy to make the decision to see if she was still at home, and have an even franker conversation than they'd had prior.

So, telling himself the startling intimacy they'd shared the night before had nothing to do with his plan, he turned on to Bromfield Road, knowing her property was somewhere along it, not too far from town.

Bromfield Road cut through the hills from south to north and his hope to find Mellie's place before he got too far away from Port Michael came true sooner than he expected. Rounding a corner revealed a wide, flat valley sloping away to the right while on the left the land plateaued the way it sometimes did in the midst of the rolling hills. The land on the left was fully enclosed with a high chain-link fence and, standing on the driveway, hanging on to two ropes, one in either hand, was Mellie.

At the end of the ropes were a pair of goat kids that seemed determined to play tug-of-war with Mellie in the middle. Her arms were stretched out wide to either side, while the goats appeared to have dug their little hooves in, resisting with all their might whatever it was she was trying to get them to do.

But what caught and completely arrested Delano's attention was the mirth on Mellie's face.

She was laughing, head thrown back. Sheer, unfettered joy radiated from every line and curve of her body and face. At that moment, bathed in the subtle early morning light, she was almost more beautiful than he could bear.

And he wanted her beyond all reason.

Pulling his car onto the grass verge near her gate then turning off the ignition, he sat watching her a moment more before getting out. As he was about to close the door, one of the kids reared up on its hind legs and cocked its head to the side in a motion that anyone familiar with goats would instantly recognize. But as the little rascal tottered toward Mellie, it lost its balance and tumbled over, and Mellie's peals of laughter turned into howls.

Delano couldn't help laughing too at the ridiculous expression on the kid's face. It sprang back to its hooves and looked around, as though to check whether anyone else saw its embarrassing fall.

The snap of the car door closing attracted Mellie's attention and, on seeing him, her laughter intensified.

"Did you see that?" she gasped, trying to stem the hilarity and only partially succeeding. "These two crack me up."

"I did," Delano replied, his heart pounding like a hammer on an anvil. It was the sight of that grin, and the light visible in her eyes even from a distance that made him feel as though the earth had tilted, and he was about to fall off. "He's a real silly Billy, huh?"

He could have kicked himself for the corny joke, but Mellie went into another spate of giggles.

"Right? Frick and Frack never stop making me laugh." She cocked an eyebrow at him. "You coming in? The dogs are all locked away, so it's safe."

The property was encircled by a six-foot-high chain-link fence with an automatic gate, but there was also a pedestrian gate and Delano lifted the latch and pushed it open. "Frick and Frack?" he queried, as he closed and locked the gate behind him. "Where'd you get those names?"

"Originally these two jokers were Harry and Ron, but they get into so much trouble, and are so hilarious, I renamed them. Frick and Frack are what my dad calls any mischievous pair of people, so it seemed to fit. I think they were comedic skaters, way back when. At least, that's what he said."

"Suits them, then," he said, smiling back at her, hoping he didn't look as goofy as he felt. "Although the original names would be just as apt."

She nodded in agreement.

As though his presence inhibited the kids, they'd

scampered over to Mellie and stood, one on either side and just behind her legs, peering around at Delano.

"What brings you here so early?" Mellie asked, shortening the ropes and starting to walk toward a nearby pen. "Did you need directions to Dad's farm?"

"No." He fell in beside her, as the goats trotted off ahead of them, clearly knowing where they were supposed to go. "I'm just coming back from there actually."

Mellie sent him a quick sideways look. "How's Lawrie?"

"He'll be fine. I put on a poultice and suggested he be allowed to rest for at least a week."

"Dad must have been disappointed. He has a polo match this coming weekend, and Lawrie is his favorite mount."

"He seemed to take it all right." Delano stepped ahead of her to open the gate to the pen. "Your father strikes me as a man who'd prefer to ride his second string, rather than risk the well-being of his horses."

"He is," she agreed, shooting him an approving glance as she bent to remove the ropes from around the goats' necks. When she straightened, she asked, "So, with that settled, why are you here?"

He searched her face for a moment, but found only curiosity. Had she put their kiss out of her mind so quickly?

"Well, I thought we could have a conversation."

Now he was the one subjected to an interrogative look, and it was impossible to miss the flash of her eyes, or the light blush that rose to her cheeks.

So she did remember their kiss, and thought that was what he wanted to talk about.

Why that filled him with a ridiculous sense of masculine pride was something he didn't want to consider, and made an effort not to let it show in his expression.

But she sounded calm and collected when she pointed with her chin toward the cottage, and said, "Okay. Want some coffee?"

"Sure."

But then they stood there a moment longer, as though delaying what was to come. Watching the kids gambol and frisk toward a shaded area where a flock of chickens and a rather threadbare turkey were pecking the ground. There was also a lone sheep grazing along the fence line.

"Quite an array of animals you have here," he commented. "Somehow, I thought it would be mostly dogs and cats."

Mellie shrugged.

"I take any animal that needs help." She pointed at the sheep. "Dolly's owner had no idea what having sheep entailed. Thankfully, she only got the one, but when she decided to get rid of Dolly, I took her when it became clear no one else would.

"The chickens I raised myself, but Horatio, the turkey, was running wild and chasing people all over a neighborhood in Port Michael. No one seemed to know where he came from, but he can be quite ferocious, and I rescued him before he got run over or otherwise killed. I have a donkey and a pair of pigs too, at the back."

There was a note of defiance in her voice, as though she was continually having to justify the existence of the shelter. It made him sad, and a little angry too.

"I think what you're doing is admirable." That drew her attention, and he was sure he saw skepticism in her eyes, so he rushed to add, "I get so tired of seeing stray animals half-starved and neglected on the streets. If more people were like you—willing to try to do something about them—the world would be a better place."

She turned abruptly away, reaching for the latch on the gate before he realized what she was about to do.

"Come on," she said, her voice a little hoarse and almost brusque. "Let's get that coffee, and you can tell me what it is that brings you here at this time of morning."

Obviously she thought he was blowing smoke, but that wasn't what he was doing at all.

Hopefully her reaction to what he'd said wasn't an indication that she'd soured toward him again.

But he was reassured when, halfway across the space between the pen and her cottage, Mellie suddenly said, "I've found that most people want to do right by their animals. Some just don't know how, while others don't have the financial means to do it.

While we do see clear cases of cruelty, those are in the minority. Mostly it's injury and disease caused by a lack of knowledge or funds."

"So, what's the answer?" he asked, more to keep the conversation going than because he didn't have some ideas of his own.

"Education, primarily," she answered swiftly. "What a lot of people don't want to talk about is that not everyone is going to turn into a mushy animal owner who talks about their pets as 'fur babies.' For a lot of people, animals have particular purposes. If you can convince them those purposes are best served when the animals are taken care of, and give them the means and ability to do so, they'll be on board."

They'd climbed the three steps up to her veranda by then, and as she pushed open the door, a barrage of barks and furry creatures were waiting on the other side.

"Enough," Mellie said firmly to the dogs. "Outside, all of you."

The dogs obediently streamed out the door, along with one cat that stalked past Delano and gave him a snooty *who do you think you are?* look. Sheba paused to lick first Mellie then Delano, but also ran outside.

Once she shut the door, Mellie waved him through the living room to the back of the house, where he found himself in a kitchen just big enough for the appliances and a small table.

"Sit," Mellie said, walking over to the coffee

maker, which was burbling away. Delano took one of the wrought iron chairs, as directed, and shifted it so he could stretch out his legs.

"So, go on with what you were saying," he urged.

"Uh, where was I? Oh, yes. People who view animals as useful tools, rather than pets you bring into the house and coddle. There are certain myths around about what happens when people spay or neuter their animals—like they get lazy, and won't do the things they used to. People also do things like feed their dogs hot peppers, and keep them chained and unsocialized in the hopes of making them fiercer and better watchdogs. Those are some of the things we talk about, not just with the adults, but also through school programs arranged by the St. Eustace SPCA."

She gave a little chuckle as she took down a mug from the cupboard, putting it beside the one already on the counter. "I tell people to walk by the gate here, and then tell me fixed dogs don't bark or look fierce. Every one of the animals here, except for the very young or very sick, are spayed or neutered, and I'm sure you heard the racket when you drove up."

"I did," he agreed, with an answering laugh.

"Then I ask people what happens when their bitch or a neighbor's bitch goes into heat. We talk about the fights the dogs get into because of it, and how many animals die because of the wounds. I point out that while the dog is roaming the streets or the bitch is running, trying to escape the pack, they're not doing the work of guarding the house, so what's the use?"

"Does the logic work?"

She shrugged. "Sometimes. We take the wins where we can." The coffee was ready, and she turned off the machine. "Our best bet, I think, is with the kids."

Delano couldn't help noticing Mellie's straight-backed posture, the sweet flare of her hips beneath her long T-shirt, and had to drag his attention back to what she was saying as she poured their coffee.

"We take animals into the schools, especially at the primary level, to talk to the children about how to look after their animals. With the older ones, we talk about how they can tell if an animal is sick or in need of help." She crossed the kitchen in a couple steps and Delano took the proffered mug from her hand. It gave him a little thrill to note that although he thought she'd been ignoring him all this time, she obviously knew he took his coffee black, since she didn't offer cream or sugar. She went on: "The theory is that if we educate the children early on, we can change families' and communities' attitudes toward animals over time."

"And, in the meantime, you take in any of the animals that need help."

She'd already sat down across from him and she gave another shrug, accompanied this time with a little upward twist of her lips.

"As many as I can. Although I'm running out of space just now." Then, as though tired of the topic,

Mellie raised her eyebrows and asked, "So, what did you want to talk about?"

A little surprised by the swift change of subject, Delano took a sip of his coffee before saying, "I wanted to reiterate to you that there's no chance I'll be staying here in St. Eustace and taking over Dad's practice. My plan is, and always has been, to go back to Trinidad as soon as Dad's feeling better."

Mellie didn't answer right away. Instead, her gaze dropped to her hands, and Delano's followed. In the momentary silence, his words seemed to echo as he watched her turn the mug back and forth, back and forth between her fingers. It was as though she was searching for an appropriate response, and Delano's heart started pounding as he waited to hear what she'd say.

Was she thinking of their embrace the night before, rather than the clinic? He was honest enough to admit he'd be happy to know that. The attraction he felt toward her, that he was sure she felt toward him too, made him wish she'd say how disappointed she'd been when he left.

"That's..." She hesitated, eyes still downcast. "That's a shame."

Surprised by her response, Delano leaned back in his chair and the wave of emotion—hope and excitement—that welled inside him, rendered him mute.

CHAPTER NINE

AN EMOTION FLASHED across Delano's face that Mellie couldn't recognize and didn't know how to interpret. All she knew was that it sent a wave of goose bumps down her back, and made her heart turn over.

She'd been unsure about how to express what she thought, and now she realized how it might sound. That he might think she was speaking personally, rather than professionally, and a wave of embarrassment rose from her chest into her face.

Quickly, before he could comment or question her, she said, "Of course I'm hoping to carry on the practice when your father retires. I've put my all into it, helping to modernize and expand it, but that's just business. Your father means a lot to me—even more than the practice—and I know how happy it would make him if you decided to move back here and take over his work."

Delano nodded, leaning back in his chair, and his hooded regard made her want to squirm.

She'd spent far too long the night before reliving their kiss, to the point where she'd almost forgotten their frank and confiding conversation. If she were being totally honest, she'd have to admit that was where the real intimacy had bloomed between them.

She was ashamed to admit how judgmental she'd been when, realistically, she'd known very little about him. It brought to mind the way her mother acted, and Mellie had always promised herself never to emulate that behavior. Getting to know Delano had changed her attitude toward him, although part of her still wondered if she could trust him.

Her judgment of character was suspect, after all.

It was the kind of conundrum she really didn't need. But she was in the middle of it, whether she liked it or not, and had to find some way to navigate through to the best solution for them all.

How to manage that was the question.

Maybe the conversation would be easier if they weren't sitting so close together, and she had something to do with her hands other than hold her cup. Setting down her coffee, she stood up.

"Do you mind if I check on the kittens while we talk?" she asked, heading back into the living room without waiting for his agreement. "I've already fed them but might need to clean them up a bit before I leave for work."

He didn't reply, but she heard the scrape of the chair legs as he got up, and his measured footsteps as he followed her down the short hallway to the powder room door.

"It's a good thing I don't have a lot of visitors," she said, knowing she was babbling but not able to stop herself. "My guest bathroom seems to constantly be in use as a nursery."

Delano snorted: a sound she'd come to recognize denoted amusement, and somehow it made her relax, just a little.

When she pulled open the door, a tiny ball of black fur rocketed out, scooting between her feet then past Delano to disappear down the passageway.

"Gilligan!" They both shouted at the same time, just as an almighty crash sounded in the living room.

Mellie closed the bathroom door before rushing after Delano into the next room, and what she saw there brought her to a screeching halt.

The curtain rod across her large living room window was hanging down on one side, clearly brought down by the kitten, who was hanging onto the fabric with what looked to be one claw. The falling curtain had also knocked a metal lamp off a side table too.

"Good grief," Delano muttered, stepping over the lamp and reaching up for the kitten, who tried to scramble farther up the curtain but couldn't get his claw free. "Gilligan, you're more of a menace than your namesake was in the show."

For an instant, Mellie couldn't move, or even breathe. Delano was at full extension, both arms raised as he extricated the kitten from the curtain, and the view was mouthwatering. Shoulder and arm muscles flexed and his shirt rode up, revealing not just that perfect ass, but also a toothsome strip of dark, smooth skin above his low-slung jeans.

What was it about this man that caused her to burn inside, even while she knew it was best to stay away?

Closing her eyes for a moment and taking a deep breath, she sought calm although inside emotions tangled around her brain, making her wonder how to move forward. Delano drew her in by his magnetism and his seeming understanding of what drove her to rescue. Part of her wanted to run away before things went horribly wrong, but the other, larger part, wanted to get to know him intimately.

The dichotomy was enough to drive her a little insane.

A touch on her arm brought her back to herself, and her eyes flew open.

"You okay?"

He was close—too close—looking at her with such concern and curiosity, she felt herself blush furiously.

"Yes. Yes, I'm fine," she said. While she was trying to sound firm, she knew her voice was more breathless than she'd like. Sinking down onto the couch put some necessary distance between them. She'd been tempted to lean forward and kiss him.

Which was the last thing she should do.

"Listen," he said. Still holding the kitten close to his chest, he sat in the chair across from her. "I know you're thinking of my father's feelings, and I'll really think about what you said last night, but

St. Eustace isn't the place for me. When I left, I decided I wouldn't come back to live here, and that hasn't changed."

Looking down at her hands, Mellie chewed on her bottom lip, wanting to ask why, but knowing it wasn't any of her business.

"On a totally different subject," he said suddenly, making her look up in surprise. "Will there be a repeat of that kiss?"

All the breath left her lungs, and once more heat stained her cheeks and gathered low in her belly.

Damn him for making her feel like a giddy and unsophisticated schoolgirl!

"I don't know," she said, watching his expression—the slow upturn of those sinful lips, the gleam deep in his dark eyes—her heart rate spiking. "It probably wouldn't be wise."

His smile deepened into a grin, and he shook his head. "Wisdom is overrated, and a very minor part of my portfolio."

"I've learned to look at least twice before I leap," she rebutted. "We're working together. That complicates things."

"Not much," he replied. "Since I'll only be here for another week or so. Give me another excuse."

There were a hundred other reasons why kissing Delano should be on her no-no list, but for the life of her, when he looked at her with that smoldering intensity, she couldn't think of another one.

"It's not an excuse. I don't need an excuse not to kiss you." She made her voice as firm as she could, but it still wavered a little. "I need a reason to kiss you again."

He chuckled, and got to his feet in one lithe move. Holding Gilligan out to her, he said, "Well, I can give you a really good one, if you're interested."

Automatically taking the kitten and cuddling him close, Mellie met his gaze, and felt like she was drowning in it.

"What?" was all she could manage to ask, with her heart in her throat.

Delano bent, so his mouth was right beside her ear, and whispered, "It was superb."

Then, before she could catch enough breath to respond, he'd touched his lips to her cheek, and was on his way out the door.

"Dammit," she said to Gilligan, once Delano was gone. The kitten was looking at her with his bottle-green eyes, as if waiting for her verdict. "He's right."

Darn him!

Delano strode out, threading his way through the dogs, happily making a fuss over them the way they demanded. Going out through the gate, he unlocked the car then got in, grinning as he starting it, although his hands felt a little shaky.

Okay, so he'd done a complete one-eighty to what he'd intended when coming to Mellie's home, but that wasn't a bad thing. He had, after all, reiterated his determination not to stay and take over the practice, so Mellie could feel assured of her place there. As far as he knew, she had no reason not to believe him when he said he'd be going back to Trinidad.

But, even more importantly—to his mind anyway—he'd let her know he'd be more than happy to repeat their mind-blowing kiss. And take it further, if she was game.

Just the thought had his body hardening, and sent a wave of goose bumps along his back. He'd need a cold shower if he didn't stop thinking about Mellie. Those soft, full lips and silky skin. The way she'd pressed closer to him the night before and tangled her tongue with his in the most erotic of duels.

Whew.

She was one in a million, and if he was offered the privilege of an intimate, erotic encounter with her, there was no way he'd refuse.

His phone rang just as he drew up to his father's house and, recognizing his cousin's name and glad of the distraction, Delano answered it once he'd parked.

"Hey, Jason. What's up? Are you back?"

His cousin, who was an attaché to the minister of local government and culture, had been in Jamaica for a conference.

"Yes. Got in last night. Looking forward to seeing you. What you doing Saturday night? There's a big fundraiser out at Cable Farm. I thought we could go together. It'll be like old times."

"I hope not," Delano replied with a chuckle. "We drank way too much back in the day."

Jason laughed, the hearty sound buoying Delano's spirits even more, albeit in a very different way than his time with Mellie had. "We tore up the place, for sure. I'll make sure you don't overdo it at the fete. You're not as young as you used to be."

"Man, you're only a few months younger than me, so I don't get what you're yammering about."

"But I *am* younger than you, so there's that," his irrepressible cousin teased, making Delano laugh again. "I'll pick you up at about eight, if that works for you?"

"Sounds like a plan." It would be good to do something fun. "I'll see you then."

He was about to hang up and get out of the car when Jason said, "Wait, there's something else I need to speak to you about."

Sinking back into the driver's seat, Delano said, "Oh?"

"Yeah."

Jason paused, and the hair on the back of Delano's neck stirred. His cousin was usually both frank and completely self-assured. For him to hesitate didn't bode well for the conversation.

"Go on," Delano urged, wanting to get whatever was coming over with.

Jason's indrawn breath was loud enough for Delano to hear through the phone.

"For the last few years Uncle Milo has been talking about setting up a scholarship fund in Aunt Iris's memory, to help kids who want to go on to tertiary education. It was something he wanted to do long ago, but…"

When his cousin's voice faltered, Delano repeated, "But…?"

"Honestly, he wasn't in the financial position to do it." Jason's voice was firm, as if he'd come to a decision to tell it like it was. "After you left, the practice started to deteriorate a little at a time. Uncle Milo's heart wasn't in it. It's only since Mellie came to work with him, and started making improvements, that it's picked up again."

Delano leaned his head back against the seat, heartsore and swamped with guilt.

As if he didn't have enough of that on his plate.

"Anyway, he and I have been talking about how he wants the trust structured and other issues about the administration of it, and we're planning a big fundraiser next year." There was another pause, but brief this time. "Uncle Milo wants you to head it up."

"The fundraiser? Me?" He didn't know why he was so surprised, but shock had ricocheted through his body at his cousin's words.

"Not just the fundraiser. The entire thing."

CHAPTER TEN

MELLIE WAS CHECKING Rufus's incision site when Delano strode into the hospital, his expression stern and somehow abstracted. He acknowledged her presence with a grunt, and started pulling open drawers, one after the other, then closing them without taking anything out.

Not exactly the way she'd expected their next encounter would be, after his final sexy salvo that morning.

"What're you looking for?" she asked, finally.

"Hmm?" He didn't look up, but kept rifling through the suture drawer. "Exam room two needs some…" Stopping suddenly, he straightened and shook his head. "Dammit. I can't remember."

"Dude. You're not that old," she said, unable to suppress a chuckle, even though his behavior had her a bit worried. "What's going on?"

Delano closed the drawer and turned to face her with an interrogative look.

"Do you know that Dad's planning some type of memorial scholarship in Mum's name?"

Mellie nodded warily. "He's mentioned something recently—asking for fundraising ideas and stuff like that. Because your mother was a teacher, he thought it would be a fitting tribute to help kids who might not be able to afford a higher education."

He frowned. "Why am I only just hearing about it? And the fact that the practice was going down-hill over the years?"

Rufus shifted on the examination table, and Mellie put both hands on him to keep him calm. She wished she could do the same to the confused and upset Delano.

"I don't know." That was the truth, if not what she thought. "Maybe your father didn't want to worry you while things were unsettled?"

Still with that fierce expression on his face, Delano shook his head.

"We both know that isn't it. He didn't tell me because he thought I didn't care."

What could she say to that?

"Well, he's told you now."

"That's the worst part," he growled. "He didn't tell me. My cousin Jason did instead."

"Oh." Delano still looked angry, but Mellie wasn't fooled. He was hurt.

Before she could think of something worthwhile to say, Delano slumped onto the stool across the table from her, and absently reached out to pet Rufus. As though the contact with the dog's fur and the little lick Rufus turned his head to bestow upon Delano's hand released some of his anger, Delano sighed.

"I'm at a loss, Mellie. Neither Dad nor Aunt

Eddie told me he was struggling to keep the clinic going. If I'd known..."

The unsaid words hung between them, and Mellie pursed her lips. It seemed unfair to press him, but until he faced his dilemma head-on, there was no way he could solve it.

"What?" she asked softly. "What would you have done? And be honest about it."

The silence between them was broken only by the whir of the ceiling fan and the sound of Rufus's breathing. Delano was looking down, his face creased into a frown. Then he looked up, and Mellie's heart ached at the torment in his eyes.

"I don't know."

Moved and sad for him, she put her hand over his and gave it a squeeze.

"And you won't ever know, because that moment is gone. If your father had told you, if you'd had to make a choice about what to do. If...if...if. The ifs will drive you crazy if you dwell on them too long. The truth is, this is a different moment in time, and the only way you're going to get any peace out of this trip is to sit down and talk honestly with your dad."

His mouth twisted slightly. "I'm out of practice doing that."

Mellie shrugged one shoulder. "Well, he's not the type of person who's going to bite your head off, or refuse to have a conversation. Not like my mom."

He turned his hand so he could hold hers, making her silly heart do a little flip.

"You're not in contact with your mother?"

"I reach out every now and then, but not really."

Now his expression was one of sympathy, and she was glad to give him something else to think about, and lift a little of the cloud hanging over his head.

"I'm sorry."

"Don't be. I had to come to the understanding that my mom chose not to be in my life, because her criteria for us having a relationship is too high for me to meet."

Curiosity seemed to war with his natural good manners, and the sight of him battling with the urge to ask questions made her smile.

"You can ask me whatever you want," she said. "Just not right now. The clinic's about to open, and Rufus doesn't know it yet, but he's going home today. Mr. Brixton is coming for him this morning."

She lifted Rufus down from the table, placing him gently on the floor. With one hand under his abdomen, she kept the dog standing.

"That's good," Delano said after a little pause, as though he was still thinking through their conversation. "Hopefully that'll improve his mood."

"Both their moods, I think." Keeping her voice cheerful was a bit of a chore since she suddenly felt as though she'd run an emotional marathon. "Mr. Brixton looked so sad when he had to leave him after the operation."

At Mellie's urging Rufus took a few tentative

steps, looking up at her with the saddest puppy dog eyes imaginable.

"You got this, Rufus," she said, letting go of his belly so he was moving on his own, albeit jerkily. "You can do it."

And, as she led the dog out of the exam room, Mellie touched Delano's shoulder, saying, "You got this too. Remember, the future doesn't have to be the same as the past. Have that chat with your father..."

"If he'll let me.

"He'll let you," she replied. "He's missed having you in his life, whether you want to acknowledge that or not."

Then she took Rufus out to do his business, so when Mr. Brixton came to pick him up he'd be ready to go.

Delano found himself considering Mellie's words all morning, in between seeing patients. The volume of clients was still high enough to keep them both busy, but when he heard Mr. Brixton was there to pick up Rufus, he made sure to take a few minutes to say goodbye to the dog.

"He looks so much better," Mr. Brixton said, smiling widely as his hand first stroked his dog's head, then scratched behind one floppy ear. "And he's walking on his own."

Rufus's tail was wagging for the first time since he'd come in, his eyes were noticeably brighter, and where before his nose had been dull and dry, now it shone.

"It'll take him a while to fully regain his balance and agility," Mellie told the older gentleman. "But dogs generally do well after an amputation, and the best place for him now is at home with you. Being back in familiar surroundings with his favorite person will be better than any medicine we can give him."

She had such an easy way about her, and a really lovely voice. Remembering the husky timbre of it after they'd kissed gave him all kinds of naughty ideas he hoped to be able to put into practice.

Even in the midst of his personal turmoil, there was no ignoring the effect Mellie had on him, but it was up to her whether their relationship ever got to the next level. Not only wasn't he the type to push, but he also respected her cautious attitude. If she decided it wasn't worth the potential problems, he'd have to respect that.

Not that he'd like it.

Quickly saying farewell to both Rufus and his owner, Delano excused himself to see his next patient. But he kept listening to Mellie as she gave Mr. Brixton instructions about how to care for his dog until he couldn't hear her anymore.

Bearing in mind what Mellie had said earlier that day, about how he might be able to move forward with his father, Delano took a moment between patients to call home.

When he asked Aunt Eddie if he could come back there for lunch, she replied, "Of course, boy. Plenty of food here."

He got to the house as his father was sitting down at the kitchen table.

"Just in time," Dad said, giving Delano a sideways glance. "I was afraid you'd be late and Eddie would make me wait until you got here."

"Thank goodness Delano keeps better time than you do," was Eddie's tart response. "The number of nights dinner got cold waiting on you..."

"All right. All right." Dad tried to sound put upon, but he was smiling, since they all knew it was true.

Delano washed his hands and helped Aunt Eddie carry the dishes of chicken, boiled green bananas, cassava, yam and salad to the table. Impossible not to feel a pang of nostalgia as he surveyed the food. His father, unlike many of his countrymen, didn't eat a lot of rice with his meals, preferring ground provisions, like the cassava, and other kinds of carbohydrates. It was how Delano had grown up, and he realized now that he'd missed it.

There was so much to love about his homeland. And so much pain associated with it too.

After his father had blessed the meal, and Aunt Eddie passed around the dishes, his father said, "I haven't had a chance to ask you how obedience class went."

That was a safe enough subject, so Delano gave

them a rundown of what had happened, making his father laugh.

"Did you really fall down?" he asked, still chuckling.

"Flat-flat," Delano assured him. "On my back, looking up at the sky, wondering how I'd gotten myself into such a position."

"I don't know what you're laughing about, Milo," Aunt Eddie said, her lips twitching as she tried to hold back her own amusement. "Remember the time the bull chased you into the pond?"

That set the tone for the meal, and although Delano hadn't asked his father about either the trust or what had happened with the clinic, it felt like a success. They hadn't really spoken much since Delano arrived, and now it was as if they'd partway crossed the barrier between them.

On impulse, Delano asked, "How about coming to obedience class next Wednesday, even just for a little while? We can set you up in the pavilion, where you can see everything, and get you a taxi home if you don't want to stay until the end."

He wasn't sure where the suggestion sprang from, but the pleasure on his father's face let him know it was the right one.

"I will," Dad said, smiling broadly.

"Give him a megaphone," the irrepressible Aunt Eddie muttered. "So he can boss you around from the sidelines."

"Cho," was his father's response, but he was still smiling.

After lunch was over, Aunt Eddie got a telephone call and went out onto the veranda to take it, leaving Delano and his father alone at the table.

That was as good a time as any, Delano thought. "Dad, I spoke to Jason today."

"Oh, yes? I didn't know he was back already."

There was no change in his father's demeanor.

"Just got back today. He was telling me about the memorial trust you want to set up."

Dad definitely stiffened, and his gaze searched Delano's face.

Then he huffed.

"I told your cousin I'd talk to you myself when I was ready," he said, the corners of his lips turning down.

"But I don't know why you wouldn't have spoken to me about it from the start—when you first had the idea."

With a little shrug, his father leaned back in his chair, trying to look nonchalant, even though his gaze stayed fixed on Delano's face.

"It was just an idea. And Jason would know who I needed to talk to if I decided to set it up. Lawyers and so forth."

A spurt of annoyance made Delano lean back in his own chair, trying to match his father's casualness. If Dad didn't want to talk about it—be honest with him—then what was the use of even trying?

Then, like a whisper in his ear, he heard Mellie's voice: *The future doesn't have to be the same as the past...*

And neither did the present. But one of them would have to break the habit of silence and deflection if there was to be any chance of making a change.

Clearly, it would have to be him.

"Dad, I couldn't help you navigate the laws here, but I would be able to give you some idea of what it entails to set up the kind of foundation you're thinking of, although mine's on a pretty small scale."

His father's gaze sharpened.

"Oh?"

Putting his elbows on the table, getting physically closer to his dad, Delano nodded.

"I set up one, myself, a few years ago. Once a year it pays for sports equipment for a primary school—cricket bats and pads, or soccer balls and cleats, that sort of thing—up to the limit of what the fund can afford. The schools apply, showing their need, and I have to pick one to benefit. That's the hardest part, to be honest."

Eyes wide now, Dad stared, and Delano would have laughed at the way his mouth moved and nothing came out, if the moment itself wasn't so important.

"You have a...?"

Delano nodded. "A foundation? Yes. Took a while to get going. Stella wasn't on board with it, so saving and investing a reasonable amount of funds was the work of years."

His ex-wife had hated the fact that he was saving money for a cause she didn't think was terribly important. Or, in hindsight, maybe what had upset her was not being in on the planning stage. Looking back, he realized he'd downplayed the importance of it to her.

He'd held his pain close, denying her access to those emotions that had shaped him into the man he was.

It was the only way he knew how to deal with them.

But that was in the past, and now he needed to move forward into the future and rebuild a relationship with his father. Even if it meant opening up the wounds they shared.

Swallowing hard against the lump forming in his throat, he said, "I called it the E.G. Foundation."

His father blinked, and his mouth moved again, this time not with shock but in an effort to speak.

"Everard Gopaul." Dad's voice wavered, and he lifted a hand to cover his eyes for a second. When it fell away, Delano could see the moisture in his father's eyes, and his own prickled too. "Everard loved sports. I remember him racing down the soccer pitch, leaving everyone in his dust." His father reached across the table and squeezed Delano's forearm tight. "That's a perfect memorial, son."

And for the first time in too many years to count, Delano felt connected to his father again.

CHAPTER ELEVEN

FRIDAY WAS THE kind of day that made Mellie want to go back to bed from the moment she woke up. Johnny Luck had an asthma attack first thing in the morning, one bad enough that it had Mellie rushing him to the hospital. After promising him she'd be back to check on him as soon as possible, she returned to the shelter to take care of the animals on her own.

Knowing it was going to make her late to the office, she called Delano once she thought he'd be awake to let him know what was happening.

"No problem," was all he said.

After hanging up, she started on her feeding chores, but before she'd gotten more than halfway through, she'd been surprised by a knock on the gate.

It was Delano, dressed in a pair of old jeans and a T-shirt that fit him way too snugly for her equilibrium.

"What are you doing here?" she asked, after she'd waved him in.

"I figured you'd need some help," he replied, a broad grin on his face. "Many hands make light work, as Aunt Eddie is fond of saying."

"Well," she said, reluctantly, "I'm not going to turn you away. I appreciate the help."

But in a way he made her work harder, because she found herself watching him as much as concentrating on what she needed to do.

Although he hadn't reiterated his invitation to indulge in more kisses, the thought of it—and what else might happen between them—hadn't left her mind, at all. At the most inconvenient moments she found herself remembering, and was awash with pleasure and need.

Yet, they got everything done in time for both of them to make it to the clinic before it opened, even though Mellie stopped at the hospital to see Johnny.

"I didn't get a chance to ask you earlier," Delano said when they met up in the office later that morning. "What plans do you have for the weekend?"

The question made heat rush through her veins.

Was he inviting her out?

Mellie resolutely pushed that thought aside.

"I have a meeting of the shelter board this evening, to finalize the plans for the spay and neuter clinic next week. Then, if Johnny isn't feeling better, I'll have my work cut out for me on Saturday and Sunday, as well as laundry and all the other stuff I need to do." She couldn't help sighing. "Not exactly how I'd planned to spend this weekend, but that's how it goes sometimes."

"If you need my help, just call." He was still smiling, although he was already shaking his head.

"Don't be so darned independent that you wear yourself out unnecessarily."

Wishing he wasn't being so nice to her—since it just made her want to melt—Mellie nodded. "I'll call, if I need help."

Which totally meant she had no intention of calling. It wouldn't be the first time she'd managed the shelter feeding and cleaning on her own, and it was doubtful it would be the last.

"What do you have planned?" she asked in return, curious, although she knew she shouldn't be.

"Spending tonight with Dad, whether he likes it or not." That made Mellie chuckle, but she was glad he was making the effort. "Then going out with a cousin of mine tomorrow night. We haven't hung out together in a long time. Not since the last time he came to Trinidad, about four years ago."

"Nice," was all she had time to say before they were deluged with patients, including a couple of emergencies, that had them both staying later than either one had planned.

She'd arranged with one of the clinic workers to go by her house to take care of the animals since Johnny, although he was out of the hospital, needed to rest. Mellie only had enough time to get to the restaurant where the shelter board was meeting, and then only because she didn't go home to change.

The directors were all there ahead of her, sipping drinks and chatting. Amity got up to hug her, but it was Janice Gopaul that Mellie looked at first. The older woman appeared tired, her face thinner and a bit drawn. And during the meeting, when it was mentioned that Delano was on the roster for the clinic, Janice's gaze dropped to the glass she was holding and her lips tightened.

It took them a couple of hours to get everything hashed out and, as they all got up to leave, Mellie thought Janice might hang back to talk, but the other woman said a terse good-night and left immediately.

It was Amity who walked out with Mellie, slinging her arm around Mellie's shoulders. "Hey, listen. I have an extra ticket to the party up at Cable Farm tomorrow night. Come with me, nuh?"

"I wish I could." Mellie stifled a yawn behind her hand, exhausted at the thought of going home to look after her house dogs. "But Johnny had an asthma attack this morning, and I'll probably have to take care of all the animals by myself tomorrow. I'll be too tired to go out afterward."

"That never stopped you before," her friend teased, bumping her hip. "You getting old?"

"Yeah, maybe."

"Stop it! You have to come. It's for a good cause, and you haven't been out in ages."

Knowing her friend wouldn't stop until she at least agreed to consider it, Mellie gave in.

"I'll try, but I won't know until the afternoon whether I'll be able to or not."

But Amity crowed as if she'd already got her way, and did a little calypso shimmy on the way to her car.

By the time Mellie finally fell into bed that night, she had already decided not to go to the party. If Delano was going out with his cousin, it stood to reason they might end up at Cable Farm. It was one of the biggest parties of the year. With the attraction she could no longer ignore simmering between them, seeing Delano there, socially, might lead her to do something silly.

Like invite him home with her.

And if he wasn't there, she'd be disappointed.

Somehow, at that moment, it was a toss-up as to which seemed worse.

The following morning, the dogs barking and people talking were what woke her. Squinting at her phone, she realized she'd overslept, and she rushed to pull on some clothes and peek outside.

Delano and Johnny were in the dog pen, laughing together like old friends.

Letting the house dogs out, she decided to make some coffee before going out there and giving both of them hell, but by the time she'd taken the first sip of caffeine, she'd lost the urge to quarrel.

"What are you both doing?" she called when she was within earshot, causing the men to turn to face her.

"Just cleaning up, as always, Dr. Mellie." Johnny grinned, exposing an expanse of gum.

"Aren't you supposed to be resting?"

That earned her a rude sound from Johnny.

"I fine now, Dr. Mellie. No fuss mi."

Turning her gaze to Delano she gave him a narrow-eyed glare.

"And don't you have other things to do?"

He grinned, one of those winning smiles he utilized so well.

"Not really. I've already taken Baldur for his run, and had breakfast with Dad. Nothing else on the agenda right now, at all."

Mellie sighed.

"And I suppose you're going to want coffee on top of everything, huh?"

She said it as if grudgingly but smiled at the same time, letting him know she was both grateful for his help and forgiving of his assumption that she needed it.

Delano tried to look rueful, but failed. His eyes were twinkling and crinkled at the corners, and he couldn't control the upward tilt of his lips.

"I don't want to put you out…"

She snorted, and headed back toward the cottage, saying over her shoulder, "The temerity! Just for that, meet me in the kennels. I'm putting you on cleanup duty."

And his shout of laughter made her grin, knowing he wouldn't see the evidence of her amusement.

Taking care of the animals in the shelter was hard work, but Delano didn't mind, particularly as it had become easier and easier to open up to her about his journey with his father. While he couldn't yet bring himself to speak about their conversation about

Everard, just telling her that the ice had been broken was a big step for him.

"What did you end up doing last night?" she asked, after saying she'd fallen into bed and was asleep as soon as her head hit the pillow.

"Your father came by with Mr. Andy, and we ended up playing dominoes."

She sent him an amused glance. "Not the type of pastime I would recommend for a man who's supposed to be resting. Not the way your father plays, anyway. He always gets so worked up."

Delano chuckled with her. "Aunt Eddie read us the riot act before we started. Said if she heard tiles banging on the table or raised voices, she'd put a stop to the game. And Dad was happy because he and your father won six-two. No need for him to get upset, although I'm sure he'd have been even happier if it was six-love."

"Of course he would," she agreed. "And Daddy would have been too, but at least your ego was spared that humiliation."

"I'm not as radical as they are when it comes to winning," he replied, honestly. "Mr. Andy wasn't happy with me, but obviously keeping on Aunt Eddie's good side was more important than expressing his frustrations."

"Oh, hell yes," Mellie agreed with a snort. "Everyone knows your aunt isn't to be trifled with. My father loves her, but freely admits to being completely intimidated by her. He says although she's younger, she used to keep him and Dr. Milo in line even when they were children."

"I can believe that."

"It must be nice to have friends of such long standing," she said, a wistful note in her voice. "As close as family, but even more treasured because you chose them, you know?"

Delano thought of Everard, and sadness swamped him; it wasn't as sharp as it used to be, but still there. Then he pushed it away, wanting simply to enjoy the day with Mellie, rather than being bogged down with regrets.

"You don't have anyone like that?" he asked, hoping she wouldn't turn the question back on him.

"No." The way she spoke suggested it was all she was going to say on the subject. A complete sentence. So it was a bit of a surprise when she continued, "When I was very young, we moved around too much. And even when we settled in Chicago—after Mom married Tony—I didn't really know how to make friends." She paused, a thoughtful expression pulling her eyebrows together. "To be honest, my mother was too unpredictable for me to feel comfortable bringing people to the house. It was too much of a risk.

"And now, ever since I got in touch with Daddy, she's been unhappy with me. Her criteria for us having a relationship is that I go back to the States and not keep in contact with my father."

"That's harsh," Delano said, shocked and saddened.

Mellie just shrugged, though. "If you met her, you'd understand. She wants everything her way. Thank goodness I realized a long time ago that I deserved to make my own decisions, whether she approves or not, or whether they turned out to be good or bad."

Trying to lighten the mood, he said, "I can't see you making any really bad choices. You seem really methodical and levelheaded, like you have everything together."

That made her burst out laughing. "You have no idea just how terrible some of my decisions have been." Before he could ask, she held up a hand, and continued, "Maybe one day I'll tell you about it, but not today." She looked out into the sunshine and said, "It's too nice a day to go down that road."

"Okay," he teased, "I'll wait until a rainy day, then ask you."

"And if it's gloomy enough, I just might tell you. Where are you and your cousin going tonight?"

He followed her lead, turning down this new conversational path with her.

"Some charity do, out on a farm."

"Up at Cable Farm," she said, nodding. "My best friend, Amity, invited me too, but I haven't decided whether to go or not yet."

"Well, if you decide to come, save me a dance."

He made an effort to sound casual, but when she slanted him an enigmatic glance his body heated. For a long moment their gazes clashed, and the electricity sparking hot and arousing between them singed him down to the bone.

Then she turned away, and he thought he heard her take a deep inhale.

"We'll see," was all she said.

And he had to content himself with that.

CHAPTER TWELVE

MELLIE DILLYDALLIED ALL day about whether to go to the Cable Farm party. While she'd pretty much decided from the night before not to go, there was no escaping the fact that knowing Delano would be there made it more appealing.

Especially if he made good on his request for a dance.

Just the thought made her break out in goose bumps.

Of course, maybe he was thinking of a fast calypso or reggae tune, but her brain kept insisting on imagining a slow, smoochy number, where they'd be locked in each other's arms.

There was no mistaking the rising awareness flowing back and forth between them, which had reached new heights that day as they worked side by side. More than once their gazes had locked, and Mellie hadn't been able to ignore the heat gathering beneath her skin and in her core.

It was probably just because she was in the midst of a sexual drought, she told herself. The last relationship she'd had was two years ago, and calling it a *relationship* was really stretching it. The truth was, she didn't have time to devote to being a part of a functioning couple, between work, the shelter and all the other projects she had going on. She'd gone out with Rafe over the space of three months, slept with him a few times, but when he'd started complaining about her lack of availability, she'd had to call it quits.

And, in reality, she had felt only a brief moment of guilt and sadness.

She'd enjoyed the companionship, but hadn't been that into him, no matter how handsome and nice he'd been.

There certainly hadn't been the sparks she felt whenever she was around Delano.

Telling herself it was ridiculous to even consider getting involved with Dr. Milo's son hadn't worked. In fact, the more she argued with herself about it, the less ludicrous it sounded.

She had no time or wish to be in a serious relationship, and Delano had assured her he was only here for a short time. If he was interested in a brief, sex-only relationship, it would suit her fine.

Without the worry of getting too emotionally involved, she could simply enjoy him and not fret about his trustworthiness.

Not that she mistrusted him the way she had at first. The more she got to know him, the less she believed her initial impressions and assumptions were correct. His belief that his father didn't want him around hinted at a deeper issue Mellie wasn't privy to, but was desperately curious about.

But she was the last person to delve into other people's pains and sorrows, knowing she didn't really want to share her own. Only her father knew fully what had happened back in Miami, since he'd been the one to help her clean up the mess she'd found herself in. Dr. Milo knew a part of the story, but he was like a clam when it came to gossip, which Mellie completely appreciated.

There was no way she'd have been able to build her new life here in St. Eustace if everyone had known the shambles she'd made of her previous one. It would have been too embarrassing.

Amity was overjoyed when Mellie called to let her know she'd go with her to the party.

"You want me to pick you up?" Mellie asked her friend, since she could drive past Amity's apartment on her way to the farm, while Amity would have to go way out of her way to get Mellie.

"Better we drive separately," Amity replied. "Since I know you're going to want to leave before I'm ready to go home. Meet me here, and we'll drive in convoy."

Laughing, Mellie agreed. Amity would probably be among the last to leave the party, while Mellie had to be up early in the morning.

When she arrived at Amity's place later that evening, her friend gave a *whoop* of appreciation.

"Look at you, Miss Thing. I haven't seen you dressed up like this in forever. I knew that outfit was perfect for you, remember?"

Mellie felt the heat rise into her face, but tried to act nonchalant.

"Yes, I remember. I just felt like looking pretty,"

she said, as though it hadn't taken her over an hour to figure out what to wear. What would turn Delano's head enough that he'd make a move, or give her the opening to make one herself?

Finally she'd chosen a bright coral pink dress, the fabric as ethereal as a sigh. From the shoestring strap that held it up and gathered the material along the neckline, it fell to midthigh, leaving her shoulders bare. On the hanger it looked frumpy, making Mellie wonder why she bought it each time she saw it in the closet, but when she put it on, and saw the way it caressed her curves, she remembered.

Amity's perfectly shaped eyebrows rose.

"You always look pretty, even in scrubs," she said stoutly. "But I can see you put in extra effort tonight. For anyone in particular?"

"Myself." Then, knowing her friend wouldn't stop until Mellie came clean about why her cheeks were now burning hot, she added, "To give me courage."

Amity snapped her fingers. "Delano Logan, right?"

"Why'd you jump to that conclusion?"

Amity held up her hand and counted off on her fingers each point as she made them.

"One—he's gorgeous. Two—he's available. Three—he's the only man you've been in close contact with recently."

"That you know of," Mellie interjected, earning herself an eyeroll from her friend.

"That I know of for certain. Four—he's just your type—smart, jovial, hardworking, oh, and did I mention gorgeous?"

"That's twice now," Mellie muttered.

"I rest my case," Amity replied, the smugness in her voice making Mellie chuckle.

"You missed a point, though," Mellie said as Amity locked her front door, and they went down the steps to the car park.

"Which point?"

"He'll only be here for another week or so."

Amity stopped and shook her head.

"One of these days you're going to have to get over your commitment-phobia, Mellie."

"But today is not that day," Mellie rebutted. "Today, all I'm interested in is seeing if I can get Delano Logan into my bed."

"And more power to you," came Amity's reply, although she was still shaking her head, as though in disbelief.

Cable Farm was a coffee plantation in the hills, the main house built of stone and registered as a historical building by the Ministry of Culture. It had been repaired and refurbished back to its former glory, and was operated as a bed-and-breakfast by the owner, who lived in a smaller house on the property. For the charity function the house was lit up. There were tables and chairs on the lawn and, from there, down a short flight of stairs on the terraced hillside, a wooden dance floor had been erected.

Mellie and Amity paused on the lawn, surveying the crowd of people already in attendance.

"My parents are here somewhere," Amity said,

glancing at the occupied tables. "But I'm guessing they'll leave right after they've eaten. Is your father coming?"

"He has a polo match tomorrow, so no. When I asked him, he said he was too old to be feting the night before a match."

"Sounds reasonable. You see your guy yet?"

It was on the tip of her tongue to say Delano wasn't her guy, but it was too late to close the barn door on that one.

"No."

"The bar," Amity said, with her usual determination. "And even if he isn't there, I want a drink."

As they strolled along, returning greetings and hugs with all the people they knew, suddenly there he was, and Mellie's breath hitched when she saw the way he was looking at her. As he strode toward her, he was smiling, but it looked more predatory than amused, and his eyes gleamed behind half-closed lids.

"Mmm-hmm," murmured Amity, just loud enough for the sound to reach Mellie's ear. "You're definitely getting lucky tonight."

And all Mellie could do was hope the evening shadows hid the rush of color to her cheeks.

Delano could hardly believe his eyes.

From the first moment he'd seen Mellie he'd been attracted to her, even though she was threatening him with a machete. In his eyes she was beautiful, and had only grown more so as he'd spent time with and gotten to know her.

But tonight…

Tonight she was radiant. Sexy. Sinfully sensual.

Her pink dress flowed around her body, touching it the way he longed to—softly caressing with each move. Through some feminine alchemy she appeared to be naked beneath the silky fabric, as each and every curve and dip was alternately revealed and concealed. The light evening breeze added to that illusion, making the dress froth and swing with each gust.

It took everything he had within not to grab and kiss her, before dragging her away from the party and all the prying eyes around them.

All he could think about was running his hands all over her, bringing her to full, shivering arousal, before stripping her naked and making love to her in every way possible.

The intensity of his reaction pulled him up short, though. It wasn't his way to come on strong. It never had been. So he resigned himself to waiting, and letting her set the pace, if that was what she wanted.

But that didn't mean that he couldn't express his appreciation.

He walked right up to her, hardly aware there was someone else standing beside her and completely forgetting his cousin Jason, who was keeping pace with him as he made a beeline to Mellie.

"You look fabulous," he told her, wanting to

touch her in some way, but hesitating because he wasn't sure he wouldn't do something ridiculous, like full-on kiss her. "Absolutely stunning."

Rather than slough him off as he expected, Mellie gave him a long look, her lips pursed in a winsome pout.

"Thank you," she murmured. "I felt like dressing up a bit this evening."

He couldn't even reply, because as she spoke she ran her hand along her side, molding that magical fabric to her curves, and making his palm itch with the urge to follow her example.

"Jason," came Amity's half amused, half resigned voice, "Come let's get a drink. I know when I'm not wanted."

"Me too," was the laughing answer, and Delano was hardly aware of them leaving until Mellie's gaze broke from his and followed the other couple as they walked away.

"Oh, I don't think I've ever met your cousin," she said. "And you didn't introduce us."

"I'll do it later." Hooking an arm around her waist, he turned her toward the dance floor. The DJ was playing calypso, and while it wasn't the ideal musical genre for how he was feeling, there was still an opportunity to pull Mellie close every now and then. "I'm claiming my dance now, before anyone else beats me to it."

"There's no rush." When she laid a hand on his chest, he was sure she could feel his heart thumping through his shirt. "Let's wait until they play something a little slower."

That was when Delano was absolutely sure that she wanted the same thing he did. And that some-time soon, perhaps even tonight, he'd get to know Mellie as intimately as he craved.

Shifting his hand so it lay against the small of her back, trying to ignore the heat of her body through the thin material, he cleared his throat and asked, "How about a drink, then, and an intro to my cousin?"

"Sure." She slanted him a glance from the corner of her eye, her smile almost sly. This was a different Mellie again from the one he'd experienced earlier. A little more subdued, definitely with an increased sultriness quotient. "There definitely is no need to hurry."

His heart stopped, the double entendre making his entire body tighten.

But her voice was serene when she continued, "Come on. I see Kiah Langdon and his wife, Mina. You'll like them. They're really fun."

And he was forced to marshal every ounce of control and nod, following meekly after her, when what he really wanted to do was throw her over his shoulder and race away.

Get her somewhere private so he could kiss that tempting smile right off her lips.

CHAPTER THIRTEEN

MELLIE KNEW SHE was teasing Delano, both with her flirtation and her determination to wait, despite wanting him almost unbearably already. The truth of the matter was she had two very good reasons to delay what she now considered to be the inevitable conclusion of the night.

Him. Her. Together. In bed.

If he'd asked, she'd have told him that although he was still a stranger to many of the people at the party, she wasn't. Also, by night's end, because of his father's popularity, anyone who wasn't acquainted with him certainly would know who Delano was if they wanted to.

It stood to reason that if they ran out of the party before it even properly got going, both his father and hers would hear about it by the following morning. If she and Delano decided to sleep together and prolong their affair for the rest of the time he was in St. Eustace, that would be soon enough to run the gauntlet of parental scrutiny. But since they hadn't even got to that point yet, Mellie didn't see any advantage in getting either Dr. Milo or her dad too excited about their offspring falling into bed together.

The second reason was that she realized the anticipation would only make the entire situation sweeter.

The little touches they exchanged. The heated glances. The knowledge that soon whatever erotic fantasies they were weaving in their heads stood a good chance of coming true. All those heightened the sensation of a monumental event on the horizon, slowly building, waiting for the right instance to burst forth into pleasure.

And she liked that. A lot.

So she took him over to where a group from the hospital was standing, integrating into the crowd and introducing him.

"You know Kiah, from obedient class," she said. "And this is his wife, Dr. Mina Haraldson. This mischief-maker is Dr. Gen Broussard—one of our best surgeons—and her husband, Zach Lewin, who all work at Port Michael Public Hospital. This is Dr. Milo's son, Delano."

Gen laughed, and swatted Mellie on the arm.

"How dare you introduce me that way?" she asked, her Southern accent enhanced by a newly acquired island swing. "Please don't listen to her, Dr. Logan. I'm an angel, as everyone else will attest to."

"Not if we don't want to be struck by lightning," her husband muttered, earning a glare. But when everyone else chuckled, Gen was laughing with them.

This was one of the reasons she'd chosen this particular group. Their levity and comfort with each other helped ease the tension between her and Delano somewhat. Amity and Jason also came over, and the hilarity increased exponentially. Gen and Amity were friends, and teased each other unmercifully, and there was no shortage of comical stories told.

"Did Gen have a stroke?" Delano whispered into Mellie's ear at one point, giving her goose bumps as his warm breath wafted across her cheek, and his delicious scent ignited her olfactory senses.

Leaning close so her lips were against his ear in turn, and resting her hand on his arm, she murmured, "Bell's palsy."

There was no mistaking the shiver that traveled through Delano's body, and Mellie couldn't help smiling to herself as she rejoined the general conversation.

They chatted, laughed and danced, and the entire group commandeered a table when dinner was served. Although surrounded by all the others, and sometimes separated from him, Mellie was constantly and completely aware of where Delano was at all times.

And whenever she ventured a glance in his direction, it was often to find his gaze squarely on her, as well.

The night took on an almost dreamlike aura. Mellie couldn't remember when she'd had so good a time, or felt so confident and beautiful. Despite them both seemingly making an effort to not appear to be together, she and Delano orbited each other, connected by a thread of attraction.

She'd nursed a glass of red wine all evening, but it struck her, suddenly, that she felt tipsy with happiness. And while she could freely acknowledge to herself that Delano had a lot—more than a lot—to do with that, there was also a part of her that insisted she remember not to get in too deep.

That while she no longer distrusted him the way she had in the beginning, there was no upside to risking more than her physical self with this man.

And she was determined to share nothing else but that.

It turned out that Kiah's grandmother, Miss Pearl, and Delano's aunt Eddie were old friends from church, and that led to more jokes and laughter, as the two men compared stories.

This was a Delano Mellie hadn't experienced before. Although he'd seemed charming and sociable from the beginning, she realized he hadn't been truly relaxed. Not like he was now, surrounded by uncomplicated company.

Just then, as Kiah was telling Zach about Miss Eddie, and the way she and his own grandmother seemed to know everything happening in Port Michael, Delano looked across at her, and Mellie's heart stopped.

Beneath the laughter in his gaze was heat to match her own, and the intensity of it made her breath catch deep in her chest.

Looking away was difficult, but imperative if

she didn't want everyone else at the table to know how much she desired him.

Amity nudged Mellie.

"Isn't that your dad's neighbor, Mr. Ramos?"

Thankful for the interruption, Mellie looked in the direction she was pointing, spotting the elderly man walking toward the car park.

"Oh, yes. I should go speak to him."

Without sparing Delano another glance, she got up from the table and took off after her father's friend, glad to have a chance to catch her breath, away from Delano.

Delano watched Mellie hurry after the older gentleman, enjoying the view of her swinging hips in that bewitching dress.

The woman he'd seen this evening was the one he'd been longing to interact with. Mellie had laughed and teased and shone, bright as the Caribbean sun at midday. Her beauty and personality had dazzled him all over again, but whereas before he'd been on the outside and looking in, tonight she'd drawn him right in.

And he couldn't get enough of it.

He'd felt at home with her in a way he had to acknowledge he hadn't experienced in a long time. Oh, it was easy to be cordial and make casual friendships that didn't take much to sustain. He'd been doing it all his life, and had no complaints. Yet, somehow, tonight he'd had to face the fact that he'd actually been missing out on something important.

Just like he'd missed out on being an integral part of his family too.

"She looks gorgeous tonight, doesn't she?"

Amity's question jerked him out of his ruminations, and he turned to find she'd slid into the seat beside him and was watching him with a sly smile on her face.

"She always looks gorgeous," he said, before he'd thought it through.

The grin Amity sent his way let him know she'd made note of his reply and happily filed it away.

"I'm sure she'd be glad to hear you say so." They both watched silently for a moment as Mellie looped her arm through that of Mr. Ramos and the two of them strolled toward the parking area. "I'm glad to see her enjoying herself so much. She's a wonderful woman, and friend, but she works so hard she doesn't have much fun."

"I'm surprised," Delano said, tearing his gaze away from Mellie and giving his full attention to her friend. "With a crowd like this, I'd have thought she'd be out all the time."

Amity shrugged lightly. "We try, but she gives her all to everything she does, and she's fiercely independent to boot. Often that means running herself almost into the ground to get everything done, because she's trying to do it all herself. Doesn't leave much time for parties or even socializing much."

"Hmm. And she's planning to take on even more—either with taking over from Dad at the clinic, or expanding the shelter."

"She'll manage," Amity said with conviction. "I don't want you to get the idea that she's not capable, because she is. We're putting plans in place—I'm on the board of the shelter—for the eventual expansion. It's set up as a not-for-profit, and runs on mostly donations, but Mellie has made some impressive connections and there's a chance for some sponsorships and other moneymakers in the works."

"How long can she go on where she is, before she has to expand?"

"She's already there," Amity replied. "The shelter is just about at capacity. The outreach programs can continue, of course, but unless she gets a bigger place, or gets a bunch of animals adopted, Mellie's going to have to halt intake."

He shouldn't care, but Amity's words struck him like a blow to the solar plexus. From seeing her with the animals, from the kittens the taxi man had brought to the clinic, and the dogs, other cats, goat kids, and the pigs Jane and Bingley, he knew rescue was where her heart lay.

"I don't see her stopping. If an animal needs help, she'll do what she can to take it in," he said. After all, he'd seen that with his own eyes in the case of the kittens, which she'd taken into her house since the cattery nursery was already full.

Amity's lips quirked. "You know her better than I gave you credit for."

For some unfathomable reason, her words made heat rush up from his chest and into his face. Thankfully, she glanced away just then, and he saw her frown.

"Oh, darn it."

When he followed her gaze, he saw Mellie standing on the edge of the car park, speaking to a man who definitely wasn't the elderly Mr. Ramos. He was about the same height as Mellie, and was standing way too close, his face just inches from hers.

The sight caused such a rush of annoyance that he had to swallow to speak lightly.

"Someone doesn't appreciate the concept of personal space, does he?"

Amity snorted. "And Mellie doesn't much care for him. Look at how she's leaning away. I wonder if he has bad breath too?"

It was Delano's turn to snort, but there was no amusement in the sound. His annoyance was edging toward anger.

"Who is he, anyway?"

"Martin McGovern. An American working in the accounts department of one of the new hotels. Mellie went on one date with him about four months ago but didn't like him. He's been trying to get her to go out with him again ever since." Amity nudged him with her elbow, hard enough that Delano grunted. "You should go rescue her."

"I'm pretty sure Mellie can rescue herself," he

replied, but he was already on his feet, and Amity laughed as he walked away.

Plastering a smile on his face, he strode up to Mellie and slung an arm around her waist. Startled, she turned to look up at him, and he planted a smacking kiss right on her lips. When he let his mouth linger on hers, she didn't pull away.

Instead, she leaned into his embrace, and Delano almost forgot what it was he was trying to achieve.

Only when he heard the other man clear his throat did Delano pull back.

Not releasing his hold on Mellie's waist, he looked at the accountant and grinned.

"Hey, sorry to butt in, but they're playing my favorite song and Mellie promised to dance it with me. Come on, sweetheart."

Spinning her around, he danced her away, using his hip to bump hers in time to the music, and her laughter was sweeter to him than chocolate fudge.

And he loved chocolate fudge.

"You realize you just said a thirty-year-old song about a donkey is your favorite, right?"

"Sure. Why not? I'm a vet, aren't I? And specifically known as an equine vet too. It's apt."

She was belly-laughing when they got to the dance floor and when he spun her, making that magical dress flare around her thighs, Delano realized he was lost.

Gone.

Destroyed by her beauty and sex appeal.

It should have scared him, this intense flare of

emotion, but somehow he just accepted it, deciding to contemplate what it meant at another time.

Right now, he was too busy enjoying her company, and her joy.

When the song finished, Mellie took his arm and steered him off the floor and back toward the table where the others sat.

"Thank you for the dance," she said demurely. "And for saving me from Martin. I thought he was going to take a bite out of my face, he was so close."

"I doubt he was thinking about biting. And I don't blame him. You're eminently kissable."

She stopped, her hand tightening on his arm, and turned a shining expression his way.

"If you feel that way, come home with me."

For a moment he couldn't move. Couldn't reply. His heart was thumping harder than the bass coming through the speakers, and an erotic rush almost took him to his knees.

Catching his breath took real effort, but as soon as he had he replied, "Gladly."

CHAPTER FOURTEEN

DELANO WASN'T SURE how Mellie wanted to handle their departure. He didn't care if her friends knew they were going home together, but there'd been no time to discuss it with her before she'd started walking again. The best he could do was let her take the lead when they got back to the table.

Once there, she picked up her clutch and smiled brightly at all their friends.

"Okay, folks. I'm heading home."

"Already?" Amity asked, looking at her watch.

"Oh, yeah. I know, I know. Early mornings...blah-blah-blah."

"Not everyone can have a leisurely weekend like you," Mellie rebutted, as she bent to hug her friend. "My neighbors would be all over me like a cheap suit if the animals started kicking up a fuss because I hadn't fed them first thing."

The men all got up to say goodbye, and Delano stood to one side, wondering if Mellie would give him some kind of signal to show she meant what she'd said.

Then he decided to take matters into his own hands. After all, Mellie never said what she didn't mean, at least as far as he'd seen to that point.

"Hey, do you mind giving me a ride home?" he

asked. "I came with Jason, but I promised Dad I'd help out around the house tomorrow, so I don't want to stay out too late."

"And you very much would be going home when the sun was up if you wait around for me," Jason said, with a chuckle. "Amity and I are known for being the last to leave parties like this."

"That's right, my brother from another mother," Amity said, getting up and pointing at the dance floor. "Let those old folks go home to bed, while we dance the night away."

And with one last wave they went off together, while Delano and Mellie started walking toward the car park.

"I'm parked about halfway down the driveway," she said, sounding a bit more subdued than she had earlier.

He hoped she wasn't having second thoughts, although he wouldn't blame her if she was. There was a part of him that wondered if sleeping with her was really a good idea—but that part wasn't strong enough to stop him from doing just that, if Mellie was still willing.

"I had a great time tonight." He didn't say it just to fill the silence between them, but because he really wanted her to know. "Your friends were great fun. But it was watching you enjoy yourself that really made it special."

She slanted him a glance. "I had a fabulous time too. I don't get out as much as I'd like to anymore, but work is more important."

"Is it?" They were approaching her vehicle, which was backed onto a strip of grass between two trees alongside the driveway, and she fished her keys out of her bag.

"Of course." She said it impatiently, as they left the dimly lit driveway, and entered the darker area beneath the trees. "What I do makes a difference— at least to the animals. I can't do it half-heartedly or let anything else get in the way."

"But what about you?" He reached for the handle to open the door for her, but paused. She was so near, and in the warmth of the night her scent wafted out to him, calling him closer. "Don't you deserve more than just work?"

"Deserve?" Mellie turned to him in the dark, and in the slight illumination coming from the party he saw the gleam of her eyes, and the sweet curve of her lips. "I don't think any of us deserve anything, except what we work for."

Just a step more, and their bodies would be almost touching.

Delano took that step.

"Have I worked hard enough to deserve a kiss?"

He heard her indrawn breath, then saw the flash of her teeth as she smiled.

"I believe you have."

Mellie leaned closer, leaving just a breath between their mouths, and Delano did what he'd been itching to all night. He ran one hand lightly down her side, over the silky fabric of her dress, from just below her breast until it came to rest on her hip. The experience didn't disappoint. In fact, it was even better than he'd imagined. The sensation of her curves beneath his fingers, the question of whether her skin would rival the smoothness of the material, almost undid him.

And feeling her shiver at his touch made waiting even one more second impossible.

He kissed her, but softly, holding back, teasing her lips with his, rubbing lightly back and forth, learning the contours of her mouth anew, inhaling each rushed breath as she exhaled. An electric charge fired between them, as though one of them was holding a live wire and the other one was grounded.

It was too much.

Not enough.

Not nearly enough.

When her tongue swept, soft and slick, across his lower lip, Delano's brain short-circuited.

The hand on her hip clenched to pull Mellie's body fully against his, his other hand going up to clasp her nape. She already had an arm around his neck and the other around his waist, clearly offering no resistance to either how tightly he held her nor the way he'd deepened their kiss.

Made it carnal and almost rough in his eagerness and need.

She turned so her back was against the car, pulling him with her, and he went willingly. They were fused, lips and torsos, her hand on his lower back, holding him as close as possible. Shifting slightly, he brought his knee up between her legs, settling her on his thigh, and she moaned low in her throat. He could feel the heat of her through his pants, and the sensation—coupled with all the others battering him—made him lose all sense of time and place.

Gripping her bottom, he pulled her a little higher and urged her to rock against him. He swallowed her next moan, and a gasp, and a truncated cry, as she sought her pleasure against his leg and he facilitated the hunt.

Mellie's head fell back against the car, breaking their kiss, and Delano took advantage of the motion to move his lips to her neck while his hand sought and found one breast. Beneath her bra her nipple was pebbled tight, and he pinched it and was flooded with savage satisfaction when she jerked and her movements became more frantic.

"Delano..." It was a whisper, wild and sweet. "I want... I need..."

"Let go," he said, his voice rough even to his own ears. "I have you, babe."

She grabbed his head, pulling it back up, and when their lips met again it was so he could absorb the sounds of her orgasm into his mouth, muffling the desire-struck moans and sighs of release.

Mellie came back down to earth, glad that Delano had her firmly in his embrace, since she wasn't sure her legs were even working. Resting her head against his shoulder, she attempted to catch her breath, enjoying the lingering echoes of her orgasm.

When last had she lost herself in passion that way? She couldn't remember. Wasn't even sure she ever had before.

Then the absurdity of the situation struck her befuddled brain, and she started to giggle.

Delano's arms tightened fractionally. "What?"

"I feel like a teenager again. Hiding in the shadows, making out. So horny all it takes is a well-positioned thigh to bring me off."

He was quiet for a moment, and then, as if he couldn't help it, he began to vibrate with suppressed laughter too. They'd been speaking in whispers, in case anyone else was around but, thankfully, Mellie saw no sign of onlookers.

What a view they would have had!

The thought made her giggle even harder, and she pressed her face into his shoulder to muffle the sound.

"Let's get out of here," Delano said, his voice a low growl, and Mellie became all too aware of his erection pressed against her belly.

The sensation brought another wave of arousal that made her shiver and killed her amusement.

"Yes." It came out rushed and a little harsh, and she took a deep breath before continuing, "I think my legs are working again."

He eased away, as though reluctant to let her go, and Mellie had to fight the urge to hang on to him.

Ridiculous to experience a sense of loss when he was still right there.

She stepped aside and reached for the door handle, but Delano's hand got there first.

"Such a gentleman," she said, laughing up at him.

"Seems incongruous to say, after what just happened," he rebutted, amusement rife in his tone.

"I don't know," she said in a demure tone, as she got into the driver's seat. "I was more than satisfied by your behavior."

He snorted, but when he bent into the car, bringing his face close to hers, there was no amusement evident in his expression.

"I hope to always bring satisfaction."

Before she could reply, he closed the door firmly and began to walk around to the passenger side. Just as well since her entire system had gone into overdrive at his words.

If he could achieve that, she'd be the happiest of women!

She started the car as he got in, and once they both had on their seat belts she backed out of the space beneath the trees and headed down the hill.

It was funny, but she didn't feel the need to fill the silence that had fallen between them. Usually, in a situation like this, which was still fraught with tension—albeit of the sexual kind—she'd chatter away, holding off any type of too-serious conversation. However, with Delano beside her, she didn't mind the quiet.

There was one thing she should speak to him about, though, before this went any further.

"You know that if you spend the night with me, your father will probably hear about it by sometime tomorrow. Port Michael is a hotbed of gossip, and whether I drop you home after a couple of hours, or you don't get home until morning, someone is sure to spill the beans."

"Unless someone saw us making out, at which point Aunt Eddie is getting a text right now." Mellie chuckled, but because she couldn't tell whether he was amused or rethinking their upcoming tryst, she didn't know how to respond. Luckily, Delano continued, "Does that bother you—that my father, and yours, would know we were together?"

"Not in a general sense," she replied, carefully. "I just don't want your dad to get the wrong idea. He's already hopeful that you'll come back here to live permanently, so if he thinks I'm an additional incentive for you to stay, it'll just make things worse for you."

"If that's all that's worrying you, put it out of your mind. I'll handle Dad if he asks me about us. Make it clear we're just enjoying ourselves, not getting serious."

"Okay." She made her reply as casual as his, but couldn't ignore the sudden pang of what felt like disappointment.

Not that she wanted him to be serious about her, right? The fact that Delano was only going to be around for a short time made him a safe, temporary partner. So why did it hurt to hear him say that?

Then she put that emotion aside.

After all, hadn't she once succumbed to the idea of everlasting love and happy-ever-after, and got burned by the delusion?

No. Being with Delano, who was hell-bent on going back to Trinidad as soon as possible, served her purpose well. Her long sexual drought would be over, but without strings and complications attached.

"What about your father?" His question made her glance over at him, but his face was too shadowed for her to see it. "Will I have Mr. Charlie coming after me to ask my intentions?"

"No." She said it decisively, very sure of the answer. "Daddy knows I can take care of myself."

He was the only one who knew exactly what she'd been through with Kyle. And that, thereafter, she was determined not to allow anyone to highjack her life or endanger her future.

Lesson learned!

"You know what's been driving me crazy all night?"

Delano's question jerked her out of her thoughts, and she was glad. They weren't what she wanted to be considering just now.

"What?"

"That dress you're wearing."

Again she tried to see his expression, but couldn't. She turned her attention back to the road, unable to stop herself from smiling. "Why?"

"It looks so soft, and it moves around you like

the definition of *temptation*. I was practically sitting on my hands in an effort not to touch you."

Mellie giggled. "If you're imagining some lacy undies beneath it, I'm going to have to disappoint you. The reason it moves the way it does is thanks to shapewear, which is anything but sexy."

"I'll be the judge of that," he growled in return, sending a rush of excitement over her skin to then arrow into her belly.

"I don't want you to be disappointed," she replied, but her voice quavered. She was still contemplating what else could happen once he got her underwear off.

She'd been fully clothed—shapewear included—when he'd given her an orgasm. Who knew what he was capable of when she had on less?

She'd taken the back way through the hills to her home, rather than go back into Port Michael proper, and as they approached her driveway Mellie's heart started thumping. She hit the button to open the gate. Once they'd driven inside, she closed it behind them and steered the car around to the back of the house, where she always parked.

Turning off the ignition, she said, "Do you mind closing the gate at the side of the house for me? That way I can let the dogs out of the house, but they'll be confined back here."

"Sure."

He got out of the vehicle before her and, as she locked the car, she watched him walk to the side of the house, enjoying the view. A shiver worked up her spine; the anticipation of what was about to happen made her legs tremble.

She waited for him by the back door, knowing the dogs would be startled to see him coming across the yard, and preferring to have him encounter them while he was with her.

When she opened the door, they dogs swarmed around them, but when she commanded them to go outside, they obeyed without a problem.

"They're well trained," he commented as he came up behind her. "They don't jump, and do as they're told, even though I'm sure they were looking at me sideways, wondering what I'm doing here at this time of night."

"I work at training them," she said, happy to be talking about something so mundane. "All the dogs that come here get some basic obedience instruction, either from me or from Johnny, but once I decide I'm keeping one, I do advanced training with them. With the number of animals they have to interact with, I can't afford to have any problems."

She heard the door close and the latch being turned as she waited in the dimness of the kitchen to lead him through to her bedroom. But after she'd taken just one step, Delano put his hand on her upper arm, bringing her to a halt.

"I can't wait," he whispered, coming up close behind her, his lips finding the tender flesh at the base of her neck, where it met her shoulder. "Let me touch you."

CHAPTER FIFTEEN

"COME THROUGH TO the bedroom." Mellie tried to keep her voice light, even amused, but it came out laden with desire all the same. "Isn't one teenage stunt enough for you tonight? The kitchen isn't the most comfortable place for lovemaking. At least, mine isn't."

His chuckle, rumbling into the skin of her nape, made her shiver.

"Perhaps you're right, but I don't want to let you go." His hands skimmed down her arms, leaving goose bumps in their wake, and then transferred to her hips, to skim up along her sides. "Your skin is even softer than this dress," he sighed.

"You're only letting me go for a minute." Grasping one of his hands, she led him through the house. "I promise, you won't be disappointed."

He didn't reply, but his fingers tightened on hers.

When they got to her bedroom door, Mellie turned the knob, commenting, "Slip in quickly. I don't want any of the cats in here tonight."

Delano chuckled. "Agreed," he said, and snugged up to her back, so they ended up going through the door practically fused together. As she giggled, it suddenly struck Mellie that she'd never enjoyed a sexual encounter as much as she was this one.

The undercurrents were heavy. The desire very real and arousing. But being able to laugh and tease and just be free with Delano was a new experience, and one she found remarkably appealing.

As soon as they were in her room, she turned on the light. He kicked the door closed behind them, and then there was no more time for laughter, because he'd spun her around and was kissing her.

No more hesitation or slow seduction now, but full-on passion that she returned wholeheartedly. Delano's hands skimmed her body as though trying to learn her shape, and when he tugged free the bow at her nape, which held her dress closed, he inhaled her gasp of acquiescence.

But when he began to gather the hem of her dress in preparation of taking it off over her head, she held on to the fabric and broke their kiss to tease, "Are you sure you're ready to be exposed to what I'm wearing underneath this?"

He was smiling, but the gleam in his eyes had nothing to do with amusement.

"I told you: I want to judge for myself whether it's alluring or not. You've whetted my interest with talking about this… What did you call it?"

"Shapewear."

"Yeah. The shapewear."

Still hanging on to the dress so he couldn't take it off without tearing it, she asked, "Surely you've seen it, or something similar, before?"

"Not that I'm aware of. At least, not on anyone,

in person. Now, will you let me see, before I explode with curiosity?"

Giggling again, she released her hold and raised her arms. Delano wasted no time in pulling the dress over her head, and Mellie kept her eyes closed for a long moment, letting her arms fall to her sides.

It was amusing, sure, but also a little embarrassing too. She hadn't really considered this part of the evening when she was getting dressed. If she had, she might have chosen a different outfit. One that could be worn with silk panties and a lacy bra. But all she'd thought of was how great the dress looked on, and what would best enhance the movement, which Delano had claimed to like so much.

Now here she was, trussed up a bit like a sausage in a high-waisted pair of shorts that went down to midthigh and a strapless boned long-line bra that met it, leaving not even a sliver of skin between.

She could hardly contain her laughter, as she cracked one eye open to find him examining her very closely indeed.

"Seductive, yeah?" she said, trying not to giggle-snort.

Those intent, gleaming eyes rose to hers, and quelled her amusement. But he didn't answer her question, either to agree or disagree.

Instead, he asked, "How on earth does this stay up?"

But she had to swallow a gasp when he accompanied the question with a sweep of one finger along the curve of the bra cups, skimming over the swell of her breasts rising above it. She licked her lips, which suddenly felt dry, as did her throat. Clearing it allowed her to speak.

"Are you really asking me to explain the physics of my underwear right now?"

"No." He circled her slowly, and when that inquisitive, arousing finger slid just below her bottom, outlining the lower curve, she realized for the first time just how sensitive those particular parts of her body were. "I'm actually trying to figure out the best way to get it all off."

"Should I give you a tutorial?" she asked. "Or just take it off myself?"

"No, no, no." There was something feral in his tone, and Mellie shivered to hear it. "That's definitely my job."

His hands explored—softly, but filled with determination. And she stood there, trembling, feeling each touch like a mini electric shock.

When he found the hidden zipper at the side of her bra, he made a sound of such satisfaction, goose bumps fired across her arms and back.

Nudging her arm out of the way, he found the tab with a deftness that surprised her, and pulled it down.

"You've done that before," she said, and although she'd wanted to make it sound accusatory and amused, her voice wouldn't cooperate.

"I'm a quick study." Oh, no mistaking the desire roughening the words as he gripped the bottom of the bra and she lifted her arms so he could free her from it.

Then he was standing in front of her, and something in his gaze made her want to cross her arms over her breasts. Not because it made her uncomfortable, but because the moment felt too raw and hot and real.

He growled a curse, his hand rising, his finger extended to circle her nipple, making it pull even tighter, sending a shockwave of pleasure through her body. There was no suppressing the moan that rose in her throat, and Delano echoed it.

Stepping closer, he dipped his head to pull the other nipple into his mouth, and Mellie arched, locking her knees so as not to melt into a puddle on the floor.

It took her a moment to realize Delano was, at the same time, working his hands into the sides of her shorts, stretching the elasticized fabric, pushing it inexorably down. When it got to her thighs, he released her nipple from his mouth and concentrated on getting the garment lower.

"I'm one of those people who likes taking my time to open my presents," he said, as he pushed the shorts down to her knees. "So I'm enjoying this immensely."

"That's a good thing." Mellie wanted to laugh, but her breathing was too erratic for that. In fact, it took real effort to get the words out past the lust tightening her throat. When he knelt at her feet, his

face level with her stomach, she lost the ability to
speak completely.

She could feel his breath against her skin, and
the sensation made her belly flutter, the internal
muscles rippling with desire.

Delano had unbuckled her sandals before she
knew what he was about, and in an instant had
both them and the shapewear shorts off. She expected him to rise, embrace her again, but he stayed
where he was.

He traced a line across her thigh, where the elas-
tic edge of the shorts had left an indentation. "This
looks uncomfortable."

A wave of tenderness shook her, and she caressed his head, running her hand over the crisp,
dark hair.

But she made her tone amused, as she said, "It's
not painful. Just a small price to pay for fashion."

He looked up, and the expression in his eyes
rocked her, although she didn't know exactly why.

"There's a price for every pleasure," he said.

Before she could figure out his meaning, or form
a reply, he crouched farther and followed the path
his finger had inscribed with his tongue.

"Oh!" Mellie gasped, her fingers tightening on
his scalp.

Then he did it again, before switching to the
other leg.

It shouldn't be an erogenous zone. It was the
front of her thighs, only a few inches above her

knees, but somehow those slick, sweet touches had her quaking with need.

Looking up at her again, Delano gripped her left ankle, urging her leg up. Unable to resist—not wanting to—she let him lift her leg and hook her knee over his shoulder. Then his hands came up to hold her bottom, and Mellie shuddered at being so securely held. Captured.

And he didn't break his gaze away from hers as he leaned forward and licked a line of what felt like erotic fire along the inside of her thigh.

Up, and up, that torturous tongue swept, stopping just short of where she so desperately wanted it to be, then reversing course to swirl and tease back toward her knee. The entire time he watched her face, and Mellie felt his attention like another touch.

Just as teasing.

Just as arousing.

Little nibbles now, along her thigh. Mobile lips sipping and tasting her skin, hinting at the variety of ways Delano was prepared to use that delicious mouth to bring her to completion.

She wanted to beg, to plead, but bit back the words. This was a new type of eroticism to her, and she found intense enjoyment in the anticipation. He was in no rush now. Not even for his own satisfaction.

Unlike most of the other men she's known, who'd have probably been finished and snoring by this point.

One hand still on his head, the other braced against the nearby wall, she let him have his way.

Gladly.

She was wholly unprepared for when his tongue finally swept through her folds, electrifying the already oversensitized flesh. Crying out in ecstasy, she fell forward, using his head and free shoulder as props to stop herself from falling, her body shuddering, yearning, reaching for the orgasm shimmering just beyond reach.

All Delano had promised with his lips and tongue on her thigh he delivered, and more. As she shook, and held his head in place, her hips rocking with a primal rhythm against his mouth, Mellie knew he was still teasing. Ratcheting her need higher with each skillful movement, keeping her hovering on the brink until, with a muffled shriek, she came.

But it was unlike any orgasm she'd had before. It continued, racking her, turning her inside out and rendering her insensate to everything but his mouth on her and the shocks firing out from that point to every inch of her body.

She was only vaguely aware of Delano standing, somehow keeping her on her feet until he could pick her up and carry her to the bed.

The coverlet under her skin was cool, and somewhat soothing, but couldn't quench her excitement. Forcing her eyes open, she was in time to see Delano toss his wallet onto the bedside table. He unfastened only the top two buttons of his shirt before pulling it off over his head, his rush to undress completely in line with her eagerness to see him naked.

How could it be, she wondered, that after that incredible orgasm, she still was aroused and wanting him in the most intimate way possible?

She thought about sitting up and helping him get his pants off, but besides her limbs feeling like overcooked spaghetti, she was enjoying the view too much from where she was.

Rippling muscles across his chest and abdomen. Not the kind gained at a gym, but from working with the horses, probably, and his propensity for running each morning. Then he was bending to push his pants down, and Mellie lost her ability to breathe, even before he'd straightened.

Gorgeous.

She would have told him that was what she thought, but he had lowered himself onto the bed and was gathering her close, and she realized she'd rather kiss him than speak.

But she could let her hands and lips do the talking.

Delano felt as though he was about to vibrate right out of his skin.

Being with Mellie was everything he'd dreamed it would be, and so much more.

It wasn't just that she was passionate and so responsive it blew his mind. There was something else between them that took his desire for her to a whole new level.

And despite not being sure what that something was, he just wanted to revel in it.

In her.

She'd twined her arms and one leg around him as they lay face-to-face on the bed, and although he was so aroused it hurt, Delano felt no urge to stop kissing her. Instead, what he wanted was to bring her to orgasm one more time, because watching and hearing her achieve bliss had been the biggest turn-on of his life.

But Mellie was running her hands all over his body, fingers smoothing and squeezing his arms and back and thighs, and the sensation was sublime. It was as if she wasn't just learning his body, but admiring it at the same time. It was probably just his ego speaking, but that didn't stop him from feeling amazed and amazing.

Before he lost his mind completely to passion, still intent on pleasuring her again, he reached down and hiked her leg higher so it rested almost at his waist. Then he snaked his hand over her thigh and found the wetness between her legs.

"Delano!" She pulled back to gasp.

"Do you want me to stop?" He kept his fingers poised at her opening, but still gave her the option to say yes or no.

"No," she moaned, as though the word hurt to utter. "Definitely don't stop."

Elated, he bent to kiss and suck along her throat, and was rewarded when she arched, bringing her hips closer while baring her neck to his marauding mouth.

She was panting, little moans of delight breaking from those luscious lips. The heat between them intensified, and her inner muscles tightened around his fingers, making him groan in turn. She was so tight and wet and hot, he was sure being inside her intimately would be better than any other sexual experience he'd ever had before.

Suddenly she rolled, pushing him onto his back, breaking free from his hand and lips and grasp. When she leaned over him, she was more beautiful in that moment than he could bear. Her lips soft and swollen, her cheeks flushed, eyes dark with desire and gleaming. Rumpled and needy and determined.

And his.

"Condom."

She didn't ask a question but made a demand, and, without breaking eye contact, he reached back over his head to where he'd tossed his wallet. Mellie leaned over him to get it, and he took advantage of the motion to pull a succulent nipple between his lips. Her little mewl did nothing to dissuade, but after a moment she sat back, and he had to let it go.

She'd found the prophylactic, and tore the packet open carefully.

"I can do it," he said, his voice like gravel with the force of his need.

Mellie just smiled, and palmed his erection. When she stroked it from base to tip and back again, his hips lifted of their own accord, and heat gathered in the small of his back.

"Mmm…" she hummed, having her way with him, even when he gave a pleading groan. "No. I'll take care of it."

It was, he thought hazily, payback of the sweetest sort. If she'd asked, he'd have admitted to teasing her, wanting to give her pleasure that stretched and soared before reaching the final crescendo. But she didn't ask, and he knew she didn't need to, because she'd already sussed him out and didn't hesitate to repay him in kind.

All her movements were slow, and sure. Stroking, squeezing, caressing, until Delano closed his eyes as tightly as possible, hoping the star-shot darkness would help him maintain some semblance of control.

Yet, he wouldn't stop her, even when he felt he had to, or risk coming at a time, and in a way, he least wanted to. It was more important to cede the control to her right now than it was to try to snatch it back.

As though knowing the exact moment she had pushed him just shy of his limit, Mellie ceased her torture and smoothly rolled on the condom.

That, in itself, was almost too much for Delano, who clenched his jaw hard against the sensation. At least the tightening of the sheath around the base of his erection quelled some of his urge to orgasm, but only a little.

Before he could move, Mellie straddled his thighs, and the breath left his throat in a rush.

"Wait," he said, so dazzled by the desire in her eyes he knew he'd be lost as soon as she took him into her body. "Give me a minute."

She smiled and nodded, but her fingers danced over his hips to his belly, and stroked across his abs.

"You know, you're really quite beautiful without your clothes."

Her words surprised a bark of laughter from him.

"So, I'm ugly with them on?"

Mellie wrinkled her nose. "Now you're just fishing for compliments. But seriously, some people look amazing when they're dressed, but not so hot naked. You, however, look fabulous whether clothed or not." She tilted her head, as though considering her own words. "I think it has something to do with the way you carry yourself—although the muscles don't hurt either."

Silly to be awash with pride. Especially since he didn't place much store in good looks, either in himself or others. But it was impossible not to be pleased with the knowledge that Mellie found him attractive, although if she hadn't, he doubted they'd be where they were right now.

And the conversation had given him the breathing room he needed, tempering his arousal just enough that he believed he wouldn't embarrass himself like a schoolboy having his first sexual experience.

Sitting up, he wrapped his arms around Mellie's

waist and she leaned in to kiss him. The passion between them flared white-hot again, and she lifted gracefully in his embrace, positioning herself, and then lowering to take him in all at once.

They both froze, panting, and Delano thought his heart would pound out of his chest at the sublime sensation.

"Oh," she gasped, as if having made a shocking discovery.

Then she captured his lips again, and began to move. Flowing, rocking, rising, falling, as he held and touched and kissed her, never wanting to stop. Never wanting this feeling of pleasure and belonging and happiness to end.

When the end came, as it had to, Delano had no control over it because it was the sight and sound and feel of Mellie's orgasm that threw him over the edge and sent him into the stratosphere.

CHAPTER SIXTEEN

DELANO AWOKE TO a light weight on his chest, and an unmistakable sound humming in his ears. When he opened his eyes, it was to meet the green-gold gaze of the black kitten, who was happily making biscuits in the covers draped over Delano's torso and purring like crazy. Weak predawn sunlight came in through a chink in the curtains and semi-open bedroom door.

"Gilligan." Mellie's voice came from the doorway, and Delano turned to watch her walk in, searching her expression for her reaction to their night together. She looked calm and cool, and was already dressed, which made him conscious of the fact he was completely naked beneath the sheet. "How did you get in here? You're a menace and a real escape artist."

"But you love him," Delano said, hearing the fondness in her tone, and lifting said menace so he could sit up.

Mellie smiled ruefully. "I do. I think he might be a foster fail. If I were a witch, I'd have him as my familiar. He's so full of personality and life." Then she sent Delano a mischievous glance, as she held out a cup of coffee to him. "But he seems to love you even more than me. Maybe you should have him."

"Oh, I don't think so. Baldur is great with other animals, even cats, but something tells me there may be a jealous streak in Gilligan."

"Maybe," she said, brushing her hands down the legs of her jeans. "And I'm guessing Baldur sees you as his, alone?"

"I'm not sure how he'd feel about sharing his space with another animal. It's been just the two of us living together since I got him. My older dog had died just a short time before."

Mellie sat carefully on the edge of the bed so as not to joggle his hand and spill the coffee. Strange, and yet heartening, to have such a commonplace conversation after a night of spectacular sex!

"I think you're the only vet I know who doesn't have a houseful of animals. Well, at least three or four."

He blew on the hot liquid and took a cautious sip before replying. "You know I was married, right?" She nodded, so he went on, "My ex didn't like animals, but still married a vet. Go figure. She would only agree to us having one dog—no cats, she couldn't stand them—because she said any more than that would make too much of a mess in the house. I just kind of got used to it."

Her snort was slightly derisive, but more amused than anything else.

"You should have brought one of the horses home instead of a dog."

He couldn't help laughing at that, and when Mellie leaned forward and kissed him lightly, it felt so natural he was taken aback.

She didn't give him time to reply, or even to deal with whatever the strange emotion washing through him was.

Picking up Gilligan, she stood and said, "Drink your coffee and get dressed so I can take you home and get back here to deal with the animals."

"I could help."

She shook her head, grinning, as she headed for the door, the kitten held firmly in her grasp.

"Not in your party clothes. You're better off doing the walk of shame back at your dad's at sunrise than turning up later in the day looking like you went through a hedge backward."

She was right, of course, but Delano couldn't help feeling let down. Like it was an anticlimax after what they'd shared the night before.

The truth was, he realized as he took a quick shower in her neat and tidily arranged bathroom, he didn't want to leave.

Okay. Didn't want to leave Mellie.

He'd enjoyed himself last night, even more than he'd thought he would. Sure, the sex had been off-the-charts hot, but it was more than that. Mellie herself had made it special. With her laughter, wry humor, playfulness and passion.

It had been an experience unlike any other, and he didn't want it to end.

He would have liked to spend the day with her,

carrying on the conversations, sharing the laughter, and, yes, tumbling her back into bed and making her cry out with ecstasy.

But he really had promised his father to take care of some things around the house. That hadn't just been a line to excuse his leaving the party with Mellie the night before. So, although he regretted the necessity, he really did have to go back to Dad's.

Besides, it was too soon to have everyone know he and Mellie were having—

What were they having, exactly?

Sex only?

A friends-with-benefits-type thing?

A fling?

None of those seemed quite right but, as Delano dried off, he couldn't find the proper description.

Not that he should be trying to categorize it, anyway. In a couple of weeks, at the most, he'd be gone. Back to Trinidad, and his comfortable, normal life.

Giving their relationship a title would just make things more complicated.

"Hey, how're you getting on in there?" she called, as he was pulling on his shirt.

Man, she was eager to get rid of him!

"Just coming." He shoved his feet into his shoes, a little annoyed now, but more with himself than with Mellie. They'd both known this wasn't the beginning of a love affair, but here he was, acting like she'd promised more than she was willing to deliver.

When he went into the living room, she was coming back in from the attached cattery.

"The last of the older kittens will be going off to their new homes today, so I can put Gilligan and his sisters in the nursery, and get back my powder room," she said.

"Unless you have more kittens come in," he said, half teasing, half serious.

She snorted, and shook her head. "Or a pregnant bitch. My whelping boxes are full too. If you're ready, I'll just grab my bag and keys, and we can go."

"Sure."

He'd taken his cup into the kitchen, and by the time he'd washed it and put it to drain, she was standing by the back door, ready to leave.

"You're well trained," she said, using her chin to point to the sink.

"Aunt Eddie raised me to be able to take care of myself," he admitted. "Her advice has always been *Never be a burden to anyone, or let a woman tie you by your stomach.*"

"What did she mean by that?" Mellie asked, obviously amused. She unlocked the car as they got near to it, and Delano realized the side gate was already open. "I don't think I've ever heard that expression before."

"Just that I should learn to cook, and do whatever I needed to do to live comfortably by myself." He opened the car door and then slid in, as Mellie did the same on the other side. "Some of the older generation of men were so used to being catered to, she was determined I wasn't going to be like them."

"Makes sense. And good for her."

As Mellie started the car, there was a cacophony of barks from the kennel building, and the dogs started streaming out. Johnny Luck must be up and letting them all out, and Delano was reminded of what Amity had told him the night before, about the fact that the shelter was at capacity.

It worried him, for a couple of reasons.

Mellie wanted to buy his father out and take over the clinic, but she also needed to expand the shelter. From what Aunt Eddie had said, and Amity intimated, Mellie couldn't afford to do both.

If that was the case, and the shelter was at capacity, would she be tempted to prioritize the shelter over the clinic, when it came time to decide where to spend her money?

Although Delano had no interest in taking over the clinic himself—since it meant staying in St. Eustace—he'd feel sad and guilty if his father had no choice but sell it to someone else. There were other vets in Port Michael who'd probably be happy to buy out the practice, and take Mellie on as an associate. But he knew both Mellie and his father really wanted it to go to her.

"You're very quiet."

Mellie's voice pulled him out of his ruminations. She seemed to be trying to sound casual, but there was no mistaking the question in her tone.

"Woolgathering, and still a little bit sleepy," he

replied, intercepting a sideways glance from her as he turned to look her way. "Can you blame me, after such a fabulous night?"

Her lips turned up in a sly smile that made him want her all over again.

"It was rather nice, wasn't it?"

"Nice?" He didn't have to feign his outrage. "Nice?"

Mellie giggled, her cheeks darkening with a blush. "Very, very nice, indeed."

"Well, I'm going to have to try harder next time, aren't I? How about tonight?"

"I think that will work. Come by whenever you're free."

Yet, he realized he was reluctant to part from her, and the only sop to his longing was the sweet, lingering kiss she gave him before he got out of the car.

"See you later," she said, with a little wave.

And Delano watched her back out of the driveway, discontentment chasing away much of his lingering pleasure.

Mellie spent the day working at the shelter, and grinning.

A lot.

She found herself swinging from elation at the night just gone and surprise that no one called to ask what she thought she was doing, having Delano overnight at her house. It never occurred to her that it might still not be common knowledge, nor to consider not having him over later.

No use quibbling over how Delano had made her feel.

Beautiful.

Desirable.

More than enough.

The last thought brought her up a little short, and she rested on the rake she was using to clean the fowl coop for a moment, considering it.

In hindsight she could see the way Kyle had gaslit her into thinking there was something not quite enough about her for him. Even when he was using her, he'd subtly complained about all she was doing, and even about her attractiveness. He'd come home in the evenings, after she'd spent the day working on the house, nitpick at what she'd done and sniff at her clothes.

As though he'd expected her to be dressed in a ballgown after putting in baseboards, hanging crown molding or painting all day. And when she'd said she was tired, he had no qualms about going out without her, and telling her she was getting boring.

He'd hoped, of course, she'd be so dispirited by it that when he'd ultimately betrayed her, she'd be inclined to take the blame on herself. In fact, knowing about her fraught relationship with her mother, who expected everyone else to accept responsibility when things went wrong, he'd anticipated it.

Mellie shook her head sharply, and went on with

her raking. Although at the time she hadn't fully evolved out of the doormat mentality she'd grown up with, she was well on the way. And she'd made sure Kyle hadn't got away with what he'd done.

Coming out on the other side of that contretemps, bloodied but unbowed, vindicated and determined never to be lied to and used that way again, had been one of her life's highlights. The final step on her path to true, independent adulthood.

Happiness came with finding her place, here in St. Eustace. In seeing a need beyond her work, which was satisfying in itself, and filling it as best she could. She didn't try to fool herself into thinking she'd always be able to manage both the practice and the shelter. Rescue in itself could easily become a full-time job, which was why she'd sought advice and set it up as a not-for-profit, with a board of directors she could depend on to help the shelter grow.

No, it was all worked out; or it would be, once Dr. Milo made up his mind what he wanted to do.

It was a shame that Delano didn't want to come back and live on the island of his birth, but he seemed adamant. Unlike his father, Mellie could only respect his choice, although she speculated about it. Being a racecourse vet and even an associate in someone else's clinic wasn't the same as having your own establishment.

It made her wonder what the real reason was for his refusal to come home.

Then she reminded herself that it was none of

her business, no matter how curious she was. There was an agreement between her and Delano, tacit, if not specifically spelled out, that there would be no emotional attachment. And even if she found herself mooning over just how fabulous he was in bed, and how much she enjoyed his company outside of it, she'd do well not to pry.

Finished with her chores, she put away her rake and headed to the cottage, pushing all the weighty thoughts aside and turning her attention to a very important question: What was she going to wear tonight, besides her favorite peacock blue lace undies?

Or should she bother to wear anything over them at all?

Just the thought was enough to make her laugh, and cause a frantic wash of lust through her system.

Yes. She liked that idea a lot.

And was sure Delano would too.

CHAPTER SEVENTEEN

SOMETIME—AND SHE wasn't exactly sure when—
Mellie had decided to simply enjoy Delano while
she could. And she'd been glad of that choice after
talking to him later in the evening.

He'd been honest about his intention to go back
to Trinidad as soon as he could. Looked at from
that perspective—that maybe she had as little as a
week with him—Mellie could relax and just enjoy
their time together.

And she did enjoy him, to the fullest. Delano
was the most selfless and attentive lover she'd ever
had. Waking up each morning, filled with memories of the night before, had her smiling and in the
best of moods.

If there were any clouds in her blue-sky attitude,
they manifested whenever she actually allowed herself to think about what her life would be once he
was gone.

The truth was that he'd become more than a lover
to her, and although she staunchly refused to give
a name how she felt, it was useless to deny she
would miss him.

Terribly.

She'd forgotten how it felt to be with someone
who not only stimulated her sexuality but also her

mind. They could talk about almost anything, laugh together, work together. She'd taken to sharing her thoughts and plans with him, without reservation. Telling herself she felt that free and comfortable with him because she knew he wouldn't be around much longer became a refrain she wished she fully believed.

On the Wednesday before the spay and neuter clinic, Delano came into the office at lunchtime, Baldur at his heels.

"Hey," he said, coming to lean against her desk. "I had an idea I wanted to pass by you. Have you considered arranging a freedom flight for some of your animals? Sending them to the US or Canada to be adopted?"

Mellie rocked back in her chair, and nodded slowly.

"I have, but I don't have any contacts abroad to make it happen."

His grin made goose bumps fire out across her chest, and tightened her nipples.

The man was too damned sexy for his own good—and hers!

"I do. My friend Sam Nichols runs the Vaughn Shelter just outside of Toronto. I've known her and her brother for years, and I called her and asked her advice. She's thrilled by the opportunity to help."

Mellie sat back, staring at him. It was, on the surface, a great idea. A shelter in Jamaica had done something similar in the past, sending over a hundred dogs to Canada and new homes. If they could pull it off, it really would give them some breathing space. However, to Mellie, there was the other side of the equation.

Delano hadn't asked if this was something Mellie would consider. He'd just gone ahead and reached out to his Canadian friend.

It smacked of him sidelining her, despite the fact that the shelter was *hers*.

"What's wrong?" Delano's eyebrows dipped into a frown, and he tipped his head to the side, as though trying to figure out why she wasn't over the moon about it.

"Nothing," she said quickly, not wanting to sour his pleasure at what he'd done, although at the moment she couldn't share it. "How do I contact your friend Sam?"

"I gave her your number, and she said she'd call you." He was still eyeing her narrowly. "Are you sure you're okay?"

It was the perfect opening to express her annoyance, but she didn't take it, needing time to figure out why she'd had that knee-jerk reaction. Putting it aside for the moment, she smiled and, instead, asking if he was ready for obedience class that evening.

"As ready as I can be. Dad is coming with me, so I better bring my A game."

"He's not that much of a stickler." Mellie jumped to Dr. Milo's defense. "Also, he'll probably be so happy to get out of the house, he won't care if the entire class is a shambles."

Delano chuckled in agreement. "That's probably true. Dad's not used to being stuck at home like this with Aunt Eddie hovering over him and making him rest—not if all the chores he's given me since I arrived are any indication."

"Very true. Your father has slowed down a bit over the last couple of years, but was still one of the busiest men I know."

Delano was slowly stroking his hand along her neck, from just beneath her ear to her shoulder, giving her goose bumps. Not that she minded.

"Do you have time to have dinner with me this evening, before obedience class? Then we could go together. Dad's been asking for you."

That was something she really liked about him. He never demanded her time, but always asked if she was available. In the past she would have been quite content to say no, citing work at the shelter, but she was already considering how best to accommodate him.

"I think so."

"Great." Bending, he placed a lingering kiss on her lips, before getting to his feet. "By the way, what time should I be ready to go to the spay and neuter clinic on Saturday?"

It was an opportunity to ask when he was planning to go back to Trinidad, but Mellie let it pass, wanting to know and yet not wanting to, as well. She was just glad he was actually sticking around, at least until then.

"It's about an hour to Grand Harbor, depending

on the traffic, and I usually try to get to the venue by about seven thirty to set up and help with registration if necessary."

"I'll be ready then." He paused, halfway to the door, and continued, "If I'm not already with you."

She was smiling to herself as he went out the door. If she had anything to say about it, they definitely would be together on Saturday morning. Then the smile faded, to be replaced with a wave of melancholy. By then she suspected they'd be on a countdown to his departure, and she wanted to spend as much time with him as possible.

Unfortunately, she had to cancel their dinner plans that evening, and tell him she'd probably miss obedience class.

"Your friend Sam contacted me and wants to teleconference tonight to start making plans." Mellie had forgiven Delano about the freedom flight too, knowing she was being unreasonable. His excitement about possibly helping the shelter had been palpable. "The board and I will be talking to her about what we need to do to get it off the ground."

"Okay. I'll miss you at obedience class, but that's more important. Can I come by your place afterward?"

They were alone in the office, the last patients for the day seen and the staff already gone. Mellie couldn't resist moving into his arms and kissing Delano, reveling in the surge of desire that immediately swamped her.

"Of course," she finally replied, a little breathlessly, when they finally parted. "I'd be very disappointed if you didn't."

Obedience class went better than Delano expected, mainly because most of the lookie-loos from the week before didn't bother to come back. And when everyone saw his father walking in, the jubilation was unmistakable. A good half an hour went by, with everyone crowding around him in the pavilion, before Delano could get the class started.

"Where's Mellie?" Kiah Langdon asked, just as Delano was getting everyone situated.

"She had some business to take care of this evening," he replied, hoping no one noticed the disappointment in his voice.

His father had been disappointed too, when told Mellie probably wouldn't make it. Although they spoke on the phone almost every day, she hadn't been by the house since Delano had arrived.

"You tell Mellie I want to see her, okay?" Dad said, as Delano was in the process of dropping him back off at home after the class.

It was the only time his father had intimated he knew where Delano was spending his evenings, and nights.

"I will, Dad," he replied, half expecting for his father to segue into a more detailed line of questioning about the relationship between his son and his associate, but nothing more was said. Maybe just knowing Delano was going back to Trinidad soon was enough to make him hold his tongue.

When he got to Mellie's it was to find her in a state of cautious excitement.

"Sam was very helpful, and we have a tentative action plan in place," Mellie told him as she paced back and forth across her living room, the dogs' heads following her movements as if they were watching a tennis match. "Next week, we're going to start picking the dogs we think will do best, and photographing them, sourcing kennels—although Sam thinks she can help with that—and speaking to the government vet. Luckily, I know him well, and can count on his discretion. We're going to keep this as quiet as we can, until we know whether we can bring it off or not."

"Have you thought about contacting the shelter in Jamaica and asking how they managed?"

Mellie shook her head. "Sam is speaking to one of the people who was involved in that freedom flight, and they're advising her how best to go about it." She paused then, and turned her gleaming gaze his way, and something in that look made his heart gallop. "Have I properly thanked you for this?"

"Sure," he replied, as she stalked closer to where he was sitting on the couch.

"I'm pretty sure I haven't," she said. "I was annoyed about it at first because you didn't ask me before contacting Sam."

The shock of her words had him sitting up, horrified.

"Why didn't you say something, Mel, so I could apologize? I didn't mean for it to look like I was doing an end run around you, or something. I was just so excited by the idea, I went ahead with it."

She smiled then, shaking her head.

"It was a knee-jerk reaction." She seemed to consider for a moment, before lowering herself into a chair so she was facing him across the coffee table. Was it intentional that she kept a distance between them? "I have a problem with anything that seems to threaten my autonomy. I'm not very trusting, as you know all too well."

He wasn't sure if she'd answer, but it seemed important to ask, "Is there a particular reason?"

"A couple." Her brow wrinkled, as though she was wondering why they were talking about it, but then she gave a small shrug and continued, "I told you a little about my mother, and her reaction to my contacting Daddy."

"Yes." Something held him still, poised at the edge of his seat, surprised she was opening up to him in this way.

"Well, that was the final break, but the rift between us had been growing for a long time. All my life she's been demanding, wanting me to do whatever she said, without question. But as I got older, I realized she also lied, a lot, to get her way. When you're a child, and realize you can't depend on your parent to be truthful, you stop trusting everyone."

She took a deep breath and shook her head.

"She didn't want me to be a vet. She told me she and my stepfather couldn't afford my tuition. I took out loans and worked to get through vet school, only to find out afterward that Daddy had been sending her my college fees. When we figured it out, he made her give me the money so I could pay off the rest of my loans, but that sense of betrayal intensified."

Delano wanted to go to her. Hold her. But everything about her posture told him it would be the wrong thing to do just then.

So all he said instead was, "I'm sorry, Mel."

The movement of her lips might have been an attempt at a smile, but it didn't succeed.

"You'd think I'd have learned my lesson, wouldn't you? But I didn't. I was engaged to a man who treated me almost the exact same way. He isolated me from my friends by getting me to move to Miami with him, took my savings as a down payment on a house, used me to help fix it up, then sold it out from under me. Kyle kicked me out on Christmas Eve, leaving me with almost nothing."

Now she smiled, a ferocious grin that eased the anger welling inside him.

"But he'd underestimated me, you know? He knew what I'd gone through with Mom, and figured I'd be too embarrassed or weak to do anything about it, but I'd learned from Daddy that you don't let people get away with things like that. The money I have put away is what I won when I sued him for both my savings and punitive damages."

He couldn't bear it anymore. Delano got up and strode around the intervening table, Mellie's gaze following his movements. When he reached her, he opened his arms, his heart thundering in his ears, as he waited to see if she'd accept his offer of comfort and solace.

When she did, rising to step into his arms, Delano closed his eyes, more thankful than he could express, even to himself.

"Oh, sweetheart," he said, when he'd gotten control of his anger, sorrow and voice. "I'll never lie to you, ever. And now that I know how you feel, I'll always ask your opinion before I interfere in your business."

Mellie didn't answer, except to pull his head down and kiss him. Not passionately. At least, not at first. Instead, it felt like a promise, as well as an act of forgiveness and understanding.

But it didn't take long for the desire that always flowered when they were together to rise into a flame, and then a conflagration that wouldn't be quenched without the ultimate intimacy. And Delano didn't resist when she led him to her bedroom, although a part of him whispered that they'd crossed a dangerous line, and there could be no going back.

Even if he'd wanted to retreat.

CHAPTER EIGHTEEN

THE NEWS OF the commission's findings in the racing scandal was in the newspaper that Friday morning, and Delano was reminded, once again, that he should be booking his flight back to Trinidad.

His father was doing well. The doctor had assured Delano that in a week or so Milo would be cleared to resume working, although he was advised to slow down somewhat.

"You're not getting any younger, Milo," Dr. Fleetwood had said. "And I think this infarction was a shot across your bow. A warning you'd be wise to heed."

There'd been some grumbling from Dad, but resignation too.

In fact, Delano thought his father was looking forward to turning more of the clinic matters over to Mellie.

"I don't think I'm ready to retire fully," he'd said, when Delano was driving him back to the house after his appointment. "These past weeks have been too quiet for me. But it was also nice not to be rushing around and worrying about everything."

"Mellie kept everything running smoothly the whole time. Once you decide what you want to do, I'm sure she'll be willing to discuss it with you."

His father had only grunted in reply, and Delano hadn't pushed for anything more.

Their relationship had definitely improved over the time he'd been back in St. Eustace, and Delano didn't want to do anything to jeopardize it. Taking Mellie's advice to start from where they were, and look to the future rather than the past, had proven to be the right course.

They hadn't spoken much about his mother, but it was a start. Delano knew he would never get over his guilt, and his father might never fully recover from his son's part in his wife's death, but they could make the most of the time they had left.

Perhaps that was why each time he thought of booking his ticket, Delano found something else to occupy his time, or an excuse for waiting?

Yet, even as he thought it, he knew he was lying to himself.

It was Mellie keeping him on St. Eustace.

But he was set on returning to Trinidad, and his life there. The haunting recollections had faded, but he knew it was just temporary. The weight of his responsibility never left him, had only abated in the face of the passionate relationship he had with Mellie.

The clinic was busy, and they'd already agreed that he would finish up the last of the clients that evening, while Mellie prepped for the spay and neuter clinic the following day. At about two thirty, she came into the examination room, as soon as the patient he'd been with left.

"Okay," she said, looking down at the list in her hand. "I think I have everything, and whatever is forgotten I can take with us tomorrow. I'm heading out to Grand Harbor with this load."

"What time will you be back?"

She shrugged. "Not before about five. Probably a little later. We could have dinner, if you're free."

"Sounds good. Drive safely."

The exam room door was open, so he didn't try to kiss her goodbye. Although everyone at the clinic probably knew they were sleeping together, they did their best not to flaunt it.

But as he watched her bustle out, he wished he'd had the chance.

Soon those sweet salutes would be a thing of the past.

It hurt to think that, and he was honest enough to know it was because he'd fallen for Mellie. Not far enough to overcome his antipathy toward the island of his birth and all the painful memories that resided here, but enough that the thought of leaving her was a wrench.

He wouldn't express his feelings to her, especially not after hearing all she'd been through. She had good reason not to trust when she'd been so horribly treated. To confess he was more than halfway in love with her, but wouldn't do anything concrete about it, would sound a likely story.

He'd considered asking her if she'd consent to a long-distance affair, with one or the other of them traveling back and forth, but knew that made no sense. Mellie's life was full. Between the clinic and the shelter, she had no time for flying to Trinidad to see him, and once his father retired, or semiretired, she'd be even busier.

It wouldn't be possible for him to fly back regularly either. Races were run at the track twice a week, and he worked three or four days at the vet clinic where he was employed. When could they ever coordinate with schedules like that?

No.

A clean break was what would suit them both.

Besides, Mellie had given no indication of wanting him to stay, or to extend their affair. He liked to think they could sustain the friendship that had grown between them, but there was no room for any further development of their relationship.

A depressing thought, but the truth nonetheless.

There was one patient left to be seen for the day, and Delano was prepping the exam room when the door flew open and Leila, the vet tech, rushed in, holding a pet carrier.

"Wounded cat," she said. "The owner says dogs got at it."

A teenage boy came in behind her, the fear and distress on his face unmistakable.

"He's an indoor/outdoor cat, but he usually stays in our yard," he babbled, as Delano and Leila put on their gloves. "I don't know why he went down the road and into the neighbor's yard."

Looking into the carrier, Delano could see one of the cat's eyes was swollen shut, and blood matted the fur around its neck and flank. The animal looked to be in shock, and hissed as soon as it saw Delano's face through the door.

"Get the bite-proof gloves," he said over his shoulder to Leila. Then he sent the young man a questioning glance. "What's your cat's name?"

"Hero," he replied, his voice cracking a little on the word.

"And yours?"

"Marcus."

"Okay, Marcus." Delano kept his voice calm and reassuring. "We're going to take the top off the carrier, and make sure he doesn't try to run away, but I can see he's in a lot of pain, so Hero will probably fight us. If you're up for it, will you stay and try to calm him down by speaking to him? If he hears a familiar voice, it might help."

"Sure," the teen said, trying to sound confident, but his voice wavered.

Hero was traumatized and, from his attempts to bite and scratch, just wanted to be left alone, but they were able to get him out of the carrier and subdued on the table long enough to be sedated. Once he was asleep, Delano examined him, while Leila began cleaning him up, looking for any missed puncture marks or wounds as she went.

"Hero has a number of bite marks," Delano told Marcus, "but they're not from dogs. If it had been dogs that had attacked him, the bites would be bigger, and deeper." And the cat probably wouldn't have survived, but he didn't add that part. "It looks as though he was fighting with another cat. How old is he?"

"Umm…" Marcus seemed to be doing sums in his head before he said, "Just about a year old, I think."

And still intact. That would explain a lot. He'd probably strayed into an older tom's domain, on the trail of a female, and gotten into a fight.

"He's reached sexual maturity," Delano explained. "And that means he's going to start going after females. The only way to stop that from happening is to get him neutered."

"I thought about doing that, but it's real expensive, and my mam won't pay for it."

Delano was stitching up the worst of Hero's cuts, and Marcus was gently stroking one of the now-still paws. It was clear that the youngster really cared for his cat, and was worried.

"Dr. Mellie, who also works here, runs spay and neuter clinics," he told the young man. "They do it at low or no cost. Unfortunately, the next one is tomorrow, and Hero is too hurt to have surgery right now. But if you keep checking, I'm sure there'll be another one soon."

"I think I heard Dr. Mellie say they're planning one in three or four weeks, right here," Leila added. "Hopefully Hero will be well enough then, but you'll have to bring him and let Dr. Mellie look at him to make sure."

Delano felt a pang, like loss, at the thought that by then he'd be long gone. He still hadn't made a decision on when he was leaving, but he knew it would have to be soon. The longer he stayed, the harder it would be for him to leave.

They patched Hero up, and Delano told Marcus he'd like to keep the cat in the hospital for a couple of days.

"Unless you think you'll be able to put the medicine in his eye yourself?"

The teen looked doubtful. "I don't know if he'll let me. He scratched me up good when I was putting him in the carrier, and he's usually good about that."

So it was arranged that Hero would stay at the clinic over the weekend, and Marcus left to go home and treat his own wounds.

"Did the last client stay?" Delano asked Leila when she came back into the room from putting Hero in a cage down in the hospital.

"She did. Her dog's just here for boosters, worming and a wellness check."

"Thank goodness," Delano said with a chuckle. It was almost five o'clock, and the appointment had been for four. "When you send her in, you can go on home. It doesn't make sense for both of us to be late."

"Thanks, Doc." Leila grinned as she sanitized the examination table. "No word of a lie, but I'm starving."

He was just finishing his notes when he heard the door behind him open, and a voice he hadn't heard in over twenty years said quietly, "Delano?"

He froze, his brain seizing for an instant. An icy wave rushed through his body, and when he turned to face the woman behind him, it was with the stiff, jerky movements of a much older man.

"Mrs. Gopaul?"

She smiled, but Delano didn't think it got all the way to her eyes.

"It's good to see you, Del," said his friend Everard's mother. "It's been a very long time."

Mellie left Grand Harbor to head back to Port Michael, her head full of lists and plans for the following day. At some point in the future, what she really wanted was to buy a mobile veterinarian clinic, or make one, if necessary. An old RV would work, and that way she could go into the nooks and crannies of the island, instead of having to find a clinic where the spay and neuter events could take place.

So many plans and ideas, and seemingly not enough time or money to bring them to fruition!

Yet, the thoughts of animal care and husbandry that usually took up the majority of her mind slipped away before the first mile of her journey was behind her, replaced by a more troublesome matter.

Delano.

A rueful smile touched her lips as she considered that not very long ago all she'd wanted was for him to be gone, back to Trinidad, and out of her hair. Now, she actually dreaded his leaving.

It was a quandary, and she'd been avoiding giving it too much thought. But there was something about Delano that had opened her heart in a way no one else ever had.

Looking back on her relationship with Kyle, she could see where—emotionally struggling as she'd been then—she'd made herself an easy mark. After a lifetime of walking on eggshells and trying to navigate her mother's moods and whims, all he'd had to do was pretend to offer calm, stability and love, and she'd fallen into his arms.

She'd had no set boundaries, no barometer to gauge whether what she was experiencing was real or false. It had taken time and effort to examine herself, and build those parameters. And even her reaction to Delano's attempt to help the shelter showed there were still sore places in her psyche she needed to work on.

Not, she thought, because of Delano, but for her own sake. Because if the affair with Delano had taught her anything, it was that she still craved closeness and companionship. That life with him was far better than it had been before, or would be after he left.

Even now, having gone that far in her thinking, she couldn't bring herself to go the final step. To consider her true feelings for him—give them a name— would be too painful, in light of his imminent departure.

But she was just kidding herself. She'd realized how into him she was when she opened up to him about her mother, and Kyle. Not even Amity knew the full story, because Mellie couldn't bring herself to tell it. She'd gotten past the anger, but the shame lingered. Convincing herself she was a different, better, stronger person who didn't need to look back or tell anyone else what a fool she'd been had been easy.

She was about ten minutes out from Port Michael when her cell rang. It was Dr. Milo, so she answered it using the car's hands-free capability.

"Dr. Milo, how are you?"

"Mellie, have you seen Delano?"

Her heart stopped. She'd worked with the older man for years, and had never heard him sound anything but calm and cool. But now, although he was obviously trying to sound normal, there was tension in his voice.

"Not since about two thirty," she replied, trying to match his casual tone, although her heart rate was through the roof. "What's wrong?"

She heard Miss Eddie in the background, but couldn't make out what she was saying. Then Dr. Milo said, "It's probably nothing but I've been trying to reach him, and he's not answering his phone."

"I'm just outside Port Michael," Mellie said, forcing herself not to break the speed limit. Not by too much, anyway. "I'll check at the clinic, and let you know if he's there."

"Thank you, my dear. I… I'm sure he's fine."

"Did something happen to make you think otherwise?" It wasn't like Dr. Milo to fuss or go off half-cocked.

"No. No. Please don't worry. I'm sure he's fine," he repeated, but Mellie didn't believe him.

Skirting the edge of town saved her a few minutes and instead of going home, she went straight to the clinic. The relief she felt on seeing Delano's car still in the parking lot was immediate and immense.

After she'd parked, she rushed into the clinic, about to call his name when she heard the murmur of his voice from the office. Either he had someone with him, or was on the phone, so Mellie walked the few steps to the office, a sudden feeling of déjà vu making her pause at the door.

He wasn't hunting in the cupboard, as he had been the first night she saw him, but now, like then, he had his back to her.

"Yes," he said into the phone. "Nothing sooner? Okay, I'll take that."

Not wanting him to feel as though she were eavesdropping, Mellie stepped silently back out of the office and went down into the hospital area, turning on the lights as she went. There was a cat she didn't recognize, looking dazed and battered, one big golden eye blinking at her through the cage. Taking out the chart stuck in the holder, she read Delano's notes, and had just finished when she heard his footsteps in the corridor. They paused, and for a moment she thought he would leave without saying anything to her, but then she heard him striding toward where she was.

Clearly, Dr. Milo's behavior had rubbed off on her, making her paranoid. Of course, he wouldn't just take off once he realized she was there.

But then he stepped into the doorway and her heart sank, her expression freezing before the smile she was planning to send him could blossom.

He was pale, his complexion muddy, and although he was smiling it didn't reach his eyes, which looked at her with what seemed like blank indifference.

"I'm glad you're back," he said, and the distance she felt between them widened at the sound of his casual tone. "I wanted to tell you I'm leaving on Tuesday."

She couldn't answer, couldn't even ask him what was going on. Everything inside her was churning: brain, stomach, heart. Rendering her mute and unable even to move. Finally, after what felt like an age, she found her voice.

"What's happened?"

"Nothing," he said, but she heard the lie, even as he smiled again. "I need to get back to work. Dad's doing better. Aunt Eddie has everything under control. It's time."

"Okay." Inside she was screaming at herself to ask, *What about me? Us?* But the words stayed stuck in her head.

"I'll see you in the morning out in Grand Harbor. I'll get there for eight."

Mellie gathered herself then, pushing the hurt and shock down deep, drawing on every ounce of pride she could muster to nod, as if everything was normal.

Not falling down around her ears.

"Thanks," she replied, happy to have been able to keep her voice level. "See you then."

And when Delano walked away, she fought the urge to call him back, or run after him, even though it was what she most desperately wanted to do.

CHAPTER NINETEEN

DELANO WASN'T SURE how he got through Friday night but, somehow, he managed it.

Seeing Janice Gopaul had sliced his heart and soul into pieces again, and he wasn't sure he'd be able to put any of it back together.

As she stood there, unsmiling, he'd been thrown back in time. Suppressing the recollection of the last time he'd seen her, so he could speak to her normally and treat her dog, had taken everything he had inside.

He hadn't known she was back in St. Eustace. After Everard's death, she'd gone back to Guyana where she'd been born. No one had mentioned she'd returned, or was a client at the clinic and, he'd realized as they spoke, a board member of Mellie's shelter. Her sudden appearance had floored him, and brutally reminded him why he hated St. Eustace, and all the memories associated with it.

It also made him angry.

Why hadn't Mellie mentioned Mrs. Gopaul to him? Surely she knew their history, and would realize how devastating it would be for him to see her unexpectedly? Her failure to do so felt like betrayal and the worst type of cruelty.

He pled tiredness to his father and Aunt Eddie

and went to bed early, but couldn't help being aware of the worry in their eyes as they watched him. Yet, just like they had when he'd started seeing Mellie, they didn't comment or ask any questions, and he was thankful for it.

Lying in bed, staring at the ceiling, there was no way to stop the flow of memories.

Standing behind the almost closed door on the day of the funeral, hearing her voice from the living room, where she and Dad were.

"Someone should have stopped him," she'd said, in a hoarse furious tone that was forever etched in his mind. "Del should have, or you."

"Yes," Dad replied, so sadly and softly, Delano hardly heard him. "Yes."

But Dad hadn't been there, down by the water. Only Delano had known. Had seen Everard running into the surf.

Only Delano could have stopped him, but hadn't.

Had failed Everard, and Mum. Dad and Janice Gopaul.

And had paid for it, every day since.

Eventually, emotionally exhausted, he fell asleep, but woke up the next morning still weighed down with renewed sorrow and guilt.

The spay and neuter clinic was busy and bustling with vets, clients and volunteers. Thankfully, there was no sign of Janice, although she'd mentioned it to him when he'd seen her at the clinic.

It was easy to avoid Mellie, but Delano was constantly aware of where she was at all times. She didn't search him out, nor did she go out of her way to ignore him, but on the few occasions when they had reason to talk, she treated him with the same cool contempt she had when he'd first arrived.

It should have hurt, but there was a barrier between him and all emotion that couldn't be breached.

Sunday morning dawned overcast and drizzly, and suited his mood perfectly. Baldur hadn't left his side since Friday night, staring at him with questioning eyes, and lying as close as possible whenever Delano settled anywhere. Despite the dreary weather, Delano took the dog for a run as usual, but even a punishing, wet five miles did nothing to improve his mood or break him out of his emotional bubble.

As he was getting out of the shower, Aunt Eddie knocked on the door.

"Delano, your phone has been ringing nonstop. It might be important."

"Thanks," he called back, toweling off.

It went off again as he walked into his bedroom, and he picked it up. Not recognizing the number, he was a little brusque when he answered.

"Hello?"

"Dr. Logan?"

"Yes."

"Is Chappie Robinson, Doc, from up Preacher's Mount. We have a jackass caught down in a hole, and we trying to get him out. Dr. Mellie said to call you because you the best horse vet around."

At the sound of Mellie's name, something shivered to life inside, and Delano said, without hesitation, "I'll come up. Where are you?"

He rushed out of the house, leaving Baldur behind, followed by Aunt Eddie's grumbling about his not having breakfast yet, and how he'd catch his death in this weather. His anxiety was rising, breaking through the wall that had come down around him just days before, and he drove as quickly as he could on the slick roads.

Donkeys, like people, came with all different types of temperaments. Depending on whether the animal was hurt or not, the size of the hole and its depth, whoever took on the task of going down into it could be in danger.

And he had no doubt in his mind that if there was anyone in the hole, it would be Mellie.

If she was even on-site.

The sudden realization that the man he'd spoken to hadn't actually said Mellie was there brought such a rush of relief, Delano felt lightheaded for an instant.

But when he got to the site, that relief turned out to be misplaced.

Mellie was very much down in the hole, which was about six feet deep and perhaps eight across, with the frightened animal. She was damp and muddy, and utterly lovely, even while standing in inches of mud.

Without a second thought, he swung himself over the rim and landed next to her, squelching into the ankle-deep mud and making the donkey jerk against the rope halter Mellie was holding.

"Delano, you made it."

How incredibly calm she sounded, while his heart was trip-hammering in his chest, and his mouth was dry with fear.

"I'll take over down here," he said, when he could get the words out. Then he gestured to the men standing above them, around the hole. "Why don't you climb out and direct them as to what to do?"

The look she gave him was scornful and amused.

"Do you know me at all? I've already sent for straps, and one of the men has gone to see if his cousin can bring his bulldozer. The only thing we can do is wait, and make sure the animal is okay."

"Both of us don't need to do that." It felt imperative to get her out of danger…to safety. "I can manage on my own."

She didn't even bother to reply to his words.

Instead, she said, "Take a look at his left front cannon. I think it's hurt."

Resigned to her not budging, he replied, "Better to wait until we get him out of here. If he's in pain and I touch the area, he might kick."

"Or bite," Mellie said, clearly not too worried at the prospect. "I do say, though, he's one of the calmest donkeys I've had to work with, although I know that could change at any time."

Especially since the beast was, at that very moment, rolling its eyes at Delano, while its nostrils twitched.

There was a shout from above, and the earth beneath them rumbled.

"Shorty bring the excavator, Dr. Mellie. And he has the straps too."

After a few more minutes of what sounded like confusion above, a different man stuck his head over the side, and surveyed the scene.

"Dr. Mellie," he said, then twisted his mouth to the side. "What you want me to do?"

"You think you can hoist him up with the bulldozer, Shorty, if we get two straps under him?"

Another few seconds went by as Shorty's mouth twisted from side to side, and his eyes roamed the hole, the donkey and then the ground around the hole.

"I have to bring the dozer close up, and as long as the ground holds it that can work."

"Good. Tie the straps onto the bucket, and let's get this done."

Before Delano could object, Shorty disappeared.

"Did you hear what he said, Mellie?" Delano realized he was holding on to her arm in a too-tight grip, and forced himself to let go. "He's not even sure the ground around the hole can hold the weight of the bulldozer."

She shook her head. "If he was worried, he wouldn't agree to do it. Shorty is one of the best bulldozer operators on the island."

The rumbling of the engine got louder, and the donkey shifted nervously as the ground vibrated. Then the bulldozer bucket appeared, a man standing in it, holding the straps that had been tied onto the teeth.

Delano held up his hands, prepared to catch the strips of webbing, and the donkey brayed and bucked.

"Whoa, now." He could hardly hear Mellie over the racket. "You're okay. Don't go crazy on me now."

Laser-focused on getting them all out of the situation as quickly as possible, Delano passed the first strap under the donkey's belly, just behind the front legs. When he realized the strap wasn't long enough to be thrown back up to the bucket, he gestured for the bucket to be lowered farther, and the man above them passed the request on to Shorty.

After what felt like a year, he got both straps positioned, with Mellie too busy trying to calm the distressed animal to help.

When he shouted for the bulldozer bucket to be lifted, all he could do was hope the donkey wouldn't freak out, and kick itself out of the straps before it was back on solid ground.

Mellie was on one side of the animal's head, while Delano was on the other, both watching and keeping out of the way of the hind legs, as the donkey started rising out of the hole. It was still braying, like it was being murdered rather than rescued, but thankfully kept relatively still.

Delano had just let out the breath he'd been holding, when a shout rang out.

"Watch out! Watch out!"

The timbre of the bulldozer's engine changed, and the bucket swung to one side, sending the donkey swinging, just as the side of the hole gave way and a cascade of mud rushed in. Delano shouted with fear, as Mellie disappeared under it.

Mellie had felt the shifting of the earth behind her and, although bogged down in the mud at the bottom of the hole, had the chance to move one leg forward as the mud pushed her over. Although she went down on her knee, hard, the landslide didn't have a chance to engulf her, and she was in no real danger.

Not that you'd know it from Delano's reaction.

He went nuts, using his hands to try to free her, even when some of the other men jumped down with shovels and made quick work of it. Someone lowered in a ladder, and in short order they were out of the hole, although caked in mud.

Chappie came over, all smiles.

"That fool jackass. As soon as we take off the straps, him take off down back to him pasture. Thanks, you hear?"

"Get your fence fixed, Chappie," Mellie told him. "I'm not coming back up here to rescue him again."

"Yes, Dr. Mellie. I will."

The men were moving away in twos and threes, and the bulldozer had been shut off, and Shorty was walking over to join a group. Mellie was aware of Delano standing close beside her, but hesitated to turn to him.

She hadn't gotten over his behavior on Friday, and then yesterday at the spay and neuter event, when he hardly even looked her way. And when he did, it was as though they were strangers.

In the depths of Friday night, as she lay awake, determined not to cry over him, she'd admitted to herself just how much she felt for him. In her mind, it was too soon to call it love. Or maybe she just didn't really know what love looked like, to make the comparison. All she knew was that the end of their relationship had left a hole in her she wasn't sure would ever be filled.

What she really wanted was to walk away, to pretend he was already gone.

But he'd helped her just now, and shown concern in a way that told her he cared for her, even if it wasn't enough for him to be honest about how much, or why he was acting the way he was.

Mellie was fair-minded enough to at least thank him.

She turned, looking up at him, finding his gaze fixed on her. But it was the blank, shocked expression on his face that made her breath catch in her throat.

"Delano."

He blinked, but otherwise didn't react, like a sleepwalker, she thought. And when she put her hand on his arm, she realized he was shivering.

Impossible to leave him this way. He was in no condition to drive, and Mellie knew she'd rather take care of him than leave him to his own devices when he was obviously in some kind of distress.

"Come on," she said quietly, tugging his arm until he started walking with her toward her car. Thankfully, none of the other men seemed to notice anything unusual, since they were still chatting and laughing amongst themselves.

Getting him into the car, she quickly jumped in as well and started it.

As she bumped down the farm track toward the main road, she was trying to figure out how best to handle the situation. If she took him back to his father's house in this state, it might upset Dr. Milo.

Besides, if she was honest, she wanted to be the person to take care of him, to find out why he had reacted this way. It might also be a chance to figure out what had happened between them.

She was resigned to their affair having ended, but it would be nice to know why he'd done a one-eighty without any kind of explanation.

Getting to the house, she was relieved when Delano opened the car door himself and got out to walk with her to the back door. Before going inside, he even took off his mud-encrusted shoes; a sure sign he was coming out of whatever funk he'd fallen into at the rescue site.

Then he wandered over to the small kitchen table and sat heavily in a chair. Mellie followed, and took the seat across from him. When he reached for her hand, she didn't hesitate to take it.

"You scared me, Mellie." His voice was rough,

the timbre raw and pain filled. "When I saw the hole collapsing…"

His fingers tightened almost painfully, but Mellie didn't pull away.

"But I'm fine, Delano." She didn't add that in her opinion he was overreacting. She'd never make light of his distress that way. "You can relax now."

He shook his head, his gaze never leaving hers.

"It was my fault you were almost hurt. I should have protected you. Stopped you from staying down in there."

"You're not thinking straight." There was no sugarcoating it. "You couldn't have stopped me. I do what I need to, to help and rescue animals. That's who I am, and no one tells me what I can and can't do."

"Not even someone who loves you?"

CHAPTER TWENTY

THERE WAS ANGUISH in his words, and for a moment Mellie couldn't answer. There was too much in his question to fully comprehend. Before she could articulate her confusion, Delano continued speaking.

"I know I messed up the other night, walking away from you, but I realized today, when you were in danger, how much I love you."

Her heart was racing, joy flooding her, but Mellie knew there was something missing from his story.

"Why did you walk away, Delano?" His mouth tightened, as though in pain, and she knew she was on the right track. "What happened on Friday?"

He got up abruptly, releasing her hand. For a moment she thought he was going to walk away, but instead he paced across the kitchen, as though the effort to sit still was too much for him. He stopped at her kitchen window, his hands gripping the edge of her sink.

"Do you know how my mother died?" he asked, surprising Mellie with what sounded at first like a change of subject.

"Yes," she replied, stiffening, her hands clenched so tightly her fingers ached.

He'd only once ever spoken about his mother.

"The boy she was trying to save was my best friend, Everard."

"I know," she admitted.

"Mum and Dad had taken us to the beach." He spoke quietly, but with a gravelly edge, the words seeming to come reluctantly from his throat. "Mum was laying out the food. Dad went back to the car for something, and told us not to go into the water until he got back, because the sea was rough."

Mellie's hands tightened into fists, until her short nails were digging into her palms. She wanted to tell him to stop, not to relive the pain, but knew he needed to. And he needed her to listen.

Just like she'd needed to share her pain and embarrassment with him.

"Everard…" He paused, shaking his head. "Everard wasn't afraid of anything. He said he was going swimming, dared me to go with him. I wouldn't. I told him that if my father said not to swim until he got back, that's what I would do. I tried telling him that he wouldn't have to wait long, but he just laughed and ran into the water. There was a rip current and an undertow."

"I'm sorry." How inadequate those words sounded, but it was the best she could do through the lump in her throat.

"When he first called for help, I thought he was kidding, and shouted for him to stop. Mum ran down and dove in. Then, just as she got to him, they both disappeared."

He stopped, and swallowed. There was no need

for him to continue. Mellie could imagine the scene. The chaos and attempted rescue. The devasting news being delivered to not one but two families. The fear and guilt a little boy would feel at witnessing the death of two people he loved. With jerky movements he paced back across the kitchen and dropped into the chair again.

"You asked me what happened on Friday? Everard's mother came into the clinic. I hadn't seen her since just after the funerals. Since I heard her blame me for Everard's death." He shook his head slowly, then his expression changed from sorrow to a kind of desperate determination. "Now you know why I can't stay here. The memories come at me when I least expect them, and I know whenever Daddy looks at me, it must bring it all back for him, as well."

Oh, she could hardly bear to see his agony, but, at the same time, she couldn't leave him wallowing. She knew how detrimental it was to live in the past, castigating yourself without end.

"Delano." She sought the words, said a little prayer that she would get this conversation right. "Whatever Janice said to make you believe she blamed you, was said in the midst of the type of pain that would make anyone lash out. It's not something you can ever forget, but don't you think it's time to forgive yourself—and Janice—and put it behind you?"

"I don't blame her. How can I? She was right.

They died because I didn't stop Everard from going swimming. If I had—"

"How would you have stopped him?" The question popped out of her mouth before she even thought. "You said he wasn't afraid of anything. Was he the kind of child you could stop when he made up his mind to do something?"

Even in distress, Delano couldn't help the upward twitch of his lips. "Not him. He was adventuresome and hardheaded. Even his mother said so, more times than I could count, after we'd gotten into some scrape or other."

Mellie got up then and moved close to him, looking down into his face, willing him to listen to what she had to say.

"You've been living in the past. Beating yourself up for something that wasn't your fault and you couldn't have stopped even if you'd tried. And you know what breaks my heart, Delano?" When he shook his head, she said, "It's the thought that you could have died that day too. That I might never have had the chance to know and love you."

"Mellie."

Her name came out of him like a breath, almost too quiet to be heard, but the wonder and joy in it made Mellie's heart leap and race.

Then he was on his feet, holding her close, and it felt exactly like coming home.

"Come back with me," he said. "To Trinidad. You can start a shelter there. God knows there are enough stray animals to keep you busy."

And her heart, which had been sent soaring by his declaration of love, plummeted.

For a long moment she stayed where she was, her arms tight around his waist, her cheek pressed into the curve of his neck. Savoring his touch. His love.

When she pulled back to look up at him, her desolation must have shown, because the hope and joy in his expression faded.

"I can't do that, Delano." She said it softly, aching with the need to comfort him, but also with the determination to speak her truth. "This is my home. Where I've built a life for myself, found a place where I belong and can make a difference."

"But you can do that in Trinidad too." The note of desperation in his voice tore at her heart. "With me."

"I don't know that I can." She held Delano's gaze, as his eyes widened and his lips firmed into a straight line. "Even if I put aside everything I've worked for, abandoned my father and yours—just when Dr. Milo most needs someone to depend on—I'm not sure our relationship would work."

He released her, and stepped back, leaving her to shiver with the chill filling her center.

"I don't understand. Explain."

There was no plea in his voice, only demand. Anger, she suspected might come later, but for now he was shocked and hurt. Only honesty would do.

"The losses you suffered when you were young are horrendous, something you will never completely get over. But you've blamed yourself for that loss—*for twenty years*—and, as far as I can see, run away from every reminder of what happened. Every reminder of your mom and Everard, who were both so important to you. You've even run away from your father, who loves you so much and needs you now, and I'm sure needed you long before now too."

She could see his face tightening, his eyes going flat, but she couldn't stop now. Not when everything she wanted was at stake.

"If something were to happen—something bad—I got sick, or we lost a child, or I was hurt, would you run away from me too?"

He flinched, as though she'd struck him, and his face paled.

Had she gotten through to him, or would this be the end?

Delano shook his head, and anguish flashed across his face, then was hidden as he turned away. She saw his chest expand on a huge breath, and she waited for his response, the air pent in her own lungs.

"I don't know."

As his words registered, all sensation left her legs, and Mellie blindly reached for the back of the nearest chair, holding on to it for support. Her mouth was dry, and the thumping of her heart was harsh, made her feel sick.

Then she found her courage, and strength, and although she knew the pain of loss was hovering, waiting to swamp her, she straightened. When she reached out to touch his shoulder his muscles were locked and tight.

"Figure that out, Delano," she said, proud of how steady her voice came out. "Figure it out and let me know."

And when he strode out the door, she let him go.

Delano made his way out to the road, and stood there for a moment, lost. Mentally and emotionally battered.

And angrier than he could remember being for a long time.

How could Mellie not understand?

She was the first person he'd spoken to about what had happened all those years ago, what he'd seen and heard. Why couldn't she comprehend that he couldn't stay here, in this place so full of memories and reminders that crept out of doors or jumped out around corners?

That the pain of it was something he couldn't wait to get away from?

The rage boiling inside him was preferable to any other emotion just then, and it sustained him long enough for him to call a taxi to take him back to his car. In fact, he nurtured the anger, welcomed it, stewed in it all the way to his father's house.

But once there, he turned off the car and sat in it without getting out, reliving all Mellie had said, unable to sustain his fury.

Knowing she was right.

He had run away.

It had been the only thing he'd known to do, to deal with the agony of loss.

His entire world had fallen apart, and he still didn't know how to put it together again.

Wasn't sure he even wanted to try.

There was another world, removed from all of this, waiting for him back in Trinidad and it would be simpler—easier—to go back to it. Leave all this turmoil behind.

Finally, he got out of the car and made his way into the house, standing for a moment in the formal living room, which hardly ever got used.

It's for when visitors come, his mum used to say; a sentiment echoed by Aunt Eddie.

All of his mother's knickknacks were still on the shelves, and in the cabinets. The paintings she'd collected on the wall. He wouldn't be surprised if the rug was the same as it had been twenty years before too.

While he'd run away, his father seemed to have stayed stuck.

How had he been able to bear it?

Suddenly, it was imperative to know, and Delano went through to the patio, looking across to where his father sat beneath the shade of the poinciana tree.

Dad was leaning back in his chair, his eyes closed, and Delano hesitated, not wanting to disturb him if he was asleep. But before he could go back inside, Dad opened his eyes and smiled.

"Hi, son. Were you looking for me?"

The carefully searching way his father looked at him spoke volumes. Very little got past Dr. Milo and, although he hadn't commented, Delano knew his dad had noticed the change in him since Friday.

Suddenly, Delano was overtaken by waves of love and gratitude, sadness and longing.

Love for one of the best men he knew.

Gratitude for the fact that man was his father.

Sadness for the lost years, and an overriding longing to have them back.

Or, he thought, as he crossed the lawn to sit on the grass at his father's feet, longing to have the relationship they'd had before back, rather than the years.

The future doesn't have to be like the past...

Mellie had said it, in a variety of ways, and she was right.

Of course she was.

Looking up at his father, who was still and silently waiting, Delano felt as though perhaps Dad was feeling the same way too, and something inside him cracked open.

Never to be repaired.

"Dad..." It was a hoarse whisper, and he couldn't clear his throat enough to make it any clearer. "I want to talk to you about Mum—and the day she died."

And his father's nod, along with the hand he laid on Delano's shoulder, was everything he needed right then.

CHAPTER TWENTY-ONE

MELLIE DIDN'T KNOW whether she'd see Delano again, and refused to allow herself to speculate.

He'd been gone for half an hour before she'd collected herself enough to remember he hadn't had his car, but when she'd driven up to the farm where they'd rescued the donkey, his vehicle was no longer there.

Their conversation ran around and around in her mind, as she finally showered off the mud she'd accumulated during the donkey rescue, but she was sure there was nothing she could have done differently.

She loved Delano. More than she'd ever thought she'd love anyone. But she couldn't and wouldn't love blindly. That was the old Mellie; the one who would do anything to hold on to another's affection and attention, putting her own needs last, even when it was to her detriment.

How could she, in good conscience, abandon Dr. Milo, the clinic and her rescue? Especially when she wasn't one hundred percent sure of Delano's feelings.

He'd said he loved her but then, in the next minute, assumed the life she'd built for herself could and would be discarded without a second thought. No discussion necessary.

While there was a part of her that wanted to run away with him—go wherever he demanded—that wasn't healthy. Not for her, and definitely not for him.

There were deeper issues he needed to deal with, to be honest with himself about, before they had any chance of a real, lasting relationship.

It had taken him thinking she was in danger to even admit to his feelings for her and talk to her about the past. While Mellie had opened up to him, telling him things she'd never told anyone else, he'd been carefully curating what he shared with her. Keeping parts of himself—really important parts—locked away, and out of reach.

Needing something to keep her hands busy, Mellie dragged herself out into the cattery and started cleaning. Sheba came with her, much to the delight of the kittens, who acted as though the little dog was nothing more or less than put on the earth for their entertainment. Yet, Mellie couldn't even find joy in their antics. She wanted to cry, to scream, but couldn't.

She was frozen inside, waiting for the pain to hit.

When her phone buzzed, she almost ignored it, but habit had her looking at the screen, in case it was someone calling for a rescue.

It was from Delano, and Mellie's heart did a little flip as she stood for a moment without opening the message, trying to catch her breath. Exhaling deeply, she tapped the screen with her finger.

Meet me at Ludlow Beach, please.

Ludlow Beach? Wasn't that where his mother's accident had happened?

She didn't wait to change her clothes. Dressed in cutoff shorts and a stretched-out T, she hustled the dogs inside and rushed to the car.

The fifteen minutes it took to get there were some of the longest in her life, simply because she had no idea what to expect.

It was getting late, and since Ludlow Beach wasn't as popular as some of the others closer to Port Michael, there were few cars parked along the road. One of them belonged to Delano.

As she trotted down the path, which threaded its way through palms and sea grape trees, she could hear the sound of the ocean pounding on the nearby rocks. Coming out onto the beach itself, she looked up at the flagpole and her heart rate slowed when it was empty.

No red flag warning today.

Then she saw him, standing back from where the waves rolled up onto the shore, looking out over the water, his arms hanging down at his sides. The sun, low in the sky, limned him in golden light, emphasizing the breadth of his shoulders and the muscles of his legs, bare beneath the hem of his shorts.

She didn't know why, but she was cautious approaching him, and although her steps in the sand were soundless, before she got to him, he turned to look at her.

Then, he returned to gazing out to sea.

"I've never been back into the ocean, since that day," he said softly when she was standing beside him. "Dad says he hasn't either." He inhaled deeply, and shook his head. "We used to go sailing and fishing and of course swimming, all the time. I only just realized how much I miss it."

"I'm not surprised you stopped," she said, equally quietly. "What happened was traumatizing."

"It wouldn't be so bad if I'd been afraid for a while, even for a few years, and then got over it. But I allowed my fear to rule me. In that respect, and way too many others."

Mellie wanted to pull him close and tell him everything would be fine, but held back. Maybe all he needed was to talk, to get it all out, so he could move forward, with or without her.

"I didn't want to let anyone close." He said it in such a matter-of-fact way, he could have been talking about the weather. "Not Dad or Aunt Eddie, definitely not my ex-wife. When you let people in, they have the power to hurt you. To turn your life upside down, and tear out your heart."

"That's true," she agreed, aching for him—for the boy who'd learned too young the pain of loss.

"But they also have the power to heal, if you let them in. I spoke to Dad." Mellie's little gasp of surprise and pleasure couldn't be suppressed, but she didn't know if he'd even heard it. "We talked about Mum, and Everard, and what happened here that day. And what happened afterward too. I think… I think it was good for us both."

"I'm so glad, Delano." And she was, wholeheartedly. "For both of you."

He turned to her then, cupping her cheeks so he could meet and hold her gaze. "For the first time in a long time, I feel as though happiness is within my reach, Mellie. But it won't be complete without you. Will you give me another chance? Let me show you how much I love you, and value you and all that you do? Make it up to you for trying to use our love to coerce you into making a choice you didn't want to?"

How could she say no to that?

"Yes." Reaching up, she kissed him gently, before repeating, "Yes."

He smiled, his face and eyes lighting up, all his love in full display in his expression.

"We have options," he said, rushing the words, as though wanting her to know he meant what he said. "Dad has offered us both the clinic, in equal share, as long as he can consult and come in a few days a week. Or you can concentrate mostly on the rescuing and educational work, and work part-time at the clinic. Or—"

Mellie shut him up by kissing him again, thoroughly. So that by the time their lips parted, they were both breathless and aroused.

Somehow she found the breath to say, "We'll talk about it, and decide. Together. Later."

Picking her up, Delano swung her around, then put her back down to bend and unlace his sneakers.

"Come on," he said. "Come into the water with me."

And she was crying with joy as they walked into the sea together, leaving fears behind on the shore. Swimming toward the future, and into an ocean of love.

EPILOGUE

MELLIE SAT ON a stool outside the stable door, smiling and shaking her head.

"Now I remember why I didn't specialize in large animal medicine," she said.

Delano looked over at her and chuckled as he removed the arm-length disposable glove he'd worn to reposition the foal prior to delivery.

"It's not too bad, once you get used to it," he said, shrugging off the surgical gown.

"And with this result, it's all worth it," her father added. He was gently wiping the bay foal down with handfuls of straw, while the mare, Marmalade, sniffed and snuffled her new colt.

"He *is* awfully cute," Mellie conceded.

"And it's just as well I'm the one Mr. Charlie called to deliver him." Delano gave her a pointed look over his shoulder as he washed his hands. "You could belly up to the mare, but your arm would be too short."

Mellie stuck out her tongue at him, even while acknowledging he was right.

Being thirty-nine weeks pregnant did make it difficult to get too close to anything!

"Speaking of which," her father interjected, "aren't you supposed to be resting?"

It was a mark of her father's concern for his mare that he was just bringing it up, and Delano snorted in response, earning himself a narrow-eyed glare from his wife.

"I'm on maternity leave," she replied, wondering how many more times she'd have to say it. "Not bed rest. The doctor said to keep active, just not to overdo it. Sitting here watching you two—and Marmalade—do all the work isn't exactly stressful."

"Aunt Eddie has already texted me three times this morning," Delano groused to his father-in-law, while drying his hands. "And Dad isn't much better. I don't dare tell them she isn't at home with her feet up."

Mellie snorted, but the warm sense of contentment she felt at his words was undeniable.

She and Delano had been together almost three years, and the time had flown by in a whirlwind of experiences. Through their marriage and taking over of the clinic, as well as arranging freedom flights for dogs and expanding the shelter, they'd lived, worked, laughed, teased and grown together.

And, most of all, loved.

So much loving that she couldn't picture her world or life without him.

For the first time ever Mellie felt truly secure, surrounded by family and friends, with Delano always by and on her side. And with their baby due any day now, who could ask for more?

"Let me get you home, babe," Delano said, coming over and holding out a hand to help her up. "Maybe stop and get you some ice cream on the way?"

"That would be perfect."

Taking his hand, she stood and was enfolded in his arms, where she longed always to be.

Safe.

Happy.

Home.

* * * * *

Her Forbidden Firefighter
Traci Douglass

MILLS & BOON

Traci Douglass is a *USA TODAY* bestselling romance author with Harlequin, Entangled Publishing and Tule Publishing and has an MFA in Writing Popular Fiction from Seton Hill University. She writes sometimes funny, usually awkward, always emotional stories about strong, quirky, wounded characters overcoming past adversity to find their forever person and heartfelt, healing happily-ever-afters. Connect with her through her website: tracidouglassbooks.com.

Visit the Author Profile page
at millsandboon.com.au for more titles.

Dear Reader,

In this third installment of the Wyckford General Hospital series, we're following physical therapist Luna Norton and firefighter Mark Bates on their journey to love. As you might have gathered from the previous stories, Luna is very much a sarcastic, strong, independent kitten when it comes to relationships, and now we find out why. We also learn more about Mark, the surfer-boy gorgeous, always-carefree protector who seems to be able to charm the pants off every woman in town—with the exception of the one he wants. But is Mark's sunny facade shielding something darker and wounded inside? Well, you'll just have to read their story to find out! I hope you enjoy Luna and Mark's grumpy-sunshine, opposites-attract road to happily-ever-after and, until next time...

Happy reading!

Traci <3

CHAPTER ONE

"I'M NOT LOST," Luna Norton said to the chipmunk watching her from across the wooded path. "I've been down this trail a million times. But I don't suppose you know which way to go?"

His nose twitched, then the chipmunk turned tail and vanished into the underbrush.

Well, that's what she got for asking for directions from a wild animal.

Luna stood there another moment trying to get her bearings, with the hazy winter sun seeping through the evergreen branches, her phone in one hand and her sketch pad in the other. The forest around her was a profusion of greens, thick with the remnants of the latest snowstorm a week ago. Even with the chilly mid-January temperatures, the place was abuzz with activity, and she constantly had to leap away when birds and squirrels chattered at her. Luna was used to life in the tiny town of Wyckford, Massachusetts—quaint shops, cozy diners and people constantly around. Coming out here to the wilderness, which she did at least a couple of times a month, was her escape. From stress, from work, from basically everything she didn't want to deal with. At thirty-five, she supposed she ought to have better coping skills than running away, but hey. If it wasn't broken, don't fix it, right?

She yawned and turned in a circle, searching for the trail out, which was easier said than done given all the snow on the ground. She'd been up since before dawn that morning, first working a full shift as a physical therapist at Wyckford General before driving out here to the trails this afternoon, and she was still on her feet, if a little unsure about which direction to go.

With a sigh, Luna tried the GPS on her phone again, but it was still out of service. Great.

She hiked for what felt like forever, going in the direction she was pretty sure was right, searching for more bars. The terrain looked so much different in January than it did in the summer, but Luna was usually spot-on when it came to the trails. And she'd come prepared for the cold in her winter gear, as well. She wasn't one of those dumb tourists who got stuck out here at least once a week. She knew what she was doing. Or at least she thought she did. Luna wasn't exactly a wait-and-see kind of girl. Never had been. Patience wasn't a virtue she possessed. At least that's what her parents always told her growing up anyway.

She'd always been more of a mess-around-and-find-out kind of person. Or she had been until life had other ideas.

Ugh. Life.

She'd spent her whole life in Wyckford, and she had what most people would consider success—a good job, a nice apartment, loving family, great friends. And while she was beyond grateful for those things, recently she'd noticed an inconvenient yearning for something more. Probably because her two best friends—Cassie Murphy and Madi Scott—had found their forever person over the last year, and their happiness had suddenly made Luna uncomfortably aware of what was lacking in her own life. And it was inconvenient because with all their love in the air and in her face, she felt a bit left out, even if she didn't really believe in happily-ever-after.

As she continued walking, Luna dodged obstacles like rocks, jutting tree roots and, in two cases, downed trees with trunks bigger around than her car. But Luna knew a thing or two about taking detours and getting back on the right path. So she kept moving, amid sky-high evergreens she couldn't even see the tops of, feeling small and insignificant.

And awed.

She just needed to find a new direction, a goal. Some peace would be good, too. And love? Well, she didn't care so much about that. Love, of the romantic kind anyway, was scary and dangerous and best avoided, in her opinion. Her past run-ins with romance had included a bunch of one-nighters and a few relationships that had lasted a few months even, but nothing beyond that, which was fine. Luna preferred her freedom and her safety over "till death do us part" anyway. Especially the death part.

When she finally stopped to check her GPS again—still out of service—she took a break and opened her backpack, going directly for the emergency brownie she'd packed earlier. Luna sat on a large rock and sighed from the pleasure of resting for a moment.

Then a bird dive-bombed her with the precision of a kamikaze pilot, and Luna jumped up and eyed her fallen brownie, lying forlorn in the dirt. With a sigh, she checked her smartwatch and saw it was 4:30 p.m. It would start getting dark soon, and Luna figured she had maybe another half hour to find her way out of here before nightfall. She slung her backpack over her shoulders and decided to retrace her steps back to where she'd started when an odd rustling sound had her swiveling fast as the hairs on the back of her neck prickled. "Hello?"

The rustling stopped and she caught a quick flash of blue in the bushes. A hoodie, maybe?

"Hello?" she called again, her heart racing and throat dry. "Who's there?"

No answer.

Luna reached into the pocket of her parka for the pocketknife she kept there just in case.

Another slight rustle, then a glimpse of *something*—

"Hey," she yelled, louder than necessary, but she *hated* being startled.

Sudden stillness fell, telling her she was alone again.

Blood still jackhammering in her ears, Luna turned around. Then around again.

She walked back along the path for a minute, but nothing seemed familiar, so she did a one-eighty and tried again. Feeling like she'd gone down the rabbit hole, Luna tried her cell phone again, but still no service.

Don't panic.

Luna never panicked until her back was up against the wall. Eyeing an opening in the evergreens, she headed toward it. Maybe if she could get into a clearing, she could get better reception. But she emerged through the trees to find herself standing at the edge of a steep embankment down to a frozen creek bed, sharp, jagged pieces of ice jutting up like knives waiting for a hapless victim.

The ground beneath her feet was slick, and somewhere behind her, Luna heard rustling again.

She inched back from the edge of the embankment as the scent of pine made her nose itch, looking around and wondering what sort of animals were nearby, hunting for their next meal. She'd read online there were bobcats in the state, but primarily in the central and western parts. Also, black bears. In fact, there had been more recent reports of them coming closer to town because of the food. She should have brought bear repellent.

Why didn't I bring bear repellent?

With the sun rapidly setting, she needed to get a move on before the temperatures dropped below zero that night. She resettled the comforting weight of her knife in her palm and wished for another brownie.

As she headed back into the forest, the noises started up again. Birds. A mournful howl echoed in the distance, and goose bumps rose over her entire body. Luna nearly got whiplash from checking them all out. But as she'd learned long ago, maintaining a high level of tension for an extended time was exhausting. Eventually, she heard footsteps coming up the path from the opposite direction she *thought* she'd come from. They weren't loud, but Luna was a master at hearing someone approach. She could do it in her sleep. Her heart kicked hard as old memories resurfaced, heavy, drunken footsteps heading down the hall to her bedroom…

"You owe me, Luna."

The footsteps got closer, sounded heavier. A man, who was apparently not making any attempt to hide his approach. Luna squeezed the knife in her palm, just in case. Then, from around the edge of a towering evergreen, he appeared. Tall, built, gorgeous and, best of all, *familiar*!

She knew him. Mark Bates. A local firefighter. They saw each other around Wyckford General regularly, and from when Luna taught stretching classes at the fire station to help the guys reduce occupational injuries. All the ladies of Wyckford fawned over Mark, which Luna attributed to the electrifying mix of testosterone and his uniform. Women loved a man in uniform.

Well, women except Luna. She'd learned long ago not to trust appearances.

He stood near an evergreen, wearing a black down jacket with a reflective Wyckford Fire Department logo on the front and a red knit hat covering his blond hair. Dark sunglasses hung around his neck, his light blue gaze missing nothing in the gathering dusk. Those sharp eyes were in complete contrast with his lazy smile, all laidback and easygoing, but Luna suspected Mark was trouble with a capital T, *mainly because he was just so darn attractive*, and she'd given up trouble a long time ago.

Dammit. Out of all the people in town, he would have to be the one to find her.

She was still and silent, but Mark's attention tracked straight to her with no effort at all. "Kind of late to be out here on your own, isn't it?"

If he wanted to hear Luna admit she was lost, he'd turn to a block of ice first.

When she didn't answer, Mark's smile grew.

Childish and immature? Yeah, probably. But Luna didn't like the way her pulse tripped and her skin heated when he was around. It scared her, and she refused to be afraid again. Or ask for his help. Even if he did look like he knew exactly how to get her out of this forest.

"You need help getting back to your car?" he asked after a while. "I'm pretty familiar with the territory since the fire department trains out here a lot."

Luna squared her shoulders, hoping she looked more capable than she felt. "I'm fine. I know these woods, too. I wouldn't have come out here if I didn't."

He smiled, his teeth even and white in the growing darkness. "Great, then."

"Great." For some reason, his smug grin annoyed the crap out of her. Like he knew she was lying. Which was impossible, because if there was one thing Luna knew how to do, it was hide her secrets. Whatever. She didn't have time to stand around chatting with him. Luna waved her hand dismissively as she passed him. "See you around. I'm sure you have kittens to rescue or something."

"Kitten rescues *do* actually take up a lot of my time," he agreed good-naturedly. "But if you're heading out, maybe I'll just tag along, then. For the company."

His voice always did funny things to Luna's stomach. And lower, too, but she ignored those things because it was safer that way. And all that unwanted tingling only made her more determined to get away from him. Injecting as much sarcastic venom as she could into her words, she gave him a saccharine smile. "I don't need company."

"Okay." Mark shrugged, looking completely unbothered as they continued walking side by side. "You might not know this, but on top of all the kitten wrangling I do, rescuing fair maidens is also part of my job description."

"I don't need rescuing—" Outraged, Luna turned and prepared to let him have it, but something screeched loud directly above her, and she crouched instead, covering her head, and ruining her tough-girl cred.

"Owl." A hint of amusement edged Mark's tone now. "They're getting ready to hunt."

Luna straightened as another animal howled

in the distance. She pointed in the direction of the noise. "What about that? *That* was no owl."

"Coyote," he agreed. "Lots of predators in these woods."

"I know that." The words squeaked out of Luna's suddenly constricted throat before she cleared it and turned away. "I'm usually just gone when they come out. I need to get home."

Mark shrugged, looking completely unperturbed as he followed beside her. "I'm sure you've heard about the recent bear sightings and—"

Luna kept her attention focused straight ahead, not answering. With his charming, "I'm here to help you" facade, he was everything she didn't trust. She'd fallen prey to that once before and had the internal scars from her attacker to prove it. Easy smile, easy nature, easy ways—it all had to be an act, no matter how sexy the packaging.

Mark loved his job. Having come from first the military, then Chicago FD, the current shortage of high-rise blazes, tenement fires and Jaws of Life rescues in his workweek was a big bonus. But his day at the Wyckford Fire Department had started at the ass crack of dawn this morning, when two of his fellow firefighters—there were only five of them total—had called in sick, forcing Mark to give up his much-needed day off, a chore that ranked right up there with having a root canal.

After spending a long day stocking supplies at the station and cleaning the fire truck inside and out, he'd then helped on a couple of EMT runs in town. Nothing major—suspected heart attack, allergic reaction to shellfish, Viagra mishap at the town's local retirement home. Then he'd gone back to the station to handle some dreaded paperwork, until he'd been ordered out here to check the fire gates on the trails.

Finding Luna Norton had been an unexpected bonus, standing there with her mile-long legs encased in faded jeans beneath her big puffy parka, winter boots and her stormy gray eyes that gave nothing away except her mistrust.

As usual when he saw her, Mark felt a punch of awareness hit him in the solar plexus.

Man, she was so beautiful. And so very much radiating serious "keep away" vibes.

He couldn't help wondering why, even though it was none of his business.

Besides, she wasn't even his usual type. Still, something about Luna drew him in like a bug to a zapper. Ever since he'd moved to Wyckford, he'd had his eye on her, though not much else since she seemed to go out of her way to avoid him whenever they were in the same vicinity. Which was a real feat given that they seemed to run into each other a lot, between the hospital and the fire station and the Buzzy Bird diner, which her parents owned in town. And in the two years he'd been here, he'd never once seen Luna date anyone.

Another thing that intrigued him.

Not that he was exactly a Casanova himself. Nope. He was done with relationships, after his marriage had blown up back in Chicago. Once the divorce was final, he'd said sayonara to love and was happy being on his own. No commitments. No complications. No problem. He'd stayed away from dating since he'd been in Wyckford and was perfectly happy about it.

And maybe the nights did get long and cold, especially this time of year.

He was fine on his own. Just fine and dandy.

They continued walking, in the exact opposite direction of the parking lot, but far be it from him to correct a woman who was obviously on the warpath. If she wanted to continue to be bafflingly stubborn and adorable, so be it. He hazarded a side-glance at her in the quickly fading light. Took in her short black hair spiked around her face from beneath her pink knit hat, her pink lips glistening slightly from the balm she used, her ever-present tough expression and the proud tilt to her chin, not giving an inch.

He tried a different tack. "You hike out here a lot in the winter, huh?"

She glanced out at the last rays of the setting sun, then back to him with a tight smile. "Yep."

Not for the first time, Mark wondered what it would be like to see her smile with both her eyes and her mouth at the same time. He also noticed the tightness at the corners of her mouth and eyes. Luna was scared, which stirred not only his protective nature but also his natural curiosity and suspicion—good for the firefighter in him, dangerous for a man no longer interested in romance.

"That's good," he said agreeably. "Because you know we're going the wrong way."

She stopped short and faced him, hands on hips, lips compressed. "You could've said that half a mile ago."

"I could, but I value my life." He leaned back against a tree, enjoying the flash of annoyance on her face. It'd been a hell of a long day, and it was shaping up to be a longer night. There wasn't enough caffeine in the world to get him through it, but this was a nice distraction. How someone who'd been here before could get so completely turned around was a puzzle he suddenly wanted to solve.

Luna sighed, then stalked off in the opposite direction, which was also wrong.

"Need help?" Mark called from behind her.

She slowly turned to face him; her teeth clenched. He still leaned against that evergreen, arms crossed over his broad chest, his shoulders looking sturdy enough to carry all her burdens. Which only made her angrier. He watched her like he had all the time in the world and no concerns.

Maybe he didn't. *He* wasn't lost.

The air between them crackled, and it had nothing to do with the wildlife.

It'd been a long time since Luna had allowed herself to experience this kind of tension with a man and she wasn't sure how to react, so she went with her default. Anger. Because men were dangerous, in more ways than one, and she knew beneath their chosen veneer, whatever it may be—nice guy, funny guy, sexy guy, whatever—their true colors lurked, lying in wait.

In his defense, she'd seen Mark around for two years now, and he was always just… *Mark*. Amused, tense, tired, regardless he remained cool, calm, even-keeled. Nothing seemed to get to him. Luna had to admit she was confused. *He* confused her.

She crossed her arms. "No."

He arched a brow, his expression filled with polite doubt.

Admitting defeat sucked, but the sun was nearly gone now, and the temperatures were dropping fast. "Please just point me in the right direction."

He did.

Right. Luna stalked off in the correct direction.

"Watch out for bears," Mark called after her. "Three o'clock."

She froze and glanced sideways to see a huge, hulking shadow. A bear. A *big* bear. Enjoying the last of rays of the day and scratching his back against the trunk of an evergreen, his huge paws in the air, confident he sat at the top of the food chain.

Luna held her breath as every bear mauling she'd ever seen on TV flashed in her mind. It had been a while since her last trip out here to the forest and now it might be her last because she'd not prepared properly. Great.

Definitely bringing bear repellent next time. And an old-fashioned compass.

Slowly, she backed up a step, then another, and another, until she bumped into Mark and nearly screamed.

"Just a black bear," he whispered near her ear, his warm breath on his skin nearly as unsettling as the wild animal in front of her as he gently rubbed his big hands up and down her arms. "You're okay."

Okay? That bear was the size of a bus as he wriggled around, letting out audible groans of ecstasy, latent power in his every move. Luna swallowed hard. "Does he even see us?"

The bear tipped his big, furry head toward them, studying her and Mark.

Guess that's a yes.

Reacting instinctively, Luna turned fast and burrowed her face into Mark's chest as his strong arms closed around her, warning him, "If you tell anyone about his, I'll kill you."

For once, he didn't even smile, his blue eyes unreadable as she looked up at him. "No worries. And anyway, I'm hard to kill."

CHAPTER TWO

As Mark held Luna, his wariness grew. She'd nearly leaped out of her own skin a second ago, and he'd swear it hadn't all been because of the bear. That bothered him. A lot. "I've got you."

"I've got myself," Luna mumbled defiantly against his chest, sounding a bit more like the sarcastic ray of dark sunshine he was used to. He'd take that any day over her fear, whether toward a wild animal or him. "I'm just not much of a bear person."

Before he realized what he was doing, Mark started stroking her back, soothing her quivers, trying *not* to notice how good she felt against him. Or how...*fragile*. In all the time he'd known her, Mark had never thought of Luna Norton as fragile. He'd seen her teaching a room full of beefy firefighters how to nurse their sore joints during her bimonthly clinics at the station, confront bullies at every turn and assist patients twice her size at the hospital to move around during their physical therapy sessions. He'd always thought she was as physically and emotionally strong as her attitude suggested.

But maybe not…

Either way, he didn't have plans for either of them to become a bear appetizer tonight. Gently, he eased Luna away, then guided her around to stand behind him, putting himself between her and the bear. "Don't worry. We won't be bait. Not tonight anyway."

She grabbed the sides of his down coat and pressed up tighter to him to peer around him at the bear, which was still pretty much ignoring them as he scratched himself on the tree. "How do you know?"

"Well, he'd have to go through me first and given my muscle mass, I'd make a filling snack. Also, black bears are extremely skittish. I bet if we take a step toward him, he'll take off."

Luna hesitated. "Really?"

"Really. Watch." Mark waved his arms. After a look of reproof, the bear lumbered away, vanishing into the trees with a disgruntled snort. Mark took a deep breath to calm his own nerves, then turned back to Luna. "Considering you said you're out here a lot, I'd figured you'd be ready for anything."

"I am ready for anything. Usually." The rising full moon highlighted her as she moved back onto the trail. "But I don't come out here much at night," she said, then added under her breath, "or get lost."

Ha! So she was lost, then…

The knowledge made him feel happier than it should. And brought his protector instincts racing back to the forefront. He followed her down the trail. "I'll just escort you out, then."

She gave an unenthusiastic snort as she walked ahead of him. Just as well, he supposed, since now that he was here with the only woman who'd intrigued him in years, he wasn't sure what to do. Honestly, he was out of practice with women. Several years out of practice, in fact, after his divorce. He kept an eye on Luna as his radio squawked, and his dispatcher came on. "We have a problem."

Immediately, Mark's senses sharpened, and he stopped in his tracks, pulling the radio off his belt and holding it closer to his ear as Luna continued down the trail toward the public parking lot. "Bates, where are you?"

"Forest," he said. "Checking fire gates. Why?"

"Bad news." The female dispatcher's gruff voice made her sound like a twelve-pack-a-day smoker, but she was a huge fitness guru who'd never had a cigarette in her life. "One of the standing dead fell about twenty minutes ago across the road back into town. A crew is on the way now to clear it, but based on the size of the tree, they estimate it will take until daybreak to clear it."

Great.

Honestly, it wasn't the worst news in the world. He'd camped out here many times in the winter, and he had all his gear with him in his truck. Yes, it was cold, sure, but his coat was polar rated, as were his gloves and hat. He'd be fine. "Looks like I'm staying, then. Take me off the board."

"Ten-four."

He followed the direction Luna had gone in again, stepping off the trail to take a shortcut back to the public lot. With the full moon, he didn't even need a flashlight and didn't hurry through the stands of spruce, hemlock, pine and cedar. He still beat her back and had just gotten to his truck when Luna came around a blind corner at the trail entrance, apparently not seeing him.

"Hey," he called hoping not to startle her again.

No such luck. She whipped around, her feet planted wide and her gray eyes alert, clearly ready for a fight.

"Just me," Mark said, holding his hands up and keeping his tone easy as his breath frosted on the frigid air.

"What the hell are you doing here, besides trying to scare me to death?" She limped a little as she walked over to him, and Mark frowned. "How'd you get back here so fast?"

"Shortcut," he said, narrowing his gaze on her ankle. "Did you hurt yourself?"

"I'm fine," she said, because that was always her answer, even when she clearly was not. Breathing heavy, she narrowed her eyes at him in the moonlight. "And you didn't think to mention this shortcut to me?"

Mark bit his lip and turned around fast so she wouldn't see him grin at her snarky tone. He did love a fighter. "Unfortunately, we have another issue to deal with now. The road back into town is blocked. My dispatcher called it in."

"Blocked?" Luna repeated, sounding skeptical. "Blocked how?"

"By an old-growth tree that fell across the road. Crew won't have it cleared until morning."

She blinked at him, her dark brows slowly drawing together as she worked out what that meant. "Wait. So, we're stuck here for the night?"

"Yes." Mark tipped his head back to study the star-filled sky. "It's not so bad, though. Promise. Have you ever been camping out here in the winter?"

She glanced up uneasily. "No."

"It's cold, but also beautiful. All that pristine white snow. No streetlights, no illumination from town, nothing. Just the galaxy above."

"What about frostbite?" she asked, rubbing her arms. "Hypothermia?"

He studied her jacket and boots more closely. At least she was prepared there. "Your gear's built for it. As long as we stay close together and get a fire going, we'll be good. I have blankets and supplies."

"Stay close?" Luna snorted and stepped back, giving him a flat stare. "Yeah, this is not a booty call, okay? We will not be 'staying close' for body heat, buddy. You think I haven't seen all those cheesy rom-com movies?" She rummaged around in her backpack and pulled out a flashlight, flicking it on with a gloved thumb. "And I have an early shift in PT in the morning. I can't stay here tonight."

"Well, unless you have a chain saw and a crane to lift that tree out of the way, you don't have much choice. Or I guess you can walk back to town, but given that bear's still out there, and the coyotes, I wouldn't want to take my chances." Mark put his hands on his hips and waited, their gazes locked across the span of several feet. In truth, she'd probably be fine once she reached the highway, but given it was a major route between Boston and the north, he really didn't want her taking that chance. Too dangerous. Finally, when she didn't budge an inch, he tried a different tack, turning back toward his truck to pull out more gear. "Listen, I'm not interested in 'sharing body heat,' either. Not the way you mean anyway. Not that there's anything wrong with you, I'm just not looking for that right now. So no worries there."

He pulled out two sleeping bags and a large nylon bag containing a small tent and set it all on the ground near his feet. "Plus, I camp out here a lot. I have a tent, warm blankets, food, water. And your coat looks polar rate, same as mine, plus your gloves and hat. And those boots look close to military issue."

Luna scowled. "They are. I bought them at the supply store in Boston last month."

He nodded. "Good. Then we're all set."

Regardless of what he'd said, Mark still planned to stick close to Luna tonight. Not because of a booty call, but because even with her experience out here and her gear, things could go quickly wrong and that made her a statistic waiting to happen. She still stared at him, though, her lovely gray eyes shadowed by things he didn't understand but wanted to, before he tamped those unwanted urges down. Now wasn't the time or place, and he wasn't the right man for her. Or anyone really. His ex-wife had made sure Mark knew that. He worked too much, took too many risks, was too focused on helping others and ignored what was best for his own life. At least according to his ex-wife. He picked up the tent bag and one of the sleeping bags, nudging the other with the toe of his boot to indicate that Luna should pick it up. "C'mon. We'll find a place to set up, then build a fire to keep the coyotes away."

Luna's steps faltered behind him as she shifted the sleeping bag from one hand to the other. "You think they'll come close to us?"

"Maybe." He was glad he was leading the trek back into the woods, that way she couldn't see his grin when he couldn't help but tease her a bit— especially given how she'd treated him when he'd first shown up earlier. He called back to her over his shoulder. "And remember to keep your jean legs tucked into your boots when you lie down. You don't want any extra critters crawling inside them to keep warm."

She stopped then, staring down at her black, heavy-duty boots. "Critters? Aren't they hibernating this time of year? I heard squirrels earlier and saw a chipmunk, but that was during the day."

"Some stuff is sleeping at night, yeah, but other creatures are nocturnal and stay out all year. And like we saw earlier, the black bears aren't true hibernators, either. They still come out of denning every so often, too."

They stopped at a small clearing and Luna swallowed hard, taking a long, uneasy look around them.

Mark shrugged and set down the tent, then took pity on her. "I'm sure we'll be fine, okay? And hey, sometimes, being alone out here isn't all it's cracked up to be. Safety in numbers."

She seemed to consider that for a moment, then

exhaled slow, as if coming to a decision. "Are you sure you have enough supplies for two?"

"I do," he said. "Always prepared. That's my motto."

"That's the Boy Scouts' motto." Luna gave him a long once-over. "Though you were probably one of those, too, in the past."

He laughed. Couldn't help it. "So what if I was?"

Luna shook her head. "Figures I'd get stuck in the woods with my very own Dudley Do-Right."

Rather than answer that, Mark turned and started collecting wood to build a fire before setting up the tent. Then he walked back to his truck to raid the lockbox, pulling out bottled water, some beef jerky and a bag of marshmallows. As he walked back to their campsite, he did his best to ignore the knot of tension building in his gut. Not because of the camping, but because his ex-wife had called him the same thing as Luna, Dudley Do-Right, the night they'd finally broken up for good. She'd always said he was too good, too willing to sacrifice himself for other people, too naive. And maybe he was. But he wasn't stupid. And he wasn't naive, either. He'd known their getting married was a mistake almost from the start. They were too different, wanted different things in life. But he'd been determined to try and make it work because he also wasn't a quitter. In the end, she'd been the one to file the papers, leaving Mark to feel like he'd failed. Again. And yes, sometimes, he worried he was missing something in life, even more so now that both his best buddies had paired off with the women of their dreams to start families of their own... Mark loved kids. Always thought someday he'd have a bunch of his own.

But maybe that wasn't in the cards for him.

Maybe his ex-wife was right and he was too much of a Boy Scout. Always prepared.

Too bad his preparations had failed him the one night he'd needed them most.

He reached their makeshift camp again and tossed down the food beside Luna, who sat on a big log near the fire. "Dinner's ready."

She looked from the food up to him, her gaze far too perceptive for his comfort. "What's wrong?"

"Nothing," he said, plopping down on the other end of the log from her.

The temperatures were falling fast, and Luna huddled as close to the flames as possible without singeing her eyebrows. The stars glittered like diamonds in the huge, fathomless sky. One more thing Mark loved about living in Wyckford. Didn't get skies like this in Chicago. He soaked it in.

Luna held her hands toward the fire as a slight

icy breeze blew. Her position made her puffy parka ride up, giving Mark a nice view of her butt in those jeans, but he wasn't looking. Nope. Instead, he returned to his truck and grabbed a couple of more emergency blankets, then returned and tossed her one.

"What's this for?" She stared down at the box containing a shiny silver Mylar blanket.

"To help stay warm. Put it on."

Luna didn't answer as he dropped another log on the flames. Finally, she opened the box and wrapped the blanket around herself, shielding her face from him. "Thanks."

Mark's curiosity finally got the better of him, and he couldn't resist asking, "Why are you so prickly all the time?" Her side glance said it all, and Mark wondered what kind of life she'd had in the past. "Don't get me wrong. I love a good zinger as much as the next person, but I'm pretty sure you gave me third-degree burns earlier with your snark."

Luna smiled then, a lovely thing that made her eyes shine. "It keeps unwanted attention away."

He grinned back before he could stop himself. "Unwanted attention, huh?"

He'd never really thought about that before, but he supposed it was a problem for women. Especially ones who looked like Luna.

She shrugged, staring at the fire. "Guys only think about one thing."

Mark chewed on that for a few minutes while he finished setting up the tent and tossing the sleeping bags inside. Then he took a seat on the log again and pointed at the beef jerky and bag of marshmallows sitting near her feet. "Sometimes we think about other stuff, too. Like food. Which course of our dinner of champions do we start with?"

Luna laughed out loud this time, and Mark felt like he'd won the lottery. She eyed both choices, then opened the marshmallows. "Life's short. Dessert first."

"Agreed." He stoked the flames, then pushed aside the two burning logs to reveal hot ashes—the sweet spot for roasting marshmallows. Near the edge of the clearing, he located two long sticks and handed one to Luna. She gave him a marshmallow for his stick. They roasted in silence for a while.

"Being out here makes me want to draw," Luna said eventually, staring into the fire.

Mark blinked at her. "Wait—did you just offer me a piece of personal information?"

"I'm not completely antisocial." She rolled her eyes. "I can do casual conversation, too."

"But your drawing isn't casual," he said.

She held his gaze. "No. It's not. It's how I relax."

Forget her great laugh. *Now* Mark felt like he'd just won the lottery.

"Do you draw?" she asked him.

"Nah. Unless you count the stick figures I use on fire reports." He blew on his marshmallow before eating it. "This place is inspiring, though. What kind of stuff do you draw?"

"Landscapes, mostly." Luna glanced around at the dark night. "Been doing it since I was a teenager. It centers me."

"Are you any good?" he asked, licking some sticky marshmallow from the corner of his mouth, not missing the way she tracked the movement with her eyes or the tingle that started low in his gut. A tingle he quickly squashed.

Luna shrugged and looked away fast. "I've sold a couple pieces around town, but mainly it's just a hobby."

She handed him another marshmallow from the bag, and this time their fingers brushed. Her breath caught, the sound going straight through Mark. Not good. Not good at all. She busied herself with her toasted marshmallow, popping one into her mouth, then sucking the remnants off her finger. Mark averted his gaze, but not before he noticed the way her mouth and tongue worked… His throat tightened and he shifted his seat on the log to distract himself. Suddenly, it seemed like all the frigid air had been replaced with tropical heat.

This was not happening. This could not happen. Mark was not looking for a relationship. He wasn't looking for anything romantic at all. He'd finally gotten his life back together after moving to Wyckford two years ago and he wasn't looking to blow it all up now by getting involved again. He was better off alone. It almost felt like an atonement, of sorts, for the life his little brother, Mikey, would never get to have. Another punishment for his failures. He'd tried being a couple. It didn't work. So Mark was determined to keep to himself. No matter how beautiful Luna might look by the fire's glow.

Of course, the fact she kept looking at him now like she'd never really seen him before didn't help matters. They'd somehow moved closer to each other, too, so their thighs touched. Mark's fingers itched to reach for her, but he forced himself to stay perfectly still. Then, thankfully, a coyote howled—the cry immediately answered by another, louder howl echoing off the trees.

Luna gave a startled gasp.

"They're not as close as they sound," Mark mumbled as he tried to slow the racing pulse that had nothing to do with the wild animals in the distance and everything to do with the amazingly attractive woman beside him. He couldn't sleep with Luna Norton tonight. Couldn't sleep with her ever, really. He didn't need the complications. And he certainly didn't need the recriminations when she realized he was not what she was looking for. No. Better to keep things strictly platonic between them.

She fiddled with her boot, scooting closer still to him. Then more coyotes howled, and Luna grabbed his thigh before she snatched it away fast. Mark nearly swallowed his tongue. "Sorry."

He cleared his throat and scooted a couple of inches away, needing some space, parroting her words from earlier back at her because his brain couldn't think of anything else to say. "It's fine. I'm fine."

To keep himself busy, he threaded a row of marshmallows onto her stick for her, then did the same for himself, watching Luna eye the forest around them like if she concentrated hard enough, she'd be able to see through the dark.

Finally, her tense shoulders relaxed a little and she stuck her stick in the fire again. "Where are you from originally?"

"Chicago," he said, pulling his marshmallows from the fire. "Born and bred in the rat race."

"Wow. Can't get much farther from that than Wyckford. You ever miss it?"

"Not at all." Not the weather, not the job, not

the ex… Although he did miss his family. "I like the slower pace here. Are you a town native?"

"Yep." She shrugged.

"What year did you graduate high school?"

"I didn't. Took the GED instead."

"Oh." That spawned more questions than answers, but he didn't want to ask just then and risk her clamming up again. So, he told her a bit more about himself instead. "I graduated in 2007, then joined the navy. Spent four years overseas, before joining Chicago FD."

"I know," she told him, sounding smug. "One of the other firefighters told me during the last class I taught at the fire station."

Mark wasn't surprised. Everyone in Wyckford knew everyone else's business. He just wished he knew more about hers so he wasn't so intrigued by her, but Luna's past was a closed book where he was concerned. Finally, he asked the question foremost in his mind. "Why'd you go the GED route?"

Instead of answering, she stuffed another marshmallow into her mouth.

Conversation over, apparently.

And that was just as well because now all Mark could apparently concentrate on was how she seemed to savor each morsel of food like it was a special prize.

Stop it.

When they were high on sugar, they balanced it out with the beef jerky. Luna unzipped her backpack, allowing him to peek inside and see a drawing pad, colored pencils, a hiking guide, lip balm, a pocketknife and an apple. Luna pulled out the apple and the knife, then zipped the bag closed.

She was a puzzle. And a whole bunch of other things he couldn't quite put a finger on yet, nor should he, probably. No matter how much he tried to ignore her, or his reactions to her, he couldn't. Which was a problem. A major one.

Luna carved up the apple, then handed him half. They shared the fruit, drank their waters, then both yawned wide.

"Sorry. I'm exhausted," she said.

Mark checked his watch—6:30 p.m.—then stoked the fire, before moving the pup tent closer and zipping the two sleeping bags together for maximum warmth. "It's a little early for bedtime, but you said you have an early morning, so…" He gestured toward the tent. "You sleep in here."

Luna frowned. "What about you?"

"I'll stay out here and keep the fire going. I'm not tired yet. I'll be fine. Don't worry."

She shook her head. "I can't let you do that."

He sighed and pointed at the tent again. "Our only other option is sharing that."

Luna chewed on her lower lip again—which

drove him insane because now all he could imagine was *him* doing the same thing.

Stop! What's wrong with you?

"Right," she finally said, turning toward the tent. "Good night."

"Good night," he called behind her, feeling like he'd dodged a deadly bullet. "Zip up behind you."

With her safely tucked away in the tent, Mark wrapped both emergency blankets around himself before sitting on the ground and leaning back against the log, getting comfortable—or as comfortable as he could wrapped in Mylar—then stared at the sky. Normally, the starry expanse never failed to relax him, but tonight it took a long time.

The problem was a few of his body parts were at odds with each other, but in the end, his brain reminded him of the bottom line. He'd come to Wyckford to get peace and quiet, to be alone.

To move past his mistakes in Chicago. To learn to live with his past failures.

Even all these years later, the night his youngest brother, Mikey, had died still haunted him. The roar of the fire, the heat of the flames puckering Mark's skin, the screams as Mark had tried to reach his brother before the roof came down, burying them all.

He shook his head and stared into the small fire before him now. His ex-wife had claimed that was one of the reasons he worked himself into the ground. To make amends for what happened that night, even though none of it had been Mark's fault—at least according to the adults at the time. He'd only been twelve at the time, still a boy himself. No one blamed him for what happened. No one except himself. If he'd just been faster, smarter, stronger, maybe he could have saved Mikey that fateful night. It's why he'd become a firefighter. It's why he pushed himself so hard every day to save those who couldn't save themselves. And another reason he'd come to Wyckford. To try and restore some balance in his life again. Perhaps work a little less and live a little more, even if that life was by himself.

Mark eventually fell asleep, only to be awakened by Luna's scream.

CHAPTER THREE

BREATHLESS AND HEART POUNDING, Luna lay flat on her back in the pitch dark. She'd needed to use the bathroom and had snuck out of the tent, tiptoeing out into the woods. Not far, just far enough for a bit of privacy. But her downfall had been the walk back to camp. Despite her flashlight and the thick-soled traction of her boots, she'd slipped on the ice and ended up sliding down an embankment, losing her flashlight in the process.

Now all she could see was the vague black outline of the tree canopy far above—at least she hoped they were trees. Claustrophobic from the all-encompassing blackness, and still worried about those critters Mark had mentioned earlier, she sat up and winced. Her left wrist burned. So did her butt. Great, she'd probably fractured her coccyx. And it was her own fault.

She'd been too cocky, thinking she could handle herself out here at night simply because she'd done it so often during the day. But she should have known better—bad things could happen anywhere, anytime. Usually when you least expected it. A lesson she'd learned all too well when she'd been attacked…

A beam of light shown on her from above as Mark called her name.

"Down here," Luna yelled. *Where all the stupid people fall.* "I think I can climb up myself."

"Don't move."

"But—"

"Not a muscle." Seemed the laid-back firefighter wasn't so relaxed now. "You know as well as I do that's rule number one for an injured person." He climbed down the embankment, then crouched beside her, holding Luna still with one firm hand. "Where are you hurt?"

"Nowhere."

"Hold this." He put his flashlight in her good hand, his light blue eyes narrowing on the wrist she hugged close to her chest. After a gentle inspection of it, he asked, "Can you move your fingers?"

Luna nodded, shining the light around them to make sure there weren't any bears. There weren't.

Mark scowled. "Did you hit your head?"

"No."

He took his flashlight back. "I don't think your wrist is broken, but you've got a good sprain. What else hurts?"

"Nothing."

He obviously didn't believe her since he ran a hand over her limbs with professional efficiency.

She pushed him away with her good hand. "I said I was fine."

Mark looked into her eyes and held up his hand. "How many fingers do you see?"

"Two. But one's more effective."

He smiled and despite the situation, Luna's ovaries did a little flip. "You're fine."

Mark rose to his feet, then helped Luna to hers. Pain radiated out from her tailbone, causing her to wince as they slowly made their way back up the embankment.

"Next time wake me up if you need to go out," Mark said once they were up top again.

They returned to their campsite, and Mark nudged her back toward the tent. She crawled inside and into the sleeping bag, pulling it over her head, pretending she was at home in her nice warm bed. But Luna never had to worry about bears or critters in her apartment. And she certainly never shivered. When had it gotten so cold?

"Let me see your wrist," Mark said a few minutes later after zipping them both inside the tent. He pulled the sleeping bag off Luna's head and ducked low to accommodate the ceiling. He had a first-aid kit and an ACE bandage, which he used to wrap her wrist. Then he slapped an ice pack against his thigh to activate it and set her wrapped wrist on it before pulling out a second ice pack and eying her.

Luna gave him a wary stare. "What?"

"You gonna let me look at it?" he asked.

Without thinking, her free hand slid to her tailbone. "No way."

He sighed and dropped his chin to his chest for a moment, either praying for patience or trying not to laugh, she wasn't sure which. Then, when he'd gathered himself again, Mark moved with his usual professionalism, unzipping the sleeping bag and yanking it away. He ignored her alarmed squeak and placed a hand on her waist. "Be still."

Dudley Do-Right indeed. "Listen, I'm—"

"You're bleeding."

"What?" Luna frowned and twisted to see behind herself. "Where?"

"Your leg."

From the corner of her eye, Luna caught sight of a growing dark red stain covering the back of her jeans over her thigh. The fact she hadn't felt the injury meant the wound was probably deep. She was used to treating other people, but it was another thing entirely when you were the patient. Luna suddenly felt a bit woozy.

Mark rifled through the first-aid kit. "Lower your jeans. We need to clean that up."

His words sobered her up fast. "No."

He kept his tone calm and reasonable, as if he

dealt with difficult people every day. Considering his job, he probably did. "I'm a certified EMT. You need first aid. Strictly protocol. Trust me."

Too bad she'd given up trusting men a long time ago. "Give me the stuff. I'll put it on myself."

"You can't see what you're doing, and the cut needs to be thoroughly cleaned first. And since I don't have sutures, we may have to glue it closed." His polite voice was laced with unmistakable steel. "Now lower your pants, please, or I'll have to cut them off."

Unwanted awareness shimmered through Luna's bloodstream. She didn't often allow herself to notice men these days, but with Mark she couldn't seem to help herself. She huffed out a breath, then did as he asked. "Fine." Then to distract herself, gave in to her interest in him a little. "This isn't your first middle-of-the-night potty accident, I take it?"

He laughed softly, the sound warming her. "Uh, no. My first one was when I was nine."

"You were a paramedic when you were nine?"

"No." Mark slid her a look before continuing. "My older brother took me camping. He warned me not to go anywhere without him, not even to take a leak." He shrugged. "So, obviously, that's the first thing I did."

His smile was contagious, and Luna relaxed a little. "What happened?"

"Woke up and thought I was way too cool to need an escort…" He paused meaningfully, and she grimaced. "I went looking for a tree and walked straight into a wall of bushes and got all cut up. Nearly wet myself before I got free. My brother reamed me a new one when I got back. I told him everything was fine, but by the next afternoon, I had a hundred-and-three temperature. We went home and my mom found a nasty gash on my arm that had gotten infected."

His low, slightly gruff voice worked like a magic drug as Luna listened to him, lulling her into a daze. Mark's affection for his family was obvious as he talked. She was an only child herself, the epitome of a latchkey kid. Not that her parents hadn't loved her. They had, but starting a business required a lot of time and effort, which meant there wasn't a lot left over for her by the time she'd reached her tenuous teenaged years. She'd had to make decisions on her own. Which is where she'd gotten into trouble. Started running with the wrong crowd, started trusting the wrong people. And it had nearly cost her everything.

"Poison oak," Mark continued, jarring her back to the present. "Everywhere."

"Oh, no!" Luna cringed on his behalf. "That sounds awful."

"It was. But know what would be worse?" He waited until she shook her head to continue. "*Your* cut getting infected. Which is why I'm glad you let me look at it."

Aware of Mark's big, solid presence beside her as he worked, cleaning her wound with antiseptic, which stung like hell, Luna distracted herself by concentrating on the feel of his long, calloused fingers against her skin.

It had been a long time since she'd let someone touch her, care for her. She felt both soothed and panicked in equal turns, an odd, unsettling mix. And yet, she couldn't move away, didn't want to.

"There," he said as he finished bandaging her up. "All done. You can pull your pants up and turn over now."

Luna hesitated, risking a glance up at him. Mark's face was more angles than curves in the flashlight's glow, his silky blond hair brushing the collar of his coat. He was so broad in the shoulders he blocked out the entire entrance to the tent, but she wasn't afraid. Because somehow, she knew she was safe with him, even with the chemistry between them.

After she'd gotten herself situated again, Mark handed her a second ice pack for her tailbone. She put it in place, then got back inside her sleeping bag.

"You're still shivering." He stretched out beside her on top of it. "Come here. Probably shock."

Mark pulled her in close, wrapping her up in his

warm arms, holding her close until she stopped shivering.

"Better?" he whispered against her hair eventually.

Luna nodded, burrowing farther into his rock solidness, unable to stop herself as his arms tightened around her. "Much, thank you."

When Mark finally tried to pull away, Luna let him, too scared to hang on, too scared to think about what that might mean for her.

He sat up, stroking a hand down her back. "Better?"

She nodded, not trusting her voice, feeling far too vulnerable. To move further away from dangerous territory, she said, "Did I tell you I thought I saw someone out here earlier? Before you arrived? In the bushes, watching me. A face and a flash of a blue hoodie maybe."

"People hike out here all year," Mark said, seemingly unconcerned. "Did you feel threatened?"

She always felt slightly threatened, like her attacker might suddenly reappear from nowhere, but she wasn't about to tell him that. Instead, she shrugged.

"On my first night here in the forest, I was stalked."

Shocked, Luna gaped at him. "By whom?"

"Every horror movie I'd ever seen."

She laughed. "Was the big, bad firefighter scared?"

He shook his head and chuckled. "I set up camp. Turned on all the lights. But even afterward, I still felt eyes on me." His hand still glided up and down her back, soothing her. "I searched the perimeter several times, then fell asleep holding my two-way radio. At first light, I was startled awake by a curious bear."

"Oh, God. What happened?"

Amusement laced his tone. "I screamed and scared us both. I ran away, and the bear did the same. He went into the woods, and I hightailed it home."

She giggled. "I can't imagine you hightailing it anywhere."

He grinned. "I've had my moments."

They sat there for a while before Luna asked, "Tell me about your family in Chicago."

"Well, there's my mom and dad. And my other brother. He's got three kids now. I talk to them all every week. My parents ask every time if I'm going to give them a few grandkids, too." He sighed, his smile fading. "And there was Mikey. He was the youngest. He died when I was twelve in a house fire. I tried to go back in to save him, but I couldn't. He's the reason I became a firefighter."

"I'm so sorry."

Mark shook his head. "It was a long time ago."

Luna nodded but could tell from his reaction that the pain was still fresh for him. She wanted to ask more, but didn't feel comfortable at that point, so let it drop.

"I should get back outside and check the fire," he said, starting to move away.

"No." She grabbed his wrist, not wanting to be alone. "Stay. Please."

He watched her closely a moment. "Are you sure?"

She nodded and he settled back down beside her, not touching, just letting her know he was there. A comforting warmth in the cold night. They stayed quiet after that, and Luna surprised herself by falling asleep. When she awoke hours later, dawn was creeping in, poking at the backs of her eyelids. For a moment, she stayed still, feeling quite warm, because she'd wrapped herself like a pretzel around her heat source. She cracked open an eye and found Mark watching her, looking amused.

"Hey." His voice was early-morning raspy, and he looked sleepy and sexily rumpled. "How are you feeling?"

Not exactly a morning person, it took Luna a moment to process the fact he was lying next to her, and their legs were entwined and at some point in the night, the sleeping bag had fallen away so there was no barrier between them and…

Luna's inner barriers softened, and her hands rested on his chest as he slid a hand into her hair, tilting her face up to his so he could search her gaze. "Everything okay?"

CHAPTER FOUR

TOUSLED AND SLEEPY, Luna looked softer than usual, which could be normal or could be a sign of confusion, disorientation, a possible head injury. Mark's internal analyst ticked through all the possibilities. Well, except for the most obvious one because yeah, he wasn't going there. Bad enough he'd somehow ended up with Luna in his arms, wrapped around him like a second skin, during the night when he'd sworn to keep his distance. Now, with her warm and cuddled against him, it was sending his senses into overdrive. Not good, since it made him want to throw all of his good intentions to keep things platonic between them out the window and kiss her silly. But he'd stayed close because he had to make sure she was all right. That was his duty as a firefighter and a paramedic. That's the excuse he was going with anyway.

He studied her from across the few inches separating them. Her short, dark hair spiked around her head in disarray, her smudged mascara, her mile-long legs that were currently tangled up with his. His fingers suddenly itched to unzip her coat, shove her shirt up and nuzzle every luscious inch of her. He swallowed hard and loosened his hold on her instead. "I think I should—"

Before he could finish that sentence, the sound of pine needles crunching on the frozen ground outside the tent made them both freeze. Mark frowned toward the entrance of the tent as he slowly sat up.

"What is that?" Luna whispered. Her gray eyes widened with fear. "Another bear?"

Mark shook his head and held a finger to his lips for her to be quiet. The footsteps sounded more of the human variety to him, and the last thing he wanted was to tip whoever was out there off that they were onto them. There'd been a rise in transient people living temporarily in these woods and he really didn't want to start his day by having a run-in with any of them. Pushing to his feet, he straightened his coat and hat, then slipped his gloves on before whispering, "Wait here."

The morning was so foggy he could barely see more than a few feet, but he carefully searched the clearing and found it empty of any mysterious intruders. But the fresh footsteps in the snow indicated someone had been here. Mark checked out his truck next. Everything was the same there, too, except for a flashlight he'd left on his rear fender. That was gone.

With a sigh, he started back toward the tent and that's when he heard the soft *cush* of footsteps running away in the snow. Mark turned and saw a hooded figure dodging from a hiding spot on the other side of Luna's parked car and toward the exit to the highway. He took off after them, yelling, "Stop!"

Of course, they didn't stop, so he sprinted forward, catching the back of the person's blue hoodie and yanking them to a halt.

"Hold still," Mark panted when they fought to get free, adding a small shake to get his point across. That's when the hood fell back, exposing their face—a snarling mouth, eyes spitting fury, female. A scrawny, lanky, lean teenaged girl, *maybe* sixteen, who looked like she hadn't had a decent meal in days.

"Let me go!" She kicked Mark in the shin with sneaker-covered foot. "Don't touch me!"

He cursed, letting her loose to hold his sore leg as he glared at her.

She lifted her chin in a show of bravado, arms crossed tight. "I didn't do anything wrong."

"Then why did you run?" Mark countered.

"Because you chased me." She didn't add the *duh*, but it was heavily implied.

"Where are your parents?"

Her expression turned sullen. "I don't have to answer any of your stupid questions."

Even though he wasn't wearing his uniform, Mark gave off his best public safety vibes. "You're a minor alone out here in the woods."

"I'm eighteen." She produced a card from a ratty-looking backpack, careful not to let him see inside. Her actions reminded him of another cagey female he'd come across last night in the forest.

The ID gave her name as Astrid Jones and was issued by the Washington Department of Motor Vehicles. The picture showed a cleaner version of the face in front of him, and the birth date did indeed state she'd turned eighteen two weeks ago.

Handing the card back, Mark hiked his thumb toward the trail. "Was that you outside the tent earlier?"

Her gaze darted away. "No."

"What's in your backpack?"

She hugged it to her chest. "*My* stuff."

Mark took a deep breath for patience. "What are you doing out here by yourself?"

"None of your business."

This was going nowhere fast, so Mark tried a different tactic. "The road back into town was closed last night, but it should be open this morning. If you need a ride, I can give you one."

"No!" She shook her head. "I don't take rides from strangers. I'm leaving."

There was little Mark could do to stop her. "My name is Mark Bates," he said as she started to turn away. "I'm a firefighter in Wyckford. And I just want to help you."

She stopped and looked back at him over her shoulder, her cheeks and nose rosy from the cold, and that's when he spotted something sticking out of a side pocket of her backpack. Something familiar. "Where'd you get that flashlight?"

"I've had it forever." She shrugged, keeping her bare hands tucked in the front pocket of her hoodie to keep them warm. "Why?"

"Find anything?"

Mark turned to see Luna walking toward them, a Swiss Army knife in her hand, open and ready for action. Her short hair was still wild, her wrist bandaged, her stance making it clear she was ready to rumble. Her clothes were a bit rumpled, and her face pale, but even so, he didn't think he'd ever seen anything so sexy. Which was the totally wrong thing for him to be focusing on in this situation, but he couldn't seem to control his stupid thoughts this morning. Which meant he also needed to get a grip. Rather than deal with his attraction to her, he went with Luna's regular standby, snark. "Nice job on the waiting thing."

"I don't do the waiting thing," she countered with a shrug. "Sue me."

Right. Luna could take care of herself. Message received loud and clear. The best thing he could do was to back off and let her get on with her life.

Except there was his inner Boy Scout again, his inner guilt over Mikey, compelling him to serve and protect, making him stay put.

More than anything, with his adrenaline spiking and his senses on high alert, Mark needed to remember he'd moved to Wyckford for the peace and quiet, a fresh start, an uncomplicated life. He liked being on his own, liked it a lot, and didn't plan to change that status anytime soon.

Still, none of that stopped his attraction to Luna Norton.

He turned back to Astrid, just as she looked ready to sprint away again. "Don't run. It's too early for another sprint. Where's your family, Astrid?"

Astrid's slouched posture screamed defense. "I'm not with my family. But you saw my ID. I'm eighteen now. I'm an adult."

"What are you doing in Wyckford?" he asked as Luna joined them.

"Visiting friends."

He sighed. This conversation was running in circles. "Who?"

She crossed her arms. "I don't have to tell you anything."

"Fine." He gestured toward his truck. "Get in."

"What?" Astrid's eyes got huge, and she scrambled back a few feet. "I'm not going anywhere with you."

"Look, I'm just going to drive you into town. To your *friends*." Just as soon as he tore down the campsite and packed away his gear again. Then he planned to contact the local police force to run Astrid's ID and see if she was a person of interest or reported as missing.

She looked away. "I don't need a ride."

"You can't stay out here. You don't have the proper gear and it's too cold without shelter."

Astrid seemed to notice Luna then because she hiked her chin toward the other woman before asking Mark, "She your girlfriend? Because the way she's looking at you right now, she doesn't seem to like you much."

Mark glanced over to see Luna glaring at him with raised a dark brow. "I am *not* your girlfriend."

"I never said you were." He glared at Astrid.

The girl flashed her first real smile. "So, you camp out in tents with your friends a lot, then? Awful tiny tent for such a big guy."

Heat climbed Mark's cheeks as he realized what it must look like, his being there with Luna, and the fact the girl obviously knew they'd been in that tent together since she'd been right outside it earlier. But before he could say anything else, Luna stepped closer, and her frown deepened to a scowl.

"Wait a minute," she said, narrowing her gaze

on Astrid. "I know that sweatshirt. You were watching me in the forest yesterday."

Rather than stand outside and get frostbite, they kept the girl with them as they packed up the campsite then returned to the lot. While they finished packing his gear away, Mark got the all clear from his dispatcher on the road. Because they both still had a lot of questions for the young runaway, and they were all starving, they decided to head to the Buzzy Bird in town and discuss things over breakfast. There were only two restaurant options in town, and the local bar didn't open until after 6:00 p.m., so...

Luna followed Mark in her car. He'd insisted Astrid ride with him, though it was obvious to anyone looking that the girl didn't trust him any farther than she could see him.

Smart girl.

For better or worse, she reminded Luna a lot of herself at that age—alone, full of bravado to cover the fact that underneath she was scared and lonely and hurting. At least, that's how Luna had been. And regardless of the tough-girl image Astrid tried to project, Luna knew how vulnerable she was underneath, how easily she could be taken advantage of, and she couldn't stand by and let that happen to someone else if she had the power to stop it.

They drove out of the public lot and onto the highway, waving to the crews still working to cut the old, dead tree down into manageable pieces to cart away to turn into firewood for town residents. On the way back to town, Luna remembered the day before, how she'd felt watched. She knew she'd recognized the blue sweatshirt she'd seen through the bushes. The teenager's face was dirty, bruised, too, meaning someone had hit her. Luna's gut squeezed.

After they'd managed to park in the Buzzy Bird's crowded lot, they went inside and got lucky, snagging a corner booth just as another family was leaving. Used to working in the diner off and on since she could remember, Luna quickly bused the table, then got them all waters before sliding into the seat beside Astrid, effectively blocking her from escaping, while Mark sat opposite them. Luna grabbed a menu for Astrid from the holder. She didn't bother with one for Mark or herself. They both already knew everything the diner served.

Mark tapped on the top of Astrid's menu. "Get whatever you want. My treat."

After they ordered, Mark sat back and crossed his arms, watching Astrid warily. "I'd like to get you back home where you belong, if you'll tell me exactly where that is."

Astrid looked up with a panicked expression. "I don't want to go home."

Luna grimaced, painfully aware of what the girl might be escaping. "Listen. Some people run for a reason."

Mark gave her a grim look, suggesting he understood more than Luna had given him credit for. "I know that. I just don't like the idea of her out here on her own, without support."

Luna stared at him. He stared right back. He wasn't kidding. Finally, she shook her head. "I want to say hello to my parents." She looked over at Astrid. "Stay here."

The girl blinked at her but didn't argue as Luna got up and walked back behind the full counter and through the swinging door into the kitchen. Instead of stopping to talk to her parents, though, Luna continued through the back exit, where she stood on the back stoop and took a deep breath of icy air to clear her senses. Her emotions were a rioting mess. Ever since waking up beside him in that tent, Luna had felt that unwanted prickle of awareness racing up her spine, settling at the base of her neck, followed by a rush of warmth she seemed to feel whenever Mark was near.

That wasn't good.

Having Astrid there—who reminded Luna so much of herself at that age it was like looking in a mirror—only made things worse, more confusing. Not good at all. But like Mark had said, they couldn't just turn her loose to fend for herself now that they'd found her. Luna felt a deep karmic purpose to help her, whatever that meant. After a few more deep breaths to fortify herself, Luna went back inside and found her mom checking the ice machine in the kitchen.

"Is that Mark Bates, the firefighter, I saw you come in with?" her mom asked as Luna stood nearby. "Always such a nice guy. So friendly and thoughtful. Charming, too. Are you seeing each other?"

"We're not."

Her mom gave her a look that said she knew exactly her daughter was putting up walls again, but dammit, Luna was perfectly happy with her safe, secure little life. And even if it did feel like sometimes something was missing, well, she'd live with it. She liked things just as they were. Predictable. Controlled. And what Mark did to her whenever he was around wasn't something Luna could control. Not yet anyway. And until she could, it was best to keep her distance from him whenever possible. She glanced out the small, round window of the swinging door to the kitchen and saw Mark and Astrid. He sat with his long legs sprawled out in front of him and his broad shoulders resting back against the booth. Based on his perpetual tan, he spent a lot of time outside, regardless of the season, and each time she closed her eyes, Luna still remembered his scent—salt and pine and soap, with a hint of sweat.

She shook off her reactions to just the thought of him because they were annoying and embarrassing. Rolling her eyes at her own idiocy, she looked over at her father behind the grill. John Norton had been born and bred in Wyckford. The only time he'd left the small town was to go to culinary school for two years in Seattle. After graduation, he'd returned and married Luna's mom, Mary, and they'd bought the Buzzy Bird. Her dad claimed cooking healed his soul. Wyckford certainly seemed to feel the same way because the diner was always busy.

Her mom joined Luna at the window. "Mark's a good guy. And he likes you. You should give him a chance."

"I don't want to give him a chance. I'm fine on my own."

I'm fine. Luna's go-to mantra. Whether it served her or not. Besides, Mark didn't like her, certainly not more than he liked anyone else. He barely knew her. She watched the server bring their order and refill their drinks before returning to the booth just as Mark stabbed a huge bite of his stack of pancakes slathered in butter and syrup with his fork, then pointed with it toward Astrid. "Eat up."

Astrid sighed, then did as Mark asked, poking at her scrambled eggs as Luna settled in beside her again and dug into her own breakfast skillet with sausage, eggs and cheese. After a few bits of yummy goodness, she glanced over at Astrid and asked, "Where are you from in Washington, Astrid?"

"Around," the girl mumbled, not looking up from her plate.

Right. Luna tried again. "I spent a lot of time on my own when I was your age, too."

"Hmm," Astrid hummed around a mouthful of eggs, avoiding eye contact.

"How long did you say you were staying in town?" Luna continued.

"I didn't."

Luna met Mark's gaze as Astrid devoured a triangle of whole wheat toast.

He waited until the girl swallowed a bite before saying, "You've been on your own for a while."

The girl shrugged.

"I was alone a lot at your age. My parents were busy here at the diner, so I had to fend for myself." Luna tried again to make a connection with the girl to see if they could get more information about her. "I'd eat peanut butter and ramen noodles for dinners because they were cheap and easy to make."

Astrid was halfway through her eggs now. "On Tuesdays the grocery has other stuff cheap, too."

"Grocery Tuesdays?" Mark asked, a brow raised.

Astrid hunched over her plate like she was afraid someone would steal it.

Luna's throat tightened as she answered Mark. "It's when they throw out their older stock to make room for the new."

Mark looked between the two women but didn't say anything more.

Finally, when they'd all eaten their fill but were no closer to finding any clues about Astrid than they were before, Luna gave Mark an I-did-the-best-I-could look and shrug before checking her watch. "Sorry, but I need to get back to my place to get ready for work."

She slid out of the booth and walked away, torn.

Part of her wanted to stay and help with Astrid, but the other part of her, the guarded part that never let anyone in for fear of being hurt again, knew better. That girl was a walking ball of headaches, heartaches and complications, and the sooner Luna left Astrid and Mark behind, the better. She had enough on her plate without adding more to the mix. Still, as she glanced back over her shoulder before heading out the door, Luna couldn't seem to squash the small pang of regret that rose inside her.

CHAPTER FIVE

AS MARK WATCHED Luna leave the Buzzy Bird, certain things began to click in his brain. She didn't like being approached unexpectedly or startled. She'd once survived on peanut butter and ramen. She was slow to trust. All the signs suggested something bad had happened in Luna's past, possibly worse than he could imagine. It wasn't any of his business, and certainly wasn't his job, but that didn't stop Mark from aching for both Luna and Astrid, even knowing neither wanted his sympathy.

Astrid was just a kid. A kid in trouble. And the protector in him felt obligated to help.

Based on the little he knew about the girl, she was probably on the run, maybe from abuse or, at the very least, neglect. She'd eaten everything off her plate and even snagged a leftover piece of toast off Luna's plate. "Better?"

After they paid the bill, Mark took Astrid back out to his truck in the parking lot, where he stopped and faced her. "You have two choices now. Tell me where your friends live in town so I can drop you off, or we'll go to the police station, and they can run your ID and figure out the truth of where you belong."

He planned on doing that second one either way, but Astrid didn't have to know.

They stared at each other until the sound of a clearing throat shattered the silence. Luna stood near her parked car, keys in hand, seeming to come to some decision. "Astrid, if you need a place to crash, I have a spare bedroom at my apartment. It's more like a glorified closet, but it's all yours for the night."

"No," Mark said immediately. It was one thing for *him* to get involved with a troubled teen they knew nothing about but entirely another for Luna to take the girl home with her. Until he'd had a chance to do some checking into Astrid's background, she could be dangerous, a wanted fugitive. He couldn't let Luna take that risk.

"What do you mean no?" Luna said, her gray eyes spitting fire now.

Astrid shifted her weight, looking uncomfortable. "Thanks, but I just want to go back to the forest."

"Like I said before, that's not an option," Mark insisted. "It's too cold to sleep there this time of year without the proper gear. You'll freeze to death. As a first responder, I can't allow it."

Luna sighed and moved closer to them. "Just come to my apartment, Astrid. It's safe and warm, and you'll have a hot shower and a roof."

Mark started to protest again, but before he could, Astrid walked over and got in Luna's car. *Well, damn.*

Luna watched him with an expression of grim determination in the overcast morning light. It was clear that this was personal for her, that he'd somehow touched on something in her past or a sore spot or whatever because of Astrid, and he wasn't sure how to handle that now. "Look, when I suggested we try to find out more about her, I didn't mean—"

She held up a hand to stop him. "We can't just leave her here, Mark. Where else is she going to go? She obviously won't go home with you. She doesn't trust men." Her words twisted the knife deeper within him. "Don't worry about us. We'll be fine."

Then Luna walked away and got in her car. Before she could close the door, though, Mark stepped into the open V and crouched. "Be careful, please."

"Always am," she countered, her tone defiant. "Now, can you move please so we can go? You're letting all the cold air in."

Since he had no further reason to detain them, Mark straightened and closed the door, watching as Luna cranked the engine, then drove off. Nothing about this situation felt good to him, sending a possible juvenile delinquent home with a woman he liked more than he should. If something went wrong, he couldn't live with himself.

So, Mark ended up following them home, parking on the street outside Luna's apartment building as they went inside. A minute later, lights came on in a corner unit on the second floor. From his truck, Mark called the desk sergeant at the police station and asked the guy to search for a missing person named Astrid Jones. He also gave the cop Astrid's physical description from her ID in case that wasn't her real name. While he waited to hear back, he kept an eye on Luna's building and played solitaire on his phone.

Then a sudden knock on his window nearly gave him a coronary.

"If you're not going home," Luna said through his window, "you might as well come in."

Her hair was damp from a recent shower, and beneath her puffy parka she'd changed from her outdoor gear from yesterday into scrubs for work. Mark rolled down the window and caught the scent of her floral shampoo and soap in the frosty air. With less reluctance than was probably wise, he shut off this truck and followed Luna up to her apartment. It was a tiny two-bedroom studio, emphasis on the tiny. Small as it was, though, it was also cheerful. Sunshine-yellow paint in the kitchen, bright blue and white in the living room, which wasn't exactly what he'd expected. Maybe it had come decorated that way. Luna was a lot of things—smart, loyal, beautiful, edgy—but not exactly cheerful. She had more of a goth vibe.

Luna fixed a cup of coffee for herself and offered him one, then pointed toward the couch for him to sit. He took off his coat and hat and hung them on a peg by the door before taking a seat.

"Thanks," Mark said.

She nodded, then sank down on the opposite end of the cushions from him.

Their gazes held, the air humming with possibilities, all of which were dangerous to the well-ordered, quiet life he'd built for himself here. He cleared his throat and asked, "Where's Astrid?"

"In the guest room," Luna said, watching him over the rim of her mug. Finally, she said, "About this morning, in the tent. I don't usually wake up with men I don't know."

"Same," Mark joked, but it fell flat. He nodded and stared down into the dark abyss of his cup. "It doesn't have to be anything. We were both exhausted and cold and we shared body heat, that was all." He looked up at her, his gaze flicking to her pink lips before he caught himself. "We didn't even kiss. Nothing happened."

Except, deep down, he knew that if Astrid

hadn't interrupted them, he might have kissed her. Might have lowered his head and known for sure if she tasted as spicy as she looked. Whatever showed on his face must've shocked her because her breath caught and for a moment time seemed to slow. But kissing Luna Norton was almost certainly a very *bad* idea, especially with Astrid involved and now that Mark suspected Luna might have a similar traumatic past. A past he'd stirred up by bringing Astrid into her life. He should stay away from Luna now as much as possible. She'd made it clear neither of them needed the complication.

And yet, somehow, he couldn't seem to stop himself from leaning closer, just as she did the same. As if drawn together by some invisible cord. Her pulse beat at the base of her throat and her pupils were dilated, nearly obliterating her stormy gray irises, her gaze darkening with the same tormented wanting that turned him inside out.

Then their lips brushed, once, twice, before Mark locked on, her soft mewls of need going straight through him. Only their mouths touched, but it was enough and, yes, Luna tasted spicy and sweet. She tasted like heaven. Then she murmured his name, and just like that, Mark was in far deeper than he'd ever intended.

Good thing Astrid banged out of her room and

across the hall where she closed herself in again without a glance toward them.

Mark broke away with more effort than he'd expected it to take. He and Luna sat there, staring at each other in stunned silence for several seconds before he stood and set his basically untouched coffee aside.

The distance didn't help. Nor did the sight of Luna on the couch, still blinking up at him as if in a daze. He wanted her more than anything to sit back down and kiss her again, see where this thing between them might go, but no. That wasn't allowed. Not anymore. Not today anyway.

Mark pulled on his coat and hat before striding to the door. "I need to make a call from my truck."

An hour later, Luna stared at herself in her bathroom mirror after putting on her makeup and drying her hair. "You *kissed* him."

Her reflection stared back, pleading the fifth.

Luna had no idea what she'd been thinking. Or maybe she *hadn't* been thinking. She'd been *feeling*. Far too much. That was the problem.

At least there'd been no witnesses. Well, except for maybe Astrid, but the girl seemed to be in her own world since they'd gotten inside the apartment. And besides, she already thought Mark and Luna were a couple, so… Luna made a mental note to set Astrid straight on that point. She and

Mark weren't dating. Not now. Not ever. No matter how amazing that kiss had been.

Luna had worked hard to turn her life around after what happened all those years ago, and she had a good career going as a physical therapist now. She didn't need a man complicating her life, and she didn't need one to be happy, either. She didn't want love or romance or hearts and flowers, and yet she couldn't seem to stop herself from being drawn to Mark. Nerves tickled her stomach.

She wasn't exactly sure why, but she felt anxious now about…well, *everything*.

As she smoothed a hand down her blue scrubs with the Wyckford General Hospital logo embroidered over the chest pocket, Luna wondered if maybe her worry came from whether she'd ever find the peace and fulfillment she wished for. And if she did, would it make any difference? It had been so long since she'd felt fulfilled.

With a sigh, she walked out of the bathroom and slipped her feet into her comfy white walking shoes. She'd been on her own a long time. Growing up with parents who'd spent 98 percent of their time at the newly opened Buzzy Bird Café, Luna had basically been the poster child for latchkey kids, forced to mature a lot faster than many of her peers. Because of that, she'd acted out, been reckless. Back then, she'd thought she could handle anything.

She'd been wrong.

As a rebellious teen with a badass reputation, she'd always been able to intimidate anyone who'd invaded her space without permission, but not him. The twenty-two-year-old guy, a trusted friend, who'd seemed so nice and cool, until he'd demanded she live up to the reputation that preceded her. A reputation that was all lies and swagger, but he hadn't believed her. Luna's stomach still cramped with remembered trauma. Afterward, he'd scared her enough to prevent her from telling anyone what had happened. Gaslit her into believing the assault was her fault, that she'd wanted it, that she'd led him on somehow. And with her carefully cultivated bad-girl reputation, with her short skirts and suggestively tight tops, no one would have believed her anyway. So, she'd kept it a secret until she couldn't anymore. Back then, for once, her parents' constant distraction with the diner had been a blessing, preventing them from asking too many questions. And when she'd finally told them what happened, they'd felt so guilty it had nearly broken her all over again, and for a while, her parents had treated her like she was made of glass and would shatter easily, but eventually they'd put it all behind them and moved on. Her memories now seemed like they'd happened to someone else.

Her therapist had called it dissociation. Luna called it survival.

It was fine. She'd worked through it. She was fine. She didn't need anyone.

Every so often, though, someone or something would break through Luna's carefully built barriers and make her wish things had been different, that her life's journey had followed a different path.

Like Mark Bates.

She sighed. She wanted more. No surprise. What *was* a surprise, though, was the sparks she'd felt with Mark from such an innocent kiss. She'd felt him vibrate with the same need she felt and it had been both thrilling and terrifying. Giving in to that kind of potent attraction scared the daylights out of her, so she wouldn't. She'd steer clear of Mark from now on. They could discuss Astrid and that was it.

She finished her coffee in the kitchen, along with a piece of peanut butter toast, then headed out for the hospital.

Her first patient of the day was Riley Turner, Brock's sister.

Of course, she'd known Riley for years. They'd both grown up in Wyckford, through Riley was three years younger than Luna. Riley had been a bit of a wild child, too, around town, at least until the car accident she'd been involved in a few years ago. Her parents, who'd also been in the car, had been killed, while Riley—who'd sat in the back seat—had survived but been paralyzed from the waist down. Since then, she'd been living with her older brother, Brock, and working as a radiologist at Wyckford General. On the surface, Riley seemed to have adjusted well to her new life, but underneath, Luna had always sensed a restlessness just waiting to come out.

Which, it turned out, was what had brought Riley to see Luna now.

"I want my independence back," Riley said.

She sat in her wheelchair across from Luna, who sat at her desk in a corner of the PT department. Equipment and colorful balls and mats filled the brightly lit space. Besides Luna, there was one other person in the department, but they were part-time, so Luna pretty much had the run of the department to herself.

"And what does independence mean to you, Riley?" Luna asked while typing notes in Riley's electronic chart. A chart Luna had studied well before Riley had arrived to get a clear view of what she was dealing with from a PT standpoint. Her plan today was to evaluate Riley's status— test her modalities of sensation, both superficial and deep, above her injury point and compare them with the American Spinal Injury Impairment Scale, or ASIIS. According to the ER notes taken after the accident, Riley's spinal cord had been nearly severed at T11 and T12, which made her a paraplegic but able to sit on her own, which helped with her breathing and her ability to deep cough. Both important for general health and well-being.

"I want to move out of Brock's and have my own house again. My own life again." Riley's blue eyes, so like her brother's, burned with determination. "I love and appreciate my brother and everything he's done for me, but now that Cassie's in his life, I think it's time for us to move forward with things. I want to live again, but I'm nervous. Luna. I want a full, happy, active life again. To have more than just work and babysitting Adi. I want…love. But what if I can't find that?"

Luna nodded, understanding more than she could say. "You will. Are you seeing anyone?"

Pink flushed Riley's face and she looked away. "No, not really."

Interesting. Luna made a note in the chart, remembering that there was a new neurologist in town she'd seen Riley with several times in the hospital. Sam Perkins. He'd arrived the past summer to consult on a case with Cassie and had ended up sticking around longer than anyone had expected, taking a permanent position in neurology at Wyckford General. She wondered if Riley had had anything to do with his decision.

Luna set her tablet aside and stood. "All right. Let's evaluate you to see where you're currently at, then we'll go from there."

They went out into the equipment room and Luna had Riley perform a series of tests to check her motor and sensory abilities, which took about a half hour. Luna was impressed with Riley's upper-body strength, but her biggest concern was the decreased use of the joints below Riley's waist and her lower extremities, which Riley had zero control over.

Luna measured Riley's thighs and calf muscles, inwardly cringing when she discovered how stiff and nearly locked her hips, knees and ankle joints were. She needed to get Riley back on track or the weakness in her lower extremities would eventually impact all the strength she'd developed above the waist. Not to mention Riley's circulation and oxygen uptake to keep the rest of her going.

Once she'd finished with her exam, Luna sat back down at her desk and Riley wheeled over to park in front of her. "Okay, here's what I propose," Luna said. "We work on a regimen to improve your lower-body strength with passive range-of-motion exercises at first to preserve your hips, knees and ankles so you don't develop drop foot and to improve your overall quality of life."

"Okay. What else?"

"Aerobic exercise. Since you're sitting a lot behind a computer in radiology, this is a crucial component to the treatment plan. We need to enhance your circulation and increase your oxygen intake. I've ordered in a new stationary bike designed especially for paraplegic patients that should be here by the end of this week." Luna showed Riley a picture of the bike on her tablet. It strapped the patient's legs and feet in place and stimulated the muscles as the patient rode, according to the product description. "You'll be the first to try it out."

"I always did love being first." Riley grinned for the first time since entering the department, a spark of her old fire returning. "Can't wait to get started!"

CHAPTER SIX

MARK WENT TO the gym a few times a week with Tate Griffin and Brock Turner. The next morning, he and Tate were sparring in the ring while Brock used the weight machines. Mark ducked Tate's left hook, feeling smug—until Tate snuck a right uppercut to his gut.

Mark hit the floor with a wheeze, then it was Tate's turn to be smug. "Gotcha."

They'd been at it for thirty minutes, and Mark was exhausted, but the last one down had to buy breakfast. Kicking out, he knocked Tate's feet out from under him. Tate landed on the mat with a satisfying thud.

"You two keep going at each other like that," Brock muttered from the weight bench, "you'll end up in the ER."

Breathless, Mark rolled to his back, swiping off his forehead with his arm and keeping a close eye on Tate. The guy was a formidable opponent. They'd both been in the military—Mark in the navy and Tate in the air force. Mark had left after four years, but Tate had stayed in pararescue for over a decade.

Then, after his last rescue mission had gone horribly wrong, Tate had been severely injured. He'd had surgery to save his leg, then left to deal with the aftereffects on his own. Considering what he'd been up against, Mark thought the guy had done a pretty good job of healing. They'd met at a veterans support group online and Mark had convinced Tate to move to Wyckford last year. Since then, Tate had settled in, found a great job as team lead for the flight paramedic crew at the hospital and fallen for Madi Scott, the best ER nurse in town and the person responsible for starting and maintaining the local free clinic. Tate even volunteered there now, too, running a support group for veterans like himself who'd brought the scars of war home with them, both mentally and physically.

Mark admired the hell out of Tate, truth be told. They were best buds for a reason.

He carefully nudged a still-prone Tate with his foot.

Brock stopped lifting. "At least check him for a pulse."

Mark poked Tate again. "Not falling for the dead possum act, bud."

"I've got an EpiPen in my car I can stick him

with," Brock said mildly. "Hurts like hell going in but should wake him right up."

"Come near me with that thing," Tate grumbled, "and you'll be the one needing medical attention." He groaned and eyed Mark. "That wasn't fair."

"But it worked, right?"

Tate swore and laid an arm over his eyes, still breathing heavily.

Mark felt like he'd been hit by a bus, but at least his brain was too busy concentrating on the pain to think about his next move with Luna. Because if he didn't come up with something good soon, those few kisses would be the end of it, and they hadn't been enough for him. Not even close.

Finally, Tate staggered to his feet. "Another round."

The guy liked to push himself. Mark didn't mind doing the same, but not today. "Nah. I'm starving."

"Probably because you skipped dinner the other night." Tate gave him a look. "Thanks for standing me up, by the way."

Mark laughed. When Tate had first come to Wyckford, he'd practically been a hermit, keeping pretty much everyone away. Then Madi had broken through. She brought out the best in Tate, showing the guy connections didn't have to be scary, with the right person.

"I told you." Mark sighed and shook his head. "Something came up. Out in the forest."

"The forest, huh? This have anything to do with Luna Norton?" Tate's grin widened knowingly. "Rumor mill at the hospital has it you had to rescue her out there?"

Well, hell.

Mark gave another aggrieved sigh, then climbed to his feet. "She got lost and I helped her find the way. No rescuing necessary."

"Uh-huh," Tate said. "I bet you helped her a lot. She looks like a scary, wild time."

Suddenly Mark was ready for round two after all. Tate, who'd never met a challenge he didn't tackle, grinned and came at him, but Brock whistled sharply, stopping the action cold.

Brock tossed Mark his phone, which was buzzing on the floor near the weight bench.

Tate leaned back against the rope surrounding the ring. "Handy, since I was going to kick your ass."

"In your dreams," Mark said, but he wisely stepped out of Tate's arm range before answering. It was work, of course. They needed extra help. Again. So much for his day off. At least it got him out of buying breakfast, he supposed.

Mark showered and changed, then ran back home to get into his uniform before heading into work. He wasn't there more than thirty minutes before he was called back out. He'd taken a promotion last year and it required him to wear many hats, including search and rescue. It was the S&R part he did over the next several hours, as he and four other firefighters from Wyckford FD worked with the local EMTs and flight rescue crew over at Peter's Pond to save a couple of ice fishers who'd fallen through. They'd set up close to the nearshore drop-off, which was usually a safe spot, but the weather had been wonky this year and the ice shelf wasn't thick enough to support them. The fishermen were about two hundred yards offshore and tethering them at that distance was hard, as was getting rescue swimmers or the airboat to them.

But in the end, everyone was safe and sound.

Afterward, Mark returned to his office full of tedious paperwork. He logged and ordered supplies, went over safety inspections of all their equipment and ended up with a mind-numbing headache that followed him home.

Mark wasn't much for cooking. He could do it—his mom had made sure of it—he just preferred not to. But there were limited dining options in Wyckford. The local bar and grill on the outskirts of town—Wicked Wayz—or the Buzzy Bird diner. Wicked Wayz had great beer on tap. The Buzzy Bird had Luna. Or the possibility of her anyway if her shift at the hospital was over.

Considering what had happened the previous morning between them on her sofa, he probably should've made do with whatever he had at home, for supper, yet he pulled into the diner parking lot anyway. If he saw her, he'd say he wanted an update on the girl. He did. And if he also wanted to see Luna, well, he'd get over it.

He sat in the same corner booth he'd shared with Luna and Astrid the other day and scanned the diner, his stress levels inexplicably lowering when he spotted Luna at the counter, talking to her mother. As if sensing his stare, she turned and glanced back at him, her expression unreadable. Her mother, on the other hand, smiled and waved at him, then nudged her daughter in his direction with a glass of water and a menu. Luna walked over, still in her blue scrubs from work, the ACE bandage still wrapped around her wrist. At the least the limp seemed better now, he noted.

"How are your injuries?" Mark asked as she set his water down, then handed him the menu.

"Fine," she said in a flat tone, giving nothing away. "Astrid's fine, too, if you're wondering."

"I was, thanks." He smiled, then sipped his water, glad for something to help with his suddenly parched throat. This close to Luna, all he could remember was her warmth, the softness of her lips, those little sounds she'd made when he'd kissed her. *Good God.* To distract himself, he frowned down at the menu he already knew by heart and asked the first thing that popped into his head. "And how's the cut on your leg?"

Just then nosy Lucille Munson walked by and glanced at Luna. "What happened, honey? You cut yourself?"

"I fell out in the woods. It's nothing." Luna shot Mark a glance, as if daring him to say a word. "I'm fine."

He wasn't a complete idiot and held his silence.

Lucille nodded, then looked at Mark. "And Hottie McFire Pants rescued you? That's the rumor going around."

Luna laughed, a rare and beautiful thing. "What did you just call him?"

"Hottie McFire Pants," Lucille said. "Townsfolk came up the nickname on Facebook."

Christ. Mark slouched down into his seat.

Clearly holding back her laughter as Lucille walked away, Luna finally looked at Mark again. "What can I get you for dinner, Hottie McFire Pants?"

After she took his order, Luna disappeared into the kitchen and didn't return. Mark wasn't surprised when his food was delivered by Luna's mom, a sixty-something woman with short white hair and the same sparkling gray eyes as her daughter.

"Thanks," Mark said when she slid his plate in front of him.

By way of explanation, her mom said, "Luna's on break. Poor thing's already worked a full shift at the hospital. I tried to tell her we had it covered here, but she insisted on helping. She's so helpful, my Luna."

Yeah. She was helpful all right, Mark thought as he ate his burger and fries. Helping drive him crazy.

Later that night, Luna sat in her apartment binging the latest murder mystery show on streaming, complete with a huge bowl of popcorn and two Snickers bars, while Astrid stayed in her room, playing games on the burner phone Luna had bought for her earlier that day. Considering the girl's circumstances were precarious at best, Luna figured it was good for her to have a way to get in touch with someone if she needed help.

They'd just reached the moment where the detective gives his rundown of the crime and names the killer when her phone rang. Luna answered without checking the caller ID.

"Girls' check-in tomorrow," Cassie said. "Madi would've called but she's with Tate."

Uh-huh. Luna snuggled farther down under her blanket. "I don't know. I'm busy this week and the diner's still recovering from the whole sprinkler situation last year, so…"

"Please?" Cassie pleaded. "Between Adi and Winnie, I could really use some adult conversation time. Also, Madi said with her life and mine in order, we're now moving on to yours. Sorry."

Luna sat up, frowning. "What does that mean exactly?"

"Guess you'll have to come tomorrow night and find out. See you then." Cassie ended the call, and Luna stared at her phone for a long time afterward wondering what was happening.

Cassie Murphy had returned to Wyckford last summer to consult on a surgery case at the hospital. While she was here, she'd reconnected with her old crush, Dr. Brock Turner, and now they were hopelessly in *lurve*. Luna was happy for them, even if their sweet Hallmark kind of life made her want to throw up in her mouth a little sometimes, even if secretly she did hanker for that herself.

Then there was Madi. She and Luna had grown up together and were BFFs to the end. Except last fall good-girl Madi had fallen hard for the town's recent bad-boy arrival, flight paramedic Tate Griffin. Since then, they'd spent a lot of time together, with Tate moving into Madi's place and giving up his rental on the outskirts of town. Luna was so happy for her bestie, but with Madi otherwise occupied, it meant Luna had a lot more time alone to think. Which is what had led her to the forest the other day to clear her head and sketch.

It had also led her to Mark, a.k.a. Hottie Mc-Fire Pants.

Thankfully, a knock at the door interrupted her thoughts before she fell down that rabbit hole.

Scowling, Luna set her popcorn and remote aside. The clock in her kitchen read 10:30 p.m. Too late for a social call. She walked to the door and looked out her peephole only to the man foremost in her thoughts recently standing in the hall.

Crap.

Maybe if she kept quiet, he'd go away.

"I know you're in there, Luna," Mark called, dashing her hopes. "I can hear your TV."

Cursing under her breath, she opened the door a smidge. "What do you want?"

He rocked back on his heels, hands in his pockets, his gaze taking in her flannel PJs and fuzzy purple slippers. "Nice outfit."

Luna narrowed her eyes. "Why are you here?"

"I just came to check on Astrid."

Butterflies rioted in her stomach before she tamped them. "She's fine. You could have texted."

"I don't have your number." He leaned against the doorjamb, still managing to look sexy in his fire uniform with his work belt around his waist. "Can I come in for a second?"

She blinked at him, unsure if he was joking. "No. Aren't you working?"

"I'm done actually." He squinted one eye as he studied her. "You left the diner without saying goodbye."

"I didn't know I had to check in with you on my whereabouts."

He took a deep breath, then stared down at his shoes, his hands shoved in his pockets as he avoided her gaze. "You don't. I just thought maybe we should talk about what happened yesterday morning."

The kiss. Oh, God. The last thing she wanted to think about right then was the kiss. Especially with him standing close enough that she could have a repeat performance because no. That was a horrible idea. She needed to keep her lips and her everything else to herself where Mark Bates was concerned.

After a quick peek back into the apartment to make sure Astrid hadn't come out to see what was going on, Luna stepped out into the hall and closed the door to just a crack behind her. "We don't need to talk about it. It was a mistake. That's all. Over. Done. Forgotten. Not to be repeated."

Mark watched her for a long second, then gave a slow nod. "If you're sure."

"Oh, I'm sure. Beyond sure." She crossed her arms tighter around herself, like that would act as a shield against the beguiling warmth radiating off him that beckoned her closer. She absolutely did not notice his scent—pine and soap and a hint of sweat—or how there was a shadow of stubble on his jaw and hint of shadow beneath his blue eyes like maybe he hadn't slept well the night before, either. Luna cleared her throat, pushing all that stuff right out of her mind as she lifted her chin. "I don't even remember the kiss, to be honest."

Liar.

He narrowed his gaze, a spark of something in his gaze, there and gone before Luna could register it. Challenge maybe? Or amusement? Either way, he chuckled, then straightened, his arm brushing hers before he moved away. "Then I guess we're done here."

"Yep. Done." Luna knew she should go back inside and lock the door behind her, yet she stayed there, staring at Mark in the hallway of her apartment building as the seconds ticked by. "Have a good night."

"You, too," he said, seemingly as stuck in the moment as she was. Then his eyes dropped to her lips, and she felt it like a physical caress. And Luna couldn't help herself. Next thing she knew, she'd thrown her arms around Mark's neck and was kissing him silly again. It was like her entire body seemed to disconnect from her brain when-

ever he was around, allowing her to stop overthinking everything, allowing her to just feel and
want again. A disconcerting, dizzying change for
her. She pressed closer to him and sighed when
his arms tentatively came around her to hold her
closer, not making her feel trapped at all, just free.
Free and fully focused on her own bliss for once,
and not her fears. Because this was her choice, her
decision, even if it was an ill-advised one.

For reasons she didn't want to think too hard
about just then, Mark felt safe to her.

Safe and warm and wonderful—if temporary.

Honestly, there was no way they could do this
without everyone and their brother in town knowing, and the last thing Luna wanted was to be
the center of everyone's gossipy attention again.
She'd had enough of that as a teenager to last her
a lifetime.

Then Mark cursed and broke away, muttering under his breath as he glanced at his buzzing
phone. "Sorry," he said, huffing a little raggedly.
"One of the crew is sick, so I'm on call again."

She stepped back on wobbly legs. "Okay."

His blue gaze was heated. "Talk later?"

Not trusting her voice, Luna nodded as she
went back into her apartment and shut the door.
Then stared at it. Checked the peephole again to
make sure Mark was gone before she rested her
forehead against the wood. She had no clue what

she was doing with him. All she knew was she needed to stop before someone got hurt. Namely herself. Which right now felt way easier said than done.

CHAPTER SEVEN

LUNA GOT UP early the next morning for her shift at the hospital. She was just deciding whether to leave Astrid a note or wake her when the girl staggered out of the spare bedroom wearing the same ratty jeans as she had the day they'd found her but a different sweatshirt, this one from the pile of clothes Luna had given her to choose from, with the local high school mascot—a large, grinning ear of corn with tiny hands held up in fists and the words "Go Cobkickers" beneath it. She'd been at Luna's apartment now for two days, but so far, all the information Luna had gotten out of the girl was that she liked pizza and was scared of spiders.

"Did you sleep okay?" Luna asked Astrid as she stumbled out, bleary-eyed, into the living room.

"Yeah." The girl peeked out the kitchen window at the road below. "The fireman's not there anymore."

"Nope," Luna said, her cheeks heating as she

remembered their kiss in the hall last night. "I'm sure he has more important things to do."

"Hmm." Astrid turned around and rested her hips back against the edge of the counter, watching Luna with narrowed eyes. "I thought I heard his voice last night."

"What?" Luna froze, her coffee mug halfway to her mouth. "No. Uh… I mean, yes. He stopped by to check on you, then left again."

"Uh-huh." Astrid's tone said she didn't buy that at all. "You like him."

"Do not." Luna felt like she was a teenager again herself, arguing with her mom. Then again, given the questionable nature of her recent actions with Mark, maybe her maturity level had declined significantly. She took a deep breath to calm her zinging nerves, then poured out the rest of her coffee in the sink. More caffeine would not help the situation. "Mark and I know each other from work, that's all."

"Sure." Astrid pushed away from the counter and shook her head, smiling. "I guess shoving your tongue down your coworker's throat is part of the job these days."

Mortified, Luna felt her chest tighten as heat clawed up her cheeks. She wasn't a prude. Far from it. Live and let live and love was her motto, but seriously. She'd thought she'd been careful last night. Apparently, not careful enough. That'll teach her to give in to her stupid desires like that again. She wasn't sure why she felt the need to justify herself to an eighteen-year-old, but she did. "Okay. Look. Fine. Yes, we kissed last night. But it was just to prove to myself that I never want to do that again."

Astrid raised a skeptical brow. "With the firefighter? Or with men in general? Or with anyone?"

Lord, she kept digging her own hole deeper and deeper here. Luna inhaled deep through her nose, then pointed toward the kitchen table. Thankfully, she still had about an hour before she was due into the hospital. They sat down and Luna tried to think of the best way to say things so maybe the girl could relate. "When I was your age, Astrid…"

"Oh, boy." The girl shook her head and sat back, crossing her arms. "Tell me this isn't going to be a lecture."

"No lecture. Promise." Luna sighed, then just came out with it. "When I was your age, I started running with a wild crowd. Got mixed up in things I wasn't ready for. And one night it all went horribly wrong for me." Her throat tensed, and she swallowed hard against the old trauma. It never went away, her therapist had told her, but she'd learned how to cope with it better. At least she hoped she had. "Afterward, I rebuilt my life into what it is today. But because of it, I don't trust men."

"Not even Boy Scout firefighters?"

"Especially Boy Scout firefighters."

Astrid seemed to take that in a moment, then leaned forward, exhaling slowly. "I get that. I don't trust a lot of people, either. It's hard to make genuine connections when you're constantly moving around between foster homes."

She'd been in foster care.

Luna filed that information away for later to share with Mark if she saw him. They might be able to look Astrid up that way.

"And then, when you do connect with someone," Astrid continued, "they turn out to be a disgusting creep."

The girl shuddered, and Luna took her hand. "Did someone hurt you, Astrid?"

For a brief second, it looked like maybe the girl would answer her. But then Astrid stood and walked out of the kitchen to turn on the TV in the living room, then flopped down on the couch.

Right. Conversation over. Luna pushed to her feet as well and smoothed a hand down the front of her blue scrubs. "Well, I have an early shift at the hospital. Feel free to stay here and catch up on some sleep. There's food, hot water… TV."

Astrid looked over at her. "Thanks, but I should probably get going."

"No one will bother you, if that's what you're worried about," Luna added as she pulled on her coat. "And if someone *is* bothering you, maybe I can help—"

"No," Astrid said too quickly. "I'm fine."

Her heart squeezed because the girl was obviously not fine. Luna should know. She'd been right there where Astrid was, terrified and alone. The difference between them was Luna had had people there to support her when she'd needed, whereas poor Astrid had no one. Well, no. That wasn't true anymore. Astrid had Luna. And Mark. "You're safe here," she reiterated to the girl again.

Astrid nodded.

Luna shoved her feet into her boots, grabbed her bag with her regular shoes and her lunch in it, then snatched her keys off the table by the door before trying one last time. "Is there someone I can call for you, let them know where you are?"

"No."

"There are some more spare clothes I left out in my room for you to go through, if you're interested," Luna said as she opened the door and stepped into the hall. "And if you walk down to the Buzzy Bird later, I'll text my parents and tell them to give you whatever you want for lunch. No charge."

"Why?"

Astrid wasn't asking about the food, and Luna

knew it. "Because it sucks to not know where your next meal's coming from. I can help you not feel that way, so I am."

Two hours later, Luna had finished seeing her first patient of the day, an army veteran who'd lost a leg in Syria. They were working on getting him up to speed with his new prosthetic and so far, so good. She'd just cleared away the mats and equipment from his visit when a knock sounded on her door. She looked up to see the last person she'd expected.

Mark. He looked a little rumpled and there were shadows under his eyes, but still gorgeous.

And, man, am I in trouble here.

She busied herself with putting away dumbbells as he walked into the large open space painted in bright primary colors. It wasn't the decor Luna would've chosen, but the room used to hold the hospital day care for employees before they'd reorganized things, so Luna had been stuck with what she got. Kind of like her apartment. Cheery yellows and pinks weren't really her aesthetic, but she'd received such a great deal on the rent, she couldn't say no.

And speaking of saying no, she asked, "What do you want?"

"Good morning to you, too," Mark said, congenial as always. "How's the wrist?"

Luna rubbed her still-taped appendage and felt a sudden desire to kick him in the shin just to make him stop grinning. Either that or push him up against the wall and kiss him until neither of them could remember their names. Since neither was an option, she stalked over to her desk in the corner instead. "It's fine. And I'm busy."

"I can see that." Mark didn't seem to be in any hurry at all to leave, which irritated her even more. "How's Astrid?"

"Fine," she said, plopping down in her chair to keep the desk between them. "She was watching TV when I left the apartment earlier."

"Have you found out any more about her?" he asked, taking a seat in the chair she'd put in front of her desk for patients. "The police still haven't turned up anything about her as a missing person."

"She was in foster care," Luna said, shuffling papers so she didn't have to look at him and his ridiculously pretty blue eyes. "But if she turned eighteen, she aged out of the system. That explains why they didn't find anything."

"Wow. Good work," Mark said, still just sitting there, being all cute and nice. Gah, some people. "How'd you manage to find that out?"

"I talked to her," Luna said, leaving out the part about how she'd told Astrid about her own past traumas. "We connected a little bit this morning before I left for work."

Which reminded her...

She pulled out her phone and sent a quick text to her mom at the diner about free lunch for Astrid.

When she put the phone down on her desk again, she found Mark watching her, far too closely for comfort. "What?"

Mark shrugged, then shook his head and looked away. "Still trying to figure you out sometimes."

"Don't," she snapped. "Don't do that. I'm not your puzzle to solve, okay?"

He held up his hands in surrender. "Okay. I didn't mean anything by it. I was just trying to understand why you kissed me last night and—"

"That's it." Luna stood up and pulled him out of his seat, hauling Mark toward the door. "I do not have time for this. My next patient is due in here in fifteen minutes and I have to get ready."

"But what about that kiss?"

"Forget the kiss," she said and shut the door in his face. Rude? Yes. Necessary? Oh, hell, yes.

Because she still heard him mumble from the other side, "I wish I could."

Luna felt the same way.

"The first thing we need to do today is get you loosened up," Luna said, pointing to a thick floor mat beneath the workout bench. Riley Turner was back, and they were still in assessment mode, so today's visit would be one of discovery for them both. "Can you lower yourself to the floor?"

"Sure," Riley said, putting her hands on the locked chair wheels and pushing up until her hips left the seat, then moving herself forward, repositioning her legs, using her arm and shoulder muscles to lower herself as close to the mat as possible before plopping down.

"Great." Luna helped her lie down and straighten her legs for passive range-of-motion exercises. "Okay, you've been through PT before, yes? After the accident? And you know what I'm going to do, right?"

Riley lifted her chin, a determined set to her mouth. "Yup."

"Good." Positioning herself beside Riley, Luna took Riley's right leg, carefully lifted it and bent the knee, pressing the leg toward Riley's chest, noticing how tight the muscles felt. Lord knew Luna understood how grueling schedules could be at the hospital, but staying flexible was important to Riley's recovery. Luna ran her patient through several basic exercises to loosen her hips and knees, then concentrated on her ankles. Riley watched her intently as she repeated the same exercises on the other leg.

"Once I loosen your joints, I'll show you how to do these at home yourself," Luna said.

"Sounds like a plan."

"Yeah, so why haven't you been stretching?"

"Crazy schedule. Crazy life. You know how it goes." Riley shrugged.

Luna did know, but she also sensed there was more going on than Riley was telling her. Still, it was only her first real visit with Luna, so they hadn't built up that trust level yet. With time, hopefully they would. "Okay." Luna stood and stretched. These PT appointments were as much a workout for her as for her patients. "We're done with this part for today. You can get back in your wheelchair, and we'll move on to your favorite part."

Once Riley had gotten herself back in and situated, they worked through the planned weight program. Luna liked a balanced approach when it came to training. The lower half of Riley's body was just as important as the top and bad things could happen if she didn't take care of all of herself.

They did a couple of sets of butterfly presses with free weights, then shifted Riley from her chair to the weight bench for some chest presses. Luna leaned over her patient like a life coach, motivating her to keep pushing. Riley seemed very self-motivated, though. Luna had seen a lot of PT patients and most of them were fired up to varying degrees, but none quite as driven as Riley.

I want to live again, but I'm nervous.

Perhaps they were more alike than Luna had first realized.

She studied Riley's technique, adjusting an elbow here or shoulder there, then tested Riley's resolve by saying, "Let's up the weight."

"Sure."

Luna added more weight on the bar, and Riley went right back to work.

Okay, so the girl was fine with pushing herself.

Luna found herself mimicking Riley's facial expressions when she lifted the heavier weight over her head, moving in quickly to catch the bar, just in case. "Good job. Let's take a break?"

Riley nodded. "Could use some water."

They drank, then Riley wiped her face with a towel she'd brought with her. "That was a good workout. Thanks."

"Thank you for working so hard," Luna said before taking another long drink from her sports bottle, then checking her watch. "Okay. Let's move on to the back exercises for your last twenty minutes. My next patient comes in at one thirty."

Riley pulled herself into a sitting position and Luna helped her separate her legs on either side of the narrow bench with the machine's weight bar just out of reach above her head. Luna straddled the bench in front of and facing Riley and used her legs as support beside each of Riley's knees, with her feet guarding Riley's, keeping them in place. "We'll start with fifty pounds, then go from there."

Luna watched as her patient pulled down the weighted bar and did repetitions like fifty pounds was nothing, ready to jump in if Riley lost her balance.

"Do you know anything about Sam Perkins?" Riley asked out of the blue between breaths.

Luna tried not to act like she hadn't been waiting to talk with Riley about this. "Not really. I know he originally came here from California to assist with that surgery Cassie Murphy did last year, then decided to move to Wyckford. Why?"

Riley gave a little shrug between reps. "I just wondered about him, that's all."

"Huh. You two seem to work together a lot. You should ask him." Luna tread lightly as Riley finished her last set of reps, then grabbed her towel again. "He seems nice, the few times I've passed him in the hall. And he's cute, too."

"You think?" Riley gave Luna a curious look.

"Sure. If you like that hot nerd type." Luna shrugged and grinned. She preferred the hot surfer type herself. Face heating, Luna turned away to study Riley's chart on her computer, glad for the distraction. "You did a great job today. Once we get your lower-extremity joints fine-tuned, you'll be well on your way to the independent life you want."

Riley looked at her with those blue eyes so like her brother's. "I'll hold you to that."

"I hope so."

Luna went over the passive-motion exercises for Riley so she could start doing them at home, then they scheduled another appointment for later in the week.

As Riley rolled toward the door, she said, "See you next time."

"See you." Luna suspected they'd only touched the surface of what was really driving Riley today, but they'd get there. Slowly but surely.

Later, after her shift at Wyckford General, Luna stopped at her apartment before meeting Madi and Cassie at the diner. Astrid was gone. No note. She showered and changed her clothes, then went to the Buzzy Bird, thinking maybe the girl was there, but when she asked her parents, they said Astrid hadn't shown up for her free meal.

Luna claimed a booth near the back, worried as she waved Madi and Cassie over when they arrived.

"Long day?" Madi asked sympathetically settling into the seat across from Luna. "I saw you had a session with Mr. Martin this afternoon."

Mr. Martin was a retired schoolteacher in town,

low on motivation and high on attitude. But Luna gave as good as she got during his sessions and wasn't intimidated by his old-grouch facade at all.

"Yeah, but he's a pussy cat, honestly. You just have to know how to handle him."

Madi put an arm around Luna's shoulders and squeezed. "And I'm sure you do."

She did usually know how to handle men, keep them at bay, at a safe distance, and put them in their place. Then Mark Bates had come along and now Luna didn't know which end was up anymore. But no way would she talk about that situation tonight. It was too confusing. Too raw. So, she sighed and said, "Mark and I found a runaway girl the other day in the forest. She's been staying at my apartment."

Both women gasped.

"What?" Madi asked. "Is that safe?"

"She's eighteen." Luna grimaced and reached for her water glass. "And fresh out of foster care. I think she's in trouble, but she won't talk to me about it. I just want to help her."

Cassie zeroed in on her bandaged wrist. "What happened there?"

"Oh." Luna quickly hid her wrist in her lap again. "I was out hiking the other day and hurt myself."

"Wait!" Madi said, gaping. "That was you? A couple of the firefighters were talking about a person who got lost in the forest and Mark Bates had to rescue them. Then a tree fell, and they had to stay all night out there."

Crap.

Luna should've known better than to think she could keep a secret in Wyckford. Face flushed, she glowered at her water glass. "He didn't rescue me. I got turned around, and he pointed me in the right direction. That's all."

Cassie raised a brow. "Still doesn't explain the wrist."

Man, this night just got better and better. She sighed, knowing if she didn't come clean, her friends would just take the gossip as truth, so... "I got up in the middle of the night to go to the bathroom and fell, slid down an embankment. Mark climbed down and helped me back up, then he tended to my injuries."

"Injuries?" Madi said. "There was more than one? And that sure sounds like rescuing to me."

Luna ground her teeth together so tight she was surprised they didn't crack. "I sprained my wrist and cut my leg. He bandaged me up and that's all. He's a trained EMT as well as a firefighter. That's his job. Can we please get back to the runaway now?"

"Who's job?" Lucille Munson popped her head around the side of the booth as she passed. Her lime green sweats and chunky yellow snow boots were eye-wateringly bright. "I thought I heard something today about Mark Bates being a hero."

"He's not a hero!" Luna said, a bit too loudly. Several other diners looked over at them and she lowered her voice. "He's a firefighter who was doing his job by helping me in the forest," Luna admitted reluctantly. "End of story. Nothing more to report."

"Hmm," Lucille said, then checked her watch. "Oops, look at the time—gotta skedaddle."

When she was gone, Madi and Cassie continued to eye Luna across the table.

"So, you have a new man on your radar and a stray kid in your apartment?" Cassie asked.

That pretty much summed it up. Before Luna could say anything else, though, Madi piped in again. "Is Mark staying at your apartment as well?"

"Of course not." Luna shook her head vehemently. "But he did sit outside the first night to make sure everything was okay."

"He's such a good guy," Madi said.

Luna hated to admit her friend was right, but it was true. Mark did seem to be a genuinely good guy. Which brought a whole new question to mind for her. Why the hell would he want damaged goods like her? She had more baggage than Boston's Logan Airport.

Madi frowned. "You deserve someone like him, you know."

"You do," Cassie said. "I believe everything happens for a reason."

And that right there was why they'd all been friends since grade school. No one knew Luna better than her friends, and she them. They always seemed to know what the other was thinking and feeling, even when they themselves didn't.

After a long moment, Madi took Luna's hand and asked, "Can you tell me why you're willing to give this girl a chance and not Mark?"

Luna wanted to pull away then, to hide, but she couldn't. "I don't know," she said at last. "I think because Astrid and I are alike. But Mark, he's like this shining beacon of light and goodness. I don't know what to do with that."

Cassie snorted. "I bet he's got some darkness, too. No one's that perfect."

"She's right. Maybe you should ask him."

Luna squirmed a little bit because deep down she knew it was true. "He did say his little brother died when he was twelve. That's why he became a firefighter."

"Sounds dark to me," Cassie said before sipping her drink. "You should ask him more about that."

"I don't know him that well," Luna countered.

"Then maybe you should get to know him," Madi said, winking.

* * *

Mark had a reputation for being laid-back and easygoing. And yeah, he was a Boy Scout, too. He wasn't sure any of those things were exactly true, but part of the appearance came from always being prepared for anything at any time.

He'd first been aware of his need to have as much control over situations and outcomes after little Mikey died, and later he'd mastered his abilities first in the military, then at Chicago FD. He figured if a guy could survive warfare and a ten-story apartment fire, he could survive anything. It would never bring Mikey back, but maybe it went a small way toward atoning for his loss. He'd thought he'd come to terms with his failed marriage and put it behind him. Then along came one willowy, enigmatic physical therapist named Luna Norton, with her cagey attitude and sharp tongue, with her secret soft side and the way she sighed when he kissed her and everything had been shot to hell.

If he was honest with himself, he hadn't gone to her office earlier just to check on Astrid. He'd gone because he'd wanted to see Luna again. He'd been exiting the hospital after another EMT run where the fire department had assisted the paramedics with the Jaws of Life, and he'd spotted Luna working with a patient through one of the front windows. So, like an idiot, he'd walked back inside and gone to her office just as her patient was leaving and sat down at her desk and basically annoyed the hell out of her.

Good going, dude.

And sure, he'd been interested to hear about the girl, too. Astrid was the one reason he still had a credible reason to talk to Luna, so sure, he wanted to keep that going. He wanted to find out the truth about Astrid, too, see if he could get her back where she belonged, safe and sound, because yeah. He got off on being a hero. It was who he was. What he did.

But he quickly shoved that aside and put on his happy face again because today was training day for the nonmanagement staff at the fire station. And training day meant they'd have a special stretch class afterward taught by none other than Luna Norton herself. Normally, management didn't have to participate unless they did the training, too, which Mark hadn't, but he'd made a point to volunteer as Luna's demonstrator for the exercises because it was good to keep moving and limber and, well, because he wanted to make sure Luna couldn't avoid him again. She'd dodged his question about that kiss the other night at her apartment, but there was no denying that had been all her. Mark had promised himself he wouldn't initiate anything until he'd figured her out, and he hadn't. Of course, once she'd kissed him, then all bets were off. And she'd also agreed that they'd "talk later," whatever that meant, but so far, he hadn't seen hide or hair of her at all.

So yeah. At 3:00 p.m., just as the three rank-and-file firefighters were trailing in after a grueling day of mock fire tests and training, Mark made his way down to the workout room of the station wearing his Wyckford FD T-shirt and basketball shorts, socks and tennis shoes on his feet, to find Luna setting up at the front of the room.

"Anything I can do to help?" he asked, walking over to where she stood near a rack of weights.

Luna turned around and blinked at him for a moment before turning away again, muttering, "What are you doing here?"

"I'm your demo partner today," Mark said, unable to keep his grin hidden as her obvious annoyance bubbled over in the form of a scowl. "What? I'm at your beck and call for the next hour. What more could you want?"

"What I want," Luna growled, facing him once more, "is for you to leave me alone."

"Really?" Mark said, crossing his arms and leaning a shoulder against the mirror-covered wall. "Because that seemed like the last thing you wanted the other night in the hallway."

"Stop!" she said, far too loudly. Then Luna glanced over at the three guys who'd just walked in and seemed to be during their best to ignore the obvious disagreement happening at the front of the room, but Mark knew they were still listening. They might look like rough, tough, hero types, but inside the station they were as bad as old busybody Lucille Munson when it came to gossip. Luna cleared her throat, then leaned closer, her tone dropping to a menacing whisper. Or it would probably be menacing to someone who didn't know Luna like Mark did. To him, it just sounded kind of rough and dirty and… He shoved his libido aside and focused on her flashing gray eyes. "Stop acting like you don't know what you're doing."

Now he was genuinely confused. Mark frowned back at her. "What am I doing?"

"Trying to be all nice and sweet and kind to get in my pants," she hissed before stepping back fast, like she'd been burned. "I'm not looking for that. Not with you. Not with anyone, okay?"

"Okay," Mark said, still not sure exactly where things had gone off the rails here. He was just looking for some clarification, to figure out exactly what this thing was between him and Luna so he could make sure it didn't end up with them in bed together, because he certainly didn't want that, either.

Even if he couldn't stop thinking about that stupid kiss.

"Fine. Well, if you don't need a demo person, then…" He started out of the room.

"Wait." Luna sighed, then waved him back to her as she surveyed the three other men in the room, looking a bit wary. "Fine. You can stay and demo the exercises for me. But that's it."

"Okay," Mark agreed congenially. "What about the other thing."

"What other thing?" Luna's dark brows drew together. She had on black leggings and an over-size light blue sweatshirt with the Wyckford General logo on it across the front. Her feet were in black socks and tennis shoes like Mark's. He did his best not to notice how those leggings made her legs look a mile long or how the blue color of the sweatshirt brought out the stormy gray of her eyes. And he definitely didn't notice the flowery scent of her shampoo or the hint of spice from her perfume. Nope. Not at all.

He cleared his throat and said, "We were going to talk later."

She blinked at him again, as if processing his words. "Can we discuss this after class?"

"Fine."

"Fine."

Luna checked her watch once more, then clapped to get the firefighters' attention. The three burly men lined up in front of her in the large open area at the center of the workout room. Mark stood to one side, waiting to be beckoned for duty.

"Hi, guys, and welcome to another stretching class to help improve your performance on the job. As I think all of you know, I'm Luna Norton. I hold a doctor of physical therapy degree from Tufts University in Boston, and I'm currently head of the physical therapy department at Wyckford General Hospital." She didn't mention that she was also the only person in her department, but Mark wasn't about to say anything. Luna's credentials were damn impressive. "I know you just finished a grueling day of pumper training and fire inspection modules," she continued, "so these exercises should help loosen you up and keep your muscles stretched and ready for any emergency." She waved Mark over and he joined her at the center of the room. "Your deputy chief, Mark Bates, has agreed to demo the exercises for me as we go, so keep an eye on him for proper technique."

With that, they got started.

First up was downward dog, the popular yoga pose. Mark got into position on the mat and eased into the stretch, the muscles of his spine slowly lengthening and releasing tension as he pushed himself a bit farther into it. It felt good. He'd had several minor injuries over the years because of his work—occupational hazard in public safety, unfortunately—and staying fit and healthy was a constant challenge. It's why he kept to a regular workout schedule at the gym with Tate and Brock, and why he tried to stretch whenever he could. Especially now that he sat behind a desk pushing paper more and more with his promotion. He'd had one more serious injury last year, too—a dislocated shoulder after a fall at a fire location—which Brock had tended to in the ER and later in his office. Mark was fine now, though, so no worries, though Brock had warned him to be careful. Once a joint had been dislocated, it was always more prone to doing so again in the future. Mark tended to favor his left shoulder now since the accident.

"Good, good," Luna said, walking around the class and inspecting each man's form. Then she reached Mark and placed her hand on his upper back and all his tension returned tenfold. Not because she was being rough with him. Just the opposite, in fact. Her gentle touch reminded him of how long it had been since anyone had touched him like that, and how much he missed it. "Okay, let's move on to the next exercise."

Mark straightened, aware his face felt hot, and not just from the exertion. Why was he always so aware of Luna whenever she was around? Yes, she was gorgeous. Yes, he found her attractive. But he finally had the quiet, peaceful life he'd wanted for years and was he really going to jeopardize that now for a woman who kept everyone at a safe distance? Even if she did intrigue the hell out of him and make him want to know more about her, why she was the way she was. He knew better than anyone that some things were better off left buried. Far less painful that way.

"Let's try a kickstand stretch next," Luna said, looking at Mark. "Down on your knees."

Damn if his libido didn't sit up and beg at that. Which was odd. He'd always been the one in charge in the bedroom, but Luna made him wonder if surrender couldn't be just as fulfilling. Except no. Not thinking about that. Not at all. He got down on the floor, on his hands and knees, with one leg extended out to the side. This time, when Luna got around to him, she pressed gently on his lower back to increase his stretch, and he felt that slight touch straight to his groin. The minute she left, he adjusted himself, then stretched his other leg before standing again.

They worked through two more exercises, the Spider-Man and straight leg raises, before finishing up the hour with the last one for the day—the crossover stretch. This one involved Mark lying on the floor on his back, staring up at the ceiling while he kept both arms stretched out to his sides and stretched one leg over himself to the opposite side, loosening his spine and his hips. It felt good, but what felt even better was when Luna knelt behind him, her warmth penetrating his thin cotton T-shirt as she placed her hands on his side and helped him stretch into it even more.

Apparently, more than just his body was loosening toward her because this time his thoughts shifted from ways to stop being attracted to her to ways that maybe they could safely explore this thing between them without losing control.

Control was the thing for them, obviously. For him, because of what had happened with his ex-wife, her walking out on him, telling him it was all his fault because he loved his work too much, because he seemed to be there for everyone but her. That he used his job as a barrier, a crutch, to keep himself from getting hurt. And yeah, maybe she'd been right, a little anyway. He could admit that now.

For Luna… Well, he still wasn't sure what had happened in her past, but he could clearly see that something had. It was evident in the way she kept people at bay, from the way she purposely put distance between herself and most men, both mentally and physically, how she reacted whenever someone snuck up on her and how she hated surprises. He had some idea that maybe she'd been attacked or worse but didn't want to jump to false conclusions. And he knew enough from his own trauma that forcing someone to tell you wouldn't work. You had to come to it on your own, in your own time.

But that didn't mean he couldn't let her know he was there for her when she needed him.

"Okay, class. That's it. Thanks so much for coming today," Luna said, holding out a hand to help Mark up off the floor. Their ever-present chemistry sizzled over his skin from their point of contact, and from the slight flush to her cheeks, he'd bet good money Luna felt it, too. She let him go and focused on the class again. "And remember the effects of stretching are cumulative. I suggest doing these exercises at least three times a week to see results. If there's no questions, you're free to go. Thanks again!"

The guys thanked Luna and nodded to Mark, then shuffled out to head to the showers and locker room. Silence descended between them, until Mark couldn't stand it anymore and had to break it. He focused on what he thought was a neutral subject. "I had my buddy at the police station run Astrid's info again using the foster care system," he said as he grabbed his towel and wiped his sweaty face. "But most of that stuff is sealed, so they still haven't found anything. How are things going at the apartment?"

Luna continued to pack up the tote she'd brought with her, not looking at him. "Fine."

Her pat answer. He tried a different way past her defenses. "How's your wrist?"

"Better."

Single words did not a meaningful conversation make. Mark shifted his weight and crossed his arms, determined to figure her out if it killed him, and given the glare she shot him over her shoulder when she realized he was still standing there, it just might.

Tired of dancing around things, he decided to just go for it. "What are you doing tonight?"

Luna frowned, straightening to face him with a wary expression. "Why?"

"I thought we could grab some dinner. Discuss the situation with Astrid."

"Dinner?" she repeated, like she'd never heard the term before.

"Yes, dinner. The meal at the end of the day. Together. You and me." Mark huffed out a rueful laugh, more at himself than anything. "Unless you want to call it something else."

Luna opened her mouth, then hesitated. "What else would I call it?"

He cocked his head. "Some people call it a date."

She seemed genuinely puzzled by that. "You want to go on a date. With me?"

"Yeah."

"To talk about Astrid?"

"Among other things." He grinned.

Luna stared at him like he'd grown a second head. "I don't think that's a good idea. I'm grumpy, irritable and, frankly, not all that nice a person."

"I'll agree with grumpy," Mark said amiably. "Irritable, too. But you're a better person than you give yourself credit for, Luna."

Her expression turned suspicious, like maybe he had an ulterior motive. "Seriously, though. Why?"

The easy answer was because he wanted more time with her. But that was also the hard answer, so he went with uncomplicated instead. "Because I like you and I think we have a responsibility to Astrid to keep her safe until we figure this all out."

Luna exhaled slowly, apparently speechless for once.

"Come on. It's just dinner, not a commitment. My treat, too."

She looked at him like he'd lost his mind. And honestly, maybe he had.

Finally, she shook her head and turned around. "Fine. But just dinner, and nothing else. And I need to be home relatively early for work tomorrow."

"Got it."

When Mark left the workout room after everyone else was gone, he felt like a huge weight had been lifted off him, for some reason. And he suspected, for better or worse, that reason was Luna.

By the time she got home that afternoon, Luna's mind was in a whirl—both because of Astrid and because of her upcoming dinner with Mark. She still couldn't quite believe she'd agreed to go, and there was no way in hell she was calling it a date because that was just way too scary on way too many levels. But man, she needed someone to talk to about it. Astrid wasn't available. Since she'd returned from wherever she'd been earlier, she had locked herself in her room before Luna could say a word to her. Oh well. Besides, a teenager's perspective probably wouldn't be that helpful in the situation—especially *that* teenager—so she called Madi instead. Who wasn't available. With a sigh, Luna tried Cassie next.

"I have a problem," she said as soon as Cassie answered.

"An adult one? Great!" Cassie said over Face-Time. "I'm dying for some adult conversation that doesn't involve beeping. Maybe I should increase my hours at the hospital to get out more." She stopped for a breath, then asked, "What kind of problem?"

"I'm going to dinner tonight. With Mark Bates."

"On a date? Man, I miss dates." Cassie sighed

wistfully as the phone line beeped. "Wait, it's Madi. Let me conference her in with us."

"Hey!" Madi sounded breathless as she appeared on-screen a moment later. "Sorry I missed your first call, Luna. I'm on break now. It's a full moon tonight, and we've already had two women in premature labor and a victim from a bar fight. What's going on?"

"She has a date with Mark Bates," Cassie answered for her.

"Really?" Madi squealed so loud Luna had to hold the phone away from her ear.

"Okay. First of all, it's not a date." Luna scowled. "It's just dinner."

Cassie laughed. So did Madi.

"Dinner with the most handsome firefighter in town," Madi said. "And he seems really nice. And responsible. From the way Tate talks about the guy, he's like the second coming or something. You could do a lot worse, Luna."

"I'm not trying to do anything at all," Luna said, getting more frustrated by the second because her friends didn't seem to hear the warning bells going off in her head. This dinner was no joke. Not to her and certainly not to Mark. "I don't date people. You both know that. And you know why."

Her friends sobered then.

"Sweetie," Madi started. "I'm not trying to belittle what happened to you at all. You were assaulted, and you were made to feel it was your fault. But please hear me when I say it wasn't. None of what happened to you was your fault. You were just a kid. And you deserve someone who cares about you. Someone kind and gentle and loving. Who accepts you for who you are, awkward and cranky and all."

"Exactly," Cassie agreed. "And maybe this really is just dinner. Just two adults eating together. Does it help to think of it that way?"

It did help. Luna forced herself to breathe. "He did say he wanted to talk about Astrid, too."

She kept her voice low when she said that, hoping the teen girl wouldn't hear Luna talking about her.

"Well, that's good, then," Madi said. "Do you know where he's taking you?"

"Not yet." Something buzzed on the kitchen counter and Luna walked over to see the burner phone she'd bought for Astrid lying on the charging pad. A number flashed on the caller ID, one Luna didn't recognize. Frowning, she picked it up and told her friends to hold on, then answered. "Hello?"

A raspy male voice said, "You can run, but you can't hide."

Adrenaline kicked in and Luna demanded, "Who is this?"

Nothing.

"Hello?" Luna said again.

Click. Call ended.

Stunned, she leaned back against the counter for a moment, staring at the black screen of Astrid's phone before setting it back on the charger. She'd thought getting the device for the girl would be a good thing, to help them stay in contact if Astrid needed help, but maybe the girl had been in contact with someone other than them. Someone from her past, the past she seemed to be running from... Luna couldn't imagine why Astrid would do that, but then people did things Luna didn't understand all the time, so...

"Hey?" Madi called from the other phone, jarring Luna from her disturbing thoughts. "Where's Mark taking you to eat?"

"And what are you wearing?" Cassie wanted to know.

"I don't know," Luna said, distracted now, her nerves taut. "Why does it matter?"

"Why aren't you more excited?" Madi asked, looking concerned. "What's going on?"

"Uh, nothing," Luna said. Her friends didn't need to know about the call Astrid had just received. It would only make them worry, and question Luna's wisdom in letting the girl stay there. Plus, she had Mark to talk about it with later. He, better than anyone, would understand and hopefully have advice on how to handle it from here. "Listen, I need to go."

"Have fun tonight," Cassie said. "Dates are lovely. And Mark's a good guy. He's got a good job, a home and great abs. Besides, he's already charmed your pants off, right?"

"No!" Luna's face heated again due to Cassie's unladylike snort. "What are you talking about?"

"You said he bandaged you up in the tent after you fell."

"Oh, well…" Luna squeezed her eyes shut. "Well, yes, he did that, but that was his job. And the *only* reason I took off my pants was because I was injured and—"

"—and Mark rescued you," Madi cut in again. "Another check in the pro column."

"Enough!" Luna *thunked* her head back against the cabinets behind her in frustration. "This is all beside the point because nothing is going to happen between Mark and me tonight, okay?"

"Okay, sure," Madi said, holding her hands up in surrender. "Though it does sound like you're protesting a bit too much, hon. What's really bothering you?"

Luna blew out a breath. "Because I've never been on a real date before, okay?"

Utter silence from her friends. For so long Luna checked to make sure they were still there.

Cassie looked confused. "Wait. How old are you?"

"Thirty-five."

"And you've never had a date?"

"No. Not a real one. And stop making such a big deal out of it." She stared into the empty living room. Through the sliding glass doors to the balcony, she saw a bird had landed on the icy branch of a tree nearby, and it floundered, trying not to fall. Luna knew the feeling. "Listen, I really do have to go, so I can change before Mark gets here."

"Well, have a wonderful time and try not to worry," Madi said. "I'm sure everything will be lovely."

Luna sighed. Madi sounded super emotional today—which honestly wasn't anything new since Madi was pretty much emotional all the time these days. Ever since she and Tate Griffin got together anything seemed to set her off. Madi had even sobbed openly at one of those "save the puppies" commercials when she and Luna had watched TV together recently.

"Go out and have fun," Cassie added. "Eat and talk and enjoy your first date. You deserve good things. You deserve good people in your life, and Mark is one of those good people."

Dammit. Now Luna's throat felt tight, and there wasn't a puppy commercial in sight.

She ended the call and went to take a shower.

While she stood naked under the steamy spray, she closed her eyes and inhaled deeply, her chest burning with unexpected emotion. There was no denying the truth. She'd felt flickers of something with Mark for a while now, new and tenuous, but there. Up until now, when Luna thought about her life, she'd always been in survival mode. But he'd shown her in subtle, little ways that maybe there was more than that, and maybe he could show her. He'd never once pushed her, never demanded anything from her, just always let her take the lead. Which is what she needed, at least when it came to relationships. Ever since her attack, she'd never believed she'd have that in her life—romance, love, intimacy. In fact, she'd spent most of her time openly mocking what she'd convinced herself she never wanted. But now, tonight, on the verge of her first date, Luna didn't feel like mocking it.

And that knowledge both thrilled and terrified her.

CHAPTER EIGHT

MARK KNOCKED AT Luna's door that evening, for their date that wasn't really a date. They were both obviously gun-shy about relationships, so he was fine keeping things light. Even if that kiss they'd shared had felt anything but carefree. He cleared his throat and raised his hand to knock again just as the door opened to reveal Astrid, wearing a black T-shirt with a K-pop band name he'd never heard of on the front, jeans and stockinged feet. She looked him up and down, then called over her shoulder, "He's here."

She stepped aside to let him in and closed the door behind him, leaving Mark to stare around the small place. From the living room he could see to the other end of the place and Luna's bedroom door was open, clothes strewn everywhere like a bomb had gone off.

"Have a seat," Astrid said, tucking herself into a corner of the couch again and clutching a throw pillow on her lap. A half-empty delivery pizza box sat on the coffee table in front of her along with a glass of soda. "You look different tonight."

"You, too," he said, sitting down in an armchair diagonal from her, then glancing at the TV on the wall. "You like true crime shows?"

Astrid nodded, her eyes glued to the screen. "I like figuring out whodunit."

Mark smiled. "Me, too. Pretty sure I've seen every season of *Dateline* twice."

"Same." The girl gave him a quick look and the hint of a smile before returning her attention to the TV. Progress. He'd take it. "Luna will be out in a minute. She's nervous."

Nervous? That word stopped him in his mental tracks. Why would she be nervous? They'd kept thing deliberately cool and calm between them for the sole purpose of not stressing anyone out. And he'd been very careful to always let Luna be the leader in anything even remotely resembling anything more intimate, like the kiss. She'd definitely started that. Both times. Not that he hadn't continued it, but still...

"Who's nervous?" Luna asked as she walked into the living room wearing a pink fuzzy sweater, soft faded jeans and a pair of pink high heels that made Mark's mouth dry. He'd never pictured Luna in pink, but man, she looked good. Beyond good. Amazing. She looked from Astrid to him and blushed slightly as she took him in, letting

Mark know that she was pleased with how he looked, too. Then her gaze darted away from his fast and she cleared her throat. "Hey. I'm almost ready. Astrid and I were just discussing her getting a job in town while she's here."

"A job?" Mark sat back down, still feeling a bit dazed. His throat felt tight for some reason and his palms itched. Of course, it didn't help that he kept wondering if Luna's sweater felt as soft as it looked and how it would feel if he held her in his arms. Not a date, he kept reminding himself. "What kind of a job?"

"At the Buzzy Bird," Luna said, searching for something on the kitchen counter, then finding a pair of sparkly earrings that she stuck in her earlobes. "My parents could use some extra help busing tables and stuff at night, and Astrid needs to be able to support herself. Win, win."

A commercial came on the TV, and Astrid tuned in to their conversation again. "It could work because I'm not good at anything else."

"Not true." Luna grinned, coming around the sofa to sit at the opposite end from Astrid, near Mark. "You're a great conversationalist. And have such a sweet, sunny, friendly nature."

Astrid snorted at the gentle teasing. She looked much more comfortable than when she'd first arrived in town. More progress.

"What about after that?" Mark asked, trying to

find out more about the girl. "What do you want to do with your life?"

Shadows passed through the girl's eyes before she stared down at the pillow in her lap and shrugged. "Don't know. Never really thought that far ahead." Then she looked up at Mark. "What's a firefighter do? I mean, besides the obvious fire-putting-out stuff."

"Well." He took a deep breath. He and the other guys at the station gave presentations to the local school kids each year, so he started there. "We provide safety education to people in the community. And we're also trained EMTs, so we go out on those runs as well, arriving before the ambulance a lot of times."

"Don't forget the kitten rescuing," Luna added, raising a snarky brow.

He chuckled. "Yeah, we rescue kittens, too, sometimes."

Astrid seemed to take that in a bit. "Luna said I could shadow her tomorrow at the hospital, to see what being a physical therapist is all about. Maybe I could do the same thing with you at the fire station?"

"Oh, well…" Mark hadn't been expecting that, but hey. Why not? "Uh, sure. Just let me know when."

"And until then, you can work at the diner," Luna concluded, pushing to her feet once more.

"I already talked to my mom, and you can start there when you're ready."

Astrid exhaled slowly and sank back into the couch cushions again. "Why are you doing all this for me?"

"Because we like you and we want the best for you," Luna said, grabbing her coat from a peg on the wall, then stopping. "Is that a problem?"

The girl watched Luna closely, as if trying to read Luna's true motives from her expression. Finally, Astrid seemed to see what she needed because she said, "No. Not a problem, I guess." Astrid shrugged. "I'm just not used to people being nice to me without there being a catch."

Luna swallowed hard enough for Mark to hear the clicking noise. "Well, get used to it."

"You okay here by yourself, Astrid?" he asked.

The girl nodded, her focus already back on her crime show.

Right. He held the door for Luna, then waited in the hall with her until they heard the deadbolt lock slide into place on the door before they headed down to his truck parked at the curb. He held the door for her again as she got in the passenger side, then jogged around to slide in behind the wheel as Luna buckled her seat belt. Thankfully, the weather was better tonight, the temps a bit warmer, and the sky clear above, letting the stars twinkle down. He had no idea what the night would bring, other than more talk about the Astrid situation, but if the past week or so with Luna was anything to go by, it wouldn't be boring.

He drove through downtown Wyckford, then back out the other side of town toward the forest.

"Where are we going?" Luna asked, frowning out the window. "I'm not dressed for more camping."

Mark laughed. "No. I promised you dinner, and that's what I'm giving you."

She scowled over at him through the shadows cast by the dashboard lights. "But the two places to sit down and have a meal in town are back the other way."

"We're not going to a restaurant," he said, grinning. "I'm cooking dinner for us."

"You're cooking?" she repeated. "Seriously?"

"Seriously."

"Are you any good?"

"I like to think so. I make a mean roast chicken and veggies, which is what we're having tonight, by the way." When she continued to blink at him, he continued. "You said you wanted to discuss Astrid and I thought some peace and quiet would be the best place to do that. My house is just before you get to the forest, so we'll have some privacy."

Luna snorted then and shook her head as she

turned away. She muttered something under her breath he didn't catch.

"Sorry?" he prompted.

"Astrid warned me."

"Warned you of what?" Now it was Mark's turn to frown. "About me?"

"About how if a date took you to someplace remote, they were probably a serial killer."

Eyes wide, Mark signaled, then turned off onto the long winding drive back to his cabin. "I'm not a serial killer, I swear!"

Luna smirked at him. "But that's exactly what a serial killer would say, right?"

He sighed. She had him there. But what was more troubling was the fact that Astrid thought those things about people she'd met. Maybe she watched way too many true crime shows. Or maybe she'd had the unfortunate opportunity to meet people who might have made her think that way.

Neither idea was comforting.

A few minutes later, he parked in front of his cabin and cut the engine. He'd bought the place about week after he'd moved to Wyckford, falling in love with it at first sight. It had taken him some work to get it into shape again, but he knew every board and nail in the house and loved them all.

"C'mon," he said, reaching past her to get into the glove box, then pulling out a Taser and handing it to her. "Here. You keep this with you just in case. If at any point tonight you think I'm a serial killer, you can zap me with it. No hard feelings."

Luna stared down at the Taser, then back to Mark before taking it from him and undoing her seat belt. "Deal."

They walked inside and Mark flipped on the lights before taking off his coat and gathering Luna's to hang in the closet near the door. While she took in the interior of his place, Mark said a silent prayer of thanks that he'd managed to clean it up before tonight and headed into the kitchen to check on the chicken roasting in the oven.

Once that was done, he called over to where she stood in the living room. When he'd renovated the house, he'd transformed it into open concept, with the large, chef-style kitchen flowing into the spacious living room, where a large stone fireplace was against one wall and a huge bank of windows overlooked the forest on another. Everything was warm wood and overstuffed comfort and suited his personal style to a T. "Can I get you something to drink? Beer? Wine? Iced tea? Dinner should be ready in about twenty minutes."

"Uh…tea is fine, thanks," she said, perching on the edge of his leather sofa, looking suddenly small and uncertain. Mark's heart twisted in his chest.

"Great." He got them each a cup and carried

them into the living room, putting one down on a coaster on the coffee table in front of Luna, then settling into the other end of the sofa with his own. Eager to replace the awkwardness between them, he said, "So, Astrid. I think your idea about getting her a job is perfect. It'll keep her around town longer so we can keep an eye on her and hopefully figure out more about her. And she'll earn some money of her own while she's at it."

Luna nodded and settled back a little, some of the tension visibly relaxing in her shoulders. Mark felt his own stress levels lower. "That's what I thought, too," she said, sipping her tea. "This is good, thanks."

"You're welcome." He smiled, then searched for something else to say. "So, you're going to let her shadow you at work?"

"Yep." She sniffed, then studied him more closely. "You weren't expecting her to ask to come to the fire station?"

"No." He laughed. "But I'm happy to show her around if she wants. Always looking for new recruits."

She nodded, looking anywhere but at Mark now. "Your house is beautiful."

"Thanks. It's taken me nearly two years to get it to this stage, but I'm really happy with it."

"Wow. You did all this yourself?" Luna looked

around again. "Is there anything you can't do, Mr. Boy Scout?"

"Not if I can help it," he countered, winking.

Some of the weirdness between them seemed to dissolve after that as they got ready for dinner together, Mark getting the food ready while Luna set the table. It all felt very normal and comfortable and real. If he wasn't careful, a guy could get used to it. He gave her a quick tour of the house, then returned to the kitchen. After he'd carved the chicken and had the food on the table, they took seats across from each other and dug in. Between bites, he asked, "So, about Astrid. Any new information there?"

"Not really," Luna said after swallowing a bite of chicken. "This is all delicious. Thanks for cooking."

"My pleasure." And it was. He liked cooking. "I haven't heard anything, either. My buddy on the police force said they'd have to get a court order to unseal Astrid's foster care records, so unless she voluntarily tells us something, we won't find out much there."

Luna nodded, then looked up fast. "Oh, did I tell you a weird call came in on her cell phone earlier?"

"No." Mark frowned. "Weird how?"

"I was on my own phone with Madi and Cassie earlier when Astrid's burner phone started ringing on the charger in the kitchen," she said. "Since Astrid was holed up in her room, I went ahead and answered it, and it was some guy. He said Astrid could run, but she couldn't hide. Then he hung up."

"That is weird." Mark's frown darkened to a scowl. "Could you trace the call back?"

"I tried, but no."

"Huh." He swallowed a bite of veggies without really tasting them. "Did you ask Astrid about it?"

"I did, but she said it must have been a wrong number."

"And you believed her?" He narrowed his gaze.

Luna seemed to think about that for a moment. "Maybe. I mean, it happens, right? But given we found her running away in the forest, I have to wonder what she was running from."

"Same."

They finished their meal in silence after that, both seemingly lost in thought over the Astrid situation. It wasn't until they were cleaning up in the kitchen, Luna having volunteered to wash the dishes while Mark dried them, that he realized that unless he came up with another reason for her to stay longer, their evening was almost over. And even though he'd been a bit nervous at the start of it all, he wasn't ready for it to end. He hoped she felt the same.

"So, what should we do now?" he asked as he

put away their plates, then shut the cabinet door. "I play a mean game of Trivial Pursuit. Or, if you really want to throw down, Scrabble. But you might need the Taser for that one, because my word game can get heated."

Luna laughed then, a deep, throaty one that went straight to his groin. Dammit.

Mark folded the towel and set it on the counter, then walked back into the living room to put some much-needed space between them.

Not a date. Not a date. Not a date.

"I've never really been a big game player," Luna said, following him back to the sofa and flopping down again, this time taking off her shoes to reveal toenails painted the same shade as her high heels and sweater. And now all he could think about was kissing her again, all over this time. Not good. Seemingly oblivious to this inner turmoil, she tucked her feet beneath and rested her head in her hand, her elbow propped on the back of the sofa as she stared up at him. "You like to play games?"

"With the right partner," he said, his voice feeling thicker than usual as he sat in his spot at the opposite end from her again. "Or we could watch some TV. Or whatever. Whatever you want."

She seemed to consider his offer, then sighed. "What I'd like is to understand you more."

He blinked at her. He'd like the same thing with

her but hadn't wanted to come across too intrusively for fear of scaring her away again. "Okay. Ask away."

"What brought you to Wyckford?"

Mark shrugged. "I like my life uncomplicated."

She nodded as if in understanding. "Peace and quiet?"

"Yeah." He hadn't yet found the peace, but he *had* found the quiet, and he'd settle for that.

"Do you ever miss it?" Luna asked, studying him. "The big city, the people? Your family?"

"I still see my family a couple times a year. And no, I don't miss it. Or my ex-wife."

She perked up at that. "You were married?"

"For two years," he said, shifting slightly in his seat to face her. "Things were beyond rocky at the end." This wasn't exactly the conversation he'd planned on having tonight, but since she'd opened the door, he decided to go with it. "How about you?"

"Never been married," she said, seeming to draw in on herself a little more.

"Engaged?"

Luna shook her head. "This has been a really great first, first date."

"First, *first* date? As in your first date *ever*?"

She grimaced. "Yeah."

He looked at her for a long moment. "Explain."

She opened her mouth, then closed it again, looking embarrassed.

"Were you a nun until recently?" Mark teased, keeping his tone soft. He wasn't judging, he just wanted to understand how a woman as beautiful as Luna Norton had never been on a date before.

"No." Luna laughed. "I've obviously been with people, casually. I've just never done the whole dressing-up and formally going-out thing."

"Which we really didn't do, either," he said with a sudden pang of regret. If he'd known this was her first date, he'd have planned something grander for the night.

"Seriously, this is okay. Tonight was still great. Thank you again."

Without thinking, touched beyond reason, he reached and smoothed a lock of spiky dark hair away from her temple. "You're welcome. And it doesn't have to be over yet, either."

Once the words were out, they hung there between them a moment, neither of them responding as the air grew heavy with promise. He wasn't sure why he'd said it, just that now that he'd had a peek inside the real Luna, Mark wanted more. So much more. And surprisingly, she hadn't run, as was her usual MO. Or turn snarky and sarcastic. Another defense mechanism of hers. He'd become familiar with all of them in the days since their night in the forest. Instead, Luna sat there, blink-

ing at him as if she was really seeing him for the
first time, as well. Then, slowly, she leaned closer,
closer, until they were just a hair's breadth away
and he was caught in the lovely gray of her eyes.
"I really want to sleep with you, but…"

Mark swallowed hard, forcing words past his
tight vocal cords. "That sounded like a great idea,
right up to the *but*."

Luna shook her head and closed her eyes. "I
have…qualms."

"Qualms?"

Luna sighed, then looked at him again. "If you
want anything more than sex, I'm not interested."

Wait. What?

Mark blinked at her, processing that. Then, because it was just so unexpected, unbelievably perfect, he laughed out loud.

Luna frowned as Mark laughed, her eyes narrowing. "What? You think because I'm a woman
I need flowers and candy and fairy tales? Well,
guess what—?" She took a beat to enjoy his
wince. "Welcome to the twenty-first century.
Where women *like* no strings attached."

Mark watched her closely for a second. "Are
you—?"

Rather than letting him finish, Luna kissed
him, melting into him like butter in a hot skillet,
letting everything around her disappear—all her

worries and stress and overthinking and doubts and fears from the past—until all that was left was this incredible pleasure she always felt whenever she was kissing Mark.

If she was honest with herself right then, she'd admit that this was about as far from no strings attached for her as a person could get. Because from that first night in the forest, she'd been hyperaware of him. His scent, his voice, his touch. He made her heart pound and her blood sizzle. More than mere attraction, more than just desire. As he took control and deepened the kiss, wicked thoughts overran her mind, involving her tongue and every inch of his body. Over the years, since the attack, she'd learned to compartmentalize intimacy in her mind. Keep the physical separate from the emotional. But with Mark those lines blurred. Worse, she didn't mind, didn't want to run for the hills. In fact, she burrowed closer to him and held tighter. Unable to help herself, she licked his throat to taste the salt of his skin.

"Luna." His quiet, gruff voice thrilled her as he ran his lips along her jaw, repeating his earlier question, "Are you sure?"

Turning her head, she cupped his face and pulled it closer. "God, yes!"

He groaned and sucked hungrily on her bottom lip. And while his mouth and tongue were busy, so were his hands, teasing, caressing. She nibbled his earlobe. When he moaned, she did it again.

A reverent hush settled around them as Mark took her hand and stood, pulling her to her feet, as well. And any lingering nerves she had about what was happening disappeared. This was safe. Mark was safe because he was temporary. He didn't want forever any more than she did. He'd already proved that he respected her boundaries. He wouldn't force her to do anything she didn't want to do. She could have this tonight, feel his body against hers, inside hers, have an orgasm that wasn't self-served for the first time in a long while. And she wanted it now, the sweet little oblivion, before reality crashed down again.

They continued kissing as they fumbled toward the bedroom.

"No getting attached," Luna whispered against his lips after she'd shrugged out of her sweater and let it fall to the floor.

Mark smiled, his eyes heated as he took in her nearly bare torso. "Promise."

Luna gestured to his still fully clothed bod. "You're lagging behind."

Mark removed his own sweater and tossed it aside, then kicked off his boots and unbuttoned his shirt. Then because it was taking too long, he tugged the shirt off over his head, then stepped toward her once more.

"More," Luna commanded, hovering just out of his reach, enjoying her power.

"Oh, there's going to be a lot more." Mark's voice was husky with promise. "But first, I want you in my bed."

He took her hand and tugged her to him, sliding his other hand up her back and into her hair, kissing her slow and sweet. Not what Luna wanted. She pushed away and went for the button at his waistband. Luckily this time they were perfectly in sync. She slid his zipper down, then stroked his hardness through his boxer briefs.

Mark made a sound of pure male hunger before nudging her toward the hall. "Bedroom."

But Luna had never been one who liked being ordered around, so instead, she pushed him up against the wall to the side of his fireplace and kissed him, long and deep, before kneeling and tracing her tongue down the center of his washboard abs.

His groan reverberated in his chest, and in response, blood pounded through her body. His hands slid through her hair, and he murmured her name as she tugged down his boxer briefs and kissed the tip of his hot, silky erection.

With an inarticulate gasp, Mark's head *thunked* back against the wall and his fingers tightened against her scalp, not forcing her, just guiding her to what he liked best. Luna felt the fine tremor in his muscled legs, which turned her on even more. Made her feel even more powerful to know she had this strong and dominant male weak at the knees from one touch of her mouth on him, so she did it again, this time taking more of him in…

"Luna," he panted. "Please…"

"Please what?" she asked, looking up at him, seeing him hovering on the edge really working for her. Then she continued nuzzling him through what sounded like a very happy ending. Little aftershocks still ran through his body when Mark dropped to his knees in front of her and pulled Luna into his lap. He unhooked her bra and bent her over his arm, sucking a nipple into his mouth.

With a gasp of pleasure, Luna held him there. A minute later, she realized he'd somehow removed her leggings and panties without her noticing. Amazing, since she was so aware of him at every other time. But she was lost in the moment, lost in her passion, and too far gone now to stop. She straddled him, watching as he traced a hand down her between her thighs, his long, talented fingers making her cry out in pleasure. Shocked at the noises she was making, Luna nipped his shoulder to shut herself up.

Mark kept stroking her in a rhythm that became her center of gravity. Then he kissed her deep as he sent her flying over the edge of ecstasy. When she returned to herself, Luna found him watching her, a small smile on his lips. "Good?"

He stood and stripped out of his pants and underwear, and did the same to Luna, leaving them both completely naked. Then he scooped her up and kissed her again. She couldn't hold back her breathless moan, because Lord the man knew how to use his mouth, stirring up emotions she'd sworn not to feel. All she could do was marvel at how effortlessly he drew her out of herself, bringing her to two climaxes so quickly when usually she struggled to have even one with a partner because she was too in her head. It was wonderful. Freeing.

He entered her then in one long, smooth thrust, and oh, the pleasure, the panic... Because Luna knew. Knew even as she clutched Mark closer that she was in the worst sort of trouble now.

Because she'd lied. This wasn't just sex anymore. Not for her.

Not even close.

"Look at me," Mark said gently, cupping her cheek.

Luna's eyes fluttered open, and she focused on his face, transfixed by his expression of pure ecstasy. She had no idea whether it was the eroticism of what they'd already done, or the taste of him still on her tongue, or maybe the incredible feel of him so deep within her, but she wanted him with a desperation she hadn't known she could feel. She wrapped her legs around his waist, whimpering when he withdrew only to push back inside her.

"Okay?" he asked.

She didn't answer. *Couldn't* answer. She was drowning in sensation.

He ran his hands down her arms until their fingers were entwined, then drew them above her head. She arched into him, feeling like he was claiming her in a way she'd ever allowed. And as he did, Mark's gaze held hers in the same way he held her body—sure, steady, safe, secure.

It was too much. It would never be enough.

She had to get control of herself, the situation. So, she rolled him onto his back, holding *him* down, holding his hands above *his* head as she linked their fingers together.

His hooded eyes searched hers for a long beat before he gave her a sexy smile. "Better?"

Luna gave a shuddering sigh of pleasure as she sank back down on him.

Mark let her do what she wanted, which was to ride him hard and fast, every thrust sending electric heat sparking and crackling along her nerve endings. And in the end, after they'd both shattered, she sagged boneless and sated to his chest.

Mark gathered her in and pressed a sweet, tender kiss to her damp temple. That's when Luna realized the truth. When it came to him, she surrendered all control.

And for a girl who prized her own power, that was terrifying.

She laid her head against his shoulder as he pulled her in tight. When her breathing calmed, she sighed. "You make me lose myself."

"Good," Mark said, smiling.

She met his gaze, her expression serious as a heart attack. "No. Not good at all."

An hour later, Mark drove Luna home. She'd gone from hot to cold so quickly his head was still spinning. Apparently, they'd gotten a little too intimate, and Luna had felt it necessary to remind him again as she'd gotten dressed that "this was just sex."

He didn't need her to keep bringing that up. Her emphatic expression made it more than clear *she* was in no danger of wanting more with him, and he felt exactly the same way.

Neither of them had said anything else after that.

It was hard to tell if it'd been the good or bad kind of silence since Mark's radar where women were concerned was woefully out of practice. Still, the sex had been amazing, the kind every guy dreamed of—down and dirty, mindless. Luna had dominated, clearly not liking being vulnerable, clearly needing to be in charge. Which had been new and...*interesting* for him.

No strings attached.

Which was exactly what Mark wanted. Right? Right.

CHAPTER NINE

THE NEXT DAY, Luna took Astrid into work with her. She showed the girl around the hospital and the PT room, then sat in her office, dealing with phone calls to reschedule appointments for patients who'd canceled due to a snow squall the night before. In the end, she had a sizable chunk of time that morning to fill, and rather than sit around and think about Mark and the night they'd spent together, she decided to see if Riley Turner wanted to come in for an extra session since she was also at work that morning. Usually, Luna liked to wait a few days between workouts to let her patients' bodies recover, but Riley had insisted she was fine, and Luna had promised to show Astrid what being a physical therapist was like, so it made sense to bring Riley in. Plus, it was better than Luna getting lost in an anxiety spiral due to what was going on inside her head over the fact she'd broken her own rules with Mark.

After showing Astrid the dumbbells and pointing out the correct weight for Riley, Luna showed

Astrid how to spot the patient while Riley did reps on the weight bench. Astrid picked up the information quickly and seemed interested in learning more, so Luna explained how she formulated treatment plans based on a patient's goals and needs. All the while, though, Luna's mind kept flashing back to an image of Mark in bed, whispering in her ear, their limbs entangled, making her body tingle in places that had no business tingling while she was working. In fact, she got so distracted that when she looked over at Astrid and Riley, they were both staring at her like they were expecting a response.

Crap.

Annoyed with herself, Luna shook off her sudden, freak obsession with Mark Bates and forced a smile. "Sorry, I didn't hear your question."

It'd been so long since she'd been intimate with someone, that's what she told herself. That was why she was letting herself get distracted over a man who'd clearly agreed that this was nothing but a fling. She didn't do relationships. Neither did he. So why in the world could she not stop thinking about him now?

Maybe because being with him last night had felt different from anything she'd experienced before. More intimate than she'd been prepared for, which left her feeling vulnerable and raw emotionally. Two feelings she did her best to avoid at all times.

"I asked if we could move on to a different exercise now," Riley said, handing her dumbbells to Astrid, who put them away. "Maybe some chest presses?"

"Sure." Luna showed Astrid how to get the machine ready while Riley got into position. She set the weight at twenty-five pounds and Riley moved through the exercises like a champ. Luna could feel Astrid watching her—the girl was far too astute for her own good—and could tell Astrid suspected something. She'd been in bed by the time Mark had dropped Luna off at her apartment again, but this morning as they'd gotten ready for work, Astrid had stayed suspiciously quiet, as if letting her ideas about Luna and Mark simmer until she was ready to boil over with questions for them. Luna wasn't looking forward to that interrogation, so she tried to distract herself instead with small talk. "How are things in the Radiology Department today? Lots of cancellations, too?"

"Not really," Riley said, puffing out a breath between reps. "Whatever openings we did have were filled with inpatient tests, so…" She huffed out a breath, then let go of the weight bar and sat up, wiping her face with a towel. "Did you know Sam Perkins has a daughter?"

Honestly, still Luna didn't know much at all

about the new neurosurgeon in town, other than his name and what Riley shared with her on these visits. He seemed nice and neat and, above all, competent. All good qualities in a man who operated on people's brains and nervous systems, she supposed. "Huh," Luna said, glad Riley was holding up her end of the conversation. "What's her name?"

"Ivy," Riley said. "After his wife's favorite plant, he said. Not sure how old she is."

Surprised, Luna frowned. What was it with people keeping their marriages secret these days?

"He's married?"

"Was." Riley shook her head, looking sad. "His wife died last year. A couple of months before he came to Wyckford."

Luna straightened. "That's terrible."

"Yeah. So, when he came here to assist with Cassie's surgery last summer, he said it was like a breath of fresh air, a new start. He liked the town so much, he decided to stay. Moved his daughter and his dog and everything across the country."

They moved on to a range of motion exercises on the mat before ending the session.

Once Riley had rolled out of the room, Astrid was on Luna like crust on toast.

"So," the girl started, sitting across the desk from Luna in the same chair Mark had occupied a few days before. "How was your date last night?"

"It wasn't really a date," she said, her face hot from the lie. It had totally been a date and Luna knew it. So did Mark. They'd even joked about it, so... Why was she hiding it now from Astrid?

"Oh, it definitely was. I saw the way he looked at you. Is he good in bed?"

"What?" Yep. That was why. Unusually flustered, Luna began shuffling through paperwork without really seeing it, anything to cover her mortification. "I wouldn't know."

Astrid watched her closely for an agonizing moment, then shook her head. "He seems like a really good guy. You should trust him."

"He is a good guy. And I do trust him," Luna said, too quickly. She *sort of* trusted Mark, at least far more than she'd trusted anybody in a long time. He was kind and generous and smart and funny and protective in all the best ways. She'd be an idiot not to trust him. But then again, she wasn't exactly a MENSA member, either. Luna shook off the unhelpful thought spiral she'd fallen into. "But neither of us is looking for that."

"And what's 'that' exactly?"

"What are you? TMZ?" Luna snapped before exhaling slowly. "Look. Mark and I are just friends. That's all."

Friends with benefits.

She stacked a bunch of already neat documents, then met Astrid's gaze once more, taking back control of the conversation. "What did you think of the physical therapy session?"

"It was interesting. Riley seems nice." Astrid shrugged, then asked unexpectedly, "How long can I stay at your place?"

"Uh…" Luna blinked at her, trying to keep up, her heart squeezing. "I hadn't really thought about. It. How about until something better comes along?"

Astrid nodded and stared down at her hands in her lap, looking unconvinced about the "something better" part. Luna understood. When she'd been Astrid's age, it had seemed like sometimes nothing better *ever* came along. She wondered again about that mysterious call on Astrid's burner phone and frowned. "Why are you asking this now? Did you hear from that guy again? The one who hung up on me?"

The girl went pale, her eyes wide as she swallowed hard enough to make an audible click.

Luna frowned. "Do you know who it was? If he's bothering you, we can go to the police. Are you in trouble, Astrid?"

Astrid shook her head. "No police. I can handle him."

"So you do know him?" Luna said.

The girl remained quiet, staring at the wall behind Luna.

"You don't have to live like this, you know,"

Luna said finally. "I know it can seem like everything's your fault, and you have to deal with it on your own, but that's not the case at all. I'm here for you, Astrid. Whatever you need. And once you start at the diner, making some money of your own, you can support yourself. Stick around, maybe, put down some roots. There's a lot of freedom in that, Astrid." She took a breath and added, "And in your spare time, you could get good at whatever you wanted. Go to college or whatever."

Astrid finally looked back at her then. "I'm not sure I could stand being cooped up in an office all day."

"Then don't be. There are tons of careers out there. Eventually, you'll find something you like. It's all about choices and decisions. And you're spending a day with Mark at the fire station too, right? To shadow him? Maybe you'll like that job better."

"Maybe." Astrid shrugged again, looking defeated. "The problem with choices and decisions is I usually make bad ones."

Luna sighed in sympathy. "I majored in them myself for a long time. But I'm getting better. Having good sleep and decent food helps. And friends. And safety. Which you have now, in me and in Mark, if you want it."

"Thanks." The girl smiled, then looked out

the window, where Luna noticed it was snowing again.

Luna stood and checked the time on her smartwatch. "Good. Now, let's get ready for Mr. Martin. He's curmudgeonly and cantankerous, and I bet you two will get along great."

While Luna and Astrid worked at the hospital, Mark spent his day off hanging forty feet above the ground at Rock Steady, a local indoor climbing gym, gripping the wall hard with his fingers and toes. Brock was to his right and a foot below him. They were racing to the top, with the loser buying dinner. Brock had bought the past four meals in a row, which he'd complained about, claiming the finishes had been far too close to call. But Mark had won fair and square, though only by an inch or two.

"Move," Brock groused when Mark reached out far to his right for a good fingerhold. "You're in my way."

Mark didn't move. The overhead fluorescent lights glared down and sweat dripped down the side of his jaw. "Hey, Brock?"

"Yeah?"

"I'm having everything on the menu at the Buzzy Bird tonight, on *your* dime."

"I deal with my five-year-old daughter daily,"

Brock said. "I know how to negotiate with terrorists."

Mark eyeballed the top of the wall above, figuring out the best way to get there. "If you don't want to buy dinner, you're going to have to beat me to the top."

Apparently getting a second wind, Brock pulled himself up another few feet, putting him in the lead. Mark wasn't too worried, since there were still a few feet to go, and Brock was out of breath. "Finally succumbing to the dreaded dad bod, huh?"

Brock snorted. They both knew there wasn't an ounce of extra fat on him. "Just tired. Between Riley spending more time at the hospital lately and Adi and Cassie getting into all kinds of mischief at home, it's been...*a lot*. Not that I'd ever go back."

Up until last year Brock had raised his young daughter alone after his beloved wife had been killed in a car accident. Barely a year later, he'd lost his parents, too, also in a car accident. Brock's sister, Riley, had been in the car as well, surviving, but with a spinal cord injury that paralyzed her from the waist down. It was enough to make anyone go insane, but Brock had somehow held it all together. Then Cassie Murphy had returned to town and changed everything. They were very

much in love and Mark was happy for his good
friend.

"You and Luna do the deed yet?" Brock asked,
jarring Mark out of his thoughts.

"What? No." Mark nearly fell off the wall,
barely recovering his hold as he scowled. "Why
is that even any of your business?"

Brock gave him a look. "You're familiar with
Wyckford, right? Not to mention you get that
dopey look on your face whenever her name
comes up. And I heard you were making cow
eyes at her at the fire station the other day during a stretching class."

"Who told you that?"

"One of your guys. He comes in for cortisone
shots in his shoulder. Speaking of which, how's
yours holding up?"

"Fine." Mark had nothing else to say after
that. Was it that obvious that he liked Luna? He'd
thought he'd kept it pretty well hidden, but maybe
not. Especially after last night. Dammit. Sex with
Luna had been amazing and special, more than
he could remember it being in a long time, probably because it had felt like she'd been right there
with him the whole time, naked and exposed, and
not hiding behind her usual barriers of snark and
suspicion. But that was also a double-edged sword
because he'd felt naked and exposed, too, but she'd
made clear to him that the only connection they

had was between the sheets. Nothing more. And he'd agreed. To go back on that now and want more was really dumb on his part.

But still, that didn't stop his chest from aching when he'd tried to call her earlier to check on Astrid and gone straight to voice mail. Like they had to keep tabs with him or something. He just wanted to keep them safe was all. And maybe, if he kept telling himself that was all it was, he'd believe it someday…

"I *finally* beat you." Brock whooped in triumph, because while Mark had been distracted by his thoughts of Luna, his buddy had reached the top of the wall.

Mark grumbled as he let himself down to the floor again. Figures. That's what he got for letting himself get distracted by his emotions. A swift kick in the you-should've-known-better.

Except where Luna was concerned, he didn't know better. In fact, he wasn't sure he knew anything at all except he wasn't ready for their fling or affair or whatever it was they were doing to be over.

And he wasn't sure what to do with that.

Luna took Astrid to dinner at the Buzzy Bird after work so they could eat and so the girl could get oriented in her new job. It ended up turning out well, because one of the bussers had called in sick, so Astrid got to start training right away. The weather and the roads were still awful, so it was a nice, easy shift for her to start with. Luna sat in her corner booth alone, doodling in her sketch pad while she waited for Astrid to finish, when Brock and Mark walked in, both wearing work-out sweats under their winter coats. Mark raked a hand through his hair, his gaze roaming until he found Luna, and all the nerve endings in her body vibrated with awareness. Then he smiled at her, and oh… If his concerned once-over had done things to her, his smile undid her from the inside out.

While Luna was captivated, Lucille Munson came in and made a beeline for Astrid, who was clearing dishes from the counter, and introduced herself. By the time Luna made it over to rescue the poor girl, all she heard of Lucille's one-sided conversation was, "…featuring you on the town's Facebook page will help you make friends."

Astrid looked panic-stricken. Luna stepped between her and Lucille. "No Facebook."

At Luna's serious tone, Lucille studied Astrid's sullen face, then nodded. "I understand, but if you need anything…"

"I'm fine." Astrid fled for the door to the kitchen with her bucket of dirty dishes.

Luna hurried after her. "Hey, Astrid, wait up."

The girl paused long enough to hand her bucket

of dishes over to the washer at the sink, then immediately headed toward the back, employee exit.

Luna followed her outside, then around the corner of the building, barely catching up with Astrid before she reached the edge of the parking lot near the two-lane highway. "Wait! Where are you going?"

"I don't know," Astrid called over her shoulder. "I shouldn't have come here."

"Here as in the diner? Or here as in this town?" Luna called back. The only thing she knew for sure at that moment was that if she let Astrid leave now, she'd never see the girl again. "Stop. Please. Let's talk about this."

"Why can't you just leave me alone?" Astrid turned around once she reached the curb near the highway. "You don't even know me. Not really. You have a life here, a job, people who love you. I'm nothing but trouble."

A passing semi blasted its horn and both women stumbled into the parking lot to avoid being roadkill. The snow-covered ground glowed orange under the streetlamps, giving the scene an eerie, otherworldly quality.

Eventually, Astrid shook her head, looking baffled. "Why won't you just let me go?"

Because once upon a time Luna had been the one in trouble and had been too stubborn and ashamed to let anyone help her. Because she recognized the helplessness in Astrid's eyes, and it called to her own. Because maybe if she helped Astrid, she could finally get out from under the trauma that kept her down. But in the end, she went with, "I told you before. Because I care. Because I trust you, even if you don't trust yourself yet. I've been where you are, okay? Alone and afraid."

Astrid watched her for a long beat, then said, "You were a runaway, too?"

"No. But I've been through some things in my past. I can help you if you'll let me."

The teen still hesitated. "I don't know…"

Behind them, the front door to the diner opened, and Luna glanced over her shoulder to see Mark walking over to them, his breath frosting on the chilly night air.

"Everything okay?" he asked as he stopped near Luna's side.

Luna nodded, hoping that covered everything he wanted to know, but Mark wasn't the sort of man she could brush off. He might be easygoing, but he was also proving to be as tenacious as Luna was when he wanted something. And right now, it seemed, he wanted answers.

He looked at Astrid next. "What about you?"

The girl shrugged, digging the toe of her sneaker into the snow at her feet.

Mark looked at Luna again, then he nodded,

apparently deciding to let it go for now. "Surprised to see you both here. The roads are bad tonight."

Luna took a deep breath, more grateful than she could say that he was there to help keep the situation under control because it felt like it was slipping right out from under Luna. Just like a lot of things lately. "I was out of food at the apartment, and Astrid wanted to get a jump on her new job in the diner."

"Ah. Right." Mark studied them both for a long moment, his blue gaze sharp and assessing. Luna longed to lean against his warmth, his easy strength, and let him hold her burdens for a while. Which made no sense because since she'd gotten good at self-preservation over the years, managing to survive despite herself sometimes. And yet here she was at the ripe old age of thirty-five, and all she wanted to do was burrow her face in Mark's chest and let him be the strong one.

Reaching for her hand, Mark tugged her closer. "Hey, I was wondering…"

"Ha!" Astrid said, startling them both. "I knew it." She flashed a smug grin before starting back toward the diner. "I'm going back inside again before I freeze to death, since no one's offering to hold my hand." Then she sobered as she stopped and looked at Luna. "Thanks, for what you said."

"We'll talk more later," she called to the girl,

who was already walking away. Luna would've started back, too, but Mark tightened his grip on her hand. "Tell me the truth now. What was that about?"

Luna shrugged. "Lucille came after her, wanting to put her on the town Facebook page, and it freaked Astrid out. I talked her off the ledge. That's all."

"Has she heard anything else from that guy on her burner phone?"

"I asked her about that earlier today." Luna swallowed hard and stepped a little closer to Mark. For body heat. Yep. Because it was downright arctic out there. That's the excuse she was going with anyway. "She didn't confirm or deny it. Didn't confirm or deny she knew the guy, either."

"Damn." Mark inhaled deep and stared for a moment at the diner, where Astrid was clearly visible as she bused more tables. It was clear, to Luna at least, that the girl was doing her best to do a good job. She cared, too, even if Astrid wasn't ready to admit it yet. If things worked out, the girl might have a positive future in Wyckford after all. "But she didn't give you a name?"

"Nope." Luna felt with time, she could get the girl to open up more to her; they just had to build that trust to go both ways. Rather than stand in the parking lot getting frostbite, though, she'd much rather sit inside where it was warm and there was pie. She tugged on the hand Mark still held, pulling him toward the Buzzy Bird, not even caring that anyone inside might see them holding hands. "Come on. Let's get back inside before we freeze."

CHAPTER TEN

Two days later, Mark was at the fire station with Astrid, giving her a tour of the place and explaining what their daily jobs were. She'd been there most of the morning with him, and so far, things had been eventful, as usual, giving her a clear picture of what it meant to be a firefighter. They'd started off riding along on several EMT calls, including a trip out to Gooseberry Island near the entrance to Buzzards Bay. Despite the blustery January weather, it was still a popular destination for birders. Apparently, a group of them had been out watching waterfowl when one of their members had been injured. And since Wyckford FD helped the local ambulance service when needed, they'd been summoned to action. He and Astrid rode in the fire truck across the Thomas E. Pettey Memorial Causeway, which connected the island to the mainland, then headed down one of the wide, sandy trails toward the birders with the other EMTs and fire crew. Tate wasn't working today, and Mark said a silent prayer of thanks for that. The last thing he needed right now was another buddy of his sticking his nose into this situation where it didn't belong. He was already getting enough of that with Brock.

They arrived at the birders' base camp and Mark was surprised to see several police officers there, as well. Apparently, in addition to the injury, they'd been robbed while out near the beach watching the terns onshore and the grebes diving into heavy surf. As Mark helped the EMTs bandage a sprained ankle and treat several minor cuts from bird-watchers who'd taken tumbles off boulders, he overhead another birder listing the missing items from the camp for the cop: a tablet computer, a smartphone and a hunting knife. The birders apparently hadn't bothered to lock up any of their stuff—a situation all too common in Wyckford. Mark called it Small-Town Syndrome. People figured they were safe here because bad guys only lived in big cities. But he was from Chicago and knew bad people could live anywhere, sometimes where you least expected it.

After finishing up on the island, they walked back to the fire truck, enjoying the breathtaking views of Buzzards Bay and the concrete observation tower built during WWII as part of the coastal defense system to watch for German subs. At least he was. Astrid seemed distracted again. He couldn't tell if something was bothering her or if it was a normal teen girl thing, so he asked as casually as he could, "Enjoying the day so far?"

"Yeah," she said, staring out over the bay. "I like doing different stuff all the time and being outside."

"Me, too," Mark agreed. "Sitting behind a desk isn't my thing. I do it now, because of the promotion I took last year, but I still hate it."

"Exactly." Astrid finally looked at him. "So why do you do a job you hate? Why not go back to being a regular firefighter?"

"Well, there's bills, for one thing. I did a lot of work on my house and took out loans to pay for it," he said as they crested the dune overlooking the parking lot below. "And I do still get to go out on runs and stuff, too, but not as much as before. My new job is a lot safer, so I guess I should be happy. My ex-wife would've been thrilled."

"Wait." Astrid's eyes narrowed. "You were married?"

Her reaction was so similar to Luna's the other night that Mark had to laugh. "Yeah. For two years."

"Wow." Astrid shook her head. "What happened?"

"She didn't like me being a firefighter and I don't know how to be anything else, so…" He shrugged. "Saving people is in my blood, I guess."

His chest caved a little at that with old grief.

"What's wrong?" Astrid asked, far too perceptive for her own good. "You got all pale and sad."

"Nothing," he said, but that felt wrong, so he added, "I lost someone in a fire a long time ago. Someone important to me, so I guess that's why I feel driven to do what I do."

"To make up for your mistake," Astrid said, staring down at the cars parked below. "I get that."

Mark sensed there was more there than just a response to his words. "You ever feel like that, too?"

"Sometimes." She took a deep breath. "It's hard, living in foster care. Never feeling like anything's permanent. When something or someone does make you feel that way, you tend to cling to it, even if it turns out to be a bad thing."

There was pain in her tone. Fear, too. The fear is what put Mark's instincts on high alert. "What are you afraid of now, Astrid?"

She slid him a side-glance. "Luna told you about the phone calls?"

Ever astute, this one. Mark nodded. "She did."

"I can handle it. I swear."

"I'm sure you can," he said. "But maybe I can help."

Astrid turned to him then. "I don't think you can. I don't think anyone can."

They went back to the station then, where they had a busy afternoon filled with a group of kids from the local elementary school visiting the firehouse and asking more questions about bodily functions than fire suppression. Astrid thought that was hilarious, followed by a free self-defense class the firefighters ran once a month for the good citizens of Wyckford. Since there wasn't much else to do, Mark had Astrid sit in on the class. Well, that, and he felt better knowing the girl had some basic skills to take care of herself if someone came after her, especially after that worrying conversation on the dune earlier. He made a mental note to talk to Luna about it the next time he saw her. In fact, maybe he'd stop by her place later and see if she was home. His shift lasted until after nine that night and he knew Luna was working until at least seven at the hospital, then she was going to pick up Astrid after her first shift busing tables at the diner. Maybe if all three of them sat down to talk later, they could finally get some real answers from Astrid.

After her shift at Wyckford General, Luna went to pick up Astrid at the diner. She'd some paperwork to finish up first, so by the time she pulled into the lot it was going on 8:00 p.m., though with how dark things got at that time of year so quickly, it could've been midnight.

Her mother spotted Luna's car out through the packed diner's front windows and leaned out the door as Luna pulled into a space near the entrance. "Astrid's out back dumping the trash. She's a hard worker."

"Good." Luna cut the engine as her mom went back inside, then got out and walked around the building to find Astrid standing on the back stoop tying up a garbage bag. "Hey, you about done here?"

Astrid looked up, almost smiling. "Yeah, just need to finish this. It's been busy tonight."

"Busy keeps you out of trouble, right?" Luna grinned as she walked over to hold the dumpster open for Astrid. "Come on. Throw that thing in so we can get back in my car where it's warm. I'm parked out front."

Astrid tossed the trash into the bin, then followed Luna. "I think I'll like working here."

Luna blew out a breath and studied the pier across the street where everything was quiet and dark. "Good. My parents are sticklers, but they mean well. If you work hard, you can learn a lot from them about perseverance."

"Did you?"

Without warning, Luna's throat tightened. She nodded. "I did. I was attacked when I was your age, by a guy I trusted. He was older. I felt ashamed and worried that after my parents found out they'd blame me for what happened, but they didn't. If it wasn't for their support in helping me move forward, despite what happened, I'm not sure what would've become of me…"

Astrid sucked in a breath. "Some bad things happened to me, too."

Luna paused, waiting for the girl to continue, hoping that by sharing her past trauma it might earn Astrid's trust a little more. But when Astrid didn't say more, Luna clicked the button on her key fob to unlock the car doors, then said gently, "Well, if you ever want to talk about it, I'm here."

"Thanks. I bought these earlier." Astrid slumped into the passenger seat of the car, then pulled two lollipops from her pocket, offering Luna one. Under normal circumstances, Astrid would probably be having her first relationship with a boy, writing his name on her notebook, dreaming of proms and football games instead of figuring out where to find her next meal or who would hurt her next.

"I got my first tip tonight, too," Astrid said, sounding surprised. "I didn't think people tipped bus people, but, apparently, they do. Made a whole two dollars from that alone."

"Congratulations," Luna said as she started the engine again. She'd just buckled her seat belt and looked over to make sure Astrid did the same when she noticed the girl was just wearing a long-sleeved Buzzy Bird T-shirt and it was in the low twenties out. "Where's the sweatshirt I gave you? It's cold tonight."

Astrid smacked her own forehead. "I forgot it in the kitchen. Wait here."

She dashed out of the car and vanished around the corner of the diner toward the back staff entrance again.

Luna fiddled with the radio, her mind still dwelling on the fact of how similar she and Astrid were, as far as their experiences at that age. Luna hadn't been in foster care, of course, but being on her own so much due to her parents' working had certainly felt like it sometimes. But her parents had more than made up for any feelings of abandonment, real or imagined, she might have felt with all the support they'd given her after the assault. With all the support they still gave her today. Luna wasn't sure what she would've done without them.

She put on some generic pop radio station from Boston, then glanced out the window toward the corner of the building. What was taking Astrid so long? With a sigh, Luna shut the car off and got out again, retracing her steps to the back door only to find Astrid pinned against the wall by a guy in a black jacket with the hood up and ripped, dirty jeans. "You owe me," he growled, one hand around Astrid's throat. "You know you do."

"Hey!" Luna yelled, white-hot fury and a terrible sense of déjà vu overtaking her. "Let her go!"

Mistake number one. Because the guy dropped Astrid and came toward Luna.

Swamped with the memories of another time and place, a different man who'd attacked her, Luna backed away, tripped over her own feet and went down. Mistake number two.

She scooted back on her butt, searching for anything on the ground she could use as a weapon, but it was too late. The guy already towered over her. Reacting on instinct, Luna kicked out, knocking the guy's feet out from beneath him. His knees hit the pavement, and Luna flung her keys into his face as hard as she could.

He snarled and slapped a hand over his eyes. "That hurt, you—"

Before he could finish his curse, Astrid clobbered him over the head from behind with what looked like an empty beer bottle, shattering it over his skull. The guy's eyes went blank before rolling up in his head as he collapsed, out cold. "That's what you get for stalking me, Troy!"

Luna scrambled to her feet, wincing slightly, and grabbed Astrid's arms. "Are you okay?"

"Y-yes," the girl stuttered, clearly not okay because she was shaking like a leaf.

Luna was trembling, too. She pulled Astrid away from the guy's crumpled body and inside

the diner's back entrance, securing the door behind them. Between breaths, because Luna was
pretty sure she was hyperventilating at that point,
she managed to say, "We…need…to…call…the…
police."

"No," Astrid gasped. "I can handle Troy. I promise."

Luna risked a look through the back window over the sink only to find the area around
the dumpster empty now. Somehow, the guy
had come around and managed to escape. She
whipped back around to face Astrid as the pieces
of what had just happened sank in. "He's gone.
And you know him. Troy, right? Is he the one who
called and hung up on me? He said you owed him.
You said he was stalking you."

"I said I can handle it." Astrid stared out the
window into the night.

"How? He attacked you. He tried to attack me!"

"Look," Astrid said, taking a deep breath before continuing. Luna had a feeling nothing good
would follow that breath. "Troy's my stepbrother.
He's been following me, but I know now how to
get rid of him once and for all. I just need time to
do it. Can you give me that, please?"

With that, Astrid unlocked the back door and
walked into the night, leaving Luna to stare after
her, stunned. Dammit. She couldn't let the girl
just wander around alone out there. Not with that

guy around. Luna pulled a small canister of pepper spray from the small drawer beneath the sink before following Astrid. Her head pounded, her butt hurt from where she'd fallen hard on her tailbone again, and there was a weird, pinching pain in her left side, but she snatched her keys from the ground where they'd fallen after striking her attacker, then went around the building to the parking lot out front.

The good news was, there was no Troy.

The bad news? No sign of Astrid, either. The girl was gone.

Luna drove to her apartment first, keeping an eye out as she went, hoping maybe the girl had gone there or she'd find Astrid along the way. Instead, she found Mark on her doorstep, waiting for them.

His easy smile fell the minute Luna reached the porch and he took in her disheveled appearance beneath the light. Before Luna could explain what had happened at the diner, however, her vision blurred, then shrank to a pinpoint. From a great distance, she heard Mark call her name, but Luna couldn't seem to answer him. Weird. Her bones seemed to dissolve, but luckily Mark grabbed her before she hit the ground.

She managed to stutter out, "I—I'm o-ok-kay."

"You passed out," he said, checking her pulse before going still. "Luna, you're bleeding."

"W-what? N-no, I—I'm—" Then she looked down and saw a dark red, wet patch growing on her left side, staining her blue scrub shirt crimson. She gulped in a panicked breath, but Mark held her steady.

"I've got you." He carefully laid her down on the steps and pushed her coat and shirt aside to reveal a two-inch-long gash on her left side. Guess that explained the pinch.

Luna blinked hard against the black dots gathering again in her vision, saying weakly, "He got me."

"Who?" Mark scowled as he yanked off his own jacket and pressed it firmly against her torso. "Who got you?"

"I think it was the bottle. Astrid broke it over his head. I must've rolled on the shards."

"Bottle? What bottle?" He shook her gently. "Luna, stay with me. Where's Astrid? Is she okay?"

She struggled to stay awake, stay alert, but the pain in her side hit her hard now, stealing her breath. "She was attacked behind the diner. I tried to stop it, but he came after me instead. I rolled away and Astrid broke a bottle over her stepbrother's head, but…"

Old memories mixed with the new ones, causing a confusing muddle in her mind. Her friend's footsteps coming down the hallway.

Troy looming over her.

Luna had escaped her attacker by being strong and mean and fearless. She hoped Astrid had escaped as well tonight, but she needed help. She couldn't do this alone. No one could.

"Luna, stay with me, okay?" Mark cupped her face, his voice even and calm. Soothing, steadying, just like him. "You said Astrid's stepbrother was there. Did he attack you?"

"He attacked Astrid. I attacked him."

Mark inhaled sharply. "Are you hurt anywhere else?"

"I don't think so."

He examined her anyway before lifting her in his arms and carrying her to his truck.

"Where are we going?" Luna asked groggily.

"The ER."

"What? No." A flood of fresh adrenaline had her wide awake now. "We need to find Astrid. She's out there alone and she said she could handle him, that she knew what to do. But she can't handle him alone."

Mark didn't slow down. "We'll find her, don't worry. Just as soon as we get you to a doctor."

"I—"

"Nonnegotiable, Luna."

He carefully buckled her into the passenger seat, then jogged around to slide behind the wheel as he called Brock at the hospital on his cell phone.

CHAPTER ELEVEN

MARK HAD BEEN on untold numbers of emergency calls during his time as a firefighter, both in Wyckford and in Chicago. But none of them affected him like seeing Luna bleeding. Not even that first night in the forest had gotten to him like tonight did. Tonight undid him.

No. *She* undid him. He hadn't wanted to care again, to get in so deep again, but given his current accelerated heart rate, that's exactly what he'd done. She'd gotten around his guilt and his fears about being involved again, about failing again, and made it straight into his heart.

"We have to find Astrid," she said again. "She said she knew what to do, but I don't think she does. She's started a new life here, Mark. She has friends in us. She has a job now. She could make it out of the past she's running from. But she needs our help…"

As her words trailed off again, Mark glanced at Luna as he pulled away from the curb, but the interior of the truck was too dark to see her properly. Still, what she'd just said sounded an awful lot like Luna could've been talking about herself at that age. He wanted to ask more about that, but for now he needed to stay focused on the present, on what had happened behind the diner tonight, try to piece together the puzzle of Astrid and what was going on with her. "Did you know Astrid had a stepbrother?"

She shook her head. "I think he was the guy who called the burner phone I got her, though. The one who hung up on me after saying Astrid could run, but she couldn't hide."

"What do you think he wanted?"

"Astrid," she said grimly. "He had her pinned to the wall of the diner. Guys like that only want one thing. I yelled at him, to let her go, so he turned on me instead."

Jesus. "And that's when he stabbed you?"

"No. I tripped and landed on my butt. He was on me before I could find a weapon, but then Astrid hit him over the head with a bottle and knocked him out." Luna shook her head and squinted as if trying to remember the details. "We went inside, and I said I wanted to call the police, but Astrid said no. That she knew how to handle him once and for all. She asked me to please give her time to do that." She sighed. "When I checked again, the guy—she called him Troy—had already vanished. Then Astrid left, too. I tried to follow her, but she disappeared. That's when I drove home to see if she was there and found you instead."

Mark pulled into the ER lot and under the portico where Brock met them as promised. Madi, too, ready with a warm hug for Mark and a calm, steady smile as she got Luna inside and settled into an exam room before prepping her for stitches.

Brock examined the wound. "What happened? You were stabbed?"

Luna shook again as her face blanched, whether from pain or shock, Mark wasn't sure. He hadn't felt this helpless since the night Mikey died. "Had a fight with a broken bottle."

"Hate it when that happens." Brock glanced at Mark, who stood still as stone at Luna's bedside, wanting to do something, anything to help. He had to find this guy, protect Luna, protect Astrid. He couldn't fail again. He owed that to Mikey. He owed that to himself. Brock tore his gaze from Mark, then continued. "I have a few more questions for you. Want me to kick him out first?"

Luna shook her head. "No. He can stay."

Good, because Mark wasn't going anywhere. He held Luna's hand for support while Madi stood beside Brock at the instrument tray, ready to assist.

"Who wielded the bottle?" Brock asked.

"Astrid." Luna rubbed her temple with her

free hand. "She's a teen girl Mark and I have befriended. But it wasn't her fault. She was fighting off her stepbrother."

"Did this stepbrother hurt you anywhere else, Luna?"

"No."

Brock gently examined her cheek, where a small bruise formed. "What's this from?"

"Not sure. Maybe from when I fell."

Brock nodded, his eyes still on hers. "Sometimes victims don't like to talk about what happened—"

"*Nothing* happened." Luna met Madi's concerned gaze, then Mark's, before looking back at Brock. Mark tightened his hold on her hand. He still wasn't sure what had happened in her past; he was only more certain than ever that something had. They'd be talking about that just as soon as this current nightmare was over. He'd make sure of it. "Astrid knocked the guy out, then he must've come to and vanished before we could call the police. The end."

"So you *did* call the police afterward?" Brock asked.

"No. Not yet. Troy vanished, then Astrid did, too, and I was too concerned about finding her and…"

Brock hiked his chin at Mark, who pulled out his phone. "On it."

Mark called the police dispatcher, then took Luna's hand again. "Officer is on the way to take your statement. Then we'll find Astrid and figure all this out. Okay?"

She hesitated, her gaze searching his, then nodded. "Okay."

"Stitches first, though," Brock said, examining the wound on her side again. "I'd say five, maybe six total. Won't leave much of a scar."

"Can't you just glue it?" Luna asked.

"Not this time," Brock said. "But I'll be quick, and you'll be nice and numbed up, no worries."

Mark did his part to keep Luna's attention off things, stroking a finger over a small scar bisecting Luna's eyebrow. "How did you get this?"

"I stole a bike to get to work when I was sixteen, then crashed it." She let out a shaky breath.

Brock chuckled, working efficiently. "Check out Mark's chin. Right after he moved to Wyckford, the idiot got dehydrated and passed out at the top of the climbing wall at the gym. Slammed into it face-first. Luckily for him, I fixed him up so he can still be a cover model anytime he wants."

Luna laughed softly, then winced when it must've hurt her side. "Cover model?"

"He didn't tell you?" Brock asked, shooting Mark a look. "He made the cover of one of those hot firefighter calendars for charity last year. I'm surprised you haven't seen one around the hospital. Most of the nurses got a copy." Mark's traitorous friend grinned, suturing with smooth dexterity the whole time. He'd been trying to live down that stupid calendar ever since it came out. "You're doing great, Luna. Three stitches down, three more to go."

When he'd finished, Brock helped her sit up, gave her some prescriptions, then got paged away.

They waited for the police officer to come and take Luna's statement, then Mark helped her get her coat back on before carrying her back out to his truck to take her home. They stopped at the pharmacy for her antibiotics and painkillers, then returned to her apartment, Mark's mind running in overtime. Where would Astrid go? What did this Troy guy want? Would he come after Luna again to get to Astrid?

He parked at the curb again, then took Luna's keys from her hand. "Stay here. Let me check your place first and make sure it's safe."

He got out and walked away before she could argue. Her place was fine. Fine and empty. Which was both good and bad. Part of him had hoped Astrid might have hidden herself away in her room upstairs, but no such luck. Mark turned on all the lights, then went back downstairs to carry Luna in and put her on her bed. He helped her off with her coat and shoes and changed her into a clean scrub shirt from the stack in the corner, then covered her with a blanket, doing his best to treat Luna like any other patient and not the woman he'd fallen head over heels for. Once he'd made sure she was tucked in, Mark got her water, some snacks, the remote, her prescriptions, then stepped back. "Can I get you anything else right now?"

"No, thank you."

His phone buzzed, and he frowned down at the screen. "I'm on call but I'm going to tell them they need to find someone else. Try to get some sleep." He headed for the door before turning back. "I'll be in the living room if you need me."

Luna woke up early the next morning, groggy from the pain pill she'd taken. It felt like she'd been out for days, but the clock said it was only a little after six. Brock had put a waterproof bandage on her wound, so she was able to shower. Afterward, she dressed and walked out of her bedroom, stopping short as voices filtered in from the living room.

Astrid was there, talking with Mark.

"Uh, hey," Luna said, surprised as she walked over to where they sat on opposite ends of her couch.

Astrid frowned at her. "Mark told me you got hurt last night."

"I got cut on the broken glass, needed stitches, that's all."

Astrid paled and stared down at her hands in her lap. "I'm so sorry. I never meant for you to get hurt."

"It's not your fault. Are you okay? I tried to find you after you left, but you were gone."

Astrid blew out a breath and nodded shakily. "I'm okay. This shouldn't have happened."

Luna sat on the middle cushion between the girl and Mark and took Astrid's hand. "I'm glad I was there. If I hadn't shown up when I did..."

Astrid closed her eyes, her expression fierce. "I know. But he was after me, not you."

Luna glanced at Mark, who'd remained oddly silent the entire time. "It wasn't your fault. I know you said you could handle him yourself, but we can help if—"

"No." The girl pulled free and stood, heading for the door. "You guys have been great to me while I've been here, but I've screwed everything up. I'm going for a walk. Clear my head."

"Here." Luna got up and pulled the pepper spray from her coat pocket and handed it to the girl. "If you see him again, spray first and ask questions later. And if you're not back in half an hour, I'm coming after you."

Once Astrid was gone, Luna turned to Mark next. "What were you guys talking about when I came in?"

"I was trying to get answers out of her about

what's going on, but she's a closed book." His gaze was unreadable as he watched Luna far too closely for her comfort. "Kind of like you." He sighed, then asked, "How are you feeling?"

"I'm managing." Their eyes held for a long beat. The silence just about did her in. Finally, she broke. "I'm not trying to keep secrets from you." At his pointed look, she amended, "Okay, well, maybe I am, but trusting people is hard for me."

Rather than demand she talk, Mark just sat there waiting. Waiting and watching, like he knew what she needed. Which he did, dammit. He'd always been able to read her so well, even when she did her best to stop him. And that was why she'd let him in, regardless of all the reasons she'd tried not to. Let him into her heart and into the depth of her being where she never let anyone else, except for those select few closest to her. Her family. Her friends. And now Mark.

Luna wasn't sure what to do with that new knowledge yet. It was too new. Too scary for so early in the morning. In fact, it was probably best if she pulled back a little, put the brakes on this thing with Mark for now until they got everything with Astrid settled at least.

"Last night shook you," Mark said. Not a question.

Her gut tightened. "Well, yeah. I was terrified for Astrid."

"But it was something more, wasn't it? Like the attack triggered bad memories. What happened, Luna?" His gaze was steady, his body warm and strong and comforting beside her on the sofa as he asked his final, devastating question. "And what happened last night that reminded you of it?"

Heart in her throat, Luna closed her eyes, resting her head back against the cushions for a moment before looking at Mark again. This whole time he'd been there for her, showing her time and again she could trust him. That she was safe with him. But Luna didn't want him to see her as weak, as a victim. As if sensing her inner turmoil, Mark slowly and carefully slid his hand up Luna's spine, then into her hair and tilted her head up so she could meet his gaze. "Trust me, Luna. Please."

She did. "I was attacked, assaulted by a friend when I was sixteen."

His jaw tightened a fraction, but he just nodded. "Go on."

"I got in trouble a lot back then, being on my own so much while my parents ran the diner. I thought I could handle everything. Thought I was in control. Until I wasn't." She shifted in her seat, pulling her knees to her chest and resting her chin atop them. "I thought he was a safe person, someone I could trust." She paused. "I was wrong."

Mark's grim tone sent a chill up his spine. "What happened?"

"He was bigger, older, smarter than me. Twenty-two. He said I owed him. But he didn't want money as payment. He wanted—something I didn't want to give him. He tried to force me... But I fought him off. He beat me up pretty badly. Broke my arm and my eye socket. I was busted and bruised for weeks. Couldn't leave the house for fear people would ask questions." Her voice broke and she shook her head. "My poor parents had to deal with all that on top of everything else they were doing."

"Ah, Luna." Mark pulled her into his arms then, gently holding her as he rocked her slightly. "I'm so sorry."

She swallowed hard again, then forced more words out. "The whole time he was hurting me, he kept saying it was my fault. That I brought it on myself. That I'd led him on. That I owed him."

"It wasn't your fault," Mark said tightly. "You were just a kid. Did they arrest him?"

She nodded. "They charged him with assault and put him away for years. I wasn't the first girl he hit."

Mark cupped the back of her head in his palm and pressed her face into the crook of his neck as if he needed a moment, maybe two.

"It was a long time ago," Luna murmured. "But it still affects me sometimes. I don't trust many people, especially men."

"Trauma doesn't have an expiration date," he said, his deep voice rumbling beneath her ear. "And the fact it's still there, like a land mine waiting to be triggered, is normal. Believe me, I know. Thank you for telling me. It *wasn't* your fault. You *were* blameless."

She sniffled, then leaned back to peer into his face. "The only people who know are the ones who truly care."

"Like me?" he said, making her heart flip in her chest. She could see the truth of it in his eyes.

"Like you," she acknowledged, staring into his eyes before looking away. "I care about you, too. Probably more than I should. Mark, I—"

Before she could finish that sentence, her cell phone buzzed from the charging pad in the kitchen where Mark must've put it for her after they'd returned from the hospital. She held up a finger for him to wait, then walked over to answer the incoming call. Her mom's face showed on the caller ID, putting Luna's fears to rest that it might be Astrid in trouble again. "Hello?"

But no sooner had her heart rate returned to normal than it kicked into overdrive again at her mom's frantic words. "Madi's donation jar for the free clinic on the front counter is gone. Astrid stole it."

"What?" Luna stood, any lingering woozy effect from her pain medications evaporating under the sizzling rush of adrenaline in her system. "How? When?"

She listened as her mother explained about Astrid returning to the diner unexpectedly about twenty minutes earlier, then leaving again abruptly. That's when they'd noticed the donation jar was gone. Luna's mind raced. Astrid must have left her apartment and headed straight for the diner. The timing was close, but if she'd taken a short-cut through town, the girl could've made it there, and...

No. Luna refused to believe she'd taken that jar.

Concern and guilt congealed inside her. She should have known how desperate Astrid was. Why didn't she know? Why hadn't she insisted the girl stay with her and Mark? Why had she let her go out for that stupid walk? Why?

Because you wanted to spend time alone with Mark. Because you're falling for him.

Luna balked at the words even though deep down she knew they were true. Fear and self-recrimination tightened her chest until she could barely breathe. This. This was exactly why she'd known better than to open herself up to her emotions, to what she felt for and with Mark. Her feelings never led her anywhere but trouble. And now that trouble had spread to Astrid, as well.

She should've known better than to let her heart overrule her logic. That never worked out well.

That's what happened the night of the attack. And now with Astrid, out there alone and in danger...

"Luna?" Mark frowned as he stood as well, placing a gentle hand on her arm. "What's wrong?"

She jerked away from him, not because she didn't like him touching her but because she did. Too much. She had to put a stop to this. Had to get her focus back on what was important here—finding Astrid and proving once and for all to everyone that she was a good kid and that she didn't steal that money.

Mark's frown deepened into a scowl as Luna stepped back farther from him. "What's going on, Luna? Why are you acting this way all the sudden?"

"Acting what way?" she snapped as he turned and walked away from her. Her irritation was with herself more than anything because all she seemed to want to do was run into his arms and let him take her burden for a while. Which was not going to happen because Luna had never depended on a man before in her life and she wasn't about to start now. "Look, that was my mom. She said Madi's donation jar has gone missing at the diner, and they think Astrid's somehow involved." Needing to keep moving to burn off the restless energy now burning inside her, Luna headed for the hook by the door to grab her coat, then shoved her feet into her boots. "I have to get down there now and convince them it's not true."

Mark shrugged into his coat and grabbed his keys. "I'll come with you. Let me drive."

Luna's first reaction was to tell him she could drive herself just fine, but she'd taken those pain meds earlier and, even though she felt clearer now, she didn't want to chance it. She took a deep breath, then nodded. "Fine. Let's go." Then she stopped halfway out the door and held up a hand, needing to say it now before she couldn't. "Look, I really appreciate you taking care of me tonight, and that night on the trail, too. It's been fun—"

"Fun?"

Her jaw tightened. He was going to make this difficult. Well, more difficult than it already was. Whatever. Luna could do difficult. She'd been doing it her whole life, after all. "I need a break, okay?"

"Break?" he repeated, looking both stunned and confused. "From what?"

It was the last straw atop Luna's already teetering stress pile. "Yes! A break. From this." She gestured between them. "From you. I'm fine, okay? I don't need a babysitter. And I sure as hell don't need someone feeling sorry for me because of what happened to me. I'm not porcelain. I don't break that easy, okay?"

Mark blinked at her a moment, opened his

mouth, then closed it and waved toward the hall, his tone flat and slightly brittle now. "Let's get to the diner and figure this out."

They walked out of the apartment and Luna locked the door behind them, then they headed down to Mark's truck. She could feel him watching her periodically and it only made her feel worse, about everything. But she couldn't back down now. She wasn't cut out for relationships. She'd known that going in. To believe that had changed because of one man was beyond ridiculous. She needed to stop thinking about what could never happen and get her brain back on finding Astrid and getting to the truth.

As they pushed outside into the cold night air, Mark finally said, "So, we're done, then."

Not a question. Also, not a hint of warmth in his voice. More like firm decisiveness.

Luna ignored the stab of pain in her heart and gave a curt nod as she climbed into the passenger side of his truck and buckled her seat belt. "We're done."

CHAPTER TWELVE

"You're too good, too willing to sacrifice your-self for other people, too naive..."

His ex-wife's accusations swirled in Mark's mind as he drove them to the Buzzy Bird at breakneck speed. It was 11:00 p.m. now so at least there wasn't a lot of traffic. Which was also good because his mind was definitely not on the road-way as he continued to berate himself over how everything with Luna had blown up in his face.

Why did he keep doing this? Overprotecting, overanalyzing, oversmothering everything until the thing he cared about most was driven away. It was the situation with his ex-wife all over again. He'd let Luna in, let himself believe that this time it might be different, that he'd not suffocate her or make her feel like he wanted to control her. And yet, here he was, falling into the same old pat-terns. The same old failures.

"I don't need a babysitter. And I sure as hell don't need someone feeling sorry for me because

of what happened to me. I'm not porcelain. I don't
break that easy..."

No, she didn't. In fact, Luna was one of the
strongest people Mark had ever met. That was
one of the reasons he was so attracted to her. Like
she was strong enough to survive his kryptonite,
his failure.

Maybe she was right. Maybe they did need to
put the brakes on, perhaps permanently.

They'd both agreed to keep it light, keep it easy.
Then he'd gone ahead and trampled those boundaries for himself. Exactly why he never should've
let things get beyond the "just sex" phase for himself to begin with. That was basically the definition of insanity. Doing the same thing over and
expecting different results.

Smart guy, that Einstein.

If only Mark had taken the guy's advice, he
could've saved himself a lot of heartache.

Hell, maybe he was *that* naive. But no more.

"What happened?" Luna asked as soon as they
walked into the Buzzy Bird.

Luna's mother and father sat at one of the
booths, looking both harried and sad. "Astrid
got here right before we closed. Said she'd left
something in the back and asked if she could get
it. Of course, I said yes. It wasn't until after she
was gone again that I noticed the jar was missing.
Luckily, we emptied it out a few nights back, but

there was still probably at least another hundred bucks in there. Why would she do this?"

"Are you certain it was her?" Luna asked.

"We were the only two here, other than a couple lingering customers. I don't know who else could've done it, honey," her dad said.

Mark glanced over at the security cameras mounted in the corners of the room. "Did you catch her on the security feed?"

"We haven't had time to check yet." Her mother hesitated. "But those cameras are so finicky anyway, especially after the sprinkler incident last year. We've been meaning to replace them but haven't gotten around to it yet. And if Astrid didn't do it, why did the jar disappear around the same time she did?"

Luna's father gave a slow nod to his daughter. "Sorry, babe. I know you like Astrid, but you have to admit this looks guilty as hell."

Mark went to put his arm around Luna, who looked like she was going to be sick, but then stopped himself. They were done. No more touching. No more comforting. No more anything other than just casual, platonic acquaintances. The sooner he remembered that, the better.

And truthfully, he felt a little ill, too, and not just because of what had happened with Luna, either. He didn't want to believe the worst of Astrid, either, but there was a good chance Luna's parents were right. Especially after Astrid herself had said that her stepbrother thought Astrid owed him. Maybe the girl thought she could pay him off with money instead of her body. The thought of the latter made Mark's gut twist with tension. Astrid might seem tough on the outside, but inside she was still just a kid. Just like Luna had been. Just like Mikey had been. But still, why hadn't Astrid said something to him back at the apartment? If she'd needed money, he would've gladly given her what he had on him. It wasn't much, but from the sounds of it, it would've been about the same amount as was in the donation jar, minus the robbery. He should have made sure she knew she could trust him. Another failure on his part.

Add it to the ever-growing list.

"We called Madi, too, since it's her money," Luna's mom said. "She's on her way now, along with the police."

"I just don't think she'd do this," Luna said, apparently still refusing to believe the girl would steal from them like that. "She was staying with me. She liked her job here at the diner. Why would she risk all that for a hundred dollars?"

But even as the words emerged from her mouth, she looked at Mark and they both knew the answer.

Her stepbrother. Troy.

Before Mark could say anything else, a uniformed officer from Wyckford PD walked into the diner, followed by Madi.

It was the same officer Mark had asked to run Astrid's information the night they'd first found the girl in the public lot outside the forest. He and Luna gave statements to him about Astrid, then waited while Luna's parents did the same about the robbery, and finally Madi about the donation jar.

The officer nodded when they were all done. "I should probably interview the customers who were in here at the time, too, if you can get me a list of their names, please."

Luna's mom nodded. "Will do. What happens next?"

"Well, we'll start searching for the girl and see if we can recover the stolen money and question her to determine motive," the officer said. "Then, if she confesses, we'll press charges, depending on what you all want to do."

Luna shook her head. "Please don't press charges. I don't think she did it, but even if she did, she's really trying to make a fresh start here in Wyckford. Going to jail would destroy all of that. And we don't know the extenuating circumstances. She could've had a really good reason for taking the money and—" Luna's breath hitched when the officer's gaze narrowed on her.

"Is there something you're not telling me about this girl's whereabouts or motives, ma'am?"

Mark came to her rescue, couldn't help himself. Old habits died hard. "No. We've told you everything we know for now. We're all just tired."

Weighted silence followed.

Finally, Mark said, "Astrid Jones is a good person who's caught in a bad situation, I think. She's scared, and she needs us, whether she knows it or not."

The police officer left then with Madi.

Mark and Luna stood to go as well when Mark's phone rang. He glanced at his caller ID and scowled. "Sorry, it's dispatch. Give me a sec."

Luna went into the kitchen while he took the call.

"Bates here," he said as he answered.

"Hey, A.C.," the dispatcher said, using the nickname they'd given him at the station, a shortening of his new title to the first letters of each word only. "There's a fire in the forest. Early reports say a campfire got out of hand. All hands on deck."

Mark got the specifics, then hung up just as Luna walked back out into the dining room. Just what he needed tonight. His beloved forest going up in flames. It only increased his already bad feelings about the situation. Coincidences didn't just happen in his experience, and the fact that Astrid had been staying in the forest prior to them finding her, and her stepbrother was stalking her and Astrid was now on the run with stolen money, equaled a huge problem in his mind.

"What's wrong?" Luna asked him as he walked back over to where she stood near the entrance. "You look worried."

"I am, if I'm right." He shoved his phone back in his pocket. "There's a fire, in the forest. All personnel needed."

"The forest?" Luna said, her gray eyes widening. "You don't think…"

Mark gave a brusque nod. "My gut's telling me yes."

After saying a quick goodbye to Luna's parents, they were off in his truck again—Luna insisted on coming with him, despite his urgings for her to stay put in case he was wrong, and Astrid showed up at the diner again—heading toward the forest on the edge of town. Eventually the paved highway turned into a dirt fire road that forked off a dozen times or more. Most people who tried to take these roads got lost in about three minutes, but Mark knew exactly where he was going. When the roadway narrowed even more, he glanced over at Luna in the dim light from the dashboard, not missing how she clung to the locked door handle.

"Don't worry," he said, trying to lighten the grim mood. "I hardly ever drive into a tree."

"Good to know," she said, making them both laugh despite the circumstances and lessening the tension in the air between them a bit. Luna always did have the best snark. Not that he noticed.

Twenty minutes later, they pulled into a clearing where an array of fire vehicles had parked, including several pumper trucks from neighboring town fire departments and an ambulance. Floodlights illuminated the place like the Fourth of July.

Mark parked and got out, then leaned in the open driver's side door, his keys still in the ignition. The air outside smelled of burnt wood and heat, familiar scents to him, but ones that still brought a mix of apprehension and guilt because of Mikey. "Stay here. Under no circumstances are you to get out of my truck. If the fire moves closer to this location, I want you to slide behind the wheel and drive out of here, understand? Follow the same road we came in on until you reach the highway."

"Yes, sir." Luna gave him a flat look and a mock salute.

Mark shook his head as he jogged away toward the nearest pumper truck and the group of firefighters standing near it. Thank God it was January and there was enough snow on the ground to prevent a wildfire from spreading. Still there were enough old dead pines in there to go up like torches if they weren't careful. He ducked inside the back of the pumper truck and shimmied into his fire gear over the top of his jeans and T-shirt, then exited to find out from his men what was going on in the forest. If Astrid was in there, he needed to find her, and fast. The fire chief came over and told Mark where they'd run the lines to keep the fire from spreading, and since Mark knew the area so well already, it didn't take him long to figure out the best place for him to go in and search for Astrid.

As he headed for the trailhead, he drank down a couple of five-hour energy drinks to keep him going, then hazarded a glance back at Luna in his truck a good distance away and prayed she'd do as he asked, just this one time. Then he disappeared into the trees, the light on his fire hat illuminating the dark trail before him. Ash was falling like snowflakes from the fire nearby and smoke billowed toward the starry sky, though the slight breeze helped keep the air around him clear.

The fact Astrid was out here on her own, obviously in danger, drove the protector in him nuts. And even though he understood why maybe Astrid thought she had to do it, why her past had *made* her do it, it still hurt. Hurt that even after all they'd done for her, even though Astrid and Luna were so much alike it made his heart ache, even with all that, he'd *needed* to believe in Astrid. After everything that had happened tonight, after everything that had happened in his past, he had to keep believing in the girl because it was all he had left.

Just as he knew Astrid needed to believe in them, too.

And yeah, maybe that was naïve, but dammit. That was who he was.

Ten minutes after 1:00 a.m., the light on his fire hat died. He pulled out his backup flashlight and was halfway to the spot where he'd suspected Astrid might be hiding when his backup flashlight went out, too. This was very much not his best night. Mark tried his phone next. There was no reception, but he didn't need it for the flashlight app. Apple was his new best friend. He got close to his destination by 2:00 a.m. At 2:10 a.m., his cell phone battery ran out and his phone was relegated to the same list as the flashlight, only lower. He stopped to reorient himself in the shadows. That's when he slipped.

Then kept falling…

Luna kept her promise and stayed in the truck, even though it was the worst, most helpless feeling imaginable, watching the good guys in trouble, unable to help. She stayed and she stayed, until it seemed like a small eternity had passed, but according to the digital clock on the dashboard only two hours had passed. Finally, she couldn't wait anymore. Her concern for both Mark and Astrid had grown too great to just sit and wait. The more she thought about how she'd ended things at the apartment with him, the more she knew it had been a mistake. It was had been an instinctive reaction born from old trauma, not the current situation. She'd thought she'd moved past all that after years of therapy and work on herself, but every so often, those old, buried land mines still tripped and detonated. She felt awful and owed Mark a better explanation as to why they couldn't keep seeing each other. And she'd give him one, too, just as soon as she figured it out herself.

Needing to move, to do something other than just sit there and wait, Luna got out, glad she'd at least thought to wear her heavy coat and boots when they'd left the apartment what felt like another lifetime ago. The area around the fire trucks was still lit brightly, though there weren't many people around. They were all in the forest fighting the fire, which meant it was easier for Luna to slip down the trail unnoticed.

She'd been out here enough times during the day to know if she stayed on the main trail, she should be okay. And besides, there were enough firefighters on-site that surely if she got lost again they'd find her.

Luna kept going until about ten minutes later, according to her smartwatch, she happened upon footsteps leading off into the snow. Smaller footprints, about the same size as Luna's. Too small to belong to Mark or Troy or one of the other firefighters. Hopeful that maybe she'd found Astrid at last, Luna went off-trail and into the trees, emerging about ten minutes later in a small clearing where she found the girl with her back toward Luna, furiously shoving things in a backpack Luna had given her a few days prior. When Luna stepped closer, a twig snapped, and Astrid spun around fast with a knife in her hand. The minute she registered it was Luna, though, she tossed the blade behind her and shoved her hands into the ratty front pocket of the blue hoodie she'd worn the day they'd first found her in the public lot, her shoulders hunched.

"What's going on, Astrid?" Luna asked. "Is Troy here with you?"

"No." Astrid frowned, not meeting Luna's eyes as she grabbed the backpack near her feet. "I was supposed to meet him here, but he never showed up. So, I'm going away again."

Through the top of the unzipped bag, Luna spotted the lid of the donation jar and her heart broke. Astrid hadn't even tried to hide it. "Why'd you take it?"

"You know why," the girl answered.

"We would have helped you, Astrid. All you had to do was ask."

Astrid stared down at her battered sneakers. "I couldn't do that. Not after you guys were so nice to me. This is my mess to clean up and I thought the money would do that. I thought if I paid him off, he'd finally leave me alone."

Luna glanced behind Astrid, then waggled her fingers. "Give me the knife."

Astrid picked up the blade and handed it over.

Luna took it, then waggled her fingers again. "And the other one."

The girl stared at her, then let out a resigned sigh and pulled a Swiss Army knife from her sock.

"Any other weapons?" Luna asked.

"No."

"Fine." Luna grabbed Astrid's arm and tugged her back toward the trail. "Let's go. We'll talk about this when we get back to the truck."

Astrid hesitated, just long enough to make Luna wonder if this was going to be an issue, but then she started walking—dragging her feet really—but at least she was moving.

They'd just reached the main trail again when Luna heard something. Not the fire, not the distant chatter of the animals or the firefighters, but a loud crash, followed by cursing...

Troy?

Astrid must've thought the same thing because she edged closer to Luna in the darkness as Luna dug out her cell phone to use the flashlight app. If she'd been thinking more clearly, she would've brought a flashlight with her, but there they were. Cautiously, she scanned the light around, taking in the area and realizing they were close to the small clearing where she and Mark had set up camp that first night in the woods. Luna swallowed hard, wondering where Mark was, if he was okay. "Hello?"

No answer. That was good. Unless it was a hungry predator...

She illuminated a thicket of trees next, vividly reminded of what had happened when she'd snuck out of the tent to go to the bathroom there. She slowly moved closer to the edge of the embankment where she'd slipped and fallen to the frozen creek below, shining her light that direction, and—

Oh, God.

Something rustled down there. Something big in the shadows.

Bear?

Except a bear wouldn't call for help. In a familiar voice.

Luna frowned down into the inky blackness toward the frozen creek bed, shocked. "Mark? Is that you?"

"No, it's Tinker Bell," he grumbled, adding a few more choice expletives.

"What are you doing down there?" Luna flicked her phone's flashlight beam in the direction of his rustling again but didn't see much. "Isn't the rest of your crew up here fighting the fire?"

"Yes, Luna. Thank you." He paused, giving an aggrieved sigh. "I fell."

"Are you okay?"

When he didn't answer right away, she panicked. *"Mark?"*

"I'm fine. I jacked up my shoulder a little bit, though."

Resolve joined her panic as she stared into the abyss. "I'm coming down right now. Astrid's here with me. She'll keep a lookout for us from the top."

Luna glanced over at Astrid, who nodded, her backpack already resting at her feet.

"Go!" Astrid said. "I'll see if I can find someone to help us."

"No!" Mark called up to them. "Stay where you are. Astrid, you stay put, too!"

"I'm fine," the girl called back. "And you're not my dad. Thank God because that would be weird."

Ignoring Mark's warning, Luna made her careful way down the slippery embankment. Mark was hurt. He needed her help. Even if they weren't together anymore because she'd stupidly broken things off with him, there was no way she'd leave him down there to suffer alone. She'd already let Astrid slip through her fingers once today. She refused to lose another person she cared about.

Loved, really.

Okay. Fine. She loved Mark Bates. There, she said it, if only to herself. And Astrid had become like a little sister to her. She wanted to keep them both in her life as long as possible, grow her tight circle of trusted friends closer.

The change Luna didn't even know she needed but wanted more than her next breath revealed just when it was all about to slip from her grasp.

"Stop, Luna. Go back," Mark called, apparently hearing her scramble down the ravine. "I'm coming up right now."

That'd be great, if it were true, but she doubted it was because there were no sounds of Mark moving at all. The incline was steep, and she needed both hands to keep from tumbling herself, but she also needed the flashlight app on her phone, so she unzipped her coat enough to reveal the V-neck of her shirt beneath, then stuck the device in her bra. This mostly highlighted her own face but gave Luna enough glow to see by. Sort of.

"Luna, *stop*," Mark said again, his voice edged with pain now.

"I'm not leaving you here—" And speaking of slipping, she broke off with a startled scream as her feet slid out from under her on the icy, snow-covered slope, and Luna slid down the last few feet to the creek on her butt. The stitches in her side pulled painfully and her still-bruised tailbone throbbed, but yeah. She was okay.

"Where are you?" Mark demanded. "Are you all right?"

"Yes." She fumbled her way to his side, thankful that her phone was still intact between her boobs. "Are you?"

"You don't listen," he groused. The beam of light from her phone bounced off him as she moved, showing him sitting up, his back to a stump, his jaw tight. "Are you sure Astrid won't run away again?"

"I heard that," Astrid called from the top of the embankment. "And no. I'm tired of running."

"Me, too," Luna muttered under her breath as she noticed Mark cradling his right arm to his chest at a funny angle. She scowled. "Is your shoulder broken?"

"Just dislocated, I think."

Luna reached him and pulled the phone out of her top to inspect him more closely. Despite the chilly night, sweat ran down Mark's temples, and he looked a little green. Which meant he was probably going into shock from his injury. It had been a long time since her clinical rotations in PT school, but Luna was well-versed in the basics of first-aid triage. Assess the patient's injuries, get them to safety, then stabilize them until help arrived. "Let me take a look at your injury."

Mark held her phone in his good hand while she opened his coat and gently pushed aside his shirt. No obvious cuts and no bleeding to his right shoulder, though the area was already swelling, and the angle of the joint was a bit deformed. Yep. All the signs of a classic dislocation. Luna sat back on her heels and took the phone back. "We need to stabilize that arm before we try to get you back up the embankment." She looked around, wishing one of them had worn a scarf, since that would have made an ideal sling. Then she called up top, "Astrid, do you have anything in your backpack we could use to make a sling for Mark's arm?"

"Uh, let me look," Astrid called back. "Here. Try this."

The next moment a flash of something light in color flew down the embankment and landed near them. Luna leaned over to grab it. Her old yellow "Cobkickers" hoodie. A bit bulky, but they'd make it work. She moved in beside Mark again and began doing the thing up into a makeshift sling for him, aware the entire time of his gaze on her from the shadows. When she was done, she helped him slip his coat off his injured shoulder. "Okay. Hold still while I get this fastened in place around your neck."

"Wait." He panted, grimacing as he shifted his weight slightly to move away from the stump as he held his injured arm and shoulder at a certain angle with his good hand. "Let me do this first."

"Do wha—?" Before Luna could finish her question, Mark took a deep breath and held it, then jerked himself hard to the side, ramming his injured shoulder hard against the stump behind him. Luna winced on his behalf as a loud pop sounded. Then Mark exhaled with a huff and sagged back against the stump again. Luna straddled his legs, trying to see his face, trying to make sure he was still conscious. He was sweating profusely, but his color had improved. She cupped his cheeks. "Why didn't you tell me you were going to pop the joint back into place?"

He opened his eyes and offered her a weak smile. "Got it in one." Then he coughed and added, "I'm sorry all this happened. It's my fault. I didn't protect you or Astrid."

"Protect us from what?" she grumbled as she got his temporary sling in place and secured around his neck, then carefully slid his injured arm into the wider, bottom part. Once she was satisfied, she moved back slightly and brushed the messy blond hair that had slipped into his eyes off his forehead. "Mark? What did you think you were protecting us from? And stop making everything your fault. We can all screw up just fine on our own without your help."

"Don't know," he murmured, his eyes still closed. "I'm sorry I smothered you."

Now it was Luna's turn to smile as her heart gave a little squeeze. Such a dear, sweet man. Words she'd never thought she'd say to herself again. But Mark had changed that for her. Shown her things could be different, people could be different, if she just gave them a chance to be. "Well, sometimes, a little smothering is nice. And stop apologizing. I'm the one who should be saying I'm sorry to you. I shouldn't have pushed you away like I did at the apartment. That wasn't right, and honestly, it had nothing to do with you. It's an old instinctive response from what happened to me and sometimes when I'm stressed it just comes out. But you didn't deserve that."

"Tell my ex-wife that," he said, opening his eyes to watch her in the light from the phone. "Or no. Maybe just forget about her. I don't care what she thinks anymore. I only care about you, Luna. I know we promised we wouldn't get attached, but I couldn't help it. I'm sorry, but I love you."

She laughed then. Couldn't help it. "Pretty sure that's the least romantic thing anyone's ever said. Are you apologizing now for loving me?"

"Only if it makes you feel in any way controlled or trapped or overprotected." He lifted his head slightly, flashing her a self-deprecating grin, his teeth white against his tanned skin. "I know you don't go in for all that roses-and-happily-ever-after stuff."

"True." She shrugged, then kissed him fast just because she wanted to and it felt right. Then she sighed and sat back on her heels, an odd mix of anticipation and apprehension bubbling inside her. "I'm afraid I love you, too."

Mark chuckled. "Again, not exactly a Hallmark movie kind of confession. Fear and love."

"Eh... I never really watched that channel anyway. Give me Crime Central any day over that." She slid an arm around Mark to help him to his feet then, both struggling a bit because of their injuries. "We need to get back up to the top of the embankment, if you can, so we can get some help."

"Hey, Astrid," Mark started, then stopped suddenly, halting Luna beside him as he held a finger to his lips, then whispered in her ear, "Hear that?"

Luna scowled and shook her head, then listened harder, straining to catch any sounds from up top. Finally, she shook her head. "Nothing."

"Exactly." Mark sighed. "She's gone again."

"No. She wouldn't run away from me twice in one day," Luna said, refusing to believe it. "She wants to get out of this situation, Mark. She wants to stay here in Wyckford. She told me. There's no way she'd take off again now."

Then, suddenly, sounds of an argument drifted down the embankment.

"Don't touch me!" Astrid snarled.

"You can't outrun me, bitch," a nasty male voice said, one Luna recognized from behind the diner. Troy. "And a hundred bucks ain't gonna cover it. You and me were meant to be together. Stop fighting it!"

"I'll fight you until my last breath, Troy," Astrid growled, her tone laced with steel. "I'm done running away. I'm done letting you ruin everything for me. I've found my place here and I'm staying. Without you. It's time for you to go."

Troy laughed, a cruel, mirthless sound that took Luna right back to the night of the attack. He'd laughed, too, as he'd hurt her. Her anxiety spiked, but Mark pulled her closer into his side with his good arm as if sensing her distress. Somehow, his support kept her from tipping over the edge into panic mode like she usually did. Luna forced herself to breathe and stand her ground, allowing the memories to wash over her without overtaking her. She had control now. Exactly what she'd always wanted, thanks to Mark. She gently squeezed him back, careful to avoid jostling his injured shoulder.

"I hope he doesn't hurt Astrid," Luna said,

blood pounding in her ears from her spiked adrenaline.

"She can take care of herself," Mark whispered, causing Luna to give a jolt of surprise in the darkness. For a guy who thought he carried the burden of protecting the world on his broad shoulders, that was quite a change. Then he added, "She took a self-defense class the other day when she shadowed me at the fire station. She took out most of the other guys on my crew. She can handle one punk with a grudge."

A little reassured, but still a lot nervous for the girl at the top of the embankment, Luna said a silent prayer that Astrid would find her inner strength and fight for what she wanted, just as Luna had, despite her fears and her past. Good things waited on the other side if you found your courage.

"I *said* don't touch me!" Astrid yelled, then the sounds of a scuffle ensued. There were several grunts and the sounds of fists and feet hitting flesh, and even glass shattering, then a mighty "oof" followed by a wheezing silence.

Luna released the breath she'd been holding the whole time and finally called up top, "Everything okay?"

A few agonizing seconds ticked past without a response before, finally, a voice called back, "I got him!"

Astrid! She was okay. Luna wanted to whoop for joy but considering the fact they still had to scale the embankment again, it seemed premature.

"Stay put this time," Mark said. "We're coming up!"

Before they started their strenuous climb, however, he slid his hand around Luna's nape and tilted her head up so her gaze met his. "Thank you for rescuing me this time."

Her throat clogged, and her eyes burned before she blinked hard. Luna wasn't a crier, and she wasn't about to start now. She swallowed hard around the lump in her throat. "You're welcome."

They started up the embankment again, Mark chatting as they went, probably to keep himself distracted from the pain. Luna was grateful because it also meant she didn't have to talk, as she wasn't sure she could get past the lump of gratefulness clogging her throat. "I'm glad we didn't give up on Astrid. The kid made a mistake, that doesn't mean she *is* a mistake. She's learning. She's finding out how to make things right when she screws up. That's because of you, Luna. You helped her succeed. The *best* thing that could ever have happened to her is having you in her corner." They paused halfway up to catch their breath, Mark looking over at Luna, his blue eyes warm as they roamed her features. "Just promise you won't give up on me, either. I know I'm a Boy Scout sometimes, and I care too much, and try to protect everyone, but…"

"No." Luna shook her head, incredibly aware of his heat, his strength, beside her. "I won't. I… can't. Like I said, for better or worse, I love you, Mark. And I'm not the type of girl to go back on my word."

"Good. Because, like I said, I love you, too. And I can't give up, either. Not on her. Not on you. And not on us. And I *will* be stubborn about that."

Her heart stopped, and Mark smiled, which kick-started her pulse into overdrive again, painfully. Luna stayed close beside him as they climbed, praying neither of them fell again. Finally, they made it to the top, where they found Astrid sitting atop her backpack, a crumpled figure lying on the ground a few feet away, rocking slowly back and forth and whimpering. Shards of glass from the broken tip jar littered the snow around Astrid's feet.

Luna took the scene in, then asked, "What did you do to him?"

"Smashed the jar over his head, then gave him a good swift kick in the groin," the girl said, her tone an odd mix of astonishment mixed with pride in her accomplishment. "And I managed to get enough bars to call 911. They're sending cops to arrest him as we speak."

"Great job!" Mark high-fived Astrid, then pulled her in for quick one-armed hug before taking a seat on a nearby log. "Glad those self-defense classes helped."

"They did." Astrid grinned, then turned to Luna. "Sorry about your friend's tip jar, though. I'll pay to have it replaced with what I make at the diner. If I still have a job there, after all this…"

"I think after tonight I can persuade my parents to take you back." Luna hugged the girl tight. "I'm so proud of you."

"Thanks." Astrid grinned when they pulled apart. "I'm proud of you, too. Looks like you snagged your hot firefighter."

"I did." Luna winked, then checked her smartwatch. It was closer to dawn than midnight now, her second night out here in the forest and boy, what a doozy. She walked over to sit next to Mark on the log. "How's the shoulder?"

"Might've torn my rotator cuff again," he admitted. "Brock's going to kill me."

"Cops should be here soon to take Troy over there." She glanced over at the guy still holding himself on the ground and rolling around. If he tried to get up again, Luna herself would personally knock his lights out. No one came after the people she loved. No one. "Then we can get you to the ER."

He gave a one-shoulder shrug. "Maybe you can

be my physical therapist after the surgery. Didn't think I'd ever want one until now."

"Ever is a long time."

"Ever," he repeated firmly. Then he covered her mouth with his. She cupped his jaw, his stubble scraping against the pads of her fingers. His lips moved against hers, slow and sweet, and despite the situation, she couldn't get enough of him. By the time they pulled apart, she was breathless. Luna lifted her head and met his gorgeous light blue eyes, and that was when she knew.

He was it for her.

No matter what that looked like for them.

"I know I'm probably not the kind of guy you'd ever thought you'd be with, Luna," Mark said quietly. "And I know I have baggage of my own I need to work through. My guilt over failing to save my little brother, Mikey. My control issues. My need to overprotect everyone," Mark said quietly. "But I'd rather work through all that with you than with anyone else." Luna tried to straighten but he held her close, pressing his lips to her temple. "If you'll have me."

She nodded. "I will. We'll figure our stuff out together. I have faith in us."

"Me, too. I'm here to support you, Luna. One good thing about being a Boy Scout is we never quit. I'm not going to walk away. Not now, not when the going gets tough, not ever. You're stuck with me."

"And me, too," Astrid put in as the sound of approaching footsteps echoed. "I'm not going anywhere, either."

Luna laughed again, this time from pure joy, her heart swelling hard against her rib cage. She settled against Mark's good side and stared up at the star-laden sky, the first hints of dawn streaking the heavens as the cops approached. Except, it turned out, it wasn't just the police, but a whole entourage of people from town. Nothing brought the citizens of Wyckford like a catastrophe, apparently, even in the wee hours of the morning.

The police officers put Troy in handcuffs and kept him under guard while they dealt with the rest of the scene, setting up floodlights so the whole area was bright as a Christmas tree. While the officers questioned Astrid, Brock and Madi and Tate walked over to where Luna and Mark were sitting on the log. They both looked a mess, dirty and disheveled from their trek on the embankment, yet Luna had never felt happier or more content in her life.

Brock's gaze immediately narrowed on Mark's sling, just as he'd predicted. "Hurt your shoulder again?"

Mark gave a small shrug. "I slipped and fell. Luna had to rescue me this time."

Lucille Munson, never one to be left behind, pushed her way between the group. "Glad you're okay, Hottie McFire Pants." She smiled at Brock and Tate. "The whole gang's here, huh?"

Brock ignored the old busybody and began fussing with Mark's splint. Luna hadn't noticed before because it was so dark, but somehow, she'd fixed the thing so the fighting corncob was front and center on his sling. Brock raised a brow. "Is that supposed to mean something?"

Mark gave him a look. "Just that I'll kick your butt if you ever tell anyone about it. Where's Cassie?"

"At home with Adi. And she's on call at the hospital tonight, too," Brock said.

From where she sat, Luna could hear the cops questioning Astrid, and the girl's answers broke her heart but also gave her hope. Astrid had found a way to change here in Wyckford, a new path forward, and Luna vowed to help her in whatever way she could.

"It was me," Astrid said to the police officers, staring at her shoes. "I stole the money jar from the diner earlier. But I was going to pay it back, I swear!"

"And what was your reason for stealing the money?" the cop asked as he scribbled notes in a small pad.

Astrid sighed, her gaze locked on Troy, who

was still wheezing on his log off to the side. "I did it because I had to pay him back, or he wasn't ever going to leave me alone. Last year I had to change foster homes again. He was there. He said he'd be my brother."

The second cop questioning her scowled. "You realize being placed in the same foster home doesn't make him your brother in any sense of the word?"

"I know. But Troy insisted on calling us brother and sister and he said he'd take care of me. Then he…" She looked away. "He wanted payment. And not with money."

Both cops' expressions remained stony as the first one asked, "What happened next?"

"I turned eighteen and got released from the system." Astrid's voice grew a little stronger. "I left that foster home, but I needed money. Troy loaned me some. Said I had to pay it back, but I couldn't get a job. No one was hiring. Then I had to borrow more from him."

"Where was he getting *his* money?" cop number two asked.

Astrid shook her head. "I don't know. I got a job at a fast-food place, but it didn't pay enough for me to live and pay him back. But he kept showing up anyway…" She closed her eyes. "The manager told him to leave me alone, and they fought.

He broke the manager's nose, and the next day I got fired."

"And that's when you came to Wyckford?" the first officer asked.

"Yes. I camped out here in the forest at first, hoping Troy had forgotten about me because I'd moved clear across the country, but he didn't. He still found me, and he wanted more money."

"So, you stole the donation jar," cop two said. "Instead of coming to the authorities with the problem?"

"I didn't think you'd believe me. I didn't trust anyone." Astrid took a deep breath and met Luna's gaze. "But I do now."

Before Luna could fully react to what the girl had said and what it meant for them—*she trusts me, too!*—Madi sat down beside Luna and said, "Well, I'm glad that's over with."

"Yeah," Luna agreed, then said, "I need a favor."

"Yes," Madi said without hesitation.

"You don't even know what I'm going to ask."

"The answer's still yes."

Luna's throat burned. "Didn't anyone ever tell you to keep your guard up when someone's asking something of you?"

"You're not supposed to have a guard with good friends."

Heart feeling too big for her chest, Luna sniffled. "Dammit."

"Are you crying?" Madi asked, giving her some serious side-eye.

"No, it must be the leftover smoke from the fire."

Madi laughed. "Sure. What's the favor? Like I said, anything. Well, unless you want Tate. I'm afraid I can't share him. Not even for you, babe. He's all mine."

"Keep him." Luna snorted, then sobered. "Astrid stole your money."

"I know. I heard her tell the cops that just now," Madi said. "But I'm also thinking she had a good reason for that level of desperation. What can I do to help her?"

Both Madi and her mother had the right to press charges against Astrid, and Luna was interfering. Actions had consequences, even in Wyckford, but she could try to soften the girl's way. "Do you think if charges are pressed, you'd be willing to let Astrid make restitution?"

"Absolutely. I just started Parents' Night Out at the clinic. People in town can drop off their kids for a free night of babysitting, and I'm short of sitters. Can't think of a more fitting punishment for a teenager than watching a bunch of toddlers, right?"

Luna laughed and shook her head. "You're amazing, you know that?"

"I do," Madi said. "But I'll be sure to put out a press release."

Soon a small crowd of people had gathered around them, including Mark's crew from the fire station. From the jumbled conversations around her, Luna gathered the fire had been put out and they suspected Troy of starting it. Something else to add to his long list of crimes. With luck, the guy would be behind bars for a while. Occasionally, Mark would glance over at her and smile, and for Luna, the world fell away at those moments, as her emotions rocked her to the core. She'd never imagined feeling so much would be a good thing. Now, she couldn't imagine anything else.

Mark looked down at her, his smile seeming lit from within. And even filthy, exhausted, half-starved and a complete mess, he still stole Luna's breath away. The most gorgeous man she'd ever seen, and he was hers. All hers.

EPILOGUE

One month later...

AFTER FINISHING HER shift in the physical therapy department, Luna locked up her office and started walking to the old wing of the hospital on the other side of the campus where the free clinic was located. As she went, she passed one of the cops who'd been in the forest the night they'd arrested Troy and who'd also questioned Astrid. She nodded to the guy in the hall.

"Evening, Ms. Norton," the officer said, tipping his hat to her.

In the end, no one had pressed charges against Astrid. That honor had gone solely to Troy, who'd ended up in jail pending his formal trial on racketeering and assault charges. And true to her word, Madi had allowed Astrid to volunteer weekends babysitting at the free clinic for three months in addition to her busing duties at the diner, to repay the money stolen from the donation jar. It had all worked out the very best it could, given the situation.

By the time Luna reached the front doors of the clinic, she spotted Madi through the glass in the foyer, holding a Nerf bow and arrow set.

"Hey, girl. I'd hoped you'd stop by—" Madi whirled around and shot a soft Nerf arrow at a boy tiptoeing up behind her. He had his own Nerf bow and arrow set slung over his shoulder, but Madi was faster and nailed him in the chest.

With a wide grin, the boy spun in dramatic, action-adventure fashion, then threw himself to the ground. He spasmed once, twice, then a third time, drawing out his "death scene" by finally plopping back and lying still.

"Nice," Madi told him.

Cassie popped her head out of one of the exam rooms. All the local doctors volunteered their time at the clinic on a rotating schedule. "The babies," she declared with exhaustion, "are asleep. Zonked out like a charm."

"You've got the touch," Madi said as she loaded another arrow and eyed the hallway with a narrowed gaze. But a girl who'd come around the corner had already locked and loaded and got Madi in the arm. She sighed and lay down on the floor in her scrubs. "Hit."

Cassie continued as if Madi weren't prone on the floor. "I've certainly gotten a lot of practice with Adi." She grabbed Madi's bow and arrows and shot a second kid busily sneaking into the foyer. "Hey, Luna," Cassie said as three more boys appeared. "You gonna pitch in or what?"

"She came to check on Astrid," Madi said, sitting up.

"Hey," the first boy said. "You're supposed to stay dead."

"If I stay dead, who'll hand out snacks?"

The boy thought about this for a moment, then nodded. "Plus, now I can shoot you again."

"Not if I shoot you first," Madi said, making him laugh and run off. She stood and brushed herself off. "Astrid's doing okay. She's quiet and reflective, but okay."

Relief filled Luna. "Good. I just wanted to check on her."

"She's doing fine, big sis."

"I'm not—"

"Hush." When Madi told people to hush, they generally hushed. "Anybody with eyes can see that you and that girl are twin souls, if not by blood, then by fate."

Luna tried, she really did, but in the end, she couldn't argue that point. "Did Mark stop in today? He said he would. They collected a bunch of toys at the station during the toy drive."

"Yes," Madi said. "He's bringing some by soon. And he seemed more smitten with you than ever."

"Stop." Luna had never been so happy in love before, and she had no clue what to do about it. She wasn't exactly the type to go around in a daze of rainbows and butterflies, but man, she felt good. Happy, too. For the first time in a really long time. And that's what worried her. "I don't want to jinx it."

Madi smiled and hugged her. "Honey, love isn't magic, regardless of what you might think. It's hard work and trust and commitment. And I know you and Mark are determined to make it work, so you will. I have faith in both of you."

"You do?" Luna was learning to have faith herself, but Madi just seemed brimming with it. For everyone, always. She supposed that's why they were such good friends. Opposites attract and all.

"Astrid said she expects to be maid of honor at your and Mark's wedding," Cassie said.

"What?" Luna whipped around so fast she nearly snapped her neck. "We're not…"

"Don't panic." Madi shook her head. "She knows it could be a while."

"What's a while?" Cassie raised a brow at Luna.

"I don't know." She sighed. "We're taking it day by day. We love each other and that's enough for now."

"Do you remember when I was so stubborn about falling in love with Tate?" Madi asked, hands on hips. "Well, in the end we found our way to forever. I have no doubt you and Mark will, too. And it will end up being just as special as the two of you are."

"Who's special?" Mark asked, coming in the door with a huge box of toys in his arms. He walked past Luna and leaned in for a kiss before depositing the box on the floor near the wall. "Me?"

"Always," Luna said, grinning. "Are you off work now?"

"Yep." He checked his watch. "Just need to deliver these boxes, then I'm done for the next twenty-four hours. You want to grab some dinner?"

"Love to." Luna kissed him again, then watched him walk out to the parking lot again before Madi snagged Luna's hand and tugged her down the hall, cracking open a door. Inside the room, Astrid sat on a rug in the middle of a room, surrounded by toys and four little kids. Two climbed on her, one played with her hair, and the last one attempted to tie her shoelaces together.

They were all laughing, including Astrid.

Luna's heart clutched. She looked so happy in there and that was all Luna had ever wanted for the girl. She was still staying at Luna's apartment, which worked out fine, since Luna was mainly staying at Mark's place these days. They hadn't officially moved in together yet, but it was close.

And Astrid was using the apartment until Luna's lease ran out or she found somewhere better, like the space above the diner. Things were good all around.

Madi nudged Luna with her shoulder. "She's doing great. In fact, she's been talking about taking some classes at the local college on early childhood education. I think she'd be really good at it."

"Good at what?" Mark asked, his warmth surrounding Luna as he leaned in close behind her to nuzzle her neck.

Madi discreetly left then, leaving the two of them alone in the hall.

"Ready to go?" he asked in between kisses. "We can stop someplace on the way home or I can cook. Your choice."

In the end, it was no choice for Luna at all. She grinned, then hugged him tight. Her very own Dudley Do-Right, a man so good she might never know what she'd done to deserve him, but Luna thanked her lucky stars every day that she did.

"You know I'll pick you, babe. Always, whether we're talking food or not."

* * * * *

MEDICAL

Life and love in the world of modern medicine.

Available Next Month

All titles available in Larger Print

Daring To Fall For The Single Dad Becky Wicks
Secretly Dating The Baby Doc JC Harroway

....

Therapy Pup To Heal The Surgeon Alison Roberts
Pregnancy Surprise In Byron Bay Emily Forbes

....

Paramedic's Fling To Forever Sue MacKay
Her Summer With The Brooding Vet Scarlet Wilson

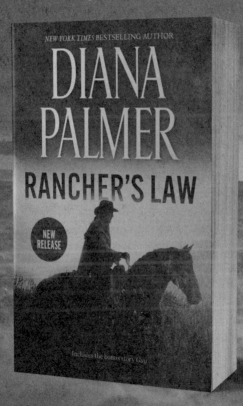